Y0-BSY-241

EX
LIBRIS

ROMANCE
Treasury

THE ROMANCE TREASURY
ASSOCIATION

NEW YORK · TORONTO · LONDON

These stories were originally published as follows:
THE VELVET SPUR 1789
Copyright © 1974 by Jane Arbor
First published by Mills & Boon Limited in 1974
THE HABIT OF LOVE 1826
Copyright © 1974 by Joyce Dingwell
First published by Mills & Boon Limited in 1974
THE EXTRAORDINARY ENGAGEMENT 1725
Copyright © 1972 by Marjorie Lewty
First published by Mills & Boon Limited in 1972

ROMANCE TREASURY is published by
The Romance Treasury Association, Stratford, Ontario, Canada.

Editorial Board: A. W. Boon, Judith Burgess, Ruth Palmour,
Alice E. Johnson and Ilene Burgess.

Dust Jacket Art by Bill Biddle
Story Illustrations by Bill Biddle
Book Design by Charles Kadin
Printed and bound by R. R. Donnelley & Sons Company

ISBN 0-373-04054-7

Printed in U.S.A.   AO 54

CONTENTS

THE VELVET SPUR

The Velvet Spur

Jane Arbor

"Stay long enough to love the island as I once did," her mother had instructed. And, obeying this last wish, Maria traveled to the island of her mother's birth.

She quickly fell under the spell of Corsica, where the elements and the savage terrain were dominant realities, and witchcraft and vendettas a part of life.

That such a feud should affect her life seemed unreal. Yet Aunt Agathe, proud and eccentric, had kept alive an ancient quarrel with the neighboring Laurents.

Since the Laurents had welcomed Maria, and Orso Laurent had set her pulses racing as no other man ever had—Maria faced a real conflict of duty and desire!

CHAPTER ONE

YESTERDAY, STANDING at a forward rail of the Nice steamer and watching the port of Calvi come into sight and sound and scent, Maria had understood gratefully all that her mother had planned and wanted for her in begging her to approach Corsica by a sea route, rather than by air.

First, by the light of the late, golden afternoon, there had been the excitement attending all landfalls—a mere pencil line of different color at the sea's horizon; then, gradually, the better defined sweep of a bay; then a clearer view of an unbroken arc of pine-shaded golden sands and its flanking by a precipitous coast where jagged rock faces fell sheer into deep water.

To the south there was a series of "bittin-in" creeks where fishing boats nestled; far to the north the red, red mass of Ile Rousse, the red island that wasn't an island at all, but a long curved promontory sheltering its own age-old resort. At the highest point of the rocks above the port and the bay reared the city's ancient capital building; behind all, the towering peaks of the Niolo mountains and—pervading all, as Maria's mother had promised—the heady scent of the spreading, greedy *maquis*, the myrtles, the cistus, the lavender, the juniper, and the arbutus, which gave Corsica its idyllic name of The Perfumed Isle and which forever haunted the senses of all those who left it, perhaps never to return—as Sorel Dane, born Sorel Juret, had never come back and never would now....

For Sorel Juret, Maria's mother, there had been childhood and girlhood in her parents' homestead in the Balagne country behind Calvi; a disillusioned young womanhood for some years in France, and then a happy marriage to the Englishman Andrew Dane. She had survived Andrew's sudden death in his fifties by only five years, after an illness that necessitated intermittent operations. Maria had nursed her during this time—a willing task, which had ended a month or two ago.

During her own young girlhood Maria could not remember that there had ever been any correspondence or contact with Corsica. Perhaps there had been some, but she had not been made confidante to it by Sorel. The three of them had vacationed elsewhere in those days. Then there had been a time of dangerous political unrest on the island, and though her mother had often talked about it, weaving its remembered magic and strangeness into a tale for her daughter's hearing, she had never suggested they go back and never seemed to want to go herself. Maria had grown up with a vague impression of some trouble which her mother wanted to forget, so she did not question her reticence about Juret family affairs, and might never have been tempted to probe further if, along with Sorel's will, which her bank duly delivered to Maria as its executor, there had not also been the letter that Sorel must have written shortly before her death.

Maria had read it with tears. It was brief, making only one point—a request which, in the circumstances, was a command. There would be, the letter said, a sum of life insurance, which her mother wanted Maria to use for just one purpose—to travel back to Corsica—("by sea, please, my darling, so that, the wind being kind, you will smell the unforgettable *maquis* offshore"). Maria was to go to the Maas Juret where Sorel knew her elder sister, Agathe, to be still living, and if Agathe should make Maria welcome, Maria should stay for a while—("long enough perhaps for you to learn to love the island as I once did, yet I betrayed it by never having the courage to go back").

Sorel had gone on to remind Maria that, though the Corsican dialect was much spoken in the island, she had seen to it that Maria had enough French to get by, and that tourism must have greatly increased the amount of English spoken. There had followed directions as to the whereabouts of the Maas Juret, and its address in Calenzana. There was, or there used to be, a bus that traveled up from Calvi.

What could Maria do? Nothing, obviously, but to see her mother's wish as a sacred trust. She had set up train arrangements to travel in the early spring; while nursing her mother she had taken only temporary secretarial posts, which paid better than permanencies and which left her free at short notice. She had savings, which, added to the amount of the special legacy, would keep her for quite a time—always supposing her unknown Aunt Agathe would "make her welcome" as her mother had hoped.

So, yesterday, she had arrived, traveling light with a knapsack and a carryall for luggage. By a curve of the coastline, the port faced east, so that by the time the steamer docked the sun was sinking behind the mountains, at first turning their peaks to flame, then bathing them in a lilac mist. Maria had taken a taxi to the two-star hotel that her agency had booked for her provisionally for one night, with the option of more if necessary. She had dined simply, afterward walking out along the front, at that hour aglitter with the lights of the café-bars and noisy with canned music and the stamp and shuffle of dancing feet. Before she had returned to the hotel the wind had risen, but she had not heeded or understood its fretting at awnings and its swirl at street corners, though during the night she had been sleepily aware that it had gained power and fury. Only this morning did she wake to dismay. The wind was at near-tempest force; beyond the windows of the hotel rain drove almost horizontally down the street; gutters ran with water and drains eddied and bubbled.

"This, I suppose, is the *libeccio*," Maria said aloud to herself and the empty dining room—though with scant satisfaction at her recognition of the Corsican version of the mean southwesterly wind, which has a different name on almost every Mediterranean seaboard. She had heard from her mother about the *libeccio*. It could rage for days or blow itself out within hours. Well, thought Maria, she couldn't wait for it to do either. Overnight she had checked that there was a midmorning bus for Calenzana, and storm or no storm, she meant to catch it.

She unpacked and donned the light raincoat and rain hat which she hadn't expected to need so soon. Knapsack on back and carryall in hand, she made her way to the small square that was the bus terminus. There was no bus shelter, nor any queue. Maria could only hope that the bus, when it appeared, would be a large one, or that all the bedraggled people huddled in shop and café doorways around the square were not all bound for Calenzana.

But it seemed they were. When the bus drove in, only a couple of minutes before it was due out, there was a concerted rush. People flung in bundles, children, and themselves. They pushed and bunted and shouted. Twice Maria reached the rear platform, only to be hurled off it again. There was no conductor. It was the driver who shouted a warning that he was filled up and about to start at the moment when Maria had one foot on the platform for the third time, only to be flung backward at the vehicle's tremendous jerk forward.

In the triumph of the victors over the vanquished, people waved to her from the crowded platform; a hairy youth blew an ironical kiss, and she herself reeled back against a supporting body—into arms that held her, saving her from falling. A cheerful male voice said, "*Tant pis*!" and then, at her unmistakably English, "*Gosh*—what a lot!" the voice translated, "Too bad! But don't you know that you English are the only people in the world who ever line up? You will have to wait for the next bus out."

Maria turned and saw a stocky, muscular figure in a pale blue uniform, which she did not recognize, and with startlingly blue eyes and curly black hair beneath the uniform cap. She said in French, "Thank you. But for you, I would have fallen. When *is* the next bus out, do you know?"

A shrug answered that. "Where for?" her rescuer asked.

"Calenzana."

"I don't know. But there will be one." He put a confident hand under her elbow. "Come into this café. They'll know about the buses, and you'll let me give you a drink while you wait."

Maria did not move. "Oh no, please—"

"Why not?" He looked her up and down. "You can't stay here. You are half-soaked already, and I'm not staying out in this, either. So come along, let's go."

She went then reluctantly. He went to the bar to order a *pastis* for himself and the fruit juice she had requested, and joined her at a table. He poured water into the clear gold liquid, swirled it until it turned to a cloudy gray and lifted his glass to her. "To our better knowing of each other," he said. "You are English, I'm sure. But you speak French excellently. How is that?"

"My French is no better than your English." She smiled.

"Ah, but then I mix with all sorts." He flicked the sleeve of his jacket. "This . . . . I'm a pilot for the local air transport—two helicopters and three car ferry aircraft strong. We ferry tourists back and forth—to Ajaccio, across to the east coast, inland to Corte, around the coasts—wherever they want to go. My off-duty day is today. My car is in dock, so I'm waiting for my brother to come down from home to pick me up. What about you now? What is your name?"

"Maria Dane. And I speak French because my mother was Corsican, and we spoke it together a lot."

"Oh. Well, I am Gian Laurent. What are you? A tourist?" He glanced at her knapsack. "A camper, or what? On holiday? And alone?"

Maria nodded. "I'm on holiday—in a way. I don't know how long I shall be staying. I only arrived last night."

"By air into Calvi?"

"No, by sea from Nice. I'm hoping to visit a relative who lives at Calenzana—my aunt. She is my only living relation as far as I know. My mother—"

"Where does your aunt live? We're not far above Calenzana ourselves."

"At a farm, the Maas Juret—" Maria broke off as she saw the blue eyes widen and stare.

Her companion echoed sharply, "The Maas Juret? But that's not in Calenzana—it's just across the valley from us—the Manoir Laurent. And you can't mean you are going to stay there—*or* that Agathe Juret is your aunt!"

Bewilderedly Maria said, "Of course I mean it—if Aunt Agathe will have me. Why shouldn't I?"

"Because . . . . Well, because I shouldn't like to think she is anybody's aunt."

"Oh, don't be silly." Maria was irritated now. "I tell you she's mine. My mother, who died a few months ago, was her sister. But why are you so shocked? Just that you don't like her?"

Gian Laurent shook his head. "She hates us," he said.

"Hates you? Your family, you mean? But a lot of families who are neighbors don't get along!" Maria protested.

"It's more than that." His eyes met hers in a hard stare. "Don't tell me you haven't heard of Corsican vendettas?" he challenged.

"The old blood feuds between families? Of course I know about them. But they're just history—completely out of date now!"

He laughed shortly. "Don't you believe it! When anyone chooses to pick a quarrel, it can still turn into a generations-long feud. Even if it is only one-sided, as Agathe Juret's is with us. Something that happened way back, around the time my brother Orso was born, and before I was, myself. On our side we couldn't care less."

"Then if whatever it was doesn't matter to you anymore, why are you so worked up about her being my aunt?" Maria asked logically.

Gian fingered the stem of his glass and swirled his drink. But before he could answer, another man came into the café, his height needing to stoop beneath the lintel. "Orso," Gian told Maria, and beckoned.

Orso Laurent raised a hand in acknowledgement and came over. He looked some years older than Gian and was, by any standards, a more dominant figure. His hair was as black, but his eyes weren't of the same bright blue. They were deep set and dark beneath heavy brows, and the lines of his face were harder, sterner. His open-necked red shirt, loosely knotted cravat and riding breeches were a countryman's gear, beside which Gian's uniform looked almost dapper.

Gian stood, asking what he would have to drink, and he chose *eau-de-vie*. But his questioning look at Maria halted Gian on his way to the bar.

"Oh yes," said Gian. "Meet Mademoiselle Maria Dane. She is English and she flung herself into my arms this morning."

The heavy brows crooked. "Into your—?"

"Yes, literally!" Gian grinned, and left Maria to explain awkwardly.

"What happened was that I was being crowded off a bus, and your brother saved me from falling."

"I see. And invited you for a drink with him!"

Telling herself she imagined a note of censure of her having accepted, she said, "Yes. Out of the rain while I wait for the next bus. It was kind of him," she said as Gian came back, bringing the brandy and a second *pastis* for himself. He edged a chair toward Orso who, however, only put a foot on its seat while he drained his glass.

"I'm not staying. *You're* not staying. I've got to get back. Did you get the stationery father wanted?" he asked Gian.

Gian spread a hand. "How could I? When I've been busy picking up—and I don't mean what *you* mean—and playing knight-errant to a pretty girl like Maria? I didn't have the time."

Orso did not smile. "Then we'll have to call for it on the way." He turned to Maria. "You'll excuse us, *mademoiselle?*" he asked.

He ignored Gian's sulky mutter of, "You don't have to *pry* me loose!"

"You are a visitor to Calvi? Where are you hoping to catch a bus for?" Orso asked Maria.

"For Calenzana."

"Calenzana?" His sharp dark glance went to Gian. "She has already missed one bus, and you haven't offered her a lift with us? Why not?" he demanded.

No answer. Then, as if his reason should explain itself, Gian muttered, "Because she is bound for the Maas Juret. Agathe Juret is her aunt."

"And so...?" Orso invited, unmoved.

"Well—"

"Well—bah!" Orso picked up Maria's carryall from beside her chair. "Your luggage, *mademoiselle?* You'll allow me? Will you come?"

He led the way out to a big station wagon. Gian, getting in, said, "You can drop me off first at home."

Orso replied tersely, "I never meant to do anything else,

my friend," and they set out, stopping off at a stationery store and a feed merchant's before they left the town.

Maria's feelings about these happenings were mixed. Though aware, with Orso Laurent, that Gian should have offered her a lift, she still realized that his reason for his reluctance to see her to her aunt's farm seemed good to him. Then why didn't Orso share it? Again, supposing, as she suspected, Orso had despised her a little for being so easy a pickup for Gian, why had he been so ready with the courtesy that Gian hadn't offered? And yet again—what was *she* thinking of, driving off into unknown country with two young men, who might be taking her anywhere, and with who knew what sinister motives? Though as to the latter scruple, she felt that if they had had kidnapping or worse in mind, they would hardly have bothered to pick up a neat packet of what looked like foolscap paper and a lumpy sack of chicken meal on the way. They had a father at home and they were neighbors of the Juret farm. No, Maria realized, she had more reason to be disturbed by Gian's dark hints about the conditions that faced her there. But she shied away from the thought of that....

As they drove, Orso Laurent put to her much the same questions as Gian had asked, but his reaction to her answers was the casual, noncommittal interest of a stranger, except when she admitted to him that she wasn't expected. Then he sent her a brief, disconcerting glance. "Is that wise—on a first visit to a relative you say you have never met?" he queried.

Though he had voiced her own misgivings since meeting Gian, she would not let him guess it for the world. "It was my mother's wish that I should surprise my Aunt Agathe," she said a little stiffly, and with a nod he accepted that.

The rain had stopped and the wind, too, after driving the clouds from the sky; leaving it clear and blue. The spread of the *maquis* on either side of the inland road was

vast; it glittered, it steamed, it scented the air. As the road
climbed, on the right there were glimpses of the sea to be
caught; on the left, beyond the *maquis* there were forested
slopes, in themselves not high, but broken along the skyline by jagged rocks thrusting far up as unassailable
pinnacles—giant needle points, no less.

The road leveled out; here there was gentler country,
pastureland bordered by rough stone walls shaded by olive
trees, some vineyards, and herds of goats. A turn in the
road brought a house into view—a large, stark fortress of a
house, seemingly hewn out of granite, with deep embra-
sured windows under the flattish, pantiled roof that was
typical of the region. It looked out and down across a valley, its immediate frontage a low-walled courtyard, where
young almond and mimosa trees, set between the paving
stones, were in full spring dress.

Orso introduced the house to Maria. "Our home—the
Manoir Laurent."

Gian got out. His gaiety recovered, he grinned at Maria.
"We must do that—and more—again some time, and
without interruption," he promised.

Maria smiled back and nodded. "Thank you for—" she
began, as Orso took the car in a big sweep round the courtyard and out into the road again.

This time it ran in a series of corkscrew bends and twists
on a shelf of the valley. In answer to Maria's question,
Orso said that the two houses were about five kilometers
distant from each other, but on foot by a short cut, not
more than two. Then, soon, he turned the car sharply
along a mere track; another turn or two, and her journey's
end was in sight. She suppressed a gasp of dismay.

If the Laurent home was like a fortress, the façade of
this one—smaller and flat faced with narrow shuttered
windows—was not unlike a prison. It made no pretensions
to a front garden, a courtyard or a front anything but a

worn stone path bordered by woody lavender that led up to the metal-studded door. Two other paths branched off around the sides of the house and the *maquis* could be seen crowding it from behind.

Orso Laurent had stopped the car and Maria was aware he was watching her reaction. At last he said, "Well, what did you expect? A dream house with roses around the door?"

She hesitated. "I thought it was a farm—dairying, and cheesemaking and honey and crops—maize and citrus fruits, my mother said. I don't see any signs of—"

Orso shook his head. "It was a farm, until the *maquis* gobbled up the pasture bit by bit. It doesn't ask permission."

"You mean my aunt has let it go?"

"I don't suppose she could help herself. You must know she is not a young woman?"

"I know she was several years older than my mother, who was fifty-two when she died."

"Yes, well . . . Agathe Juret hasn't aged well since caring for the old people, your grandparents, I suppose, until they died. And there is never a surplus of labor in these parts. The pensioners have their own little parcels of land to tend, and the young men all drift to the mainland. No, the Maas Juret, in the right hands, could be a prosperous farm again. But it's a nothing of a place at present."

Maria stirred in her seat, reluctant to get out of the car to face the worst. She said shakily, "You don't gild the lily, do you? Both you and your brother have done your best to warn me!"

"And can you wonder?" Orso flashed back. "You arrive unannounced on what most people would see as a fool's errand. No definite plans. No assurance of a welcome. All starry-eyed, no doubt, with your travel brochure idea of Corsica—eternal sun and golden beaches, *luxe* hotels and probably a delicious hint of banditry in the mountains as a touch of piquancy! Well, you saw this morning what it can do in the way of vicious weather, and you don't like what you are seeing now. And what, may one ask, do you propose to do if Agathe Juret shuts the door in your face?"

That was too much for Maria. Furious that she had shown her dismay so plainly, she despised herself for it and illogically blamed him for noticing it. She said coldly, "I came prepared to risk that. And I came the way I did because that was how my mother wanted me to come. And now—" having failed to cope with the car door handle "—may I get out, please, and I needn't keep you any longer?"

He opened the door, got out himself and took her carryall from the back of the car. He retained his hold of it. "I'll come with you," he said.

"No." That was false pride talking. Remembering her manners, she went on, "I must thank you for giving me the lift and for seeing me so far. But from now on I'm on my own—please."

He shrugged. "I shall wait in the car."

She took the bag from him, "Not that, either."

"If you say so," he agreed. In the accepted continental fashion he offered his hand and, taking it, about as illogically as she had blamed him before, she wished she could hold on to it; keep him there. On too little evidence he had judged her to be foolhardy, but his harsh concern seemed sincere; at least it went further than Gian's. Obviously Gian hadn't wanted to see her safely to the Maas Juret. Orso had seen it as his duty, and in face of the ordeal before her she would have been grateful if he had insisted on following it through. Even more contrarily, supposing Aunt Agathe was cozily apple cheeked and welcoming, she would have liked him to be there to be proved wrong.

But he had released her hand. By way of parting he said,

"We have a telephone. You do not. But if you need us, there's a public one in the hamlet of Creno—*that* way." He waved a hand down the valley. Then he backed up the car and was at once out of sight at a turn in the track. Maria felt very much alone.

Her three knocks on the studded door went unanswered, so she took one of the side paths around the house. At the back the stone paving of a small courtyard kept the *maquis* at bay. Crossing to the house from the gate to a hen-run in a corner was a woman, carrying a bowl of eggs in one hand and an empty feed-tin in the other.

Aunt Agathe . . . she was in something like folk dress—heavy shoes, black skirts just clearing her ankles, a bibbed apron, and a loose headscarf covering severely drawn black hair. She was neither apple cheeked nor welcoming. From fine dark eyes in a strongly handsome face—the nose aquiline, the cheeks gaunt—she surveyed Maria unsmilingly, inviting no opening and making none.

Maria came forward. "Tante Agathe," she said in French, "I am Maria—Maria Dane, your sister Sorel's daughter. She died last November. But you'll know that. She left you something in her will, I think, some rings and a brooch...."

"Yes, they came to me through my lawyer. And so now you have come, too. What do you want?" demanded Agathe harshly.

How to answer that? Maria did her best. She said simply, "To see you. To stay with you for a little while, if I may. Mother wanted me to come. She left me a last letter to say so, and even if I hadn't wanted to come and to get to know you, I'd have thought it my duty to her—and to you."

"*Hein*! A duty that does not seem to have troubled her in her lifetime!"

"I think she may have feared how you might receive her," ventured Maria.

"And what did she expect—the fatted calf?" Agathe paused to look Maria over. "And so she sent you. Alone? What about your father? How old are you, h'm?"

"I'm twenty, and my father died five years ago, which you may not have heard at the time."

"There was no need. I never knew him. But since you are here, you had better come in. Did you arrive from England today?"

"Not directly. I came by sea from Nice to Calvi yesterday." As Agathe moved toward the house, Maria following, there was the sound of a car starting up. Agathe lifted her fine head to listen. "What was that?"

"Just a car, I think." But for Maria it was more than that. It was the sound of reassurance—that, after all, Orso Laurent hadn't weakly taken her no for an answer. Around that first corner of the track he must have stopped and waited, giving her long enough either to be thrown out or welcomed. For some reason she was glad of that.

Compared with the grim exterior the kitchen of the house was a pleasant contrast. There was a warm smell of baking bread, and cooking pots simmered on the hob of an open fire. But there was electric light and with a "Tch! Such waste!" Agathe hurried to turn off a dripping hot water tap over the big stone sink—which showed at least a mixture of ancient and modern comforts indoors, however badly the farm had been neglected.

Agathe set down her bowl of eggs and approaching Maria, took her by the shoulder and turned her to the light. "Let me look at you, niece. Are you said to be like your mother—or not?" she asked.

Maria smiled. "I'd like to think I am, but I'm afraid not. She was so...vivid, with hair as dark as yours and her eyes a dark velvety brown, whereas this—" she ran a hand under her long corn-blond hair "—comes more from my father's side, and my eyes are gray."

"As one sees. And you are too thin for your height. At your age, Sorel had shape. As I once had, too. And of course you do not help yourself as a woman with those... garments." Agathe's disapproval was clearly directed at Maria's slacks, for which Maria hastened to apologize.

"I just wore them for traveling. I don't, all the time," she explained.

"It is to be hoped not," Agathe commented severely. She moved to the fire to stir the contents of a pot. "Have you souped, yet?" she asked over her shoulder.

"Souped." Remembering the word as Corsican idiom for lunching or dining, owing to the universality of soup at either meal, Maria said, "Not yet."

"Then we will do so when I have shown you where you will sleep, if you are staying. This way. Will you come?"

Agathe led the way through an archway without a door, across a hall and up broad stairs to one of several rooms on the second floor, pausing on the way to take soft merino blankets and bed linen, yellowed with age, but smelling sweetly of lavender, from a warming cupboard. She threw open closed shutters to show a white-walled room with a high-domed ceiling and furnished heavily in carved walnut. She made up the bed with speed and deftness, directed Maria to the bathroom, and clumped away downstairs with scarcely another word.

Maria washed and unpacked, putting away her two or three pairs of slacks in one of the magnificent *armoires* and deciding ruefully that if they were forbidden her, she must invest in some cotton dresses as soon as possible. Then she went down to find the kitchen table laid for the meal and an earthenware bowl of steaming, fragrant soup ready at her place. This was followed by a kind of hot sausage, called by Agathe *figatelli*, the ingredients of which, Maria suspected, were first cousins to those of the haggis. It was agreeably savory and was followed in its turn by hunks of crusty bread, butter and a white cheese made of goats' milk. There was a flagon of raw red wine to drink.

They made rather staccato conversation—mostly question and answer. When Maria ventured to query the isolation of the Maas Juret, with consequent loneliness for Agathe, the latter said sharply, "It is my home. It always has been, and it provides all I need. I have vegetables for the table, poultry for the pot, and eggs; milk and cheese from my goats, and olives for cooking oil are to be had anywhere at the price of a bent back to pick them up where they have fallen. Anything else I can get from down below—" she nodded in the same direction as Orso Laurent had indicated the village "—and for money I have my pension and an allowance that my father must have arranged for me, since it comes to me each month through my lawyer. No, you can spare your pity for me, niece. I manage very well."

To Maria's question as to whether she had television or radio, she admitted to radio, "for news of the *libeccio* or of forest fires," but television had as short shrift from her as had the electric cooker in a corner, which she had been persuaded to buy when electricity had been brought up the valley, but which looked as if it had never been used.

She asked whether or not Maria worked for her living, and if so, how she had been free to come to the island, and how long she proposed to stay. To which Maria explained the temporary nature of her jobs and about the legacy that had enabled her to make the trip, and added, "I think mother hoped you might welcome me for long enough for us to get to know each other and for me to see something of Corsica."

Agathe accepted this with a grudging, "Stay as long as you please, child. Better to come late than never, perhaps. Though I must say there have been many years since Sorel left, when she might have brought you and come back herself."

In reply to that Maria was tempted to point out that for some years before her death, Sorel had been intermittently ill and could not travel. Also that at no time had either Agathe, or her parents while they lived, made any move to invite Sorel back. But she said nothing, thinking it prudent, while she was a guest in her aunt's house, to respect whatever long bitterness put that edge of criticism into Agathe's tone whenever she spoke of Sorel. Sometime, Maria supposed, she would learn the cause, without realizing that her answer to Agathe's next questions would spark the smoldering fire.

Agathe suggested, "I suppose you caught the Calenzana bus from Calvi as far as Creno, and walked up from there?"

"No, I was crowded off the bus, and nearly fell. I was caught by a young air pilot, who introduced himself as a neighbor of yours, Gian Laurent. He invited me into a café out of the rain while I waited for the next bus and while *he* waited for his brother who, when he arrived, offered me a lift, and I accepted." As Maria spoke she was watching for Agathe's reaction to the name that Gian had claimed she "hated," but she was totally unprepared for the naked outrage that showed in Agathe's stare as she mouthed, "Laurent! *Laurent?* You accepted a favor from one of *them*? From two? Neighbors, indeed! *Enemies! And* their father, *and* all their family, past, present and to come. You told them who you were—what you are to me, a Juret?"

"That I was your niece, yes. Through my mother, your sister," said Maria.

"And they still dared to pretend to befriend you and to bring you here? I wonder you were not ashamed, niece, to let them—Laurents!—treat you as if you were a parcel by the carrier! Not though, one notices, that they were so bold as to face *me* on my own threshold. They dropped you at the door and ran—as one might expect!" concluded Agathe with sour satisfaction.

As quietly as she could Maria said, "That was my doing, Aunt Agathe. I rather wanted to meet you for the first time alone. It was only the older brother who brought me. He had left Gian at the Manoir on the way. And why should I be ashamed of letting them help me? The name Laurent meant nothing to me!"

"*Nothing*?" Agathe echoed. "You say that—you, a Juret and daughter of a Juret! Daughter of Sorel, who was betrayed and abandoned by a Laurent, like so much trash! Bah! Have you no pride, child? No sense of family? No injured honor for your mother's sake? Have I then to be the only one left to remember—and to hate?"

CHAPTER TWO

THERE WAS A LONG SILENCE. Evidently Agathe meant her bitter words to be given time to make their impact, and to an extravagance of virulence, which was quite outside her experience, Maria could find nothing to say.

At last Agathe prompted, "Well, now do you claim to know nothing against the Laurents? Or that you never heard the name Jules Beauloin from your mother?"

Maria could answer that with conviction. "Never," she said. "Who is—or was he?"

"A Laurent by blood, through his mother. First cousin, though younger, to old Pascal Laurent, who is the father of *your* fine friends from the Manoir. A debonair from the mainland, with money and ease with the women, he spent a whole summer here, making love to Sorel, promising her everything, short of the keys of heaven or marriage. And at the end of it, poof, he is gone—and she, too."

Maria felt hollow inside. "*With* him?" she whispered.

"Bah, no! He *deserted* her, ran away. And not only from her. One heard he had more than one little friend and *affaire* in Calenzana and Calvi, no doubt because Sorel would not let him have his way with her."

Maria breathed again. "But she followed him?" she asked.

"Against all our pleadings, our parents' and mine. She was in love, wouldn't hear ill of him and must make one last bid for him, she said. She found him. He was on the point of going abroad, and went, and he has never come back to Corsica since."

Maria mused, "Nor did she. And you never asked her?"

"At first she would not have come. She knew she had treated us heartlessly, and she was ashamed to face us until she had made good alone. Besides, she wanted to forget even Corsica. And then, later, when *I* needed her most, I was too proud to ask her, lest she would refuse."

"And when was that?" Maria asked.

"When I myself—yes, *I* with my horseface—could have married, if there had been any other daughter to care for our parents. He—my suitor—was from Bonifacio. I sent him away. That made me bitter against her. I told myself that if she wanted to come, she would come, but ask her, beg her, I would *not*!" Agathe declared.

Maria sighed. Such rancor, such misplaced pride, such stubborn silence on both sides was pitiful, when a gift, a letter, even a Christmas card might have broken the vicious circle. And on reflection, except for the tragedy of Agathe's sacrifice, what did the story amount to? Surely a very common one? The despairs of a girl's first love at the mercy of a philanderer—it had happened before and it would happen again—at least Sorel had had the courage to fight her way back to happiness alone.

Maria said defensively, "Mother was good and generous, and I'm sure she would have come back to help you if she had known."

"She should never have left us. If she had listened to us, she would have married here, and have had a happy Corsican family."

Maria couldn't help smiling. "*I'm* glad she didn't. If she hadn't married my father, I wouldn't have been myself—Maria Dane—and I'm glad I am! Besides, Aunt Agathe, it must all have happened a long time ago. Mother did get over it, and she did marry happily in the end. And this Jules Beauloin was—what? Only a second cousin or something to Orso and Gian Laurent, and it's not fair to hold it against them until now, do you think?"

Agathe compressed her lips. "He was of Laurent blood. We Corsicans have long memories," she declared.

Too long, was Maria's unspoken comment. Aloud she protested, "I'm sure they don't see you as an enemy. And they are your *neighbors*! You never know when you might be glad of their help, living alone as you do."

"If I ever needed help from a Laurent, I would not ask for it. You, niece, must please yourself. *I* cannot forbid you their company or their house. But they will never be welcome in mine." Agathe stood and began to clear the table. "Come now and help me with the dishes, child. I shall not treat you as a guest, and we must begin as we mean to go on," she added.

Glad of this dismissal of their differences, Maria helped willingly. Afterward Agathe sat down with the makings of a black shawl she was crocheting, and Maria remembered that she must ring her hotel to say that she would not be requiring her room again.

"How far is Creno?" she asked after explaining matters to Agathe.

"Something over a kilometer. Where the road divides, bear to the left, and you will see it down below."

The village had an air of having been flung at the slope of the hillside on which it was built. The gaunt stone houses stood at any angle to each other on any level that would accommodate them and the street surfaces were variously flights of steps, cobbles and hard-baked earth, runneled today by the morning's rain. Most of the streets rayed out from the largest flat area, the *place*, where the post office stood in a corner, adjacent to an ancient holm oak, whose branches, still bearing the last brown leaves of winter, afforded shade to a rustic seat.

Maria was coping with her call in the outside phone booth when a station wagon drove up; Orso Laurent alighted and went into the post office, to emerge just as she left the telephone booth.

He offered his hand. "So—you are finding your way around already. How did you come down?" he asked.

"I walked. I had to phone the hotel I stayed in last night."

"To say you would—or would not—be back, perhaps?"

"Would not."

"Good. Round One to you." He moved toward the tree seat, inviting her to sit, which she did. Then she turned to him. "Was that why you didn't drive off straight away after you left me this morning? Because you didn't expect Round One, as you call it, to go to me?"

He threw her a glance. "How did you know I waited?"

"I heard a car start up around that first corner, and I thought it must be yours."

"Yes, well...I felt more than a little responsible for you, knowing Agathe Juret's reputation for...let's call it brusquerie. Especially if you had to admit to having been delivered by a Laurent."

"As of course I did."

"And...?"

Maria stirred uncomfortably. "I think you must know," she said. "Your brother had told me something about her long quarrel with your family, and she has told me the rest."

"Which you didn't know before?" There was surprise in his tone.

"No. But you did?" she queried.

"Yes, though it all happened thirty years ago—almost before my time, though not quite. You mean you had never heard from your mother why she left home and went to France as a girl?"

"Never. I knew she had been in France for some years before she married father. And since I've been grown-up I've wondered if she left Corsica because of some unhappy love affair. But she never talked of it and—" Maria smiled ruefully "—I didn't realize I was going to collect the backlash now!"

"The backlash taking what form? Or can I guess? You were forbidden the Manoir and warned to be strictly *incommunicado* from the Laurents?"

She shook her head. "Rather worse than that. She said I must 'please myself,' meaning of course that if I did, I should lose favor with her."

"So you had pleaded the cause of the Laurents? You want to know us? One of us, or both?"

Maria felt her color rise. "I'd said that you had been very kind and that one day she might be grateful for you as neighbors."

Orso smiled faintly. "Very adroitly turned, considering you made it clear that you considered *my* 'kindness' officious! However, what did your aunt say to that?"

"That if she needed help, she wouldn't ask you for it. And when she said she couldn't dictate to me, that made me feel guilty, which I'm afraid she may have intended."

"Which is ridiculous. You obviously have a duty to her, but you must have come to Corsica with some idea of seeing something of it while you are here?"

"Mother wanted me to, yes."

"Well, you won't see much by spending twenty-four hours a day at the Maas Juret, with no available transport but the bus and your feet. Besides, I should like you to meet my father, we sometimes give a party at the Manoir, and Gian is free at all sorts of times—he could take you around."

Maria hesitated. "Thank you. But I would feel very disloyal if I accepted."

"Which again is nonsense, as long as you don't neglect any duty to your aunt. And who knows but that you might be the means of bridging a rift that ought never to have opened for such an empty reason?" Orso retorted. He stood up. "No, I propose to drive you back now, and this time I hope you'll let me speak for you. What do you say?"

"Oh—it wouldn't work. Supposing Aunt Agathe refuses to see or speak to you?" Maria demurred.

"If she opens her door and sees you, she will have to see me as well. After that I'll play it by ear."

Following him reluctantly to the car, Maria said, "You are going to a great deal of trouble for me. And how do you know Gian will want to take me around?"

Orso looked her up and down appraisingly. "Why shouldn't he?" he said. "You are attractive and about his age, I'd say. Besides, he made good opportunity from your plight this morning, and he has plenty of time on his hands, off and on."

That sounded as if, thought Maria, having clinically measured her degree of attraction, he assumed his right to dispose of Gian's time and inclinations accordingly. Just as, having taken her under his wing, he was already making plans for *her*. She knew she should be grateful, and she was—this time. But she did wonder whether anyone had ever said a great big No! to Orso Laurent—and had got away with it.

On the short drive she reminded him of his scorn of her tourist's-eye view of the island, and asked why he would want her to see it differently—if he did.

He considered the question. Then, "I suppose," he said, "because you have Corsican blood, and if you are to care for it, you should know it as it really is, away from the smart beaches and the hotels. Inland and along its coasts it is savagely beautiful, but far too empty of people for its own good. It has everything to excess—floods in winter, parching drought in summer, the *libeccio*—our houses have to be built to withstand the lot, and the *maquis* that scents it like Araby is half choking it to death." He paused to shrug. "There are those who claim that tourism can save it;

others that our forest fires could reduce it to a smoking pyre within a few generations. As to tourism, I don't know, but the other—the loss of valuable timber to fire, and good pasture to the greed of the scrub—are very much my business. I manage the Manoir estates for my father, if you didn't know?"

"I didn't," said Maria. "And is your land threatened, too?"

He shook his head. "Fortunately, no. I saw the red light in time. I am reforesting everywhere I can, though I need more land for it. I've also kept the *maquis* outside our boundaries, but it's all around us on the no-man's-land of farms that have been abandoned in despair, and the owners have gone away."

"As my aunt has had to abandon hers, you said?"

"Yes, though she could still sell. The soil of her land must still have some virtue in it." As they neared the Maas, his question changed the subject. "When you and Gian were getting acquainted this morning, how much did he tell you about your aunt?"

Maria thought back. "Only, I think, that she had had a long feud with your family, though not what it was about."

"No more than that?"

"I think not. Why?"

"Nothing. She is something of a character, as you may already know, and I wondered what fact or fiction about her he may have passed on." Orso stopped the car and they both alighted.

Agathe had moved into one of the front rooms while Maria was out. They saw her pass the window at Orso's knock on the door. At the sight of Maria she began, "You could have walked straight in, child"—then drew herself up as she recognized Orso.

She said to Maria, "So—you have lost no time in pleasing yourself as to the company you keep!" At which Orso cut in, "You should blame me, madame. We met again by chance in the village, and your niece allowed me to drive her back, so that I could ask a particular favor of you."

"Huh! A Laurent asks a favor of a Juret? That is indeed something new!" Agathe flashed.

"Yes, isn't it?" he said easily.

"And if I invite you to come in while you ask it, it is not because you are welcome in my house, but because I do not care to parley, least of all with a Laurent, on my doorstep." She stood aside, closed the door behind them, then led the way into the room, where she turned off an old-fashioned radio set and sat down with her crochet, though she left it in her lap.

"Well," she said chillingly, "the favor—what is it?"

"That you would allow us—my father, my brother and myself—to offer your niece some hospitality while she is staying with you. And to show her as much of the island as, having no means of getting around, she might not be able to see for herself."

"Indeed? Though I understood she came to Corsica to see *me*."

"*And* her mother's country, I think," said Orso quietly.

"And am I standing in her way in this?"

"If you deny her opportunities that we can offer her and you, placed as you are, cannot—yes."

"She is free to come and go as she pleases. And there is a bicycle in the *cave*, which she can use."

"Up and down our heights, and always alone? Would you really care to have her doing that, even if she could get far afield?" Orso urged.

"I meant," said Agathe loftily, "that she could use the bicycle to travel to your house, if and when you invite her there. It is a level road across the valley, and she should come to no harm. And since I had already told her I could forbid her no company she cares to seek, I must say I see no need for your making it a favor to be asked of me, monsieur!"

For a moment this sudden about-face seemed to put Orso at a loss. Then he said calmly, "The favor was necessary, madame, because your blessing was."

"My blessing was—what?" she snapped.

"Necessary. To your niece, who refuses to do anything or go anywhere or see anyone without your goodwill."

"And how many more times must I repeat that she has it?"

"But only grudgingly?"

"What does it matter, as long as she has it?" Agathe took up her crochet and appeared to concentrate on it. "No, monsieur, it is quite clear to me that your story of a favor to be asked was a ruse. You made use of it to open my door, but you came with quite another purpose, and we both know what it is."

Orso waited until she looked up. "You are ahead of me, I'm afraid," he said.

"I think not. The Laurents need more land. I, the last of the Jurets, have land to spare. Going to waste, you would say. And at a price that would suit you, you want to buy it. Don't deny it, please."

Orso said, "I don't deny it. But I assume the price would also have to suit you?"

"Ah, but no price would suit me. Or none that a Laurent would offer me. Besides, you should know as well as I do that we Corsicans think it dishonorable to sell family-owned land."

"Which is why you would rather the *maquis* would swallow yours?"

"Rather than that your family would benefit from it, yes. In short, monsieur, you are wasting your time, and I will give you *au revoir*."

"*Au revoir, madame*. You make both your position and

your prejudice very clear." Orso turned to Maria. "If I may, I shall send Gian to bring you over to luncheon at the Manoir on Thursday," he told her. Then he shared a formal bow between them and left.

Maria felt both embarrassed and irked by the scene. Sooner than she expected she had heard no said to Orso Laurent, and his failure to deny Agathe's conjecture as to his real errand made Maria wonder whether or not he had indeed made a pawn of her in order to approach Agathe about the land. She didn't want to think so, but the idea did tie in with her first impressions of him as a man who manipulated people and situations for his own ends.

Evidently Agathe had no doubts on the subject as, nodding with satisfaction over her crochet, she remarked, "There you have a fine friend indeed! A cunning one, too—making use of his acquaintance with *you* to trick *me* into a meeting, which he knew that I, alone, would refuse him! As you also heard me refuse him the land—*my* land—which I know he covets—Yes!"

At that Maria felt almost ready, if it were feasible, to go straight to her room, to pack her things and announce her immediate departure. But of course she could not, and a second, less impulsive thought doubted whether or not, given the chance, she would have taken it. She had never yet met anyone like Agathe Juret, nor indeed any man of the seemingly masterful quality of Orso Laurent. She had no experience to guide her in her dealings with either of them, yet she felt oddly challenged by her very ignorance, by her pity for Agathe's implacable bitterness for so slight a cause, and even by her doubts of Orso's motives. It was as if, she thought fancifully, she had been handed a thread, two threads, of which the full skeins were out of sight, and if she dropped both threads and ran away, she knew she would always regret not having wound them in.

She used the promised bicycle as an excuse to escape

temporarily from Agathe's self-satisfaction over her victory. She found it in the *cave*—the ground-level "cellar" typical of French farmhouses—resting on its saddle and handlebars. Righting it, Maria wondered who had ridden it last. Surely not Agathe in those skirts? It was rusty and the leather of the saddle was torn, but its tires stayed inflated when she had used its pump on them. She spun its pedals and tried its brakes—none too good, these—but she supposed that somewhere she could get new brake blocks fitted. She found a torn piece of emery paper and used it on the rusty handlebars, conceiving, as she worked, quite an affection for the old crock as her means of escape from the Maas Juret when, as she guessed it might, its forbidding atmosphere threatened to stifle her.

Dusk was falling when she returned to the house. Meanwhile Agathe had fed her hens and milked her goats, and presently she prepared supper—the inevitable soup, cold ham and very strong coffee. Afterward they listened to the radio and then, far sooner than Maria was ready to go, Agathe announced that it was time for bed; she always rose early.

Used to later hours than this, Maria could not sleep for a long time. She finished the book she had brought for her journey and hadn't another. She mentally added paperbacks to the list of her immediate needs—brake blocks, a road map of the region and a couple of dresses or skirts to meet Aunt Agathe's prejudice against slacks, though surely she would sanction trousers for cycling? There was also Orso Laurent's almost royal command to luncheon on Thursday. What should she wear for that? She must ask Aunt Agathe if, before then, she might wash her hair—it was lank and sticky after the sea crossing and the morning's rain, and for anywhere as grand as the Manoir appeared to be, she mustn't look like a tramp. Gradually coherent thought blurred and stopped. She was asleep.

She awoke with a start to sit bolt upright, listening for whatever unfamiliar sound had waked her. For something had, she knew. And though any sound in a strange house would be unfamiliar, she felt as disturbed by this one as if she had flushed a burglar in her room.

There it was again! The creaking of old boards under footfall. Someone walking, though farther away now. Going upstairs to the attic floor of the tall house? Or down to the ground floor? It was Aunt Agathe, of course. It had to be. Who else...?

On tiptoe Maria was out of bed and softly, she opened her door, which did not creak. Across the landing Agathe's door was shut fast, and the whole house was quiet now. If Agathe had left her room she had not switched on the light to either staircase, and the bathroom door stood ajar on darkness.

Maria waited for a few minutes, not liking to knock at the other door, disturbing Agathe for what seemed so little cause now. She went back to bed, and though she lay awake and alert for a long time nothing else happened to disturb her.

In the morning Agathe said nothing about having had a disturbed night, but merely asked how Maria had slept.

Maria said, "I took a long while to get to sleep, but then I slept well, I think, until I heard you about."

"This morning, you mean?"

"No, in the night."

Agathe stared. "In the *night*? I? I didn't leave my bed. What makes you think you heard me moving?"

"Not just in your room. I heard the stairs creak under your feet."

Agathe laughed shortly. "You slept better and more deeply than you knew, child. You dreamed all this. Footsteps in the night indeed!"

"But I got up to listen at my door," Maria protested. "There was nothing to see, but—"

"Then if you did hear something, it was the stairs creaking on their own. The furniture talks, too. You will often find this happening in a house as old as this one. It is nothing for alarm. You will get used to it," Agathe assured her.

Maria said no more. It was possible she had dreamed the whole thing, *if* she hadn't got up and gone to her door, and afterward lain awake. Or had she dreamed that, too? No. But if Agathe hadn't stirred, then it must have been the stairs playing a trick on her unaccustomed ears. Though she had never before heard wood creak in quite that way—as to the regular pad-pad of feet....

There was no cycle repairer in the village, Agathe told her. The nearest was at Calenzana. Yes, the road was a switchback, steep in places and with many zigzag turns. But as a girl she had often cycled it herself, and with care Maria should come to no harm.

The bicycle could hardly date back to her aunt's girlhood. But its life span couldn't be far short of it, thought Maria as she mounted its high saddle above its big old-fashioned wheels. With very little brake power and no bicycle bell at all, the journey to Calenzana was likely to be decidedly fraught.

The downhills were precipitous, the corners hairpin, and the uphills had to be trudged on foot. But she had the narrow road almost to herself, but for a few straying goats and a farm cart, which had to draw into the hedgerow to allow her to pass. "If I meet anything bigger or faster than that, *I* shall be doing the giving way," she thought, and then, on a corkscrew downhill slope that she was negotiating carefully, she met it—a long, open sports car, driven by a woman, using all the road there was at a criminal speed.

There was only one thing for a mere cyclist to do, and Maria did it. Bicycle and all, she fell against the high bank bordering the road, with less than six inches to spare between her and the careening car, which went past at such speed that she doubted whether the driver could tell whether she had been mown down or not.

Her legs shaking, she stood down on the road. The car had stopped and was coming back in reverse gear. Level with her, it stopped. The driver was young, her near-perfect complexion was lightly tanned and the wind was teasing strands of her chestnut hair from under the head-scarf tied over it. She wore a short-sleeved white trouser suit, and she removed white-rimmed sunglasses in order to stare at Maria, who stared back.

The other girl used attack as her defense. "What were you doing—weaving about the road like that?" she demanded in French. "I might have killed you!"

Maria agreed grimly, "You might indeed—the way you took that last corner and came on, though you must have seen me. Weaving! You didn't give me *room* to weave—if I hadn't thrown myself and my bicycle up the bank, you would have been within—that—" she demonstrated a tiny distance between her hands "—of catching my handlebars."

"And you were riding—so." In her turn the other girl mimicked an erratic path with a slim hand.

"I was doing nothing of the kind," Maria denied hotly. "And I was taking the hill carefully, because my brakes aren't very good."

That was a tactical error, and the girl jumped on it. "You take to roads like this without proper brakes? Really, you tourists on hired bicycles are a public nuisance! You should be very thankful that I missed you as I did," she accused.

Maria pulled the bicycle upright from the bank. "I am thankful—but not to you," she said. "And as it happens, I have been riding a bicycle since I was eight years old; I'm not a tourist and this bicycle isn't hired."

But once again her opponent was too much for her.

Looking the bicycle over, she drawled, "As one would certainly hope! For any dealer who hired out a museum piece like that should never hire another! *Au revoir, mademoiselle*. Down the next hill on your way, I would advise that you *walk*!" With which she put her car in gear and swept away, leaving Maria still shaken, but now more with impotent rage than with shock. She pedaled on into Calenzana, mulling over all the biting things she might have said, but hadn't had the wit to think of in time.

By experience she was to learn that Agathe could dispose of any circumstance or happening of which she disapproved, simply by ignoring its existence. But not knowing this on the day of her proposed visit to the Manoir, Maria expected to have to face some conflict on the subject, or at least some scathing remarks.

None came. Agathe's morning chat was as usual of domestic things. One of the laying hens had gone broodsy. She was running short of olive oil for cooking; Maria must take baskets and gather some for the press; there were always plenty of ripe ones fallen at this time of year; the monthly cheque from her lawyer was late—the postman had passed by. And she laid just her own place at the table for the midday meal without any remark at all.

Maria supposed that when Gian came to call for her, Agathe would have to acknowledge his arrival. But when he announced himself with a long blast on his horn, Agathe appeared to have heard nothing.

Maria waited, expecting Gian to come to the house. But after another blast, totally ignored by her aunt, she said lamely, "That will be Gian Laurent—for me. I'll be going now," and hurried out.

Gian, in the mufti of orange jeans and a sky-blue shirt, was standing against a small sports car, his thumb on the horn button.

"You needn't sound that again. I heard it and I'm here. But why didn't you come to the house for me?" Maria asked rather sharply.

He gave her an exaggerated bow and showed her into the car. "Because I didn't fancy being snubbed by your respected aunt. If we ever meet in the village she looks through me. The Juret-Laurent vendetta thing, you know," he said.

"Because, years ago, a relative of yours jilted my mother? But if neither side gives way, it could go on forever! And your brother came in with me the other day and met Aunt Agathe," Maria reminded him.

Gian shrugged. "Orso suits himself—usually for what he hopes to gain. Though one gathers he came away with empty hands that time. Your aunt refused him the land, didn't she?"

Aunt Agathe's suggestion again—that she, Maria, had been cast in the role of cat's-paw by Orso! Denying it to herself as much as to Gian, Maria said, "He didn't go to her with that in mind, I'm sure. It was she who brought up the subject."

"Ah well, if she hadn't, I daresay he would have done. All those good hectares of land running to *maquis* seed keep 'Brother Orso' awake o' nights, I know," declared Gian. He changed the subject. "How do you view Agathe yourself?"

Maria hesitated. "I didn't know what to expect. She is utterly different from my mother. Much more old-fashioned. Austere and rather . . . . " As she paused in search of the word she wanted Gian looked at her quickly and away.

"Sinister?" he offered.

"*Sinister?* Gracious, no. I was going to say *direct*. She doesn't waste many words, and she isn't very easy to get to know. But to me she has been kindness itself," said Maria.

"Then you'll be staying?"

"While she will have me, and until my cash runs out."

"Good." They smiled at each other, and Gian said, "We promised ourselves a date—remember? One of our own—not laid on for us by Orso. What about a flip down the coast to Ajaccio?"

"A flip?"

"By helicopter as my guest, if you don't mind sharing with two or three other passengers. If people are going for the day I have to wait to taxi them back again. So what about Sunday? Bring swimming gear, and among other things we'll have a dip. I'll call for you again."

"Thank you, I'd like that. But this time you must come in," Maria told him.

When they arrived at the Manoir Gian parked in the courtyard, saying he had to return to duty later. The inside of the house was in warm contrast to its forbidding exterior. It must have been of similar age as the Maas Juret, for the domed ceilings of the reception rooms and the hall showed the same Moroccan influence. But the Maas was a farmhouse and the Manoir a mansion, and much taste had gone into its furnishings.

The salon into which Gian showed Maria was a long room running the length of the front-to-back elevation of the house. Two French windows opened onto a balustraded loggia, and as Gian and Maria entered from the hall two people were silhouetted against the light from a window at the far end.

They were standing close together, aperitif glasses in their hands. They turned as the other two approached. One of them was Orso. The other was the sports car's reckless driver who had almost run down Maria on the Calenzana road.

Orso introduced them: "Madame Chantal Garson; Mademoiselle Maria Dane."

Chantal Garson offered a coolly polite hand. "Well,

well," she drawled, "who would have said we moved in the same circles? And do you know, *mademoiselle*, after our encounter the other morning, I doubted that you would reach your journey's end in one piece?" She turned to Orso with a laugh. "*Mon cher*, you should have seen ...! A bicycle straight out of the Iron Age, and Mademoiselle fighting to control it in the middle of the road! I'm afraid I showed I wasn't amused. But now I suppose you'll insist that we make it up? And of course we shall—to please you!"

CHAPTER THREE

ORSO SAID SHARPLY, "So you have met? How?"

"*Met?*" laughed Chantal Garson. "We nearly collided on the road between here and Calenzana. Mademoiselle's machine had no brakes—"

"I'm afraid you misheard me," Maria put in quietly. "I admitted that my brakes weren't very good, but I was riding well within my ability to pull up."

"This was the bicycle your aunt mentioned?" Orso asked her. "And you've ridden it on these roads without proper brakes?"

"To Calenzana and back to get new brake blocks fitted. It's pretty old-fashioned, but it's got wheels and tires and a saddle, and I think I shall find it very useful while I am here," Maria told him.

"You shouldn't have ridden it while its brakes weren't functioning. You could have mentioned it today, and I'd have sent a man over to see to it." He turned to Chantal. "Maria is Agathe Juret's English niece. You'll remember the Juret farm?"

Chantal widened the tawny eyes that matched her rich hair. "I remember *Agathe*!" she said, affecting to shudder. "When I was small I was terrified of her. In my own mind I decided she was a witch straight out of a Perrault fairy tale. She haunted my dreams!"

"Mine, too," claimed Gian from the background. "Meanwhile, may I mention that we haven't asked Maria what she will drink?"

He poured and brought her choice to her as Chantal

asked how long she was staying, adding in an arch aside to Orso, "I have to confess *mademoiselle* didn't like at *all* my taking her for a tourist!" before drifting over to one of the loggia French windows, where she beckoned to Orso to follow her and they both went out.

Gian emitted a long "Whew! Chantal," he commented, "in all her old form—prettily disposing of every attractive female in sight. One might have hoped that widowhood might have mellowed her. But no! She is as handy with the rapier as ever I remember her."

"Madame Garson is a widow?" Maria questioned.

He nodded. "As I said. She was born Chantal Ferrier. Her people are wealthy cork exporters in Calenzana who had her lined up for a *mariage de raison* with Orso since she was seventeen. But when she was twenty or so Papa Ferrier married her off to an even more eligible rich American named Garson. Meat for a prize vendetta between our families, one would say. But it didn't take that turn. And now here she is, back home again after three years of marriage and one of being a widow, and apparently intent on picking up with Orso where they left off."

"I didn't know arranged marriages were still practiced," murmured Maria.

"Oh, they are, over here. By parents, or even by older brothers for younger ones or for sisters. Though nowadays it is rather more of an idea that such and such a marriage would be 'suitable' than it's an ironcast pact. Our generation won't stand for it. As I certainly wouldn't, if either father or Orso tried it on me."

"They wouldn't, would they?"

"You never know. Father propelled Chantal in Orso's direction, and as it seems to be working out after all, it could give him or Orso ideas about someone for me. What isn't usual is for a broken arrangement to be patched up later, as Orso's and Chantal's promises to be. You'd think he had more pride, having been jilted once."

You'd think he had more pride. It was Maria's own reluctant reaction to Gian's gossip. From the little she admittedly knew of Orso, her imagination could not fit him into the role either of a biddable partner to an arranged marriage or that of claimant for a woman who, willingly or not, had been persuaded to reject him earlier.

From her brief experience of him, it wasn't in his character. Or if he could be flexible...vulnerable, it was a side of him she hadn't seen. Even his kindness to her had been impersonal, detached, as if he had a duty to her, though no warm inclination to help her. Gian's easy friendship was a camaraderie she understood; it was of her own age-group and set and she responded to it naturally. But her vanity—it had to be her vanity; what else could it be—was intrigued by Orso's aloofness. She wondered what or who involved him deeply. Work? Sport? Love? Chantal...?

Now she watched as Gian went down the room to meet the elderly man who came in, accompanied by a manservant and supporting himself on a stick. Pascal Laurent had Orso's black eyes in a broad leonine head, and Gian's curling hair, though his own had receded now. He sat heavily in the nearest chair, dismissed the man and looked a question at Maria.

Gian introduced them: "My father—Maria Dane," at which the old man took her hand and held it, frowning and nodding as he said, "Ah yes—Orso told me about you. You are Sorel Juret's daughter. One heard that in the end she married an Englishman, though before that a cousin of mine had done her no good service with his false courting. For which her family never forgave ours, though you, child, bear us no grudge, one hopes?"

"No indeed," Maria assured him warmly. "I'm grateful to both your sons for befriending me and asking me to your house."

"And the other sister—the last Juret left—she is less bitter against us now, since she has allowed you to know us?"

Maria shook her head. "My aunt, *monsieur*? I'm afraid not. But she has said I am free to come and go as I please while I am here."

"Then you must let us do all we can to make you welcome. This is the least return we can make you for the wrong your mother suffered at Jules Beauloin's hands." He turned to Gian. "Where is Orso? Is Chantal here?" he asked, just as they returned from the loggia. "Ah, Chantal my dear!" he added, his face lighting up at sight of her.

Both hands outstretched in greeting, Chantal went to him, touching each of his cheeks with her lips. Orso refilled glasses, and presently they were summoned to lunch by a gong.

Over the meal Maria learned that her host was researching and writing a folklore history of the island. "The scope is enormous," he said. "Our people are soaked in centuries-old customs and superstitions—some of them quaint and picturesque, others with a darker side to them. Already I have amassed an unwieldy mass of notes and handwritten manuscript, which I shall have to put into order soon—make a fair draft of the first chapters and send them down into Calvi to be typewritten."

"You don't type yourself?" asked Maria.

He smiled deprecatingly. "No. I have a machine, but the mechanics of the thing come between me and my ideas. My prose dries up. But after luncheon Gian shall bring you to my study and I'll show you how I work, if you are interested."

Maria was, and said so. But from across the table Gian said, "Sorry, father, but if I'm to take Maria home, I must whisk her away as soon as we've had coffee. I'm on the evening duty roster at four."

"Then you needn't take her home. If she can stay a little longer, Orso can drive her," the old man decided. "Orso, you can do that?"

"Of course."

They adjourned to the salon where Chantal presided over the coffee tray brought there by the manservant who had waited on the table, helped by a young maid. Pascal Laurent, who did not take coffee, went to his study, and Gian mentioned his invitation to fly Maria to Ajaccio on Sunday.

"Sunday?" queried Chantal. She looked at Orso. "Shall we go, too?"

A shade too quickly for good manners, Gian said to that, "Not on Sunday, I'm afraid. I've checked, and I shall be carrying two other passengers. The chopper will be full."

Chantal's lip curled in a half-smile. "Don't sound too eager to have us along, dear boy! And I wasn't suggesting we beg a free ride. Nor does a helicopter happen to be my first choice of transport. If we went, we would drive down. Orso, would that suit you?"

"Yes, if you'd like to go. We'll talk about it." He stood and returned his cup to the tray. Gian said he must leave, and went, and Orso, ready to show Maria to the study, looked back at Chantal.

"You won't be going yet?" he asked her.

She stood, picking up her bag. "Yes. Now," she said.

"I thought you wanted to—?"

"Forget it," she retorted crisply. "I didn't know you were going to have to play chauffeur to all and sundry. I can't wait."

"Then I'll ring you about Sunday?"

"Yes, do that." She nodded to Maria. "I wouldn't ride that velocipede of yours without sporting a red flag back and front," she quipped, blew a kiss at Orso and went ahead of them out to her car.

Pascal Laurent's study proved to be a workroom in the fullest sense. Floor-to-ceiling bookshelves lined the walls, a large map of Corsica was pinned to the back of the door, books were in askew piles on the desk and the "mass of manuscript" was very much in evidence.

"You see," he gestured ruefully. "I am not a tidy writer, either in thought or execution. An idea comes to me, and I must write it down at once. But where is it when I want to use it? As likely as not, on a scrap of paper that I have since destroyed. I have no discipline, as Orso here frequently tells me, and the result is the muddle you see."

Maria looked around her, noting the office typewriter under its plastic cover on a side table. "I think you said you had some chapters of your book ready for typing, didn't you?" she asked.

"Alas, not ready, though nearly so. They are here somewhere...." He riffled through the pile of paper on the table, detaching a bundle of sheets and squaring them off.

"Because," Maria went on, "I am a skilled typist. It's my job, and if you would trust me, I could probably help you with that. With fair copying it in type, I mean."

"You could?" His eyes lighted eagerly. "You could type from my handwritten script, and in French?"

"I think so." She picked up a sheet and read aloud from it without difficulty.

"That is splendid. But how? And when...?"

"Perhaps Maria could come over, say, on one day a week?" It was Orso who answered his father's question. "Since you've offered, could you manage that, do you think?" he asked her.

"I'd like to."

"Yes, well .... It would be better than taking the work away with you. Then you could check with father on the spot if you were in difficulty," he suggested.

"And when could you come, my dear?" asked Pascal.

"Any day. Say next Tuesday?" she offered at random.

"Good. I will have something ready for you by then. You will see...." Papers skittered beneath his busy hands as he set to work.

They left him to it, as Maria said it was time she was going. On their way out to his car, Orso said, "That was good of you, though have you considered Agathe's reaction?"

"I hope she won't mind. I shall be glad of having something to do while I'm here. I help her in the house a little, but she does most of it and all the cooking. Besides, the house—" Maria broke off.

"What about the house?"

"Well, it's rather grim. I long to be out of it, in the sun walking or doing something away from it. It's as if—" she voiced a vague feeling "—as if it were brooding over its troubles and had to groan now and then."

"Groan? How so?"

"It creaks. Makes the oddest noises. In fact, the first night I slept in it, I thought it was Aunt Agathe moving about. But of course it wasn't."

"Of course not. You must have magnified sounds that were strange to you," Orso agreed sharply.

"Or I was dreaming, which is what my aunt said."

They had reached the car, but Orso hesitated. "No, I think we'll walk," he decided aloud. "Oh, not by the road," he added to Maria's questioning look. "By the short cut through the *maquis* that I told you of, if you're willing?"

"So that I could choose to walk or cycle over on Tuesdays? Yes, please, I'd like to know it," she agreed.

"Can you make it in those?" He indicated the light pumps she wore. "The path will be dry, but it's rough going. You should be wearing sensible shoes."

"I am always up for walking. I didn't know I was going to, today. Please let's go," she begged. Two kilometers on foot would take longer than five by car, and though her conscience called her back to the Maas, her will was in no hurry to get there.

"Come along then." He led the way around the back of the house, through a kitchen garden, past some hot-houses and out into a lane.

A few minutes of this, and he struck off into the border-ing *maquis* along a path slippery with air roots and in places so narrow that Maria had to follow in single file.

She was able to brush both hands along the waist-high woody shrubs. "It doesn't smell as sweetly close up as it does from a distance or from the sea," she remarked.

"No, it needs a breeze to carry it," Orso replied over his shoulder.

"It's rather like thrusting through a field of corn. You could sit or lie down in it, and no one would guess you were there."

"Yes. Though there are easier ways of getting lost in the *maquis* than playing hide-and-seek." His tone was dry. "Believe you are keeping to a path when you aren't, and there's no knowing where you may end up. Deeper in, it all looks alike."

"I wouldn't care to have to find *this* path at night!"

The track was wider here and he waited for her to draw abreast. "Considering calling on us at night, then?" he asked, looking down at her.

She flushed. "No, of course not. But I hope it gets easier than this to follow."

"From your end? Yes, it does. You can't miss it. Or you couldn't, the last time I used it, which was the other side of the winter. It opens up from just behind the Maas. You'll see. Steady...!"

His hand went briefly across her shoulder as she slid and stumbled. They walked on in silence until he said, "I'm glad for your sake that you are going to help father. He knows more about the island and its ways than almost anyone I know, and you'll learn a lot from him."

Maria said, meaning it, "You are very good. You want to put me in the way of getting to know the real Corsica, and I can't think why you would trouble."

"Which is where we came in. You asked me much the

same thing once before ... remember?" The path narrowed and he went ahead of her again, adding over his shoulder, "And my answer is the same as then—because, as a blood-Corsican, you ought to know your own country for what it is ... feel enough intrigued with it to want to come again. Or even not to leave it at all."

She laughed at that. "I must leave it some time. I've my living to earn."

"Until you marry, perhaps. And why shouldn't you marry here?"

She laughed again more shortly. "Not very likely. I only met Gian and you by the merest chance, otherwise I'd know no one. Aunt Agathe is very self-sufficient and I doubt if she has many friends. No one seems to come to the house, not even tradespeople."

"All the same, you haven't done so badly under your own steam so far. You *did* meet Gian by chance, and he doesn't seem ill pleased with his luck."

"That sounds as if I were something he got out of a bran tub!" Maria felt she must ask a question that was easier to put to Orso's back than to his face. "The day we met, I got the impression that you thought I had let him pick me up. Did you?" she asked.

"Well, he had, hadn't he ... literally?"

She bit her lip. "Yes. But you know I meant in the other sense. That I had been too ... easy?"

A moment's silence. Then, "One can be wrong, but I admit it crossed my mind," he said.

"And yet you offered to see me to the Maas, when Gian hadn't. Why did you do that?"

"Why not? One has certain obligations to strangers, and Gian seemed to have fallen down on his."

(What was she pressing to let him know; what had she wanted to hear him tell her? Whatever it had been she was no further on, and she felt vaguely cheated.) She made one last lame attempt to force the issue (what issue?). "There was no need. I could have caught the next bus," she said.

"Nonsense. For the moment you were stranded and we were going your way. What more sensible than that . . . ?" He broke off, halted and stared ahead. "Well, that's a hazard I hadn't reckoned on," he said as if to himself.

She drew level with him. "What?"she asked.

"This." He walked on, pointing until she saw what he meant. No more than twenty paces on, the path and the *maquis* stopped abruptly at the edge of a deep chasm, running right and left out of sight, at its narrowest where the path stopped, but far too wide for striding. Yet at the far lip of the chasm the path went on, as did the inexorable *maquis*.

"What is it? I don't understand. Didn't you know it was here?" Maria queried.

"Of course I knew it was here. It's a rock fault that has always been here. But there was a handrail bridge across it at this point—you can see where the path continues, and there's no sign of it now—not even of any broken woodwork. It must have been swept away in the winter floods and no one has bothered to repair it. So now what?" He pondered his own question, measuring the width of the gap with his eye.

"Must we go back? Or could we cross it somewhere else—this way or that?" Maria's sideways nod of her head indicated the left and right length of the rift.

"No, it gets wider both ways. That's why the path was worn here and the bridge thrown over." He considered the gap again. "I could jump it," he suggested.

"But *I* couldn't!"

"I meant—carrying you, if you're prepared to risk it."

"Oh! I . . . that is, *could* you?"

He smiled. "Didn't you know we Corsican males are all born with cloven feet, like mountain goats? Come here. . . ."

She hung back. "You can't. I shall be too heavy."

"That I shall have to find out to our peril, won't I?" Moving over to her, he slid one hand behind her knees, the other arm around her shoulders, and lifted her. Black eyes looked down into gray. "Ready?" he asked, and braced himself for the jump.

At the moment of impact of their landing on the far side of the rift he grasped her body more closely, breaking the shock for her. As he steadied himself, feet apart, she felt his heart thudding from the effort of the leap. Her own, for no such reason, had quickened, too. He held her for another moment, then set her down and watched as she went through the instinctive feminine motions of smoothing down her dress and throwing back her hair. Her heart quietened, but she felt oddly shy. "I *am* knight-errant prone, aren't I?" she said. "First Gian, and now you—"

"Ah, but this was my fault," he said quickly. "I should have checked. But I'll send a couple of men over tomorrow, with the makings of a new bridge."

"Your own men? Is all this your land, then?" she asked, surprised.

"*Mon dieu*, no. If it were, it wouldn't be in this state. Though we are very near the Maas now, it isn't your aunt's either. But you heard her say that Corsicans make a point of honor of not selling family land? Well, that's so. When fighting the *maquis* breaks their spirit they tend to walk out and take jobs in the towns or on the mainland. That's why there are vast tracts going to waste; it becomes almost impossible after a time to trace whose is the title to any land one wants to buy and redeem. Or sometimes, as a last-ditch stand before they abandon a farm to the *maquis*, they'll resort to arson."

"Arson? But isn't that criminal?"

"And who is to prove that the fire wasn't caused by a camper's match, or a cigarette stub, or a broken bottle act-

ing as a burning glass? No, if a lucky accident like that
'happens' to clear a few hectares and the damage is reasonably contained, there are likely to be few questions asked.
After all, there are so many spontaneous fires—hundreds
during the summer, and nothing burns faster than
maquis—it's worth no one's trouble to investigate the few
that may be due to arson on a man's own property. A different matter, of course," Orso added, "if it can be proved
to be deliberate, to a neighbor's property."

"You mean that is sometimes done?"

"If one has a grudge against an enemy, it's one way of
settling scores."

"But what a wicked way to do it!"

He shrugged. " 'All's fair . . . .' " he quoted. "And a can
of petrol and a box of matches are handier weapons than
some."

As he had said, the path brought them out quite close to
the Maas and behind it. He left her there to go in by the
back entrance, asking first whether or not she had made
her arrangements with Gian for Sunday. When she told
him she had he said "Good," and offered his hand. "You'll
be there before Chantal and me, but we must meet somewhere for a meal and a swim. I'll fix it with Gian," he said.

IT WAS WITH SOME MISGIVING that Maria told Agathe of
the proposed trip to Ajaccio, prepared to forgo it if her
aunt made any objection. But as with her luncheon date at
the Manoir, Agathe made no comment, except to say,
"Then I shall have only myself to please as to what I have
for meals that day,"—which was Maria's second experience of her baffling refusal to acknowledge facts that dis-
pleased her. Tempted at first not to mention her offer of
help to Monsieur Laurent, Maria changed her mind and
did so—only to meet the same stone wall of apparent lack
of interest on Agathe's part. Her next remark was a re-

minder to Maria that she needed olives for the press, and Maria, half-relieved, half-frustrated, agreed readily to go and gather these.

Baskets in hand, she said, "I know they are lying thick on the ground under every olive tree. But do you really mean they are there for anyone at all to take?"

"But of course," said Agathe. "There are too many olive trees and they never have a barren season. All that are not taken by people who need them will only lie where they are until they rot."

"I've seen a lot that are shrunken and wrinkled already," said Maria. "As near to rotten as not."

"And you must not reject them because of that," Agathe ruled. "A shriveled olive yields as much oil as a fat one. I have only a small handpress, so the two panniers full will be enough for today. You can go again another time. The olives will wait for you."

It was rather like going blackberrying—in March! thought Maria as she set out. More backaching, but less painful and no need to search far for a good harvest.

She took a lane that she had earlier explored for a little way and had noted a group of the fine old gnarled trees in a small grove just off the roadway. Here the last of the crop still clung to the branches, but the main bulk of it was a thick carpet of fruit in varying stages of overripeness on the ground. She knelt, gathering them in with both hands, remembering Agathe's tolerance of the shriveled ones, but discarding on her own account those that were already slimy with decomposition.

Presently there was the sound of voices in the lane and three young village girls, carrying between them baskets as deep as full-sized barrels, made for the grove, chose a tree, laid down mats of dried sheepskin and began to shovel olives into the baskets by the handful. They glanced in curiosity at Maria, then, catching her eye, one of them smiled and came over to her, dragging a spare sheepskin. "You need something for kneeling, *mademoiselle*. The ground is hard," she said.

"Yes, isn't it?" Maria agreed. "But I have nearly finished, as you see."

The girl looked critically at the panniers. "You will not press much oil from that lot. Is that all you need?"

"For today, yes. But perhaps I can help to fill your baskets for you?" Maria offered in return for the sheepskin.

"That is kind." The girl led the way, said something in Corsican *patois* to the two younger ones, who nodded and smiled at Maria and made room for her to kneel beside them. Between themselves they chattered in Corsican, but they understood her French and could answer her in it. Their names, she learned, were Anne-Marie, Hélène and Berthine; they lived in the village and they could earn a few francs by gathering olives for the local machine press. Yes indeed—the baskets would hold many kilos, but they scorned Maria's doubt that when they were full the three of them would find them too heavy to carry. They asked her her name. They did not know her. English—so? And why had she come to the region from so far away? Was she a tourist who would go back soon? Or was she staying, and where?

It was her reply to this latter question, that had a galvanic effect on all three of them. They stared, wide-eyed and open-mouthed. Hélène quavered, "At Madame Juret's? She is your aunt? But do you not know? She is a...!"

"*Tais-toi!* Hold your wild tongue!" It was Anne-Marie, the older girl, who cut in, scowling at Hélène, who pouted and launched on an incomprehensible gabble to Berthine.

"Take no notice, *mademoiselle*. She is a gossip, with her mother as her example," Anne-Marie told Maria placatingly. "It is just our surprise, since no one visits at the Maas Juret now. You are the first one for years who...."

"But what did Hélène mean, when she began to say my aunt was a...something?" Maria interrupted.

Anne-Marie flushed. "Nothing, *mademoiselle*. I have told you, her tongue runs away with her. Or if she meant anything, it was to say that Madame Juret was a...a solitary lady, one who seems to have few friends. Or...or something like that."

It was a gallant effort but a lame one. Maria felt quite sure that Anne-Marie knew well what she had cut Hélène short from saying, and that it had been some disparagement of Agathe. What could it have been? But as Anne-Marie would be unlikely to let the younger girl repeat it, Maria thought it diplomatic to let it pass. She merely nodded to Hélène. "Yes. My mother, who is dead, was Madame Juret's younger sister."

To which Hélène returned only a blank "Oh," and they all went on amassing olives until the big baskets were full.

Then Anne-Marie slung one of them nonchalantly onto her back, holding it there by both hands put back over her shoulders. The two younger girls carried the other between them, and the little party broke up after exchanged *Au 'voirs*.

Taking up her own baskets, Maria watched the three until they were out of sight. She was remembering Gian's equal dismay on first hearing of her destination, his reluctance to see her safely there, his thoughtless quip that he couldn't see Agathe as "anyone's aunt," and his offer of "sinister" when she had been seeking a word to describe Agathe.

What *was* it then with Agathe, which kept her so friendless and people at bay from her? Even people as brusque as she was usually had *some* contacts. Yet, as Maria had told Orso, no neighbors called at the house, and when, on her first Sunday, they had walked together to the little church in Creno, Agathe had spoken to no one, not even the padre; and nobody had spoken to her.

Evidently there was a word that described her adversely, for the child Hélène had almost spoken it. Agathe was a ... what? Maria wondered whether or not, if she asked, she could expect some more responsible person to enlighten her. But she knew she would not ask. Some quirk of loyalty to Agathe would not let her.

CHAPTER FOUR

FOR MARIA, as for her fellow passengers, a young honeymoon couple, the flight to Ajaccio from Calvi was over far too soon. Never having boarded a helicopter before, she had been a little nervous of the adventure. But the scenery along the west coast was so arresting as to take all her attention, and Gian, who could be blasé about it, having done the trip so often, was as gratified by her pleasure as if he had laid out the astonishing panorama himself.

In order that they should see the jagged, broken line of the coast, for the most part he flew over the sea and low enough for his passengers to marvel at the colors, streaked purple and ocher, of the cliff walls, which plunged sheer into blue green water that heaved and sucked and swirled into the caverns at their bases.

Too soon they were flying over the great bight that was the Gulf of Porto and which scenically had everything—sapphire sea, golden shoreline, a town of gray and pink granite buildings, and inland, slopes deep in the inevitable *maquis*; foothills dark with forest trees and above all, the tooth-edged peaks and ridges of the mountains whose reflections fell in dark shadows on the surface of the sea.

Then there was more wild coastline, the smaller gulfs of Sagone and Lava, and then the outflung chain of barren islands, the Iles Sanguinaires, guarding the bay of Ajaccio like a man-made bastion.

At the heliport, under Gian's skilled hands, the craft hovered and settled gently groundward. A time was arranged for the return journey; the other couple went off on

their own, and Gian and Maria took a taxi into the town
along typical Mediterranean avenues of white villas, open-
air cafés and palm trees.

The hotel that was to be their rendezvous with Orso and
Chantal had a private beach and Gian suggested they
should go there first for a drink before a swim. But Maria
wanted to see the old town of canyonlike streets and cob-
bled squares and, of course, the house where Napoleon
Bonaparte was born. At her insistence on this, Gian
scoffed, "In Calenzana we can boast of a chap who was
much more with it—by name, Don Juan."

"Really? I didn't know that?" Maria queried.

"Yes. His people were refugees from Spain."

"Whereabouts in Calenzana did they live?"

"I don't know. But why the eager interest? Are you looking for a Don Juan yourself? If so, I daresay I could give a
passable imitation." Gian grinned.

They came out from the severe seventeenth-century
house behind the harbor onto the fishing quays where
fishermen were dyeing and mending their nets, crowding
the dark bars and watching their fellows' boats setting out
or returning with a catch. By the time Maria's interest was
satisfied and they went back to the hotel, the other two had
arrived and were drinking on a terrace facing the sea.

Chantal was exquisite in white. Though she had sunglasses, she had pushed them up to ride on her head, and
Maria noticed today that her golden eyes were flecked with
green—the perfect foil for her rich hair. Orso was casual in
shirt and slacks, dark glasses making his expression unreadable. Gian was loud with grievance that he had to be
trussed up in uniform. Once he got into swimming trunks,
he declared, he wasn't going to change until it was time to
go home.

But they agreed to lunch first, after which, though they
all changed, the girls elected to sunbathe for a while before
swimming.

When Chantal appeared in the briefest of bikinis, Maria was painfully conscious of her own lack of tan after an English winter.

She explained ruefully, "We count ourselves lucky if we get any sunbathing sun before the end of June at least." At which Chantal, rubbing in perfumed oil and disposing herself prone upon her air mattress, murmured pityingly. "Too bad for you. If I didn't keep a tan all year around, I should die of shame in a bikini. Men don't appreciate the trouble we take, not to look like uncooked sausage meat from the neck down."

They basked in silence for some time, then Chantal raised herself on her elbows, resting her chin on her laced fingers. Not looking Maria's way, she said, "I suppose you know and are rather flattered by what Orso seems to be up to?"

Maria turned onto her side, propping her head on her hand. "Orso—up to?" she echoed.

"In the matter of you and Gian, I mean."

"What *about* Gian and me?"

"Oh, my dear...."

"Well, what?" pressed Maria, genuinely puzzled but apprehensive.

"My dear, if you really don't know and can't guess, then you don't know Orso as I do," returned Chantal.

"I've only met him two or three times. How could I expect to?" Maria murmured, not without an irony, which, however, escaped Chantal.

"No, how could you?" she agreed. "After all, I've known him since before I came back from school in France to find myself promised to him! I'm sure Gian will have told you *that*. A pity, I suppose, that later my father chose a better match for me in Grant Garson, but in the meantime I had learned quite a lot about Orso's autocratic ways, and it's no secret to me that he is plotting a match between Gian and you."

At that, for all her sense of outrage, Maria laughed aloud. She sat up, turning to clasp her knees. "But that's quite, quite absurd," she protested. "I've seen Gian just about as few times as I've seen Orso, and it was entirely by chance that I met them at all. So how could Orso possibly be harboring any such idea? And why? Even if he had the power to bring it about? In *these* days! Really!"

Chantal sat up, then knelt to rummage in her beach bag for lipstick and mirror. "As you please," she said indifferently. "Though I wouldn't question Orso's power, as long as he had the will to do anything."

"Even twisting people by the arm to force them to the altar?" scoffed Maria.

Chantal threw her a slanting glance. "But in this case would he need to use force—for either of you? Gian seems quite taken by you, and you... well, wouldn't you see some advantage in marriage to a Laurent?"

"Certainly not—on those terms," said Maria promptly. "And if you can suggest why Orso would want to match-make, you are well ahead of me."

"Then I'm ahead of you," agreed Chantal. "Because I would hazard two reasons. One, that he thinks it time Gian stopped sowing his wild oats and put down some roots. Gian's enthusiastic affairs last on an average about a month, and even he would admit they're not serious. No Laurent material. For instance, as well as you, one hears he is running a pretty little Cypriot number named Anna Lesnos. She dances at the Valin nightclub in Calvi. And two—it just could be that Orso is hoping to lay his hands on the Maas Juret land through you."

"Which is about as unlikely as your whole idea is absurd," said Maria. "I haven't any influence with my aunt in regard to her land."

"But Orso may believe she will make you her heir to it. Or even that he might not have to wait so long, if an alli ance with Gian might patch up that old quarrel between the Jurets and the Laurents." Chantal smoothed color onto her lips with her little finger before returning lipstick and mirror to her bag. "Anyway," she concluded, "with that still between them, why should the Laurents be cultivating you rather earnestly, unless—" She cut short the subtle insult of that as the two men came up the beach from the sea. She offered both hands to Orso, indicating that he should pull her to her feet. Maria was already standing, but Gian took her hand and swung it.

"Time you two dipped your toes in," he said, and to Maria, "Can you make it out to the raft?"

"I think so."

But they dallied on the way. Orso outstripped them all in pace. Chantal swam and dolphin dived like a mermaid and Gian indulged in surprises and tricks—catching at people's legs, ducking their heads and forcibly lifesaving them. Orso and Chantal, swimming side by side, were first at the raft. Maria followed them and, with her hands on the edge, was attempting the bounce, which would take her onto it when Gian, behind her, lifted her and himself up bodily, retaining his hold on her waist when they were aboard. "Nice shape," he murmured, smoothing his hands down over her hips before he released her.

She glanced at Orso; saw he was lazily watching and wondered whether he had noticed or disapproved of her instinctive recoil from the intimacy of Gian's touch. But to think he was interested, one way or the other, was to admit that Chantal's mischievous surmise had some grounds to it! And that she would not believe, however self-conscious it made her with both men until she was able to forget it.

They sunbathed for a while, then swam again. The sun sank toward the horizon and the air grew cooler. They swam shoreward then and when they had changed Gian said that though he must not drink again as he was flying,

he would sit by with a mineral water while the others had
one before he and Maria must go to keep their rendezvous
with his other passengers.

Drinks were brought to the terrace, but Chantal had
taken only a sip of hers when she stood, picking up her
bag.

"I promised I would ring mother from here. I'd better do
it now."

When she came back she looked shaken. "It's my father," she said in answer to Orso's question. "He has had a
heart attack and he has been taken to the hospital in Calvi.
He is very ill."

"So suddenly? Was he all right this morning?" Orso
asked.

"Yes. No," she corrected herself. "That is, he half-
fainted while he was dressing and didn't feel well, and my
mother asked me to ring during the day to hear how he
was."

"And you didn't call her until now?"

"I...forgot."

"You didn't mention it. You shouldn't have come away.
Has he had anything of the sort before?"

"Once—no, twice. But nothing so severe. My mother
sounded beside herself—nearly hysterical, and angry that I
didn't ring before. I just caught her before she went to the
hospital to spend the night if necessary."

"If he had had two earlier warnings, I wonder that you
left her this morning." There was censure in Orso's tone,
and Chantal's lip quivered.

"Now you are angry, too!" she said piteously.

"Rather surprised, not angry." He stood. "Now I've to
get you back as soon as possible. Just as well we came in
your car; it's faster than mine. But we shall still be nearly
three hours on the road. Or I don't know...." He paused in
thought. "Gian, how long did you take to fly down?" he
asked.

"M'm... less than an hour. About forty-five minutes."

"Then you could take Chantal back, gaining at least two hours."

Gian shook his head. "No room. But I could get permission to lay on a special flight and come back for her."

"That would gain very little time. No, I'm suggesting that you take Chantal back, and Maria comes with me. How about that?"

"Oh. Well, yes ... could do," Gian agreed. "And I'm off duty when I get back, so I could see Chantal to the hospital. Or home, whichever she wants."

"Good. Then... on our way. We can all pack into Chantal's car to get you out to the airport; we'll drop you and then go on."

For all her need of urgency Chantal did not seem to care for the arrangement. "Do I have to?" she appealed to Orso. "You know I hate helicopters."

But he was firm. "My dear, you can't afford to lose any time," he ruled. "Two hours could make all the difference, if only to your mother's peace of mind." Nobody consulted Maria.

Half an hour later she and Orso were on their way north in Chantal's open car, climbing toward the pass through the first group of mountains on their journey. They had left the coast far to their left, but would drop down to it again for some distance before the next range of heights and the next beyond that, Orso said. Then again the road would follow the coast for most of the rest of the way to Calvi.

From the San Bastiano Pass the sea was just visible; on the right of the road the last rays of the setting sun were turning jagged granite peaks from gray to incredible color—pink and orange, with violet-shadowed recesses hewn by a giant hand between them. At Maria's exclamation of wonder Orso slowed the car at the top of the pass, stopping for a while until, at the final dipping of the sun, the colors faded; grays were gray again and blacks black, and a necklace of mist began to form and swirl at the level of the lower peaks. Maria sat back with a sigh of pleasure and Orso put the car to the winding road downhill.

So far he hadn't asked whether or not she had given Agathe a promise to be home at any particular hour. But now he did, and she told him no, because she hadn't known what Gian's plans were for timing the return journey. She did not add that when she had ventured a vague, "I don't expect I shall be late," she might as well have said nothing. Agathe had pretended not to hear.

Orso commented, "Too bad for Gian, if he meant to give you a night on the town when he got you back to Calvi."

"But I couldn't have gone. That would have made me too late," she objected.

"He would still have wanted to give you a meal. As I shall have to, somewhere on our way."

Maria did not care for the dutiful sound of "have to." "Oh, that's not necessary," she said. "I—"

"Nonsense. You haven't eaten since lunch and we've two hours' driving ahead of us yet. We'll stop somewhere along the coast, though I warn you the menu will almost certainly be *langouste* in some form or other. I hope you like lobster?"

Maria said a little absently that she did. But his mention of Gian had been a jarring reminder of Chantal's extravagant suggestion that he was a calculating matchmaker. She had wanted to forget it. It was too absurd. She had known quite early in their acquaintance that he was something of an autocrat, steering people and events in the way he wanted them to go. But that was in minor things. He couldn't possibly think he had the right to order *lives*...!

She turned a thoughtful look on his profile, noting the strength of the jawline and the arrogant carriage of the dark head. Why was she more intrigued with him than with Gian? Gian was so much easier a companion, whereas Orso—

She started at the sound of his voice. Not looking at her, his eyes intent on the road ahead, "Why the rapt expression?" he asked.

She laughed self-consciously. "Oh...was I staring?"

"As if you had to make sure of knowing me again. What were you thinking about?"

Wondering what she might learn if she told him the truth, she said, "I was comparing you with Gian."

His dark brows went up. "Really? To whose advantage?"

"Neither. I had only got as far as thinking how different you are from each other."

"Well, between us there are some ten years in age and about the same in experience, and peas-in-the-pod alike physically we certainly aren't. Nothing very perceptive about that. Was that all your gimlet gaze at me afforded you?"

He wasn't helping. "I've told you—I didn't realize I was looking so intent," she said lamely.

"Nor that your subject might be curious to know why?" He glanced at her briefly. "But you aren't telling, are you? So many marks allotted to Gian; so many to me, though for which qualities in each of us you are keeping to yourself?"

"I hadn't got as *far* as qualities," she protested. "I don't know you well enough."

"As well as I know you," he countered.

"Which isn't very—"

Not allowing her to finish, he nodded agreement. "You are right, of course; it's too early yet to play the truth game merely on first impressions. It could be dangerous."

"Dangerous?"

"To future relations—what else?" In his tone there was a finality that dropped the subject.

The café at which he stopped was on the quay of the first coastal village they came to after leaving the mountain road.

"It doesn't look much of a place, but I've been here before and they know how to cook. The tourists don't come here. Besides us, there will only be the locals, eating out," he explained, as he held aside the bead curtain at the door for Maria to enter the dark interior—a bar, with half a dozen laid tables, intimately candlelighted, in the far arm of the L-shaped room. Two of the tables had been put together to accommodate a family party—an eve-of-the-wedding affair for a young couple. The wine was flowing freely and the guests were pressing everyone, friends and strangers alike, to join in the infectious hilarity.

The dinner Orso ordered was simple—a creamy onion soup served with Parmesan and *croutons*, followed by lobster claws in a prawn sauce, accompanied by an amber wine recommended by the *patron.*

By the time they had finished this course the wedding party had embarked on some form of ritual that Orso had to explain to Maria, and which involved the arrival at the table of a plate of flat cakes, which might have been tarts or biscuits or sugar-dusted small fritters. The mother of the bride-to-be took charge of these, before handing them to her daughter who offered them with grave ceremony to her fiancé, and afterward to each relative or guest. The two then kissed each other and everyone ate his or her little cake amid general acclaim and congratulation.

"It's a modified survival of the *abbracciu*; the marriage rite that was enough to seal a union until the church ruled that marriages must be solemnized *by* the church," Orso said. "The kiss exchanged in front of an audience of friends and relatives, and the *fritelli*—yes, they are little fritters made of chestnut flour—eaten in the same company symbolized the future sharing of the couple's lives. In those days the *abbracciu* sanctioned the consummation of the marriage without more ado; nowadays it's just a quaint practice at the wedding breakfast, or at a party like this before the day. I wouldn't be surprised," he added, "if we aren't all asked to partake. Yes—the *fritelli* are being passed around."

While this was going on an elderly woman came in, to be greeted as Madame Signadore and invited to drink with the wedding party. She was in peasant costume of black veil and flowing basqued dress; her gaunt features were not unlike Agathe Juret's; her black eyes were luminous and darting. "Evidently the local clairvoyante; would you like your fortune told?" Orso asked Maria.

But the wedding party laid first claim to the clairvoyante's powers. Nothing would content them but that she must predict for the young couple, which she preceeded to do after various mysterious passings of her hands over a plate of mingled water and olive oil.

After that others of the party demanded her services, though as far as Maria could see, no money passed.

"Don't they have to cross her palm with silver or something?" she asked Orso.

He was shocked. "*Mon dieu*, no. She would be insulted. *Signadori* have dignity and standing. For them it's Art for Art's sake; they claim to be faith healers as well, and even the doctors respect them." He rose and went to speak to the woman, then brought her back to their table.

She gave Maria a grave smile. "For the *sgio*, too?" she asked Orso.

"If you like. But for the lady first," he said, and then in an aside to Maria said, "*Sgio* is a Corsican corruption of '*signore*'; otherwise, 'the gentleman,' meaning me."

The woman prepared a plate for each of them, tiptilting

Maria's and coaxing the separate blobs of oil to coalesce into a mass. When they did she nodded her satisfaction and broke into a gabble of Corsican, very little of which Maria understood. Then it was Orso's turn for treatment, after which he thanked her in Maria's name and his own and kissed her gnarled hand in parting.

Over their coffee Maria smiled. "I'm not much the wiser as to my fate. What did she say is to happen to me?"

"About the same things you might get out of a Christmas cracker or from a gypsy at a fair. You have suffered a bereavement; there is in your life a dark man whom you could love and who could love you. But as yet he is reluctant to embrace marriage, forgetting, as he should not, that to forbid oneself love is to give it spurs. So, if it proves too strong for him, as it may, you may hope to exchange the Kiss of Promise and have *fritelli* broken and eaten for you perhaps within the year. Oh yes—and she said that she could see you were a true woman, in that you will crave the domination of the man you love. Though in that," Orso added, "I think she may have been quoting Colette for dramatic color."

"Colette, the French writer?"

"Yes. Doesn't she say somewhere that all women need—how does she put it—'to feel the certitude, from head to foot, of being the prey of one living man'?"

A little shakily Maria said, "I don't know. I haven't read Colette. What did the *signadore* say about you?"

"Nothing enlightening as to my love life. That my oil had not massed as well as yours; therefore I must be on my guard against the Evil Eye of an enemy. That I am suffering certain frustrations at the moment, but that I plan too much; leave too little to my fate. She wanted to know when I had last acted on pure impulse, and when I told her I couldn't say—that impulse was usually a fool's errand, she shook her head over me as a lost cause. A man should leap ahead of himself now and then; behave against his character; kiss the wrong girl .... And when I said to that, 'And get my face slapped for my trouble?' she had the last word."

"Why, what did she say?" laughed Maria.

"That it did any man good to have his face slapped on occasion. It took the cold pride out of him and warmed the blood. And as there didn't seem any suitable riposte to that, I gave her best." He stood as he spoke and went to draw out Maria's chair. "If you are ready, we'll be going on."

With the sinking of the sun the air had grown colder and as they climbed to the next mountain shelf and the early darkness gathered, it was colder still. Maria, who wasn't dressed for open-air motoring, sat rigid and tensed, doing her best to control her shivers and her chattering teeth. But they had not escaped Orso, who stopped at the summit of a corkscrew climb. "I should not have let Chantal take her coat with her; you could have borrowed it. But I'll see if there is anything in the trunk; if not, you must have my jacket," he said.

He came back with a scarlet-lined parka. "You're in luck. It's one of mine; I must have left it in the car sometime when I was driving with Chantal." From his seat he turned to help her into it, wrapping its amplitude around her and turning back the jutting edge of the hood, making a scarlet frame for her face. "Now you need only a wolf and a grandmother and you could pass for Red Riding Hood any day," he remarked as he drove on.

Cuddling into the padded warmth of the parka, Maria was grateful for it. Lying back and relaxing, she compared the impersonal touch of his hands as he had wrapped it around her and adjusted its hood with the familiarity of Gian's smoothing of her hips on the raft. Orso's had been the care of a grown-up for a child for whom he was fur-

nishing comfort—no more. Gian's had been an intimacy
she had resented, but it showed his awareness of her as a
woman; he had meant that she would know it. She wondered what his plans for the evening might have been;
wondered how Orso and Chantal would have spent theirs,
if they had returned to Calvi together, instead of being
forced to change partners. Wondered....

But there the rhythmic hum of the car, the wine she had
drunk at dinner and her returning warmth must have
taken their toll. Her next conscious movement was the
start with which she awoke to find they were running
through the lighted streets of Calvi, making for the Calenzana road.

She knuckled her eyes. "I've been asleep," she said un-
necessarily.

"Like a babe," Orso agreed. "But you'll soon be home
now, and it isn't so very late." He glanced at the clock on
the dashboard. "Not much after nine."

At the house he got out of the car with her, but said that
he wouldn't go in. He must go back into Calenzana to see
if Chantal and her mother were at home or at the hospital.

"Well, good night, and thank you very much for bringing me back. Oh—your coat—"

But as she began to shrug out of the parka, he brought
both hands down on her shoulders. "Keep it until you are
indoors," he said. "You can return it any time you are
coming over to the Manoir."

"Very well. I'll do that."

For a moment they stood so—he looking down at her,
she up at him, and for one wild, heady moment she found
she was wondering what she would do or say, supposing...supposing he took the *signadore*'s advice at its literal face value and "kissed the wrong girl." But his hands
dropped away; they bade each other good-night again,
shook hands and she went into the house, after waiting to
see the car leave.

The kitchen door by which she entered was slightly ajar, but the kitchen and the house beyond were quite dark. She hadn't expected Agathe to show any interest in her day, but it would have been nice to have her return noticed and mildly welcomed. As it was, Agathe must already have gone to bed, and feeling a little cheated, Maria supposed she might as well go, too.

But in the hall, just before she switched on the light there, she heard a movement at the top of the stairs and looked up. It was Agathe who must just have gone up. But for some reason she was lighting her way with a hand torch, and to Maria's call of, "Aunt Agathe—I'm back safely," she made no sign that she had heard. She went into her room and the door closed behind her.

It was not until Maria was in her own room that she realized Agathe had been in her nightclothes and slippers. So she must indeed have gone to bed early, if between then and now she had undressed and then found occasion to go downstairs again and back. Maria remembered the open kitchen door. But surely Agathe wouldn't have gone into the yard without dressing gown or coat? And why the torch when all the lights were functioning? Maria gave it up, and, warned by the reception of her last questioning of her aunt's night prowling, she decided to say nothing about it. In the morning she would merely report the time of her homecoming, expecting no comment from Agathe and probably getting none.

SHE WAS RIGHT. All Agathe said was, "Ah, I had gone to bed before that," and went on setting up the handpress to take the olives Maria had gathered.

In spite of Agathe's refusal to discuss the Laurents or even to admit their existence, she and Maria got on remarkably well. Maria learned how to refine and bottle olive oil, to make a sweet-tasting bread of chestnut flour and to be patient with the long process of boiling and skimming of goats' milk to make the delicate soft cheese known as *brocciu*. As Agathe had said contentedly on Maria's first day at the Maas, she managed for the most part to live "off the country," needing to shop for very little.

On the day of her appointment with Monsieur Laurent, Maria remembered that she must return Orso's parka. As her bicycle had neither a carrier nor a bicycle basket, she decided to wear it on the outward journey. Before wheeling out the bicycle, she slipped on the parka in the *cave*, putting her hands by habit into its pockets and finding in one of them a folded paper.

Thinking nothing of the action, she had taken it out, unfolded it and had read a line or two of its contents before she realized she was reading someone else's letter. Written to a man—Orso—since it began, "*Chéri*" and went on:

"It was wonderful that you were not angry last night. But you must have been hurt. I understand that. I—"

But at that point Maria forced herself to stop reading. Nor, though she expected she could guess it, did she look for the signature. Carefully, making a business of it, she refolded the paper in its original creases and returned it to the pocket, thrusting it deep, as if by doing so she could make it disappear.

Of course she had known—everything spoke to it—that Orso and Chantal were on those terms. Those of a lover who could be "hurt" and a loved one who could "understand" after a lovers' quarrel. She had had no right to learn it for certain in the way she had. But now indeed, *indeed* Orso would have been kissing the wrong girl if he had shown any inclination to do so the other night!

She was welcomed at the Manoir by Monsieur Laurent, of whom she remembered to ask how Chantal's father was.

"He is much better, thank God," Pascal Laurent told

her. "He is still in the hospital, but will be allowed home soon and should not have a recurrence of the trouble if he lives quietly. We are very glad for Chantal; to lose both a husband and a father within a year would be hard for her. It is good that she has Orso to help her to forget. You know, I expect, that they were bethrothed to each other when they were younger?"

Maria said she did; that Gian had told her.

"Ah, Gian. . . . " The old man's face clouded slightly. "One could wish that his future were as clear as his brother's. Orso knows very well what he wants—to make a success of the estate and to have children of good Corsican blood to carry on our line. But Gian is the wild one. Now if only he would settle down with a Corsican girl of good family! But no. For him it is blow hot, blow cold, with one little café or nightclub type after another, though perhaps it is as well that he doesn't want to bring them home, and squires them so briefly that he breaks no hearts, one hopes."

For Maria that was an unwelcome reminder of Chantal's theory as to the family's plans for Gian and herself. If it were so, which she couldn't believe, she wondered how aware was Gian of them. When Corsican autocrats planned *mariages de raison*, did they tell either or both victims what was afoot—or not?

She had expected, from what Pascal Laurent had said, that she would be copy typing his backlog of handwritten manuscript. But instead he asked her if she could take dictation, as he wanted to get into shape the chapter of his book on which he was currently working. It dealt, he told her, with some of the darker, more sinister customs and beliefs that had survived the centuries. They might not make pleasant reading, but in a history of Corsican folklore they had to be given place, and in order that Maria would understand his later dictation, he proposed to read to her as much as he had written.

Before he began he drew his spectacles down his nose
and surveyed Maria over them. "I begin with the
signadori—nothing very sinister about them. They are
healers, they can ward off the Evil Eye; very worthy wom-
en, most of them, and in foretelling the future they sometimes, if not always, come very near the truth. But I hear
from Orso that he was able to introduce you to one the
other evening?"

Maria smiled. "Yes, he did, and she told my fortune."

"But not fair to make you blush by asking you what she
told you . . . h'm?"

"I don't think very much of it was true."

"Ah, you never know. You never know. But now I must
read. I deal next with the *voceratrice*—the singers who
gather at a funeral to mourn the dead in improvised
verse."

He began to read. Maria heard how, in the days when
the vendetta led almost inexorably to murder, the songs
chanted and the verse spoken at the victim's funeral were
always of the terrible vengeance to be wrought on the spil-
lers of blood, the singers working themselves into a frenzy
of hate during which they tore their own faces and their
hair to the ponderous music of the ceaseless drumming of
the butt ends of guns on the floor; the guns that would
later be used to avenge the dead whom that day were
mourned. The vendetta worked both ways. . . .

Pascal paused to look over his spectacles again. "Nowadays, the *voceratrice* make a good living out of the verses
they compose for peaceful deaths." He smiled. "One orders a consoling *voceru* as, in happier circumstances, one
orders the wedding cake, and in the particular circumstances, one never questions the price that is asked."

He laid aside the manuscript. "That is as far as I have
planned this chapter. There are other subjects to
come—the drum of death that is heard beating in the

maquis by everyone but the person about to die; the *attacar*, by which a man claims a woman by kissing her in public or snatching off her veil, and others. But the *mazzeri* follow naturally on from the *signadori*, so I shall take them next, if I may dictate now. You have heard of the *mazzeri*, mademoiselle?"

Maria said, "Please call me Maria, monsieur."

"Willingly, my dear, if I may."

"Thank you." She frowned as she caught at a memory. "While you have been reading I think I've heard from my mother about some of the customs you mention. But I'd forgotten them, and the *mazzeri* ... weren't they witches of some sort?"

Pascal Laurent shook his fine head. "More than that ... more disposed to evil, that is. A *mazzere* could be male, too, and there are still both men and women who are believed by their neighbors to be *mazzeri* and are cruelly shunned in consequence."

"But what is it—or was it—that was supposed to make them evil?"

"They were thought to have closer links with the spirits and with death than ordinary people. And they hunted at night—to kill. Sometimes in their own shape; sometimes they changed into dogs. Or they saw their enemies in the form of animals and attacked them. Any dead sheep or goat or dog found in the *maquis* would have its death put down to the nearest *mazzere* on the prowl. They set fire to property; they would fire the *maquis* in order to carry on a vendetta—planning that it would ▮▮▮▮ to an enemy's crops or stockyard or ▮▮▮▮▮▮▮▮ also controlled the weathe▮▮▮▮▮▮▮▮▮▮▮▮▮▮re up a *libeccio* to fan the

▮▮▮ did they live and look like ordinary people when they weren't working their evil?" asked Maria.

"Yes, indeed. It was said of some of them that they would be unaware, the next morning, of their night ex-

ploits. And you will still find people who will tell you tha
when they were children they believed their own grannie:
to be *mazzeri*! But now," concluded Pascal, "shall I try tc
put all that and more into some literary form?"

Maria prepared to take his dictation. But her penci
moved mechanically. She was hearing words and makin₅
the right symbols for them. But her mind was set upor
memories, on pictures, on things she was reluctant tc
know.

There had been Gian, on her first day in the island
Gian, who had been incredulous that she should be visitin₅
the Maas and who hadn't wanted to take her there. Anc
there had been Agathe's mysterious errand of that night
which in the morning she had denied. That other night
too, when she had been downstairs in her nighclothes
lighted only by a flashlight. And the village children, gathering olives . . . . The young one—Hélène—who had begur
to say of Agathe, "She is a . . ." only to be angrily stopped
by the oldest of the three. And the neighbors who did not
come to the house, nor speak to Agathe after church . . . .

Supposing the old house didn't "talk" in the night; tha₁
its uncanny creakings were caused by its mistress moving
about? And supposing the word Hélène hadn't been allowed to say had been "mazzere"? And supposing Agathe
was "cruelly shunned" because she was believed to be
one . . . ? Because even Gian thought so?

But that was absurd! There weren't such people; there
never had been, as no doubt Pascal Laurent's survey
would make clear. They were simply a primitive imagination run riot in search of cause and effect. What was she
thinking of, entertaining such ideas, such fears? This was
the twentieth century, not the Middle Ages!

Yet for all the bright sunlight, for all the warmth it
brought to the room, she felt chilled, as chilled as by the
momentary sensation that someone was walking on her
grave. But this chill remained.

CHAPTER FIVE

DURING THE DAYS that followed Maria wondered what had happened to her, that she could even entertain such fears as had been put into her mind about Agathe.

In England she could have laughed them off. For in England Agathe would merely be regarded as an eccentric spinster who did not mix; she certainly wouldn't be suspected of sorcery, and Maria herself wouldn't be torn between the sanity of knowing it couldn't be so and a reluctant half belief that it might.

It must be, she decided, that already she had come under the spell of this island where the elements and the savage terrain were the dominant realities and that, with its fortune-tellers and symbolic fritter eating and elusive drums of death, seemed to live by the raw stuff of fairy tale. And perhaps, by the measure by which it intrigued her, she had to respect beliefs and fears, which she would have dismissed as nonsense anywhere else, or in any other company.

But that didn't mean she wasn't going to face them in defense of Agathe! She remembered that when little Hélène hadn't quite called Agathe a *mazzere*, she had seen it as a loyalty to refrain from seeking anyone's help to fill the gap for her. But now her instinct and the clues at hand told her she mustn't afford such scruples. She had to *know*, to hear the accusation spoken in so many words before she could show it up for the falsehood it was...had to be.

Whom could she ask? Since Gian had been the first to hint that there was something sinister about Agathe, he seemed the obvious person to challenge. But how could she isolate him from his job and the Manoir long enough to question him? She must wait until he next contacted her, if he meant to. Meanwhile Agathe, going about her daily milking and baking and cleaning, and sitting down in the evening with her radio and her crochet, appeared to be as ordinary a housewife as any other—until the morning when Maria came down to find her hanging out to dry one of her ankle-length skirts which was wet through for inches above its hem.

"The evening dew in the hen-run must have been heavier than I knew last night," Agathe explained. "My yard boots are wet, too. I must cut down those nettles there today. They hold the damp too much." To which Maria found herself at a loss for a reply as she experienced again that cold shiver down her spine. For it was she who had fed the hens overnight, when Agathe had wanted to finish some ironing. The grass and nettles in which the hens scratched had been quite dry then, and Agathe hadn't gone outside before their bedtime. But after it? If she had got her skirt as wet as that from any cause during yesterday, she must surely have noticed it. And so . . . ? Maria found she didn't want to answer that.

Gian got in touch by letter. In a scribble of a note he invited her to lunch with him in Calvi. He couldn't call for her, but if she could go down by bus, he would be at Le Coq d'Or restaurant from noon onward. If she weren't able to accept, she needn't let him know. He would be there all the same. In a postscript he added that the restaurant was on the front, and if she would bring swimming gear, they could bathe afterward.

Though Maria was becoming used to her aunt's refusal of interest in her movements, she missed sadly the knowledge, which she had always had at home before her mother died, that someone who stayed behind cared to know where she was going and what she hoped to be doing while she was out. She never missed the courtesy of telling Aunt Agathe with whom she would be, and roughly the time when she would be back. But Agathe never gave so much as a nod of acknowledgement.

Gian was waiting for her when she arrived at the restaurant where, from his cajolery with the waiters and the cigarette girls, she gathered he was well known and liked. For Maria's entertainment he had a fund of stories about his pilot colleagues and his flight clients of all nationalities. He could mimic the English, the Americans, the Germans and the gesturing Italians true to life, and Maria, listening and laughing, was almost able to forget the opportunity she had to make with him while they were alone.

She postponed it until they were taking their coffee. Then, bracing herself, she asked him, "Do you remember how surprised and dismayed you were when I first told you I was bound for the Maas Juret?"

He nodded. "And with reason—"

"Which you didn't tell me?"

"As I recall. Orso happened along just then."

"And if he hadn't offered to see me safely there, you didn't mean to. Why not?"

He didn't answer that at once. Then, stirring his coffee, he said, "You sound as if you know why."

"I don't. But when someone—a child I met—began to say that my aunt was a . . . something, and was stopped by an older girl, I wondered whether you had held back the same thing."

He looked up. "That she is supposed to be a *mazzere*? But would you have understood me if I'd said so?"

"Not then. But through helping your father with his manuscript, I've learned since, and I've wondered how you *dared*, and how, in these days, you could possibly say or believe such a thing of anyone."

"And if you aren't half afraid of having to believe it yourself, why bring it up? Why worry your head? Why cross-examine *me*?" he countered. "Isn't it because you think you have some evidence of your own, and you *are* worried? Am I right?"

"No. Well . . . " Maria hesitated, "not *evidence*. How could it be, when none of it can be true? Just some rather disturbing things that would—would tie in if there were such people as *mazzeri*, which of course there aren't."

"Things such as...?" Gian prompted.

She told him, and as she finished, he commented, "Sounds as if she does go out at night."

"And that, if she does, she doesn't know she has been."

"Well, *mazzeri* don't. Or didn't, if you prefer that."

"But what does she go *for*?" Maria pleaded.

Gian shrugged. "If she doesn't know, how can you expect to?" He reached to lay his hand over Maria's. "Look," he said. "I'm sorry to have been the first to alarm you, but I'm afraid you were bound to hear this sooner or later from someone. Though if you are convinced it's all nonsense—which it probably is—you don't have to listen, you know."

Maria nodded. "Not that that will stop people saying and almost believing it, will it? And it's the effect on Aunt Agathe's life that I care about. Before I came, I didn't know how she was placed, but how can I go back to England, knowing that, however much she needed help, not a soul would go near her?" As Gian opened his mouth to speak, she added, "Yes, I know—your family would, but she wouldn't let them."

"Yes, well, as to that—" not looking at her, Gian studied the dregs in his empty cup "—there seems to be an idea afoot at home that you may not be going back to England for good."

"What do you mean?" asked Maria sharply. "They can't—"

"They think they can." His eyes met hers frankly now. "And you know what I mean, because dear Chantal says she told you, and you weren't amused."

"About...about you and me?"

"Exactly." He smiled wryly. "Would you take it amiss if I said I'm not amused, either?"

Maria had to smile. "Not a bit," she assured him.

"Good. I mean—you are a lovely person, and blessedly natural, and fun to be with. But I'm not marrying even you to please Orso and father. I'm not marrying, full stop. Or not yet, and when I do I'll choose my own bride, thank them very much."

"But why? And why me for you?"

"Because they want to pin me down as a second string to Orso on the estate, and I refuse to be pinned. I'm going a lot further in the air world first. A year ago I was turned down by Air France, but I'll make it in the end. And you—because you aren't the type I usually run around with. Father likes you. Orso approves of you, and you are half-Corsican, for which they would settle."

"When they hardly know me!"

"Ah, but you are a Juret, as generation-rooted as we are."

"But how do you know their thinking goes like this? What have they *said*?"

"Nothing to me, though I daresay Orso has discussed us with Chantal. Perhaps she put on a jealous act and in self-defense he had to tell her why he is anxious to keep you here."

"*Is* he anxious to keep me here? If so, he is very . . . detached about it," said Maria.

Gian threw her a shrewd look. "You said that almost wistfully. As if you would like to have made an impression, and feel you haven't." He reached forward again, this time to tweak the tip of her nose. "Never mind, little one. As

long as we're agreed we will run our own affairs *for* ourselves, *by* ourselves, we can still have fun." Standing then,
he held out both hands to her. "About that swim ... let's
go," he invited.

He had shrugged off both problems as a snake sloughs
its skin. How lucky he was, thought Maria. But though she
sighed for her own involvement, she knew she mustn't
blame him for being as he was—cheerful and uninhibited
and frank.

They went for their swim. In the water Gian played and
fooled as he had done at Ajaccio and he held and swung
Maria's hand as they ran up the beach afterward. Before
they parted at their dressing huts he drew her to him and
kissed her in a warm friendly salute, which she couldn't
take amiss. He had to go back on duty, but on their way to
catch her bus he said, "You must let me take you to Valin's
one night. Not next week, as I'm on night flight call, but
I'll let you know. You'd come?"

"Valin's?" Maria queried. "That's a nightclub, isn't it? I
don't think I ought to be out so late."

"But you can't go back to England admitting you've
been to Calvi without going to Valin's. It's as cosmopolitan
as—as Dean's in Tangier or Harry's Bar in Paris! And we
could make it the first floor-show, which is over before
midnight, and I promise I would see you back to the
Maas," Gian offered.

She hesitated. "I'd like to come. But isn't there another
thing? If you go on taking me out, won't Orso ...? Won't
they...?"

He took her meaning at once. "Won't they think we are
making it easy for them; falling into line? What if they do?
So long as *we* know we aren't committing ourselves to anything serious, we have the laugh on them, haven't we?"

Not sure that she wanted "the laugh" on anyone as
kindly intentioned as his father, and even less sure that

Orso would allow them to have it, she reluctantly agreed. Her bus came in then, and promising to be in touch with her about Valin's, Gian left her.

A few days later Agathe made her first trip to Calvi since Maria's arrival. She had business to discuss with her lawyer, she said, and scorning Maria's suggestion that she call a taxi, went down by bus. When she returned in the late afternoon, she made as little small talk about her day out as she ever encouraged from Maria. But over her crocheting that evening she announced baldly, "Today I made my will. With my lawyer's help and advice in drawing it up, I have left the Maas Juret to you."

Maria, idly sketching from memory one of the fishing coves she had glimpsed from the helicopter, drew a sharp breath and looked up to stare.

"To *me*, Aunt Agathe? But you can't! I mean, I can't...."

"On certain conditions with which Maître Dumas did not agree, but I overrode him," Agathe continued imperturbably. "These being, in short, that coming into possession of it at my death, you do not sell it, as I never shall."

"But you don't understand! I must go back to England, and I couldn't manage a property in Corsica from there. I know nothing of farming practice here, and besides...." There Maria stopped short of a truth that was too brutal to put into words, but Agathe took no offense.

"You are thinking, niece, that it is not worth the managing, from there or here. But this is not so. The soil is good, the area extensive. You have only to employ a manager and it will recover with a little time and some care. As our friends from the Manoir know only too well."

Thinking it best to overlook the sneering emphasis that made the word "friends" stand for "enemies," Maria said, "I couldn't afford to pay a manager. Please, Aunt Agathe, think again! Don't leave it to me. There must be someone closer to you than I am."

"Psst, child!" It was Agathe's first sign of impatience with the argument. "You talk as if it were to be your burden tomorrow or the next day, and I hope I am good for much longer than that. By the time I die, much may have changed for you—a husband, children, your whole scene different. You may be happy to come back to Corsica then. But I warn you, you must not court the dishonor of selling it. You will suffer if you do. It must not pass out of your hands or those of your children when the time comes."

"You make it very difficult for me," murmured Maria.

"By doing what I will with my own *for* my own?" Agathe retorted. "No, child. It is being drawn up and will be settled on my signature. At my death Maître Dumas will be prepared to help you. There is no need to discuss it further now."

That left Maria in a dilemma from which she could see no escape, except by enlisting the help of her mother's lawyers when she went home. For the moment she could do nothing, but more than once she had heard bluff Mr. Blantyre of Blantyre and Perrin express his disapproval of testaments that laid such a "dead hand" upon the heirs to them, and she knew she could rely on him to advise her.

When Gian made his promised date with her his note said that though he couldn't call for her himself, he was sending a car to take her directly to the nightclub, where he would either be waiting for her or would arrive soon afterward. He had already booked a table, and an usher would take her directly to it.

While she dressed for the evening Maria was trying to remember something, and at last it came to her. Hadn't Chantal hinted that Gian was currently "running" a girl who worked at the Valin club? If so, it showed how little he was serious about Maria herself, if he could take her there without having to make awkward explanations to—what was the other girl's name—Anni someone?

The place was within the citadel, high on the cliffs above the bay and reached by streets coiling around the heights. The doors were open; music poured out into the night in the plaintive wail of *tziganes*. As if she were an old friend, Maria was welcomed by a porter and was shown to her table by the headwaiter.

Gian was not there before her, and as a woman alone, she had to endure the unabashed ogling of the young men of the cosmopolitan crowds for longer than she liked. She ordered a drink and toyed with it, wishing she had met Gian somewhere else before he brought her here. Now, after more than a quarter of an hour, he was late, and she was debating taking temporary refuge in the cloakroom when she alerted to the sound of her own name being called. A bellboy was threading his way between the tables around the dance floor to his monotonous chant of "Paging Mademoiselle Dane . . . Paging Mademoiselle Dane. Message at the reception desk. Thank you. Paging...."

Maria stood up, her heart beating a little faster. It was always embarrassing to be so singled out, and here one had to run the gauntlet of soft wolf whistles and playful hands pretending to bar her way out of the big room.

The message, as she felt it must be, was from Gian. He wasn't able to come. Although not on duty officially, he had had to accept an emergency flight down to Porto Vecchio on the east coast, not returning until the morning. "So sorry. Another time lucky. Get them to order you a taxi at Valin's, and at least you'll have your beauty sleep, which I won't," the message ended.

Disappointed about her evening, but relieved to be spared waiting for him in vain any longer, she thanked and tipped the reception clerk before going to fetch her cloak. When she returned to the foyer both the porter and the desk were busy with incoming parties and she stepped outside to wait until they were free to call a cab for her.

It was a magical night, lit by a full moon, which was reflected in the far below waters of the bay. No wind stirred; walls, parapets, gaunt houses all were in silhouette, their shadows as dark and sharply etched as they would be in the strong sun of morning. Maria stood for a moment or two, very much alone with the night, and then became aware that she was no longer alone. Someone, treading very lightly, had come up behind her and had halted just off from her right shoulder.

She turned. The newcomer was a girl. She wore a hooded cape, which short as it was, hid the length of whatever dress she wore. There was a glint of silvery fabric as the cape opened, that was all. Her legs were long and exquisitely slim; she wore silver sandals with exaggeratedly high heels. Her face was fine boned and oval; her eyes, as they met Maria's, were dark with a fire that owed nothing to their heavy makeup. They flashed angrily, and the hands, which held the hood about her face, were trembling.

In oddly accented French she said, "So after all, he dared not meet you here! Where else then are you to keep rendezvous with him, *mademoiselle*?"

Momentarily nonplussed by the attack, Maria could only stare. Then, playing for time, she began, "I don't understand you, I'm afraid—" only to be cut short by the other's high false laugh.

"But I think you do," she countered. "Deny if you can that Gian Laurent booked a table to entertain you here, and that at the last minute he has decided that he cannot face me, cannot flaunt you at me—*me*, his *petite amie*, his girl—me, Anni Lesnos, if he has not told you my name!"

Maria shook her head hopelessly. "You've got it all wrong," she said.

"So? How?"

"Well, it's true that I was to meet Gian Laurent here.

But I've been paged with a message that he can't come, and so—"

"That you were paged, this I know. I saw you leave your table. I know also that he booked it for two, for dinner and the floor show in which I dance. *But* ... he does not arrive, and of course he lacks the courage, the *cretin*; he asks you to meet him elsewhere—where I cannot see; cannot know...!"

"He has done nothing of the sort," Maria explained patiently. "His message was to say that he has had to take an emergency flight over to Porto Vecchio, and so can't keep his date with me."

"And this you believe? Or no—"evidently the girl had second thoughts on that as she went on "—*this* is what he told you to tell me if I asked you; if I made trouble for you. As I'd like to, *mademoiselle*. As I *will*. Look down on me, would you? Laugh with him over your food, your wine, while I—I dance for my living and for your enjoyment! Well, wherever you are going to meet him, you shall not go unscarred, *mademoiselle*. Explain *this* away to him and your friends! And this...!"

But as she came at Maria like a fury, her painted nails almost making contact with Maria's face, an imperative hand came down on her shoulder and swung her violently around. Maria blinked behind her outspread hands, abortively raised to shield her face. Trembling with shock, she lowered them slowly, saw who her rescuer was and marveled at the chance fortune that brought Orso here.

He ignored her while he dealt with the spitting, kicking virago in his grasp. Panting, she berated him, "Let me go, *monsieur*! You have no right—I have brothers, I warn you, strong men who—" She checked as Orso cut across the flow.

"Mademoiselle Lesnos, I think? Yes—" across which she cut in turn with a stream of apparent invective, though it was not in French nor in any language Maria recognized. When she paused for breath Orso said almost gently, "That will do, *mademoiselle*. I don't understand your Cypriot Greek, but you make your meaning clear." He released her. "Meanwhile, get going, will you? I've had enough of your company and I'm sure Mademoiselle Dane has." He reached for one of her hands and looked at it. "And do pare your nails a little shorter, won't you? With a temper like yours, for your own sake you can't afford to have them handy as a weapon of attack. *Vas t'en*. On your way."

To which the girl flung a single vituperative word at him and went, and he turned his attention to Maria.

"What had you done or said to her to cause all that?" he inquired.

"Nothing," Maria assured him. "I had a date to dine with Gian here, and—"

"Yes, I know."

"Oh. Well, she claims to be his girl friend, and she wouldn't believe me when I told her he had had a message sent to me, saying he had been called to emergency duty on his job."

Orso nodded. "And wouldn't be coming back tonight," he supplied.

"You knew that, then?"

"Yes, he phoned to say he couldn't be home tonight. Also that he was having you paged here, breaking his date. Not his fault, but you couldn't convince Mademoiselle Lesnos of that?"

"No. She thought he was afraid to face her with me; and that we were meeting somewhere else. She wouldn't listen to me, but I was quite unprepared for her to come at me as she did—sort of *flailing*. If you hadn't happened to come along—"

"Except that I didn't 'happen' to arrive. I came because, as Gian had failed you, I ought to see you home."

Why had he to make anything he did on her behalf sound like a pious duty, Maria wondered. Warning her against reading any warm interest into his solicitude for her, she supposed. She said a little shortly, "You needn't have troubled. When the porter wasn't so busy, I was going to ask him to call a taxi. I'd have been quite all right."

"And were so, I suppose, at the mercy of the young harpy?" he queried dryly. "You should have stayed at your table or in the foyer. She wouldn't have dared attack you there. However, I've my car just around the corner. Unless of course you feel cheated of your evening out and would like me to stand in for Gian?"

And make a virtue of that, too? No, thank you, was Maria's silent comment. Aloud she said, "No, I'd rather go home. You can't want to stay, and I wouldn't want you to, just to indulge me. Gian will invite me another time, I expect" —which sounded lukewarm and as ungracious as his offer had sounded to her.

In the car they made desultory conversation. Orso remarked, "Your aunt will be surprised to see you back so soon."

"But she won't show it."

"What do you mean?"

Maria outlined for him the stubborn No Comment tactics by which Agathe registered her disapproval while expressing none in words.

"And this embarrasses you?" he asked.

"A little, though I realize it is her idea of playing fair by me in the matter of my association with you and Gian and your father. Or else she has a need of her own to ignore the fact that any of you exist."

He said nothing in answer to that. But when he drew up outside the Maas he got out of the car with her and announced, "I think I'd better come in with you tonight."

"Oh no, please!"

"Why not? You'll need to explain yourself to Agathe—that, through no fault of his, Gian had to let you down. And for your part I'd like to establish with her that we do exist and that we are concerned for you, which is why I've seen you safely home."

But the cool detachment of that was more than Maria's touchy mood could take. He had made a duty of going to find her at Valin's; if she had been willing he would have made another one of playing escort to her in Gian's place. And now he was making yet another of guarding her from Agathe's silent criticism, with which she had already come to terms without his help.

And it wasn't only tonight! All along, with regard to her, it had been, "I must...," "I'd better...," I shall have to..." Bodyguard, knight-errant, disinterested Galahad—you name it, and Orso Laurent *was* it to the life!

Whoever wanted to be at the receiving end of mere duty-bound charity? She didn't. And yet—the thought was a contradiction, which had to be faced—she did want quite badly this man's care of her for own sake; did crave to make an impression of herself upon him; did want to matter to him enough for it to show in his look, in his occasionsal touch, in some warm inflection of his voice. Why was that? Was it only her vanity that was piqued? Or was it...? But she couldn't afford, hadn't the right, to indulge a need that went deeper than hurt vanity, and it had to be pique that answered him irritably.

"I'm sure Aunt Agathe knows you exist for me. She only pretends not to. And I could wish, you know, that you regarded me more as a—a person, and less as a bit of a burden that our being neighbors has lumbered you with. Do you have to appear quite so responsible for me always?"

If she had hoped to rouse him with that she was to be disappointed. He said coolly, "You can't accept the common courtesy of help when you seem to need it?"

"It depends on how it's offered. You are so—so clinical with yours. You make me feel like a dropped parcel that you've picked up, dusted off and handed back to the owner—except that I'm a parcel with feelings."

"Oversensitive ones, surely? But which particular nerve centers take the rub from me?"

"Well, my self-reliance, I suppose. Everyone likes to feel they are equal to dealing with their own situations until it's proved they aren't."

"Anything wrong with someone else stepping in before that happens to their possibly overinflated ego? But go on. Any other exposed areas left raw and bleeding by my treatment?"

Maris hesitated. "Well, perhaps there's my vanity, too. My personal vanity, I mean. You—you *administer* help and advice like a poultice. There's nothing warm or flattering or rewarding about the way you give it. You'd do the same for any stranger."

Orso laughed shortly. "Poultices and parcels! You use pretty dreary images to make your point. But you make it. My approach offends your feminine awareness of yourself? It hasn't had from me the kind of tribute it expects and gets from other men? For instance, Gian for one."

He had laid his finger so surely on the truth that she had to acknowledge it. "If you like," she agreed. "Gian is certainly a woman's man and doesn't mind anyone knowing it. But yes, he can make me feel like a woman—"

"As I don't?" Hitherto there had been irony in Orso's tone. Now there was something more dire.

"As you don't trouble to. Though why should you, if you only regard me as a kind of incubus, as I suspect you do?"

"A good question—why should I indeed?" he retorted. "Not that the tricks in themselves aren't easy enough and cheap enough, if that's the kind of empty male tribute you

want. Why, my dear girl—" suddenly he drew her to him
and held her "—my dear good girl, don't you realize that
anyone, anyone at all, could make you 'feel like a woman'
at will? It only takes—this." And his lips sought hers in a
long inviting kiss to which every pulse within her responded, and suddenly and devastatingly she knew why....

At last he released her. "There. You see," he said.
"Wasn't your reflex just as easy as the trick?"

She took desperate cover. "And—and as meaningless,"
she lied.

He studied her face intently. "Exactly," he agreed.
"Which I'd say proves my point. But for you, if friendship
between a man and a woman isn't interlarded with romance, accepting it chokes you?"

"I didn't say that!" she denied. "Friendly help is one
thing. P—patronage is another."

"And I've patronized you? Well, well, I must keep my
disinterested zeal in check, mustn't I? Unless I accompany
it with the appropriate motions?"

Wretchedly she looked away. "That's not fair," she murmured, and surprisingly he agreed.

"You're right. It wasn't," he said. "Anyway, we're only
talking in theories and getting out of our depth." His hand
went to her shoulder, turning her around. "It's time you
went in, I think. Any more plain speaking between us will
keep."

Wordlessly, she turned back to offer him her hand and
he took it in a cool formal grasp. As she left him and
moved toward the house she was almost praying that custom would have sent Agathe to bed as early or earlier than
usual. Tonight she craved—*had* to—to be alone with the
heady, dangerous knowledge that all her reluctant awareness of Orso, his challenge to her, her groping need of the
warmth that he withheld from her, only meant one thing to
her heart and her mind.

She loved him; hadn't known it until that kiss, which he had used only to prove a theory; hadn't wanted to know it; didn't want to know it now. Or did she? Just for tonight perhaps—pretend it had the future it had not; imagine a little; dream....

"Please, please," she begged her fate, "let Aunt Agathe not be there!"

But Agathe was, there in the darkened kitchen, awaiting her.

CHAPTER SIX

THERE WAS A WARM yeasty smell in the kitchen, and as she switched on the light Maria's first glance went to the fresh batch of loaves on the table. Her second halted her with shock before she ran forward and fell to her knees beside Agathe's inert figure where it lay between the oven and the table. Agathe's eyes were closed, and though her face was in shadow it showed a suffusion of angry red and purple. She was breathing, but stertorously; she must have fallen—in a seizure or had tripped—and as her feet were toward the stove and her head below a corner of the table, she must have hit her head on it as she went down.

Maria smoothed back her hair and spoke to her. No answer but the continuing heavy breathing. Maria sat back on her heels, at a loss as to what to do but knowing from her small experience that she mustn't attempt to move Agathe, lest she complicate any injuries there might be to limbs or back. She slipped a cushion under Agathe's head; fetched brandy in order to have it ready if she regained consciousness and knelt again, watching and waiting.

Once, Agathe stirred and muttered. But she sank back into coma again and after a few more minutes Maria decided it was time to act.

But what to do? Where could she turn for help? Obviously to a doctor if there were a telephone. But there wasn't. Anyone but Agathe would have friendly village neighbors ready to help in a crisis. But Maria didn't know which of them to ask and dreaded prejudiced refusal. Which—though the village was nearer—made the Manoir the answer. The Manoir—and Orso. Orso, whose unasked help in other circumstances she had dubbed officious and impersonal. Orso, whose humiliating kiss had been deliberately calculated to destroy her argument. Orso, the very last man she cared to appeal to....

But it had to be done. There was nothing else open to her, and the urgent question now was how to reach the Manoir at best speed.

She had only the bicycle for transport, and having had no thought of riding it at night, she had not provided it with lights. But there would be no traffic if she were lucky; it was moonlight and she could do the five kilometers in less than half an hour. She must risk leaving Agathe for that time, and no doubt Orso would bring her back.

She hurried out to the *cave*, only to meet with a deadlock there. The bicycle's back tire was flat and her feverish pumping of it was answered only by the continuous hiss of escaping air. What now? Walk the five kilometers? She supposed she would have to. Or no—there was the short cut through the *maquis*. Dared she face its meanderings at night and alone? Before she allowed her fear to grow she left the *cave* and made for the gate that went from the yard into the open.

As Orso had promised, the bridge across the rift had been mended, but there had been a lot of growth since the day he had shown her the path. It was there, and for the most part she was able to keep to it. But in places the *maquis* had encroached so much that she had to make herself thrust through it in the hope of a clearance ahead. Surely it couldn't have overgrown the path so thoroughly while it hadn't been trodden? She must have missed it! She ought to take this branch ... or that! But that was sheer panic. By her amateur navigation by the moon, she knew her general direction was right, and at last to her relief she came onto the lane adjoining the Manoir grounds.

Her knock was answered by Pascal Laurent's man César, who was too well trained to show surprise at her arrival at that time of night.

As he showed her in, she inquired of him, "Monsieur Laurent? Monsieur Orso Laurent? If he is at home, could I speak to him, do you think?"

While she waited for Orso she looked herself over in some dismay. When she had run to Agathe she had thrown off her cloak, but in the *cave* she had put on the short rough coat she kept in her bicycle basket, and had stepped out of her sandals into the heavy shoes she wore for cycling. But the midi-length hem of her silk dress was snatched and torn in places, her gossamer evening stockings were full of runs, her hair was wild and her hands were filthy.

When Orso came to her from the direction of the salon he was not alone. Strolling close behind him was Chantal, exquisitely groomed as usual. She draped an arm over the newel post of the staircase and leaned against it as Orso hurried over to Maria.

"*Diable!*" The expletive expressed his opinion of her tatty appearance. "What has happened? What do you want?" he demanded.

"Your telephone, please. To call a doctor for my aunt. She has had an accident," Maria told him.

"What kind of accident? And how did you get here?"

"A fall. I left her unconscious, and I came by the *maquis* path."

"You came through the *maquis* in the dark?"

"I had to. My bicycle was punctured, and it would have taken too long to walk by the road. And now, please—a doctor?" Maria begged.

"Yes." As she had expected and hoped, he was wasting no words. "Who attends Agathe, do you know?"

"She has never mentioned anyone."

"Then I'll call my father's. He is a Calenzana man, Doctor Carteret. If I can get him, he should be at the Maas soon after we are." Orso held out his hand. "Come with me, in case he asks for details."

From behind Orso, Chantal's voice said, "Why don't you suggest he calls here first? Then Maria can go back with him."

Orso turned. "No, I'll drive her. But if I'm not back within, say, an hour, don't wait. I'm sorry, Chantal. I'll phone you in the morning."

She wrinkled her delicate nose. "An *hour*! In that case, I won't wait at all. I'll go now." She went to him and offered both cheeks to his formal kiss, then held out a hand to Maria. "What a state you are in, child!" she sympathized. "You really should hire yourself a car. Then you wouldn't be so painfully dependent on your friends, would you?" The implication in her tone was that though the dependence was Maria's, the pain was her friends.

Orso's comment on that, when, very shortly later, he was driving Maria back, was, "You need a telephone more than you need a car. I'll see that the Maas gets one."

Maria looked at him doubtfully. "Aunt Agathe wouldn't let you."

"She wouldn't be consulted. For speed's sake, it might have to be on a party line with the Manoir, but she could be given to understand that it was by doctor's orders. Or if she wouldn't accept that, it could be installed by a local council decree that all outlying homesteads should have one, owing to the universal fire hazard."

"Would that be the truth?"

Orso smiled. "Not strictly. In fact, as a desirable bylaw, I've just made it up. They can't force a telephone on anyone. But I think there is a subsidy for pensioners and isolated places, and with your connivance we should be able to stretch the truth of that far enough to convince Agathe. You agree?"

Knowing he meant to make himself responsible for the installation, Maria murmured, "You are very good. I'm sorry I—"

"—Questioned my enthusiastic do-gooding?" He threw her a brief speculative glance, then looked ahead again. "How galled you must have been to have to make me your only port in this particular storm," he commented.

She flushed. "I—I was grateful to know I could call on you."

"Good. Then we sign our Pax?"

"Please." (Not that any peace treaty with him could blot out the memory of his punishing kiss; the kiss that scorned a need, which until then she hadn't admitted she felt—her need of tenderness from him, of some sign of love that answered her own. Neither had been there for her, of course. Just reproof....)

When the doctor arrived at the Maas and examined Agathe his opinion was that in falling she had suffered a concussion but had no other injuries. A later X ray would have to confirm that, but in the meantime she must be got to her bed. He and Orso carried her there, and Maria helped him to undress her. By then she was stirring and regaining consciousness, but the doctor gave her an injection, which would keep her under until morning, when he would send a nurse to help Maria with her, and later an ambulance to take her to the hospital in Calvi for further examination.

Maria waited until Agathe seemed to be asleep, then fetched blankets and pillows from her own room and made up a bed for herself on the old-fashioned couch at the foot of her aunt's bed. When she went downstairs the doctor had not left. He was talking to Orso in the kitchen, and Maria gathered Orso had been describing her relationship to Agathe. She expected them to leave together, but Orso showed the doctor out and returned to announce, "When he gets home, Carteret will ring the Manoir to say that I won't be back. I suppose you've no objection to my camping here for the night?"

"Of course not," Maria said, surprised. "But do you think you need to?"

"I think I mean to. You shouldn't be alone." He looked about him and nodded toward Agathe's high-backed chair. "I'll bed down in that. By the way, do you suppose your aunt had seen to her livestock before she fell?"

He thought of everything! "Oh, surely," Maria told him. "She feeds the hens and milks the goats before sunset, and I think she hadn't fallen very long before I came in—the breads were still on their trays and still hot. Oh dear...." She paused, biting her lip. "That's something I can't do—milk the goats in the morning!"

"You've never tried?"

"No. I've watched Aunt Agathe, but she wouldn't let me. Louisa and Bella 'knew her,' she said, and she wasn't risking their going dry at the clumsy hands of a stranger. That's an expression she had when things like, say, dripping taps or blunt knives or drawers that won't open are defying someone else. 'Come, they know *me*!' she says, and more often than not, she tames them at once," explained Maria.

Orso laughed. "A character, Agathe—won't allow that she could ever be beaten by circumstance. Not unlike her niece in that," he added, as if by an afterthought.

"When I've just admitted that I can't handle the goats?"

"Merely the exception that proves the rule, and if I weren't there tomorrow morning to give you a lesson, I wouldn't put it past you to tackle the unfortunate creatures on your own."

"You mean *you* can milk them?"

"A Corsican who couldn't would be hard put for milk for his coffee," he retorted. "Agathe uses a milking table?

And—what are their names, Louisa and Bella—are docile enough with her?"

Maria nodded. "Like lambs."

"Then we'll beard them together in the morning." He paused. "By the way, you cannot have had any dinner!" he exclaimed.

"No. I'd forgotten...."

"And—" his glance was mildly critical "—you look as if you would welcome a bath. Suppose you take one, while I forage for some food? What am I likely to find?"

"Well, soup and eggs and cheese...."

"Very well. I'll have something ready when you come down."

Nothing could have been more reassuring than his matter-of-fact command of the bizarre situation that had thrown them together for the night. Nobody, thought Maria, would guess, from his present ease of manner with her, that only an hour ago he had rebuked her naïveté with that kiss. She had wondered then how she was going to face him again. Yet in crisis she had run to him and he hadn't failed her. He had made it easy for her to accept his decision not to leave her alone with Agathe, and now he was preparing a meal, which they would share. She had been allowed to draw away from him emotionally, yet felt less shy with him, more in accord, than ever before. For people who loved each other there must be such companionable levels between the mountaintops of passion, she knew, and though she was the only one who loved, while he remained uninvolved, it was good merely to tread safe ground with him for as long as he wanted to keep it so!

When she went downstairs again he was waiting to ladle soup into bowls and he had prepared a dish of hard-boiled eggs and diced cheese sprinkled with chives. He had opened a bottle of wine and had cut into one of the still warm crusty loaves. The butter melted into the slices as they spread it.

"Hadn't you dined, either?" Maria asked him.

"No. I was just about to when Gian phoned and I decided to go down to Calvi for you. Then when I got back Chantal, who had had dinner, had called, so I missed out twice. Did you look in on your aunt upstairs?"

"Yes. She was sleeping very quietly." Maria paused. "I've just realized I'm going to have a problem when she comes around and begins to ask questions. How did I call a doctor to her? How did I know which one to get? Are the hens being fed, the eggs collected and the goats milked—and so on."

Orso nodded. "You'd rather not confess to its being a combined operation? Well, let's see. I think you did what you might well have done—you went down to the village, consulted the Classified Directory in the phone book and telephoned the doctor you chose from there."

Maria's jaw dropped slightly. "Oh ... I never thought of that!"

He smiled faintly. "I'm flattered that you didn't. Then the hens are no problem. You've probably dealt with them and the eggs before. And you had watched her doing the milking and felt you knew well enough how."

"So I do—in theory. Practice could be very different." Maria's smile turned to a worried frown. "I hate having to lie to her, but I suppose I must?"

"For your own sake ... probably," he agreed. "As to the telephone line, I'll have a word with Carteret, and it can come as an order from him."

"Thank you. I hope he will make her accept it. It worries me that she would be so alone and cutoff."

That brought a questioning look from him. "Does that mean you are setting a term to your stay here?" he asked.

"Not really ... yet. I came without any definite plans, but she has made me so welcome and I am spending so little, and now this has happened, I certainly want to see her well and about again before I go. I'd rather like to see the summer out, I think."

There was a small pause. Then Orso asked, "You hadn't considered making the island your home?"

"For good? Oh...no. I'm English. I—"

"Half-Corsican, surely?"

"But what sort of a job could I do here? I would have to have one."

"My dear girl, we're not barbarians! We've heard of the invention of the typewriter, and I daresay there are quite a number of business and professional men needing secretaries in our cities. Besides, sooner or later, won't you be looking to marriage as your permanent career? After all, you've admitted to your need for romance in your life!"

That struck the first jarring note of the evening. His ironic dismissal of her arguments recalled for Maria Chantal's warning...and Gian's. Chantal's— "It's no secret to me that he is planning a match between you and Gian." Gian's own— "At home there is an idea afoot that you may not be going back to England for good." She had found the idea too absurd for belief at the time. But now she was cruelly—though unwarrantably—hurt by an anxiety to keep her here that Gian had suggested could be for only one reason. She wondered what Orso would say if he knew her aunt's will had offered her the means to stay. Precarious means, to be sure. But means with a possible future, if she cared to develop them.

Suddenly and recklessly she decided to test his reaction to the news by telling him. Ignoring his last question, she said, "In fact, Aunt Agathe has given me a problem I shall have to deal with as soon as I do go back to England—she told me the other day that she has willed this house and the land to me."

If she had thought to surprise him, she was to be disappointed. He said evenly, "Well, wasn't that rather to be expected?"

She shook her head. "It's the very last thing I expected—or wanted!"

"But surely? She refuses to sell; she must leave it to someone, and who more eligible than you, probably her nearest or only relative?"

"You mean *you* would expect her to will it to me?"

How she wished she could hear him deny it! But he agreed. "Since you came out to Corsica, I think so, yes. Financially, as it stands, it's not much of an asset. But it could be made so. Probably Agathe feels agreeable to your working it during her lifetime, and you wouldn't have to lack good management and advice. What's more, when you do marry, you wouldn't go to your husband without a dowry."

With the words he confirmed her worst doubts. So that was it! In the scheme of things at which Gian had hinted, she was not only cast in the role of anchor to him, but Orso envisaged her bringing assets to the Manoir as well. How *could* he? How could he, her hurt spirit cried, and she couldn't hide the bitterness in her tone as she scoffed, "A dowry! Any man who expected to get one as his right would have short shrift with me!"

Unmoved by her vehemence, Orso said, "There speaks the English part of you. Here, dowries are still seen as desirable if not necessary, and you shouldn't blame Agathe for looking forward on your behalf."

"If that was in her mind, I don't blame her. I realize that in making her will, she did it for the best. But it's no inducement to me, and when I go home I shall have to take advice on what to do about an estate I never expected to inherit, don't want and can't develop," Maria declared.

"And that's your last word on the subject?"

"My first and my last. I told Aunt Agathe…!"

He nodded. "I can guess. It would be in character. You arrive, a complete stranger. But she welcomes you and acts for your future as far as is in her power. Her mistake. For you aren't a gracious taker, are you? Very little provocation, and you are biting the hand that feeds you, h'm?"

At that she felt the prick of angry, mortified tears in her eyes. But she blinked them back and took what she knew was a coward's refuge from his scorn.

"I thought we'd agreed to call Pax on that?" she said, despising herself. She stood up and began to collect plates and dishes. "It's very late and I'm tired. Do you mind if I go to bed now?" she added.

"I wish you would," he agreed. "You've had quite a day. You will call me if you need me? We'll do the milking early and I'll leave after that, and with luck and some finesse from you, Agathe may not have to know that I ever came."

But on that score luck was not with them. After the short night, during which Maria had slept only fitfully, though Agathe had scarcely stirred, soon after dawn she had pulled on slacks and a shirt and had gone down to find Orso already out in the yard. He had persuaded Bella, the younger of the two nanny sisters, onto the low milking table, while Louisa was tethered nearby.

He handled Bella gently, talking to her in a low voice, and when the milk was flowing smoothly and freely, the jerk of his head had beckoned Maria to come closer and to kneel beside the stool.

"Slip your hands under mine and work with them," he had ordered, and presently, under his strong firm touch she found she had mastered the rhythm and Bella had responded. He had lifted his own hands then, allowing Maria to finish along. When it was Louisa's turn, he had made Maria do the coaxing onto the table, to take the stool herself and to persuade the nanny to yield.

Flushed with triumph, Maria's verdict had been, "It's easier than I thought!"

At which Orso's dry comment had been, "I wouldn't admit as much to Agathe too soon. As you should know, people like to foster the idea that their own skills are unique," —which made Maria wish he hadn't seen fit to preface the truism by his "As you should know." For that had an echo of the argument on which they had parted overnight. The touch of his hands controlling and guiding hers in the milking was a much more pleasant memory.

When he had left, she had gone back to find Agathe awake and, though complaining of a headache, as alert and brusque as usual.

"It is daylight. I must get up and see to the milking," she announced.

"I'm afraid you can't get up until the doctor has been. And it's all right—I've milked the goats," Maria told her before asking. "How much do you remember about your fall? You had one, you know. When I came home you were lying on the floor unconscious and you had hit your head on the table edge. Doctor Carteret helped me to get you to bed and he is coming to see you and to have you taken into Calvi for an X ray."

But Agathe was not to be sidetracked into concern for herself. "Impossible. You cannot have milked. I have never allowed you to do it. You do not know how," she declared.

Maria remembered Orso's parting advice. "Well, I did . . . somehow. I knew someone must, so I had to do the best I could," she admitted.

Agathe was not convinced. "Impossible," she repeated. "Someone must have advised you, helped you. Who?"

Maria realized that she hadn't expected quite so direct a question. But before she could answer it truthfully or otherwise, Agathe had another. "And may I ask, niece, how did you bring a doctor to me? Someone must have done that for you, too. Was it the young man who entertained you last night? If so, you must have brought him—a Laurent—into the house against my wishes. And if it were not he, then who?"

There was nothing for it but the truth. "It was Orso Laurent. Gian Laurent couldn't keep our appointment and it was his brother who brought me home," Maria admitted.

"*That* one!" snapped Agathe.

"But I didn't invite him in. It was only when I came in and found you that I knew I must have help. I went over to the Manoir and he came back with me, after telephoning his doctor, who met us here and examined you and helped me to get you to bed. He is coming again this morning and sending an ambulance to take you into Calvi for an X ray this afternoon."

"I need no such thing. I tripped, and hit my head as I fell. I remember that, but I have hurt myself nowhere else."

"All the same, you were completely unconscious, and I think you'd better do as Doctor Carteret wants." On the principle of being hanged for a sheep, Maria added, "He says too that, living alone, you should have a telephone and he means to insist that one is installed."

"A telephone! What need have I of a telephone?" Agathe wanted to know.

"Well, I needed one rather badly last night," Maria pointed out—unanswerably, she thought, though Agathe's snort evidently did not agree.

Doctor Carteret, however, had his way with her, both in the matter of the X ray check and of the party line telephone. The X ray showed no broken bones and, though she declared she would never use it herself, the telephone was duly installed. After a very few days she was busily about again and Maria missed only one Tuesday's visit to the Manoir for the typing of Monsieur Laurent's manuscript.

Evidently Gian had heard from Orso of his girl friend's

jealous attack on Maria. But with characteristic airiness he dismissed it as a mere bagatelle.

"That's the worst of your sex," he grumbled to Maria. "One admires a pretty girl; tells her so; takes her out once or twice—and what happens? She considers one to be her slave, hand and foot! Tell me, am I never to put my nose inside Valin's doors for as long as Anni Lesnos is dancing there?"

"Not if you take another girl as your guest, apparently," said Maria.

"Does that mean you wouldn't go to Valin's again? Oh, you must—if only as a buffer between *me* and Anni's wrath!" Gian wheedled. At which unabashed plea Maria had to laugh, though she was not at all anxious for another rendezvous with him at the nightclub. At least for the present she could refuse any evening engagement on the score of Agathe's convalescence.

At the Manoir she did not often see Orso, who was usually out on the estate before she arrived. But one morning, when she had stayed later than usual at her typing session, she clashed with Chantal, for whom, it appeared, each Tuesday was a firm date for lunching at the house.

Maria was alone in Monsieur Laurent's study, checking through the sheets of her morning's copying before she left, when Chantal looked in, in search of her host.

So far as Maria knew, he was not yet back from Calvi, where he had gone to collect an order of books on his subject, and she told Chantal so.

"Nor Orso? In, I mean?" Chantal asked.

"I don't know. When I come over, I don't always see him anyway," said Maria.

"And Gian, I suppose, is on duty. How very dull for you—three unattached males, and not one of them showing up!" The two girls had not met since the night of Agathe's accident, and to her small gibe Chantal added a perfunctory inquiry as to how the old lady was.

"She is very much better, except for the cut on her head
which is still stitched. In fact, it was only the blow and the
fall that knocked her unconscious. Nothing more serious
thank goodness."

"More serious?"

"Well, not a stroke or some kind of seizure, which was
what I think I feared when I dashed over here for Orso."

Chantal agreed, "You certainly were in a flat spin
Enough to impress him and to filch him from me when we
were promising ourselves a cozy tête-à-tête evening!"

Maria made a business of covering her typewriter and ti
dying her papers. "I'm sorry if you minded missing it," she
said. "But I had to come for Orso for help in telephoning
for a doctor."

"Even though it meant ploughing through the *maquis* in
the dark, and there was a public telephone in Creno at les
than half the distance from the Maas?" Chantal insinuated
gently.

"I didn't think of it," Maria flushed. "It was silly o
me—"

"Silly?" Chantal arched her lovely throat and laughed
"My dear girl, forgetting it was a minor stroke of genius or
your part! For after all, what's a mere handy telephone
compared with a real flesh-and-blood man, not quite so
handy perhaps, but—available, so long as the sob stuff i
laid on thickly enough?"

Maria asked tautly, "Are you suggesting that I *wasn*'
frightened for my aunt that night?"

"Of course you were frightened. Who wouldn't be? Bu
so frightened that you didn't weigh the Creno telephone
against the advantages of calling Orso instead?" Chanta
shook her head slowly. "No, I think not. You drew lots be
tween them, but you saw to it that Orso got the long straw
I'd say. Though I do wonder that he let you persuade hin
to stay the night."

"I didn't persuade him," Maria denied. "He insisted on staying."

"With only an unconscious old lady as chaperon?"

"He stayed in case I needed help when she came to."

"Of course. But I still wonder that he cared so little for your reputation. This isn't England or America. Here they are still in the Dark Ages about that kind of thing. Once people begin to talk, it's regarded as a kind of *attacar*. But you wouldn't know what the *attacar* is, I daresay?"

"I think I do," said Maria quietly. "Monsieur Laurent has mentioned it. Wasn't it the custom by which a man could compromise a girl by some very trivial advance, and in consequence public opinion forced them to marry?"

Chantal nodded. "Yes. Not that they always did. More often than not, the man had no intention of marriage; it was the unfortunate girl who suffered the stigma, and a vendetta between the two families usually followed. That's all in the past, of course. But even nowadays any decent man will bend over backward to avoid compromising a girl for whom he has even only ordinary regard. Because once people know she is *disonerata*, as they call it, her chances of marriage to anyone are nil. Which is why I'm surprised that Orso risked "dishonoring" you for so little cause. Especially in view of the plans he has for you and Gian—his own brother!"

At that Maria had difficulty in reining in her temper. But unwilling to brawl with Chantal in Pascal Laurent's house, she managed to say merely, "Plans which, I think, exist only in your and Gian's imaginations. For he seems to believe in the same absurdity, too."

"And who better than he to know what Orso had in mind?" Chantal retorted.

"And who," countered Maria, "better than he to know what nonsense the whole idea is? *And* to be in one of the best of two positions to have nothing to do with it whatsoever?"

Chantal's brows drew together. "The best of two?" she echoed blankly.

"Well, mine the other one—surely?" Maria could not resist the small triumph of that last word, even though by snatching it she guessed she had made an open enemy of Chantal.

CHAPTER SEVEN

NOW THE EARLY SUMMER HEAT was mounting. The morning skies were blue and cloudless but the midday sun blazed from a nearly white bowl. All the seasonal hotels were open and the beaches crowded. Between the coasts and the enclosed inland valleys there was a difference of degrees in temperature. Buildings and roughcast walls reflected back the burning glare to which they were subjected; the shade of trees was inadequate; there was a heat shimmer ahead on every road, and on almost every skyline the lazy upward curl of smoke told its own tale. Somewhere on that line the *maquis* was spontaneously on fire.

Hitherto Maria had made enjoyable use of both her borrowed bicycle and her road map. She had explored the gentle Balagne plain behind Calvi and had pushed the bicycle up to numerous hill villages and coasted exhilaratingly down. But now the heat of the middle day, broken only by the occasional thunderous fury of a summer storm, was too much for even her energies and native English hunger for the sun.

When she rode over to the Manoir for her weekly stint of work for Pascal Laurent, he was amused by her enthusiasm for quartering the countryside on her bicycle and sympathetic to her capitulation to the heat.

"You must have the chance to retreat to the mountains now and then. Not the foothills of our region, but the peaks of Monte Cinto or Paglia Orbo, which look down on us and are both nearer to three thousand meters of height than two. There the heat counts for very little—their heads are in the clouds. We must arrange a trip for you," he promised. "Orso has sometimes to go over to Corte on business and he must take you for a closer view of our proudest points."

Maria would not allow herself to enjoy any such prospect. Except for one or two passing encounters, she had last parted from Orso on his criticism of her as an ungracious taker. That had stung, and the last thing she wanted was to have to suspect that any offer he might make to take her into the mountains was at his father's prompting. The very doubt would make her gauche in accepting it; she felt his perception was sure to guess why, and even if it were forced on them, they would, as it were, set off on the wrong foot.

At that point in her thoughts she stopped. Just how hypersensitive was she becoming where Orso was concerned? If only she could be at ease and entirely natural with him as once or twice she had managed to be, and was always with Gian! Why could she be utterly careless of what Gian thought of her and forever watching her step with Orso? But she was in love. Only the best of her was good enough to offer to Orso, and in trying for the best, she probably overstepped herself and tried too hard.

That reasoning helped a little. She must not, *would* not care so much. Since there was no future in loving Orso, she must take him merely as the neighborly friend he showed himself willing to be. She mustn't dream. . . She remembered his translation for her of the *signadore*'s fortune-telling—"to forbid oneself love is to give it spurs," the old woman had commented. He being unaware, and Maria too then, of the warning it had spoken for her since. She must not allow herself to be spurred....

Gian organized several beach parties for her—at Calvi and Ile Rousse and in some of the picturesque coves along the coast. He seemed to have countless friends and acquaintances. Some different ones appeared at every party, along with a nucleus of the few who were always there. Anni Lesnos was not among them, and Gian was vague when Maria asked him about her. From the gossip she gathered from his friends, it seemed that that affair had cooled and his "latest" was a vivacious little redhead named Vivienne, who was at every party but who, it was said, took him no more seriously than he took her.

On one of the rare days of brooding storm, Maria found herself confined to the house with nothing in particular to do and nothing to read. As usual when they had dealt with the midday meal, Agathe repaired to the grim front room with her crochet and Maria joined her in the somewhat vain hope that the locked glass-fronted bookcase there might yield some acceptable reading matter.

"May I?" she asked with her hand on the key.

"Of course. Though I doubt if you will find anything to your taste. The books are very old and nothing has been added to them for years. As you know, I do not read myself, having many better things to do with my time." And Agathe's crochet hook flicked ostentatiously, as if in evidence of its superior worth over that of a book.

Maria opened the doors and sampled a shelf. Some nineteenth-century French classics, a couple of long-out-of-date yearbooks, a book on goat husbandry, half a dozen Tauchnitz translations of English best-sellers of the 'thirties, which Maria had already read (evidently someone of the Juret family hadn't despised fiction—she hoped it had been her mother), and a schoolroom copy of *Les Malheurs de Sophie* on which Maria had, so to speak, cut her own teeth in French.

She drew this latter out and read a page or two, savoring again Sophie's various naughtinesses, which always landed her in such dire trouble with her grown-ups. Yes, Maria was thinking, she could explore *Sophie* again. Then Agathe said, "There is, however, something that might interest you—you as a Juret, I mean. Our family album of portraits, the dates of family events and so on. It is there. . . ." She peered toward the bookcase. "Yes, I see it—there on the lower shelf. Bring it to me and I will explain it to you. It is right that you should recognize your mother's people."

The volume in question was a thick-leaved tome in calf leather, fastened with a brass clasp. Cut into each leaf were three or four slots containing photographs—some might even have been daguerrotypes—of people mostly so uniformly nineteenth and so early twentieth century in hairstyle and dress and stiff in pose that they might easily change places with those in anyone else's family album and nobody would guess.

But Agathe knew and identified them all, needing to refer only once or twice to the fly leaves for details of their marriages, births of their children and dates of their deaths. There was great-great (Maria wasn't sure of the number of "greats") Aunt Amélie, whom Napoleon Bonaparte had once patted on the head; and Marc and Josie who had died in infancy; and Julian, a great-uncle who had entered the priesthood; family groups, a four-generation group and, coming nearer to present day, Maria's own grandparents, Agathe's and Sorel's mother and father.

Beyond that the slots were empty. There was no photograph of Agathe and none of Sorel. Maria was rather glad of that. She had her own memories of her young dark-eyed mother and of the serene woman she became in middle age, and she would rather not see her posed against a studio potted palm. And Agathe explained the absence of her own picture with a gruff "In youth I had not a face that was worth the price of any portrait. My date of birth is there and there are no others to add, except of my death, which I shall trust you to note, niece, when the time comes."

She closed the book with finality, but in handing it back to Maria they fumbled the exchange. It half slipped from Maria's grasp; the clasp was not fastened and from between the back cover and last page something fluttered to the floor.

Maria stooped for it and picked it up. It was a snapshot, taken by an amateur, of a man and a girl, hand in hand on a beach, both laughing. The girl held her long skirts up from the wavelets lapping over her bare feet; she wore her hair in the plaited "earphone" fashion of the period, and she was unmistakably Agathe.

The man—But before Maria could register any more than that he was young and muscular in a bathing suit and that there was something oddly bizarre to his looks, Agathe was demanding, "What is it?", had twitched the snapshot from her with a harsh, "*That* has no place in a family album!" and had torn it across and across.

Embarrassed, Maria said nothing. Evidently the snapshot recalled a circumstance that Agathe did not want remembered, and she was not a person of whom one asked unwelcome questions. But Maria thought of the suitor of whom she claimed to have been cheated, and wondered. What had it been that was odd about him? With the snapshot destroyed, Maria realized she was never likely to know.

That, however, was before a tantalizing coincidence arose.

Gian, who had arranged to call for her to take her to a picnic, had telephoned that he must send one of his flying mates, "Magpie" Dinand, instead. Gian himself would be late on the rendezvous beach, but "Magpie" would stand in for him meanwhile.

"Magpie," when he arrived in a nearly vintage Renault car, was a new acquaintance for Maria. He was bronzed and chubby of feature, but the one thing that took her notice sharply, making her stare at him as if something about his appearance had suddenly broken a dream, was the swathe of white hair that grew back from his forehead in extraordinary contrast to the jet-black of the rest.

He seemed used to this reception at first sight, and he grinned. He ran his fingers through the white lock. "You are looking at my *touffe blanche*; wishing you had one just like it," he said.

Maria laughed. "Any girl would pay her hairdresser handsomely to achieve it," she said. "But on my part it wasn't only envy. It was someone with a white tress just like yours."

He feigned offense at that. "Impossible! The well-named Magpie is unique around here!"

"Around here, perhaps," Maria agreed. "This man was in a snapshot I chanced to see."

"A snapshot? Could only be of a brother—if I had one. Or of my father or grandfather. It's something that runs directly through the males of our family. If I have any boys when I marry, they will probably have it, too. Where did you see this snapshot?" Magpie asked.

They were on their way now, and Maria jerked her head back toward the Maas. "At my aunt's. It was of her with a young man who would be much older now. Tell me, where do you come from? Where does your family live?"

"Bonifacio. Just my father now. He exports timber. My mother has been dead for years. Why? Do you think he could have been the man you saw?"

(Bonifacio. The name rang a bell. "*He—my suitor—was from Bonifacio. I sent him away,*" Aunt Agathe had said.) But feeling she hadn't the right to share that bitterness with the boy at her side, Maria, studiedly casual, replied, "Just could be, don't you think? They may have met at some time or other, on some beach?"

To which Magpie said, "Yes, perhaps. When I next go

home, I'll check. And you could ask your aunt about it, couldn't you?"

But Maria, feeling she had successfully turned aside his interest, and knowing she wouldn't broach the subject with Agathe again, resolved that if her curiosity confided in anyone, it would be in Gian. And the next time they were alone together, it did so.

Gian was interested, but not very helpful. He suggested, "We could send old Magpie to the house sometime when you were out. Your aunt would have to answer the door and he could get her reaction at seeing him and his *touffe*."

"How could we, if we weren't there?" Maria objected with reason.

"I meant," Gian explained, "that something she said or did at the sight of him might register with him. She might question him, perhaps, and he would report back to us, don't you see?"

But in sudden distaste, Maria knew she couldn't agree to the plan. "No," she told Gian. "It would be too much like spying on her. She tore up the snapshot. She doesn't *want* to know."

And though Gian commented, "Pity. It would have been a smart bit of detective work," he agreed that it wouldn't be to much purpose, and they let the discussion drop.

At around that time he had a confidence of his own to offer Maria, namely that in September or October, at the end of the summer tourist season, he was hoping to be accepted to fly with Air France, along with Magpie and another of the local pilots.

"Have you told your people?" Maria asked.

"Not yet, and I'm trusting you not to let it slip. I've no wish to spend the summer under pressure to change my mind. I only thought that as my alleged marriage prospect whom I'll be jilting, you had the right to hear it first!" he grinned.

She laughed with him. "You know I never took that idea of yours seriously."

"Not my idea. Theirs, as I told you," he disclaimed. "Fostered by Chantal, too, I imagine. Even if she has nothing to fear from them as rivals for her own choice of male, she never has relished having any unattached, attractive females around. Pairing you off with me probably makes her feel much safer with Orso. After rejecting him once, she may have to watch her step. So when I bow out in the autumn, watch yours! She—if not Orso or father by then—may be on the watch for another suitable *parti* for you."

Maria felt a little sick at the implied intrigue that he dismissed so lightly. "I won't be here myself in the autumn," she said.

"No? Really? You'll be leaving your aunt again, after coming to look her up? Does she know you mean to go?"

"She knows I must—that I have to earn my living. But I may come back again. Next year, perhaps—to see her."

"Next year? Quite the tourist, aren't you? I'd have thought . . . . But it's none of my business, and life at the Maas can't be exactly a picnic. Anyway, drop me a card when you are coming, I'll come bounding back, too, from wherever I am, and we'll paint the town red. Is it a date?"

Maria smiled, "It's a date—if I come."

"You'd better!" he threatened gaily.

HER OVERSENSITIVE PRIDE being always ready to read "duty" into any move Orso made in her direction, Maria was relieved that his suggestion that he should drive her over the mountains to corte was a long time in coming. To believe that he hadn't invited her merely at his father's instigation made it easier to accept, and indeed she was thankful to do so at the end of a torrid week when the air scarcely stirred even on the slopes of the valley. Even a day on the cooler heights was welcome. And a day with Orso—dangerous but tempting.

They drove south from Calenzana to join a main road out of Calvi until it dwindled to a track through forests, at first of cork oak and chestnut in close, dark formation, and as the road climbed inexorably, of pines, their scent sickly sweet in the confined air.

The pines thinned out until only the hardiest of them clung to jagged rock. To the northeast the peak of Monte Cinto loomed; to the southwest, Paglia Orbo. Between them, at a lower level than either, the mountains had to be crossed in order to reach the good road, which led ultimately to Corte.

But there were the mountains and the mountain road first. . . . Sometimes the road was a mere shelf cut into a wall of rock; sometimes it swept down into a gorge as dizzily as the Big Dipper at a funfair; climbed again to a comparative plateau ringed by saw-toothed peaks; nosed across it to repeat the pattern—up, down naked rock face to one side, ravine to the other—until its last upthrust was its limit of height. Thereafter, beyond the escarpment, it would drop and drop to the level of a river bed and be tamed.

Up there Orso halted the car. Up there the air was cold, colder than seemed possible by contrast with the heat of the plain, so cold that it caught at the breath and flung it away.

Maria gasped, "There must be easier ways to get across to Corte than this!"

Orso half turned in his seat to face her. "There are," he said. "There's an excellent road that skirts the lower slopes by way of Asco and Ponte Leccia. But I understood the lady ordered mountains. Why, have you had enough of them, now you've got them?"

She shook her head. "I doubt if I could ever have

enough of heights like these. They ... do something for me. Challenge me in some way."

"And you enjoy being challenged?"

"Usually, I think. I need to feel equal to most situations. I tend to despise myself when I'm not."

"That has always been self-evident." He spoke dryly. "You have a touch of a child who refuses to be taught to tie her own shoelaces—she fights to do it, though she hasn't the experience. That tends to annoy people. You might try less of the 'anything you can do, I can do better' approach. It lacks feminine appeal." Before she could reply he was getting out of the car. "But come and view the limit of the heights you've achieved this morning. And the distance down again you have to drop."

When she joined him he tucked his arm into hers and led her to the very edge of the flattish summit they had reached. The drop from it was sheer precipice, and at her instinctive recoil his hold tightened momentarily.

"It's all right. We don't have to fall over it," he assured her. "We take to a mule track farther east. But challenge enough to your eager spirit for one day?"

Maria looked down into the craggy depths. There was mist down there and granite peaks reared jaggedly out of it as if their hidden bases floated. The rocks were gray, the mist was blue and such vegetation as there was was green black. She drew a long breath.

"More than ...." she said, and then, "Except that I've achieved it under your car's steam, not my own."

"Tch! There you go again," he accused. "For that I'm tempted to give you a push and make you find your own way down on the double." As he turned her back toward the car, he added, "Have you ever done any real mountaineering on foot?"

"Never."

"Nor winter sports?"

"Only once in Scotland."

"Then you should stay longer than the summer and come up with Gian, who is our expert."

Maria compressed her lips. "I can't stay that long."

"So you've said before, and as *I've* before, I'm surprised you think you can't consider it, if only for your aunt's sake."

"She is better now, and I wouldn't worry about her, if only she had some friends."

"She doesn't make that easy."

"I know. But a lot of people who don't usually have one or two who care about them."

"As she should have you."

Maria said nothing to that, wishing she knew, though fearing to learn, how much of his solicitude was for Agathe, how much for his own plans for herself. Loving him, she shouldn't have to doubt him, but the canker that had been fostered by Chantal went too deep.

Corte, when they reached it, was a disappointment, a garrison town of houses like square boxes and modern barracks in yellow stucco, beneath the stupendous rock, rising sheer out of the plain, which housed its ancient fortified citadel. There was excellent river trout from the Tavignano for luncheon at the hotel to which Orso took Maria. Afterward she explored the narrow streets while he attended to the affairs that had brought him, and was glad to escape from the stifling heat when they took to their return road.

After driving through the mountain passes, Orso chose a slightly different way on which, being less steeply daunting, there was to be overtaken the occasional muleteer and his team, drawing its load of laricio pine timber down to the coast for export. There were more frequent hamlets and farmsteads on this road, too, and once to Maria's delight, at a turn in the track a young donkey at ease, dozing in the sun, strayed from who knew where. Not that he was troubled. Orso edged the car around him, and when they

looked back he was nodding sleepily again above his
folded knees.

Lower down, they were once more in *maquis* country,
the growth now dry as tinder and encroaching on vineyard
and pasture and homestead, greedy for more than its share
of the land, as always.

Maria alerted suddenly and glanced at Orso as he lifted
his head, his nostrils scenting the air. "Do you smell it?" he
asked. "Smoke?"

"Fire?"

He nodded. "Ahead of us, I think. I wonder if it is being
contained?"

He drove on more cautiously, telling Maria to scan the
terrain on her side of the road for signs of the outbreak.
There were none for the distance of nearly a kilometer, but
there was drifting smoke, and as they rounded a bend, a
man armed with a stave barred their way.

"You can't go on much farther," he told Orso. "In
places it has crossed the road. Besides, we need aid. Even
one more pair of hands."

"Where is it?" Orso was getting out of the car.

The man jerked a head backward. "All over, just short
of the boundary of the Maas Grognard, Pierre Tillot's
place. It is gaining on us."

"What is on Tillot's farm?"

"Vines in a small way. And stock."

"How far from here?"

"A quarter of a kilometer...less."

"All right. Get in. I can go closer than this?"

"One moment." The man showed a large square of ply-
wood, scrawled with a "Danger" warning to cars and an
appeal to any males to go forward to help. He propped it
prominently against a pile of stones at the roadside and got
into the car.

Orso told Maria, "When we go on, you'll stay with the
car."

"Can't I do anything?"

"No. This is man's work." He stopped short of a farmyard and a gaunt farmhouse. Off to the right were an open
milking shed and some outhouses. There was no fire to be
seen, but the smoke was thicker here, a long cordon of it,
causing the air to shimmer in its heat.

In the yard the man produced for Orso a cloth to tie
over the lower part of his face. He rejected a stave as a
beating weapon, choosing a wide-bladed spade instead. As
the two moved off behind the house, Maria heard him ask
whether or not the alarm had been given to the district fire
patrol. She did not hear the answer, but presently a familiar drone overhead was evidence that the patrol's helicopters were on survey, ready to direct the professional firefighters to the area.

Maria felt infinitely lonely. The farmhouse was silent
and deserted; if it had any womenfolk they must have
been pressed into a service that Orso had forbidden to her.
She circled the car restlessly; she couldn't just *sit* in it . . .
waiting! From a distance that she couldn't gauge, the
shouts of men were borne on the wind. Nearer, though not
too near for danger, there was the spit and crackle of
woody stems as they scorched under the heat of the smoke.
Feeling that Orso couldn't have meant literally that she
was to remain in the car, she picked her way across the
farmyard to the back of the house, where a low wicket
fence was the boundary between it and a plantation of
waist-high vines, their grapes as yet no bigger than unripe
currents.

The smoke hung like a pall above them, but so far they
were safe from the enemy, which could reduce them to
blackened tatters in a matter of minutes. They were safe
and untouched as yet—as was the house—*or was it?* Suddenly, even as she stood there, looking back at the house
and across to the outbuildings, the smoke cloud behind

them broke into sporadic flame, which sparked and glowed
in the gusty wind; died in one place, took heart in another,
sending up errant rags of fire to lick at foliage, which
crisped at its touch ... as it drew nearer to farmyard debris
and to wooden buildings, which would prove the merest
tinder to its wild rampage, once it reached them.

And after them, the house itself .... Maria fought down
the surge of utter panic that assailed her. Where were the
men? *Where were they?* Hadn't they gone out—somewhere
beyond her puny reach or call—on their urgent errand of
stemming the tide of this very threat to one man's liveli-
hood and homestead? Fire in the *maquis* was only too
common; they must be experienced in fighting it. So how
had they let this rogue tongue of fire escape them?
Shouldn't they have been on the watch to forestall it, to cut
it off before ... ? Or had it cut them off? Couldn't they beat
through it? Out there, wherever they were, was it already
an inferno?

She found she was shouting for help, in vain. ... The
wind that was driving on the long frontage of flame threw
the sound back in her teeth. Horror-struck, she watched
the fire creep forward on an uneven line, rather as the incoming sea tide would seek the easiest levels of the shore to
follow. Now it was reaching out experimentally to the back
of the milking shed, and she must *do* something! Beat, or
stamp or throw water.... Where was water ... a yard tap or
a rainwater tank? And buckets? *Ah, what was that?*

She froze, listening to a voice of panic that wasn't her
own. It was plaintive, animal, instinctive of danger, and it
came from the outhouse adjoining the milking shed. Something alive was shut in there, and at all costs it must be
freed!

The door was of stable type, in two halves, the top half
secured by a bolt through a hasp and padlocked and the
lower by a bolt inside. That meant the bottom half must be

broken in; it didn't look too sturdy and its warped panels bulged. But what should she use for a battering-ram? She had to have one...something.

Behind a stack of tangled wire she found a four-foot iron stake and dragged it, her breath sobbing in her throat, over to the outhouse. There was a frantic scrabbling from within now, and she recognized the crying—it was the bleat of a goat. She stood sideways to the door and wielded the bar, crashing it with all her strength against the wood, which splintered encouragingly until finally one panel gave and was smashed in sufficiently to enable her to peer into the interior at not one goat nor a pair, but a nanny with two kids on tottering spindly legs beside her. At the noise of Maria's onslaught on the door, all three had retreated to one back corner of the shed. At the other there was already an ominous crackle of dry wood, and smoke with an acrid smell was beginning to wreathe.

It was a race against time. Maria beat again at the weakened wood of the door until it broke away to a hole big enough for the goats to escape by. Maria looked in and called soothingly to the mother. But as if petrified by what she saw as danger on all sides, she did not stir. A kid whimpered and she nuzzled it, but she made no move to bring it or its twin to safety, and Maria realized she would have to go in and drive them out. She beat and wrenched and levered again until the hole was large enough for her to crawl through it. Inside, she stood, slid back the bolt and swung the broken door wide. For a moment or two more the nanny did not move, but then, scenting through the open door a freedom that she understood, she bleated encouragement to her kids and galloped out.

After that everything seemed to happen at once. Suddenly the back wall of the shed began to blaze in earnest, the heat fanning Maria's face and body as, panting and spent, she stood there, momentarily incapable of moving out of danger.

Then she thought again, "Water!" She had to find some, and some means of playing it on the fire. But as she turned, dropping the crowbar she was still clutching, a shadow struck across the open doorway and she was in someone's arms—in Orso's compulsive grip in which there was no kindness; only the urgency of rescue as he bundled her un-ceremoniously out into the yard. There he turned on her and forcibly shook her. "What the devil do you think you were doing?" he demanded. "I told you to stay in the car!"

She hung her head, unable to face the naked anger in his eyes. "I—I couldn't," she defended herself. "There were a goat and two kids in there...." She nodded backward at the shed where two other men were tearing at broken wood and beating out flames. "They had been forgotten."

"Wrong," Orso contradicted crisply. "They were re-membered as soon as we spotted an outbreak we weren't fighting—one that the wind had picked on, to carry in from quite a different direction, fast toward this way. Any-way, if you felt you had to do something, why didn't you shout, or follow us, instead of trying to cope on your own? Will you *never* learn?"

At that she flared. "I did shout," she claimed. "But you weren't in sight and you must have been out of hearing. And if you've only just got here after you noticed the spread, you wouldn't have been in time. Those poor crea-tures might have been burned alive."

"And you—in possibly another few minutes? *Standing* there, as if you'd had the bonfire and were waiting for the fireworks! And how did you get in? Tillot says the door was locked."

"I found an iron bar and I beat in the bottom of the door—" she gestured to the broken door "—until I'd made a hole big enough to get through, and the goats to get out. I don't know where they went to." She looked about her vaguely and then, conscious of pain in her hands, turned them palm upward in Orso's sight as well as her own.

He reached for them and held them. "You've burned them!" he accused.

She shook her head. "No. They're only beginning to blister. From ... the bar, I suppose. It—it was rusty." Suddenly, to her shame, her voice was plaintive and tears of self-pity had welled in her eyes. She mustn't let him know his injustice had hurt her! She would *not* cry in front of him!

And the next moment was doing just that. Weeping uncontrollably into the hollow of his shoulder while he held her awkwardly, patting her back as he might a distressed child's, briefly indulging her weakness, trying to make up for his harsh judgment of her folly. But counting her only as so much nuisance value, she knew.

CHAPTER EIGHT

IT WAS NOT UNTIL they continued their return journey that Maria was able to apologize to Orso for her shaming outburst. Tears, she had always felt, were a woman's unfair weapon against a man, and she longed for him to know that she realized it. But after she had pulled herself together they had not been alone again while the fire was everyone's priority.

At last there had been a drift back of the firefighters to the farmyard and the house. By that time the professional patrols had come up from Calvi and Porto and had taken over the operation from the tired, anxious amateurs—and their womenfolk.

For as Maria had guessed, the women had turned out, too, and returning weary and disheveled had at once set about preparing a meal for the men. They insisted that Orso and Maria must join them, and everyone took their places at the long table laden with bread and sausage and cheese and bottles, and they ate. Everyone, that is, except the women, who didn't sit down until all the men were served.

As they ate, the talk was of this outbreak compared with others. But it seemed to be accepted with a shrug that it was a very normal hazard of farming in the region—the shrug implying that it had happened before and would happen again. *C'est la vie,* they agreed. That was life....

It was early morning before Orso and Maria were thanked, each forced to accept a bottle of homemade myrtle wine and set on their way. Maria bore her sense of guilt as long as she could, and then said into a silence, "I'm sorry I broke down in that idiotic fashion. I don't cry easily and I don't know why I did then."

Orso said, "You were overwrought, I daresay. I should have made allowances. You felt you had acted for the best, and you took it badly amiss that I had judged you merely foolhardy. Am I right?"

"I thought you had been rather unjust—"

"Unjust? My dear girl, I was out-and-out angry!"

"Angry that I'd dared to disobey you?"

"Don't be petty," he snapped. "Angry of course that you had taken such risks without a thought for your own safety."

"Well, what would *you* have done in the circumstances?"

Watching his profile, she saw the corner of his eye crinkle to a smile. "The same as you did, no doubt," he admitted.

"Well then ...!"

He nodded. "Fair enough. I'll allow you that round. I can afford to, since your collapse into tears showed that there are gratifying chinks in your armor; that you can be vulnerable on occasion."

Maria said in a low voice, "But of course I'm vulnerable. Who isn't ... somewhere? And the thing that always gnaws at me is being misjudged or disbelieved. I can't bear it."

He agreed dryly. "That, as we say in our idiom, jumps to the eye. And as you say in yours, it takes all sorts. ... One woman will cry in a studied bid for sympathy; another, when she isn't winning; another, because she knows that tears brighten her eyes. Others, like you, I imagine, despise them as the ultimate weakness, and when you're betrayed into them, you have to show how stoic you are by claiming they're from some cold-blooded cause like outraged self-esteem. Whereas any man would prefer to comfort some genuine emotion he can understand."

"Counting the genuine emotions as, for instance ...?"

He shrugged. "Surely? Pain, loss, contrition, despair, un-returned love—do I have to catalogue them for you?"

"No." She caught at the least dangerous one in his list. "Do you mean you would rather I had cried over my blistered hands than because I'd resented your injustice?"

"Much rather."

"But why?"

"Because, one supposes, it would briefly have made a 'little woman' of you, and me, proportionately, superior to you. An illusion, of course, and without any lasting effect. But primitive, fundamental and quite rewarding at the time."

"Rewarding to whom?"

He glanced quickly at her, smiling. "Why, to my male ego, of course. What else?"

Later she was to wish she had laughed with him at that. But for the moment she could not. On her dignity, she said stiffly, "Well, I'm sorry you feel cheated," and watched his mouth set to a hard line.

He said, "And that makes two apologies I didn't ask of you. But if they have eased your conscience, well and good. But let's leave it there, shall we? It seems to be an unproductive argument."

They had almost reached Calenzana when he said he was calling for Chantal to take her to the Manoir for dinner and the evening, adding, "I expected we would be back long before this, so she may have decided to drive up herself. But I must go to the house and see."

At her parents' villa he left Maria in the car and went in, only to return a few minutes later without Chantal but with her mother, voluble and apologetic on Chantal's behalf.

"So *naughty* of her not to leave a message for you. I had no idea . . . ! Not a word to me that she was expecting you and that she was to come to you for the evening. . . ."

"As I've said, I am very late," Orso put in.

"All the same! But you understand, there was this friend from America—a very dear friend, she said, a Monsieur Eldred, though she called him Charles—in Corsica on holiday. Or on business, was it? No, I'm afraid I don't know which. But of course he made opportunity to see Chantal, and naturally, when he asked her to dine with him, she accepted."

Sounding as if he had heard all this before, Orso agreed dryly, "Naturally."

"Yes. But *not* so, if she had promised you. She should have warned me, *la méchante*. But you will forgive the naughty one? I think she must have known you would, or she would not dare to treat you so...." Madame Ferrier broke off to beam at Maria whom she had met once. "Disappointing for you, too, my dear, if it was to have been an evening out for the four of you...."

"The ... four of us?" Maria looked a question at Orso, but it was Madame Ferrier who explained, "Why, yes, wasn't it? Orso and Chantal; you and Gian. *Une partie carrée*—a happy foursome 'on the town' as people say...."

Orso was getting into the car. "Just an evening at home, *madame*," he told her.

"So? Then, if Chantal knew that, perhaps she is not so very bad after all. But I shall still scold her. For there are some things one does *not* do to an intimate like you, and even to appear to slight you for another man is one of them. I shall say...."

But whatever else Madame was rehearsing to say to Chantal was lost on the air as Orso bowed goodbye to her and drove off.

Outside the town the road forked, one branch leading to the Maas, the other to the Manoir. Before they reached it, Maria asked, "Madame Ferrier was mistaken, wasn't she? You hadn't thought of inviting me to dinner?"

"I'd meant to, yes."

"But I can't. Not tonight."

"Gian will be at home. Why not?" Orso asked.

"Because I mustn't be late. Like you, I thought we would be back hours ago and Aunt Agathe will be waiting. Besides, I'm dirty and tired. Please. Gian will understand."

"Very well." Orso gave in more easily than she expected but taking the appropriate fork in the road when they reached it, he remarked, "Looks as if Gian and I may have to decide to 'do' the town on our own this evening. Stood up by both our partners, who could blame us if we did?"—a piece of oblique criticism that Maria resented. She hadn't even known he'd meant her to make a fourth with Gian for dinner, and to link her with Chantal's cavalier treatment of him wasn't fair. But she thought it best to let his rhetorical question pass. She was as weary as he claimed to be of futile argument.

When they reached the Maas, he brushed off her thanks for the trip into the mountains, and made his chief concern her blistered hands.

"See to them thoroughly," he ordered. "I know you washed them at the farm, but bathe them in disinfected water and keep them covered for the night. I shall send a cab to take you into Calvi for an antitetanus jab at the hospital in the morning."

"Surely that's not necessary?" she protested in surprise.

"Of course it is. Our soil is notorious for infection. I shall send the cab," he said.

MARIA WOULD HAVE GIVEN a great deal to feel she could interest Agathe in all the details of her exciting day. But though she had to explain her late return, the condition of her hands and the state of her dress, the rest of her story evoked from Agathe only a strange, almost irrelevant comment.

Agathe said, "Ah, fire in the *maquis*. There was an outbreak near here last night."

"Near here? How do you know?" Maria queried.

"I saw it and smelt it. It was on the rise beyond the house. But it wasn't serious. It died away as I watched."

"When was this? Could you see it from the house?"

"Oh no. Not possible, that. It was over the brow. I saw it while I was out on my walk."

"On your walk? But...what time was this?"

Agathe lifted a shoulder and spread a hand. "Who knows—to this minute or that? It was late and dark, but as you know, niece, I frequently take a walk before I go to my bed."

Maria, who knew nothing of the kind, felt her very spine chill. She hadn't known her aunt to "take a walk" at bedtime ... ever. So what was she to understand by this calm assertion, which was far too bland and purposeless to be a lie? What was more, she did not know how to pass it off, short of the downright contradiction that she would have offered to anyone but Agathe.

Then why not to Agathe? Because, though they had gone up to bed together on the previous night, Agathe patently believed it was her habit to go for a walk and that last night she had seen a fire start up and die down over the brow of the rise a time when, to Maria's knowledge, she could not have done.

Which meant...? But Maria, faced with an enigma entirely beyond her experience, had to admit she was coward enough to shrink from guessing what it meant. Certainly, that evening, Agathe made no move to go out before they both went to bed, and it was not until the middle of the night that Maria sprang upright from sleep, aware that memory and her subconscious had forced an answer upon her.

Agathe must have dreamed that she had gone out and had seen the fire! The dream had been so real to her that she believed it to be true. Alternatively, she had actually seen the fire when she had gone out much later, as Maria suspected she had on those other occasions. Both possibilities were disturbing, but of the two the first was the more sinister. For it meant that for a least some of her waking time Agathe was living in a dream state, when her dreams were the reality and her real life the dream. And it was that thought that had evoked the memory—even in her own sleep—that filled Maria with incredulous horror.

For this she had learned from her typing of the chapter of Monsieur Laurent's book which dealt with the *mazzeri* and the *signadori*, the sorcerers and the seers in whom people—even Gian—still claimed to believe. The *signadori* weren't sinister at all; they were common fortune-tellers, and hadn't she listened to one herself? But the *mazzeri*....

Writing of them as past folklore, Pascal Laurent had said, "Men and women both, they were credited, among other evil powers, of being in two places at once; out, hunting an enemy to his death, yet, in the flesh, still asleep in their beds. Their eyes were magnetic; they communed with the dead; they had foreknowledge of death and could bring it about. They controlled the elements, earth, air, fire and water. They were solitaries, shunned and feared by their neighbors. Yet they appeared to live ordinary lives and often claimed to have neither knowledge nor recollection of their vicious practices. Moreover, fantastic as these beliefs appear today, there are in the island still those for whom the *mazzeri* legend endures in the shape of a neighbor or an acquaintance who does not quite conform...."

As Gian believed it of Agathe! As the village children did! As...but at the point of admitting her own midnight fears, Maria knew she must shake herself free of them. Daylight would convince her of their absurdity, as could any sane, well-balanced person. And *what*, she accused herself, had she done since she came to Corsica to ensure that Agathe was accepted, was befriended, wasn't forever alone?

Nothing. Nothing at all. Yet surely there must be someone whom Agathe herself would accept? Some woman to whom she could gossip; some man to whom she could turn for advice? A thought struck Maria—the padre, the parish priest—wasn't he the obvious person to enlist on Agathe's side? Yes. On the resolve to go down to Creno to see him tomorrow, Maria felt steadier and slept again at last.

THE NEXT DAY she returned from the hospital bringing with her a card dated for a booster antitetanus injection six weeks hence and for a final one six months later. Not that she would be given her latter anywhere but in England, she thought wryly. Even six weeks ahead, near to the end of the summer, she might not be here.

Agathe, at her baking and cleaning and husbandry, seemed so normal, so little in need of anything but the work she did so briskly and contentedly, that Maria almost doubted the necessity for her visit to the padre. But after their midday meal she told Agathe she was going to walk into Creno, and Agathe found an errand for her to do.

"It is the day for my allowance to come from my lawyer, but the postman did not bring it this morning. Be good enough, will you, to ask at the post office if it has arrived, and if it has, bring it yourself?" she asked.

Maria said she would. She made for the presbytery first, in case the padre would be out and she must call again. But to her disappointment he was not merely out, but away from the parish indefinitely.

"His mother is dying, down there in Sartène," his housekeeper said. "He has leave of absence from the bishop and he went to Sartène yesterday. It depends on how long the old lady lives, or whether or not she rallies, as to when he will be back. But of course there will be a relief priest in time for Sunday, and if it is anything important—a death or a marriage or a baptism, for example—which is your business, madame, the relief, Father Brieux, can deal with that. Would you like to make an appointment with him, or shall I ask him to call on you?"

But Maria, seeing no point in enlisting anyone but the resident priest on Agathe's behalf, thanked the woman and said her business could wait until Father Goncourt returned. She would call on him another time, later on.

She left, feeling dispirited and frustrated. She had depended a lot on gaining Father Goncourt's sympathetic ear and help for Agathe, and where could she turn now? Nowhere. Father Goncourt would be coming back, and she could go to him then. But she had so wanted to strike while the iron of her idea was hot!

In the quiet of mid-afternoon the village square was empty. One car was parked under the plane trees outside the post office and its driver, an elderly man wearing a linen suit and a flat Basque beret, was inside, being attended to by one of the two assistants. Maria asked the other for stamps and stamped envelopes and then, "If you have a letter for Mademoiselle Juret which came too late for the morning delivery, may I take it, please?"

"For Mademoiselle Agathe Juret, at the Maas Juret?"

"Yes."

"So. . . . But yes, we have a letter here." Belatedly cautious as she was about to hand it over, the girl asked, "You have her authority to collect it?"

Maria hadn't, except her own word, which probably wouldn't do. But she tried it. She said, "Well, I am her niece, staying with her at the Maas. . . ."

At which the girl cut in, "Ah, of course! One has heard!" and handed over the letter.

Maria took it, gave her the customary *bonjour* and turned away . . . to be surprised by her fellow customer's obvious interest in the transaction, if his listening attributes and his long curious stare were any indication of it.

He followed her out; hesitated on the short distance to his car and approached her instead.

He said, "You are the niece of Mademoiselle Juret? Wait!" He lifted a hand. "Then you are Mademoiselle—Maria—Dane, I think...yes?"

It was Maria's turn to stare. "I don't know you, monsieur. How do you know me?"

He smiled. She liked his smile. "From my son, who knows you slightly. And you knew him—as Magpie Dinand? And I—" he swept off the flat cap with a flourish"—also a magpie, as you see!"

Maria gasped. She was picking up mental threads, knitting them together. That white lock of hair—like his son, he had it! He was the man who had been young in the snapshot Agathe had destroyed. When she and Gian had abandoned their plan to face Agathe with his son, they had both forgotten his casual promise to "check" with his father. He must have done so, telling her own name in the course of the story, and here was the original Magpie, wanting to know her—for what purpose?

He watched her confidently, as if he could follow the pattern of her thought. She smiled back at him. "Yes, I know you now," she told him. "But I had forgotten your son said he would tell you he knew me and about the snapshot I had seen that brought the subject up."

Monsieur Dinand nodded. "The likeness of me which Agathe had kept...all these years?"

Cruel to be kind, Maria said, "Yes, though I'm afraid she destroyed it as soon as she knew I had seen it by accident."

He nodded again. "Destroyed it...how? With passion? With indifference? With regret?"

"With...passion, I think. As if she were angry that the sight of it could still hurt." Maria hesitated. "You see, she had told me earlier—and she was bitter about it—that

there had been a man who wanted to marry her, whom she
had sent away, because of the duty she owed her parents.
And because she was angry, am I right, monsieur, in thinking that man was you?"

He agreed, "Sadly, yes. Unless there was someone else
whom she turned down later."

"I don't think there was. She blamed her sister, my
mother, for forcing her to refuse you."

"I know!" He looked about him. "Is there anywhere
where I could buy you an ice, and a coffee for myself while
we talk?"

"I'm afraid there is nowhere open at this time of the
afternoon. But we could sit here," Maria indicated the seat
under the holm oak.

They sat. She felt completely at ease with him, and a
quarter of an hour later they had exchanged stories.

Marcel Dinand had subsequently married in his home-
town, had fostered an export business to success and had
been happy in his marriage until his wife died, leaving him
with an only son. During the early years he had thought
often of Agathe; not so vividly later, but when, after his
wife's death, he had heard that Agathe was then alone, he
had made some discreet inquiries as to her circumstances,
but had made no other move toward her—except one.
When young Dinand, in the local air service, had been
asked at Calvi, he had not mentioned Agathe or the Maas
Juret to him.

In return Maria outlined her own story, telling him of
her worry over Agathe's chosen isolation, of her enduring
bitterness against Sorel and the distance at which she kept
the Laurents, who would willingly have befriended her if
she would let them. She herself must return to England at
the end of the summer, without having achieved anything
on her aunt's behalf. She mentioned neither Agathe's will,
nor her neighbors' dark suspicions of her.

"But you say you did make one approach to her, monsieur?" she concluded.

"Not personally. I haven't seen her since the day we parted. No, but when I learned she had inherited only the impoverished farm, I made—er—arrangements for her without her knowledge."

"Arrangements?"

"With her lawyer's connivance I opened a trust fund, by which she receives a small income each month."

"Each month? But—" Maria glanced at the letter that she still held "—this? She thinks it comes to her through her father's will!"

Marcel Dinand smiled. "She has never been told so—or not. A diplomatic type, her lawyer! And though I mean to see her now, I am trusting you, my dear, to keep my secret. When would it be best for me to call on her and make myself known after all these years?"

"Oh. I . . . don't know. You . . . must realize that she will be very much changed," said Maria, taken aback by the directness of his plans.

"So am I. I am an old man now."

"Yes, but women . . . ." Maria did not know how to point out that a woman's sensitivity to old age was the more poignant. She went on instead, "Would you let me prepare her for seeing you? I could let her believe that it was your son who made the link between us, which, except for today's chance meeting, he did."

Her companion looked doubtful. "You think it would be best?"

"I hope so. I'm sure she would prefer to hear how it all came about, and when to expect you."

His smile was rueful. "Ah, you are confirming that I am an old man and that I shall be a shock to her! But you may play decoy if you will. Here is the address of my Calvi hotel. You can telephone me? Good." He wrote the particu-

lars and gave them to her, adding, "I only ask one thing o
you, mademoiselle."

"Yes?"

"It is that you leave it to me to tell Agathe the ultimat
purpose of my coming to her after so long."

"And that is ...?"

"Can't you guess? I am going to ask her again to marr
me, of course," he said.

A COUPLE OF DAYS later Maria was to look back with won
der at the happy confidence with which she had rehearsec
and made her approach to Agathe on Marcel Dinand's be
half. She had done better than the confidant and friend i
need, which she had hoped Father Goncourt would be fo
Agathe; she had gained for her instead a potentia
husband—a man who she had once loved enough to b
embittered for years at his loss. So—Maria had askec
herself—how could she fail to ease his way again towarc
her?

But she did.

Mortified for her own inadequacy, desperately sad fo
him, she phoned him at his hotel to tell him that Agathe re
fused to see him.

He sounded as thwarted as she expected, but she coulc
give him no hope, though she did her best to soften for hin
Agathe's harsh, "He left me once when I told him to; le
him leave me alone now." He was reluctant to accept tha
as final and was inclined to blame Maria for persuading
him against the surprise approach he had planned. To tha
she had to tell him he was wrong. Agathe had said, "If h
came to me with or without warning, I should shut m
door in his face. He has had his marriage and a son; I hav
had to be content with neither, but now that I am old,
am."

There was a long silence on the line. Then Marcel Di

nand said heavily, "This then was her answer, and you think it is final?"

"She made it sound so."

"And all I can do for her is the little I have been doing over the years?"

"You are very good, monsieur."

There was another pause. Then, "Ah ... good," he replied. "Perhaps when you are older, mademoiselle, you will know that when one has loved, as I once loved Agathe Juret, it comes easily to 'good'—even if it comes too late." After that he added formally, "Thank you for all you tried to do for me. I appreciate that."

Later she heard through Gian, who had it from Magpie Dinand that Marcel had left for Bonifacio an hour after that talk. And characteristically, Agathe never inquired of Maria whether or not her refusal to see him had ever reached him.

CHAPTER NINE

MARCEL DINAND was not the only person to deplore Maria's role as ambassadress to Agathe. Orso, who heard the story from Gian, took the same view and told her so one morning when he came upon her working alone in his father's study.

"You should have let him go to Agathe himself," he said. "That was what he had come for—to propose marriage to her, and a man should be free to do his wooing in his own way. He doesn't need a troubleshooter—or he shouldn't, if he has any spirit at all."

That stung. Maria defended herself, "I did it for the best. I thought I knew Aunt Agathe better then he possibly could after all those years, and that she had the right to be cushioned a little. After all, I was the one who had seen her angry reaction to my finding that snapshot. Anyway—" turning defense into adroit attack "—I've always understood that, here, it's quite normal practice for people *not* to be allowed an entirely free hand in their courting?"

"The *mariage de raison*? Not the same thing at all," Orso retorted. "Arranged marriages are for young people, and they're not obligatory at that. No one nowadays is dragged, screaming, to the altar. One or both of them may be advised and helped, that's all."

Not quite knowing she wanted to force him into admitting he had plans for herself and Gian, Maria said, "Helped to whose advantage—theirs or their families?"

"Just helped—full stop. For their own good, as their elders see it, and nobody blames them for taking a hand to get the best *as they see it* for their own children. Sometimes they are only too wrong. That happens. . . . But in quoting marriages of convenience at me, you are just dodging the issue. That man Dinand had the right to surprise Agathe, to take her by storm in his own way. They knew their own minds about each other once, and from what you told Gian of him, it seems that he at least believed they could go on from there."

"Even though Aunt Agathe declared to me that she would have refused to see him if he presented himself?"

"He should have risked that. By coming between them you robbed him of a chance to dominate her, and he had every right to resent that."

"I still did what I thought was best for both of them," Maria returned with dogged finality.

Meanwhile, over the weeks, Monsieur Laurent's manuscript had taken shape, and as it had been commissioned by his publishers and was sure of acceptance, he declared his intention of giving a party to celebrate the completion of its final draft.

"We haven't given a party since you came, my dear," he said to Maria. "We must show you what the Manoir can do, and you can be very sure that my guests will be left in no error as to the help given me with it."

"Just a copy typist's help!"

"No, more than that. It can't have escaped you that I am a born muddler, and if I hadn't had to face your Tuesday morning greed for more and more manuscript, the thing wouldn't have been finished for months. As it is, I am going to feel quite lost without it. You and I must write another book together sometime, h'm?" Pascal chuckled.

That sounded as if Orso hadn't passed on her decision to leave before long. She wondered why. Could it be because he was confident of his ability to persuade her to stay?

Briefly, she indulged the daydream that he *really* wanted her to stay, for the same reason as she longed to herself. But she couldn't allow it to last. That Orso was concerned with her future had no substance. None at all.

As it was, she couldn't yet make a firm date for her departure. Now that a happy outcome for Agathe through Marcel Dinand had proved a mirage of hope, Father Goncourt's cooperation became important again. But he was still absent from his parish, and to abandon Agathe without trying to enlist his sympathetic help for her was something Maria could not bring herself to do. It was even possible that she might have to stay on after Gian had left—a happening that would put a decisive end to any latent hopes or plans for them both. For by now he and Magpie Dinand had each been accepted for service with Air France, though in confiding the news to her he had asked her again to keep it to herself.

"I won't spoil father's party for him by telling him before it," he said. "Time enough later for all the regrets and reproaches there are bound to be. Justified too, from his point of view, I suppose. I *am* abandoning the estate; I *am* opting out from playing reserve man to Orso. But it's my life, and the estate isn't getting it for keeps. It has Orso's already, but he likes it that way."

"Aren't you telling him yet, either?" Maria asked.

"Of course not, or he would tell father. Anyway, brother Orso has trouble enough of his own just now. Chantal is paying coquette and is going back to America. Nominally only on a trip and nominally alone, though it just happens that her friend Charles Eldred will be traveling by the same flight, and she can hardly expect Orso to be amused."

This was news to Maria. "But she isn't going for good?"

Gian laughed cynically. "What do you think? I can't see her passing up a second chance with Orso, and she knows father would like them to marry this time. No, in my view she is only turning the screw a bit, making Orso jealous. So that will be two of us gone. Funny—wouldn't it be—if we came back to find him courting you instead?"

"*Very* funny," Maria had agreed dryly, though "funny" was not the word she would have chosen herself.

That was before two untoward happenings, each as unrelated as each was inconsistent with anything that had gone before.

The first was a peace move from Monsieur Laurent to Agathe. One morning Maria opened the door of the Maas to him, leaning for support on his stick while his man waited at the wheel of his car.

As she stared in surprise, "Mademoiselle Juret—is she at home? If so, would she see me, do you think?" he asked.

"I . . . ." But she couldn't leave him, frail as he was, standing on the doorstep. "Please come in," she said, "I'll tell my aunt you are here."

That was not necessary. Behind her she sensed Agathe's approach and they both stood aside to allow him to enter.

He looked about him. "May I sit down?" he asked disarmingly. "As you see, I am not very agile; I wear my years much less well than you carry yours, madame," he added with a faint smile.

Agathe said harshly, "Since you are in my house I can't deny you a seat while you have business with me—or believe you have. This way...." And she showed him into the grim front room, where Maria would have left them together if a downward flick of Agathe's forefinger hadn't ordered her to stay.

With an air of granting a royal audience, Agathe seated herself facing Pascal. "And your business is ...?" she invited.

He said carefully, "Primarily to see you, madame. We were young together once; now we are old, and it has occurred to me what a great many neighborly years we have wantonly wasted in between."

"Wasted, if you will, through your family's fault, not through mine," she retorted.

"But through neither mine nor yours, as people," he reminded her.

"What of that, with one's family honor at stake? I shouldn't have to tell you, a Corsican *sgio* born and bred, such unpaid debts as lie between us must expect the consequences of vendetta!"

"And I," he countered, "shouldn't have to tell *you*, as truly Corsican as myself, just how much evil and cruelty and injustice any vendetta brings in its wake, making enemies where there were none before." He paused and sat forward. "Come, madame—a long time ago *one* young man of my family wronged *one* young woman of yours—"

"One from each family was enough! Too many for friendship to continue—"

He ignored the interruption. "Yet, now that two young people of my family have been privileged to come to value one of yours, doesn't that restore the balance at all? Not to mention what Maria here has done for me, an old man who had no claim whatever on her time and her skill? We—my sons and I—are all her friends. Must we continue to count you as our only enemy?"

Agathe stiffened. "I daresay you have others, did you but know."

He said mildly, "Perhaps, though I hope not. But if we have, I trust they have better cause for their enmity than you."

"Really? Surely you could allow me to judge the worth of my cause? My sister—"

"Ah, your sister! Yes, your family made loyal enough stand for her here. But since she herself had done nothing wrong, tell me—did you ever invite her to come back?"

Agathe flushed an angry red. "She could have come if she had wished. She was a free agent!"

"But whether through her fault or yours, she did not come. It was left to Maria to heal the rift, and now won't you allow her to heal another?" Pascal stood up, painfully stooped before he straightened and faced her again. "Let us welcome you in our house as we all welcome her; let any or all of us feel welcome in yours. Well, madame, what do you say?"

"Impossible." Agathe stood up, too, an implacable figure. "I would have you know, monsieur, that as I go about, I do not even willingly *pass* your house, let alone wish to enter it!"

Pascal permitted himself an ironic smile. "That must be rather awkward for you sometimes, madame?" he suggested.

"Not at all. Wherever I want to go, there is always another way."

To which he merely murmured, "What a pity!" and with a gesture of his free hand, invited Maria to show him out. Later, Agathe made no reference whatsoever to the interview.

The second isolated incident occurred one morning when Maria planned to return some books that Monsieur Laurent had lent her. She had told Agathe where she was going, and as usual there had been no comment. But as she was about to set out Agathe asked, "Are you going by the road on your bicycle?"

"No, I'd thought of walking through the *maquis*."

"Then I will come with you. It is a long time since I penetrated the *maquis* on a walk," said Agathe.

Surprised, Maria warned, "It's very rough going; very overgrown."

"And who would expect anything else at this time of the year?" Agathe retorted. "If you are ready, let us be on our way."

They set out, sometimes able to go abreast, sometimes

Maria taking the lead, sometimes Agathe striding ahead. When they neared the Manoir boundary, though not yet in sight of the house, she halted and queried, "What difficulty could there be to that, if one knows the direction one wants? A good nose to follow and a pair of stout boots for the feet, and how could one go wrong?"

Maria said, "I don't know, but I've sometimes had to wonder whether or not I had missed the path." Then she ventured, "Will you come any farther? All the way?"

"This is the end of the *maquis* at this point?"

"Yes. Now there's just the lane leading into the Manoir grounds."

"Then of course I shall come no farther. I came to join you on a walk, not on an *errand*!" With which, making a taunt of the word, Agathe turned on the heel of her "stout boot" and strode back by the way they had come.

FOR SOME DAYS before Pascal Laurent's evening party the heat had turned ugly, though lessening not at all. Now the skies from which the sun had blazed were heavy with cloud, driven ceaselessly on by an angry *libeccio* with a breath like the blast of a furnace.

Window shutters fretted and abused their fastenings, tree branches tossed wearily, sere leaves of the scrub gave up the struggle, blackened and dropped; the sea was worried and gray, and on every dry path the caprice of the hot wind would tease up miniature whirlwinds of dust to irritate eyes and nostrils and tempers, although for the most part people accepted this ill-natured interlude with a shrug and a resigned, "It is the season."

Gian drove over to take Maria to the party. "I had no idea we knew so many people," he said. "I admit I've contributed a few, and so has Orso. But father has excelled himself with his generation. I declare he must have begun at a in his address book and gone on down to x, y, z, and every man jack of them R.S.V.P.ed—'Thank you kindly—we'd love to come.' The original idea was a marquee in the gardens, but owing to this weather they are all milling in the house. I believe there are some vague relatives of ours, but I hadn't tracked them down before I came for you. Chantal, by the way, has brought her American along. Asked Orso ever so prettily if she might, and what could he say?"

"I'd have thought," said Maria, "that she should have asked your father. It's his party."

"But it's Orso she is playing like a salmon just now, and it was his hospitality she had to beg for the fellow. Once under our roof as a guest with Orso's agreement, Orso can't very well cold-shoulder him, she'll have argued. Which should give her the whale of an evening—doing the coquette bit with them both."

"You don't like Chantal much, do you?" Maria asked.

Gian smiled. "How did you guess? Though I have taken it upon myself to warn her that Orso might take just so much and no more."

Hungry for any crumb of talk about Orso, Maria said, "No more of what?"

"Why, of being stood up twice by the same woman, of course. Not that he hasn't himself to blame if she is getting tired of waiting for him to propose again."

"Then they aren't actually engaged?"

"Not officially. Just what's known as an 'understanding,' I suppose. 'Brother Orso' keeps the facts to himself. . . . Heavens, will you regard those cars? Is this a party or an automobile rally?"

Gian indicated the line of cars drawn up by the roadside and had to leave his own there as the courtyard was full. Inside the house, in the salon, the hall and other downstairs rooms there was such a press of people that Maria, who knew hardly anyone, wondered how all the others managed to trace their friends. However, to judge by the babble of chatter and laughter, they seemed to be making do with mere acquaintances, and the uproar around the chair in the salon where Pascal was holding court was such that she realized she would have to wait her turn to approach him.

Gian had left her and she was standing alone when Orso shouldered his way toward her, bringing a waiter with a tray of drinks.

When she had made her choice he stayed with her, pointing out people to her—one of the partners in Pascal's firm of publishers from Nice, some cousins of his own, some representatives of the island's complicated politics. He promised she would meet various of them, then said, "By the way, we have a guest—he hasn't arrived yet, I think—who will be a surprise to you. Inviting him was an idea of my own, which has gone awry. But he is coming all the same—with his son." To Maria's puzzled look Orso added the name, "Marcel Dinand" in explanation.

"Monsieur Dinand? But you—you don't know him!" she faltered.

"Only by repute, from you. But we got in touch with him via Gian and Magpie Junior and had already invited him when father made his unsuccessful approach to your aunt. I'd seen the possible advantage of bringing Dinand over again and father had been so sure that if he went in the right spirit he couldn't fail with Agathe that we hoped she might agree after all to meet Dinand. But as you know, father did fail...."

Maria bit her lip. "I think I could have told you he would," she said.

"And you resent our interfering?" Orso asked quickly.

"No. Anything was worth trying. Although—" she looked about her "—I can't see Aunt Agathe coming to a party as big as this."

"Ah, but that wasn't the idea. The party first, for us to get to know Dinand, and while he stays with his son in Calvi, a discreet meeting arranged between him and Agathe. And though it isn't to come off, we let our invitation stand. Ah, there's Magpie now!" Orso lifted a finger and beckoned to the boy, who came over, accompanied by Marcel.

Magpie introduced Orso to him. He said, "And Mademoiselle Dane and I have met before," as he gave her his hand. Orso obtained a drink for him and the talk was general until Orso took him away to meet Pascal.

Magpie said to Maria, "I've heard the whole sorry story now from my father, and it isn't going to have a happy ending, is it?"

"I'm afraid not," Maria paused before asking a difficult question. "But supposing, by a miracle, it had, you wouldn't resent his not having forgotten my aunt all through his happy marriage to your mother?"

"Not a bit. The last thing maman would have wanted for him is his loneliness now, and if your aunt could make him happier, I'd welcome that. Especially as, when I go to the mainland, I won't get home as often. But if she won't even see him—what a hope!"

Gian came to fetch Maria then, to introduce her to a Laurent cousin and his wife. Some more people presently mingled with them, and when they moved on Maria found herself temporarily isolated again. Watching the other groups, she saw Chantal on the fringe of one of them; saw her say something to her escort before she left him and came over.

"I thought I'd better take pity on you," she told Maria. "Of course you'll know hardly anyone here, and I've noticed that so far Gian and Orso have produced for you a pretty dull lot. Who was the oldish man Orso brought to you—the one with the white *touffe*?"

"The father of Gian's friend Magpie, who has the same white lock. I'd met his father before," Maria told her.

Chantal's expression was enlightened. "Oh . . . him?" she said. "Yes, I've heard from the Laurents about him—your aunt's faithful-unto-death suitor. But I thought you had sent him on his way for good?"

"I'm afraid my aunt refused to see him," said Maria shortly.

"But you would have had a hand in that too?"

"*I?*"

Chantal's eyes widened. "Surely? You couldn't have wanted your aunt to marry him?"

Bewildered, Maria protested, "Why not? It was I—even if only by chance—who brought them together again!"

"Yes, but . . . . Well, really, it can't have escaped you that if she had accepted him, their marriage would make her will null and void?"

"Aunt Agathe's will?" Then, as the ugly implication took meaning for Maria, she blanched and a chill ran down her spine. "What do you know about that?"

"Just as much as Orso told me, I remember. That she was leaving the Maas to you, whereas, if she married she would have to make a new will, and do you suppose you would get it then? And so, when you saw the way things were going, you'd have discouraged the whole idea. *Very* adroit of you, I must say. Besides, without the property you wouldn't be as much value to the Laurents as you would like to be, or as they would like to make you. You had to get rid of the old man if you could."

Maria told herself she must keep calm or she might do violence. She said, "I won't try to convince you that I had nothing to do with my aunt's sending Monsieur Dinand away. You wouldn't believe me. But if you think the Laurents were glad she did, can you tell me why he is here again at their invitation?"

Chantal shrugged indifferently. "How should I know? They don't make me a confidante to their power politics. I'm just a humble onlooker, watching the game. I wouldn't *pretend* to understand the moves. No, I'm merely amused to remember how indignant you were when I first suggested they were seeing Gian as your future. But you are playing along nicely now. If I were you, I'd be very pleased with my progress into the charmed Laurent circle!"

As she spoke, Chantal took a glass from the tray of a passing waiter, drank its contents at a gulp, took another before the man was out of reach and drained that. Careless of where she was putting it, she set the empty glass down on the edge of a table, where it tottered for a moment, then fell and shattered to the sound of her high-voiced laugh, which brought heads turning curiously her way.

There were titters and nudges and raised eyebrows—the embarrassed reaction of people to the prospect of a scene, as she kicked petulantly at the pieces and demanded of her audience, "What are you staring at? What's *one* broken glass at a party? Why, I've been at parties where ...." She broke off to laugh again— "But of course they weren't *Laurent* parties! *Nothing* ever happens at a Laurent party, except by gracious permission of our respected hosts. They don't countenance broken glasses. Their spe— speciality—" she had difficulty with the word "—is broken promises, didn't you know? They use people; they dangle them like puppets. Con—conscience? They don't know the meaning of it. They...."

Maria stood aghast at the wild tirade, which was a tipsy extension of the bitter resentment of their hosts, which had sounded in Chantal's earlier, more sober, and therefore perhaps more cruel, taunting of herself. Maria had never before heard her call the family "the Laurents" as she had done then and was doing now—as if they were strangers and enemies, instead of one into which she was probably at last going to marry. What could have happened? What faith with Chantal had they broken, that she could accuse them so publicly and under their own roof?

Chantal had broken off at the approach of a tall fair man, a stranger to Maria, who put a firm hand under her elbow and said in a strong American accent, "Come, honey, that's enough. You don't bite the hand that's feeding you Martinis while it's doing it. It's not polite, and what does it matter now? Forgive and forget—it's old history. So say good-night prettily and let's be leaving. You've got an early start in the morning."

"*Old* history? Making a fool of me twice?' She wrenched free of his hold. "All right, we're leaving—and soon! I can hardly wait. But not before...."

She broke off again, facing both Orso and Pascal now. Orso began quietly, "You are not yourself, Chantal. You should let Monsieur Eldred take you home, as he suggests—" but stopped as Pascal laid a hand on his arm.

"No," the old man said. "Not yet. In front of all our friends Chantal has made accusations, which she should take back or justify before she leaves. So choose, please, Chantal. We are waiting."

She glared at him. "Take them back? I'll do no such thing. I'll repeat them instead. Years ago, you—" she pointed a shaking finger at him"—made a promise to my people; they made one to you. He—" the finger shifted to Orso"—chose to break it; to shame me before everyone, and you let him!"

Pascal said quietly, "My son had every right to break a promise made in good faith in his name, but not by him."

"*And* to break one of his own, with your blessing?"

Orso put in, "I've made no promises to you that I've broken."

"Nor marked time with me while hoping to better yourself in other directions? And you—" she turned again on

Pascal and mimicked his elderly, gentle voice " '—I do hope you will allow Orso to make you one of us at last, my dear!' Bah! What was that worth, if you please?"

Pascal said quietly, "When I told you that, it was true. As from now it isn't anymore, and you obviously couldn't wish it to be. And so I am neither advising nor inviting you to leave my house. I am ordering you to go. Monsieur...?" His gesture toward Charles Eldred was too definite to be mistaken, and with a slight inclination of his head the American led Chantal away. Before they reached the door she announced, "I've changed my mind. I won't be coming back. If you want me, phone me in New York. But I hope you won't!"

No one answered her. Monsieur Laurent slung his stick over his arm and dusted off his fingertips as if in distaste. He smiled calmly at the rest of his guests. "Shall we make up our parties to go in to supper?" he said.

It was an invitation to ignore the incident, and certainly, while they remained his guests, people complied. Feverishly at first, they made small talk of other things, and though Maria's mind was a turmoil of questions as to what had caused Chantal's violent about-face, she managed fairly successfully to do the same. At the buffet supper table she talked again to Marcel Dinand, who was full of the Laurents' courtesy in inviting him, even though they feared he must concede failure with Agathe. He would be returning to Bonifacio the next morning, but meanwhile he had one thing still to ask of Maria.

"My arrangement with her lawyer—you have not betrayed me this? No? Then it can continue until—until she has no more need of it, I can hope?"

Maria said, "I hope so, too, if only because I think helping her helps you, monsieur."

He agreed sadly. "So little. But if it is all I can do for her, I must be content."

It grew late and people began to leave. Maria was won
dering whether or not on the drive back to the Maas, sh
could ask Gian what he knew of the trouble between Ors
and Chantal, when he came over to her.

"We have a problem," he said. "Who'd be on a dut
roster? Magpie and I tossed for it; he won, so I've been o
lime juice all evening, just in case. And now there is a
emergency call. Besides, he has to see his old man back
and I can't take you."

Maria said, "Well, that's all right. Perhaps you could ge
me a taxi?"

"No need. Orso will take you. I've asked him and he'l
be ready as soon as you are."

"I'm ready now, as soon as I've thanked your father. Bu
Gian...?"

He grinned. "About Chantal? You know as much as
do, *chérie*. Except that they had a session together las
night, and he didn't see her home. Ask Orso, why don'
you? He'll tell you. Or will he?" With which he blew her
kiss and was gone.

As if she could possibly ask Orso anything so intimate
she was thinking as she joined him and they went out to hi
car. Certainly on the drive he gave her no encouragemen
They discussed the party, and only when they reached th
Maas did he put a serious question of his own.

"Gian tells me you know of his acceptance by Ai
France?"

She nodded yes, and he went on, "He told me today. H
plans to tell father tomorrow. Did it come as a surprise t
you?"

She considered her answer. "Not really. He had told m
some time ago he was ambitious to leave the local air serv
ice."

"As a disappointment, then?"

"To me? No." She met Orso's glance levelly and decide

it was time to bring this at least into the open between them. "Perhaps I should ask whether or not it was a disappointment to *you*?" she said, wondering how much his reply would reveal of his intrigue on Gian's behalf.

He said, "It was a shock. It will be, to father. Something of a disapppointment, too—for his sake." He got out of the car and went around to her side. "I'm coming in with you. You and I have to talk. Agathe won't be waiting up for you?" he asked.

"I asked her not to." (Talk? At his instigation? What about, unless he thought he could persuade her to get Gian to change his mind?) She added, "If I go in by the back way it will disturb Aunt Agathe less than if I use my key on the front door," and led the way around the side of the house.

The kitchen door to the yard stood wide open though the room itself was dark. Maria looked back and up at Orso, her breath catching in her throat. "What?" he asked, and of the open door, "Why? You think Agathe wouldn't have left it so for you?"

"No. On the latch, but not open. It shouldn't be...." She went in and groped for the light switch. As it revealed the empty kitchen, neat as Agathe always left it, she flung down her bag on the table and raced for the stairs.

Agathe's room—the door open, the bed rumpled but empty. Her own room, the bathroom, the top floor. She heard Orso go into the front room and as she came down from the attic, they met on the landing. Sick with fear and almost swaying toward him, she gasped, "She's not here. Not in the house at all!"

"*Out*? At this time of night? Where can she have gone?"

"I . . . don't know." She pushed past, ran downstairs ahead off Orso and out to the *cave*; came back to meet him in the kitchen.

"Her old coat—she hangs it in the *cave* and keeps her

yard boots there when they're muddy. They aren't there," she said, her voice flat with despair.

"But what does that mean? It says something to you?" He scrutinized her closely. "She has left the house at night before?"

"Yes. That is ... I think so."

"You don't *know*?"

"I'm not sure. Once ... I thought I heard her go; but I didn't hear her come back. And another time her skirts were wet when she hadn't been into the yard in the evening...."

"And if she went, you don't know where?"

"No."

She watched his lips compress, as if in exasperation at her ignorance. He said, "Well, we're wasting time. We'll have to man a search." His hand, firm on her shoulder, turned her about. "Come ... I'm taking you back to the Manoir."

She resisted him. "You can't. *I* must help to search for her!"

"Do you think I'm leaving you here alone? I said 'man' search, and I mean that literally. Now—"

"Aunt Agathe might come back."

"If she does, all the better. But you are not waiting on the off chance. Come."

She had no choice. He left the back door as they had found it, but switched on lights. As soon as they were under way, his questions began again.

"How long has this been going on?"

"Since I've been here? The first time was on my first night. I thought I heard her about in the small hours."

"But you would have questioned her the next morning?"

"I did. She denied it, told me I must have been dreaming."

"And the other occasions you suspected?"

Maria told him of the night when Agathe, using only a torch, had ignored her as she had gone up the stairs. And of the incidence of Agathe's soaking skirts, she said, "By that time I knew she didn't answer unwelcome questions about anything, so I said nothing."

"Nor to anyone else of your doubts and your misgivings?"

"I told Gian."

"Gian?" Orso's echo was sharp. "Why Gian? Why not my father or me?"

"Because I felt I knew Gian best. Because I can talk to him more easily than to you. And it was he who first alarmed me about Aunt Agathe. He confirmed for me what I thought the village people were saying about her, which is why they avoid her."

"You mean you have heard them call her a *mazzere*?"

Maria drew a sharp breath. "You know they do? Wh—why didn't you tell me?"

"Because I wouldn't alarm you with nonsense that has no substance to it and which I didn't credit you could take seriously."

"But how could I *not*?" she appealed. "When so much of Aunt Agathe's strangeness seemed to bear it out? Her goings out at night and denying it; the claim she made once that she had been out walking when I knew she hadn't; her withdrawal from people; her bitterness. . . . I knew about the *mazzeri* from your father, from his book. About their habits, their evil! I fought against believing it; I still don't. It—it's grotesque; it's monstrous. But oh, can't you see how frightened I've been for her when . . . ."

She broke off as she saw she hadn't his attention any longer. He was staring ahead at a glow in the darkness and, as once before, was lifting his nostrils to the scent of fire.

She smelt it, too; saw the glow fan down . . . up; heard the dread crackle of burning wood, and suddenly *knew*.

They were very near to the Manoir now and he set the car rocking and bucketing around the last two bends in the road. He jumped out; she scrambled to his side. They weren't the first on the scene, for behind the house men were shouting. Orso said hoarsely, "It's the *maquis* on our boundary. Get indoors and stay there with father—"

"No!" she defied him.

"You little fool, do as I say!" he ordered.

"No, I can't. Not this time—"

"You never have done yet," he flung back at her. "But this time—"

"This time I've *got* to come with you, to be *there*. Please, Orso!" She clung by both hands to his arm. "Because *she* is out there—Aunt Agathe! It's she who has done it—fired the *maquis* on purpose. Oh, you've got to believe me. It's what she came out for tonight. I know it. My very bones know it....Please!"

He stared down at her. "Arson? You must be mad. How would she have got over here? And why?"

"She walks well, but I think she would have come by the short cut through the *maquis*."

"At night? She would never have found her way."

"She could have. She asked me to show her the path one day, and wouldn't have it that it was difficult to follow. And as to why, you ought to know how she hates you and your family. She would be waging her vendetta against you. She would think it right that she should. So please let me come. If she has done it and your men discover her, they might do her a mischief, and I must be there to protect her. She has no one else—only me!"

At that Orso detached himself from her clawlike grip and took both her hands in a firm but gentle hold. "Listen," he said. "We are wasting time. I should have been out there now. If Agathe is there—which she won't be—I promise you she shall come to no harm. So I'm asking you—not advising, nor ordering—simply *asking* that you leave it to me. You can refuse. You can come with me if you insist. But this—the first of many things I'm going to ask of you in all humility when we've more time—I beg you to do for me. Well?"

She looked down at her hands, remembered how at their very first meeting she had felt safe in the clasp of his; hadn't wanted him to let go. She said, "If you put it like that—"

"And I do. Thank you." Then, as if it were his natural habit on parting from her, he bent to kiss her lightly on the mouth. "Wait for me," he said, and ran.

She watched him disappear into the darkness, then turned and went toward the house. His kiss was warm on her lips and the puzzle of his switch from hectoring to entreaty was an excitement in her mind. Something had changed in the climate between them. But what?

CHAPTER TEN

EARLIER AGATHE HAD STIRRED, muttering, and Maria, sitting with her in the shuttered room, had gone over to her. Her murmurs had turned querulous and with one of her heavily bandaged hands, she had fumbled at the bed clothes, trying to throw them off.

"Bella. Louisa." Her voice had come thickly. "It is nearly dark, and I must milk them." In fact the twilight of the room was only caused by the shutters closed against the morning sun. But Doctor Carteret had warned that, rousing gradually from her sedation, she might not be able at first to distinguish night from day, and Maria, knowing that a man had gone over to the Maas to see to the goats and to feed the hens, had been able to reassure her that the creatures were being cared for. After which Agathe had dropped off again and Maria had returned to her vigil, which had freed the professional nurse for a mid-morning cup of coffee.

Once before, according to the nurse, Agathe had roused briefly and had seemed to accept that though she was not at home, she was in safe hands at the Manoir. But what her fully conscious reaction might be to finding herself immobilized by shock and burns in the house of her enemy, Maria had not cared to think.

Overnight they had brought Agathe in from the *maquis*, dazed, burned and barely coherent. Orso had come with her, giving her into Maria's care with the brief order, "Don't ask her to talk. Tend her, get her to bed and call Carteret urgently," before he left again to return to the fight.

Later the cruel blast of the *libeccio* had lessened and changed direction and a blessed rain had begun to fall, finishing the work that the change of wind and the dogged firefighters had begun; not before some damage to the estate outbuildings had been done, but soon enough cut a worse menace to animals, farm stocks, machinery and the house. The coming of the rain and the easing of the threat, which she knew must follow it, hardly registered with Maria, occupied with the care of Agathe, helped by the cook-housekeeper and the young maid. Later still Orso had brought back the tired estate men for drinks, by which time Doctor Carteret had arrived, had dealt with Agathe, promised to send a trained nurse in the morning and had said he would wait to see Orso.

He reported on Agathe to both Orso and Maria. "She is badly shocked and has first-degree burns to her hands and arms...."

"No wonder," Orso put in tensely. "When we came upon her, she was beating out the flames with her bare hands. She was already half-surrounded."

"And you don't know how or why she came to be there, so far from home at night?" Doctor Carteret had repeated to Maria the question he had asked her before, while he had been treating Agathe and dressing her wounds.

"Only, as I've told you, that she must have walked here, through the *maquis*," Maria had said again.

"But for what purpose?"

As Maria hesitated, Orso had thrown her a warning glance and had answered that for her. "None, so far as Maria knows." He had used her name familiarly. "As she will have told you, we arrived at the Maas to find it empty, and we came back here to find—" he spread his hands expressively"—what we did. And Mademoiselle Juret out there, in the midst."

"And she said nothing then? I may say she was in no fit state to be questioned by the time I saw her."

Orso said, "She did talk. But disjointedly, without making much sense to us."

"Nor to you?" The doctor had turned to Maria.

"When they brought her in, she only looked at me as if—as if she didn't know me," Maria said, her voice breaking slightly.

Orso went on, "To the man who first found her she said she had gone up to bed when she remembered she hadn't taken her evening walk and had come down again—"

Maria broke in, "But she never did go for a walk at bedtime. Besides, her clothes were folded on a chair, her nightgown was missing and her bed had been slept in. She must have left it to go out, as—as I suspect she has done before."

"In her nightclothes?"

"Last night she had taken a coat and boots."

The doctor had looked thoughtful, pursing his lips. He invited Orso, "And so...?"

"When I came up with her she seemed bewildered to find herself where she was. She was still beating wildly about her, muttering about 'danger'; blaming someone, we thought, for starting the fire, and asking where 'they' were. She had seen 'them'; two of them. *Malfaiteurs*—evildoers, and then suddenly they weren't there. Then, reluctantly, she allowed us to bring her away."

"M'm." Doctor Carteret had nodded sagely. "A typical illusion, that, of the somnambulist—seeing people, buildings, animals that aren't there—" He broke off at Orso's sharp movement and Maria's suppressed gasp.

"A somnambulist?" she breathed. "Aunt Agathe is a sleepwalker? That's all?"

"*All?* You are not too disturbed? Nor need you be. It can be treated successfully nowadays. But though you believed she took these nocturnal trips, you didn't suspect it as the cause? Her own doctor didn't know?"

"She never owned to having one before you first attended her. And I thought—"

But there Maria had checked at a second warning glance from Orso, who said, "Agathe was wide awake, though dazed, when she was found."

"Yes, very likely, and though the traumatic state usually continues for some time, it is just possible she did see someone—or two, as she claimed. And if she did, there and at that time of night, they could have been intent on arson. Have you enemies who would stoop to it, would you say?"

The question was the doctor's, but it was at Maria that Orso had looked as he had answered with conviction, "None that I know of. Or suspect."

And so they had left it. Doctor Carteret had departed and Orso, refusing to discuss it, had insisted that Maria go to bed in the room the housekeeper had prepared for her. He had gone upstairs with her, an arm around her weary, drooping shoulders. At the door of her room he had said wryly, "So much for the talk we haven't had! Tomorrow will have to do."

She had asked then, "Talk? What about? And why not now?" To which he had said, "Too much for now. And I mustn't take advantage—of your tiredness, for one thing. Of your relief that it seems Agathe is neither an arsonist nor a *mazzere*, for another. And for a third, your generosity toward my fears for you when I wouldn't let you go with me to find her." He had touched her cheek lightly then. "Good night, little one. We will talk, we must talk... soon."

And with that promise she had willingly let him leave her. She didn't know the pattern of the promise—only that it was good to have it, that he would keep it, and then when he did, they might be talking in more than words....

BUT THE FULFILLMENT of the promise was still to wait. Maria had breakfasted alone with Monsieur Laurent, who told her that Orso had gone out as the result of a telephone call from Doctor Carteret after she had gone to bed.

"It appears," said Pascal, "that the doctor hadn't got far on his way home from here when his car gave him trouble. He had switched it off, got out and had been working on the engine under the raised hood for some minutes when he looked up to see two youths, one of them carrying a petrol can, scramble out of the hedgerow ditch onto the road, not many meters ahead. Not having heard the car, they must have been surprised it was there, for they halted and looked back, in the full beam of the headlights, and then ran. At that point they were just a little way past the limits of our land, and Ivone Carteret thought that petrol can rather significant."

"You mean they *could* have raised the fire, and my aunt *may* have seen them?"

Pascal smiled. "Or they *could* have been a couple of motorists whose car had run out of fuel! But why travel by ditch in search of it, and why run from another car that might have had some to spare? No, though by the time Ivone was able to follow them they had disappeared—back to their ditches for safety, one supposes—he was pretty sure they were your aunt's 'evildoers' and also that he had recognized them."

Maria gasped, "He knew them? Who were they?"

"Neither of them a patient of his, but neighbors to a widow who is. Not a Corsican family—Cypriot; a daughter who is a nightclub dancer and these two youths, her brothers, less often in work than out of it, according to this old lady's gossip to Ivone. Their name—"

A sordid memory had clicked for Maria. "Is it . . . Lesnos, perhaps?" she asked.

"Lesnos, yes. How did you know?"

"Because I know them. That is, not the two young men, but the girl, Anni . . . ." She paused, watching Pascal. But giving no sign that he knew the name of one of Gian's passing fancies, he had asked, "You say you know her, my dear? How?"

Maria told him, recalling for him the night of the girl's jealous attack upon her, Orso's intervention and Anni's spitfire threats of her brothers' vengeance. He listened in silence and when she had finished, said, "Orso told me nothing of this, but he will have remembered it; and it will be evidence to put before the police."

"If the men are guilty, what will happen to them?" Maria asked.

"They can be deported. Probably the family, too. In Corsica arson is not many degrees less heinous than murder, and rightly so." Pascal paused and sighed. "It is a pity Gian's foolishness should have such evil consequences, for he is a good, fine boy at heart. But perhaps one must be patient. A year or two more and he may begin to take more interest in the estate. At least he knows my wishes for him, though that it would not be wise fatherhood to foist them on him against his will is a lesson I learned rather painfully only last night."

He paused again and looked inquiringly at Maria. "You witnessed that unfortunate scene with Chantal Garson at my party? Well, that was the direct result of a years-old mistake of mine. To think that if, young as he was at the time, Orso hadn't had the conviction and the will to defy me, he might have married that virago at my behest! How wrong and mistaken in her I was! For as I expect you know her father and I had a *mariage de raison* for them in mind?"

Maria said, "Yes. Gian told me, and that it came to nothing when he chose another man for her instead."

"Ah, that was what we had to allow our world to think.

Even Gian, too. For if it had been known that it was Orso
who refused to keep a pact he hadn't made, that would
have rendered Chantal *disonerata*, which, for a girl of good
family, would never have done. Instead, for her honor's
sake, Orso wore the stigma of having been rejected for a
better match. That it was not so was a secret known only
to Chantal, her parents, Orso and myself. Until last night,
when it seems, having despaired of her renewed hopes of
Orso, she took her public revenge, which I think she may
regret—though too late."

Maria experienced a little shiver of relief. So her esti-
mate of Orso had been right! She hadn't wanted to believe
him complacent to a match of mere advantage, nor that he
had fallen prey to the glamor that Chantal had brought
back with her from America. Chantal's wild accusations
had implied that she had been disappointed by him not
once but twice. But his denial of having made either promise had rung firm and true. Whatever Pascal might have
hoped for by her return, Orso had not shared it. Or was
that too wishful thinking? Maria longed to believe it was
not.

She realized from Pascal's continuing faith in Gian's ultimate change of life-style, that he hadn't yet heard Gian's
news, and her heart ached for him, deprived of an acceptable daughter-in-law and the shaping of a son's future almost at a stroke. How would he take Gian's decision to
make the air, not the estate, his career? She wished there
were some way in which she could soften the blow for him.
But though of course there was not, if Pascal had really
learned the lesson that he claimed to have done, he would
not force the issue to an unbridgeable rift. His hardly won
tolerance of other people's wills—Orso's in particular—might see to that.

But now Agathe was rousing again, this time apparently
fully awake, and presently as alert and blunt as ever.

After a critical survey of her surroundings she announced, "They told me last night that I was walking in my sleep—which I have never done in my life before,"—a statement that took Maria aback, but which she did not contradict. Whatever therapy Doctor Carteret had in mind for Agathe must deal with bland assertions of that sort, she decided.

Agathe continued, "However, it may have been so on this occasion. For I woke—if, of course, I was asleep—to find I had walked much further than I intended, along the way through the *maquis* that you had shown me. It was fortunate for these friends of yours that I took it. For otherwise I should not have seen those two miscreants in the very act of firing the *maquis* on their borders."

Maria felt her way carefully. "You did see them doing it?"

"Haven't I said so?" Agathe retorted. "And how did I get these—" indicating her bandaged hands"—if not through trying to beat out the fire? An act of misplaced charity, you may say, considering what the Laurent family has done to me and mine. But fire is fire, and one would not willingly stand by and watch one's worst enemies *burn*."

To that Maria ventured, "They are not really your worst enemies, you know. Nor even the least of them. *They* bear *you* no ill will, and isn't it going to be difficult to keep up your feud after their care of you now?"

Agathe bridled. "And what else could they do but care for me? *I* am not their unpaid night watchman! Though—" she paused, pursing her lips"—you have a point there, niece. Spend a night under the freely offered shelter of an enemy's roof and one's cause becomes void. Though for the time being only, of course," she added hastily. "Given new provocation, it can revive."

"Provocation that I'm sure your cause won't get from

the Laurents after this," Maria assured her with hot iron-striking opportunism. "So please, aunt, won't you forget it? If I can, can't you? After all, whatever wrong was done was done to *my* mother!"

But Agathe, adroit as ever in quashing argument by silence, said nothing and presently changed the subject to announce, "I have changed my mind in the matter of my will. I am still strong and able, and since there is no reason why I should not live for years, it has occurred to me that you might have to wait for far too long for your inheritance of the Maas and its land. Therefore, as soon as I am free and am able to sign my name, I shall ask my lawyer to draw up a deed of gift of it for you now."

If Maria had been surprised by the original proposal, she was astounded by this, but found herself with only much the same protests to make—"But you can't do that! I can't accept it! You're not serious, surely?"

To all of which Agathe replied evenly. "My mind is made up. Thus you will stay here, or return very soon. I shall ask my lawyer to advise us on raising a loan to enable us to run and improve the farm enough to make a living for us both. In this way, it will always remain in the family, as honor says it must."

"If you left it to me, as you originally intended, it would still stay in the family," Maria pointed out.

"Yes indeed. But I have a fancy to develop it now, and I cannot do this alone at my age." Agathe nodded thoughtfully. "Bees, for instance. A bee farm. The Balagne region has always been noted for its honey."

Bees! Knowing nothing of the cultivation of bees, Maria was tempted to claim a fictitious lifelong allergy to bee stings. But realizing that, up against Agathe's iron will, she was likely to lose any case against the scheme, she said nothing and was relieved when the nurse came in, bringing pills and a glass of milk for her patient.

Agathe said, "I do not drink milk in the middle of the morning. I prefer a glass of wine."

"Doctor Carteret ordered milk for you, madame."

"Perhaps. But he could not be expected to know that my habit is to take a glass of wine. Something very light—a *rosé* perhaps."

"I cannot go against his orders, madame."

But though no wine was forthcoming, neither did Agathe drink the milk, and Maria was witnessing this typical deadlock with amusement when there was a knock at the door and it was Orso's voice speaking to the nurse when she went to open it.

"Is madame well enough to see a visitor?" he asked.

"You, monsieur? Yes, I think so."

"I didn't mean myself, but a very old friend of hers. He was leaving for Bonifacio this morning, but hearing of her accident, he would very much like to . . . ." Orso did not finish the sentence. He stood aside at the open doorway to enable Marcel Dinand to pass and to approach the bed, both hands outstretched to Agathe.

"*Ma mie!*" he murmured tenderly. "It has been so long. . . " And though she drew herself up and tried to avoid his embrace, he saluted her with a kiss on either cheek and stood back.

Her fine eyes flashed at him and beyond him at Orso. "This is an outrage . . . !"

But Orso was already hustling Maria and the nurse from the room, closing the door firmly on whatever was to follow. To the nurse he said, "Leave them for a while, will you? Their meeting has Doctor Carteret's blessing." And to Maria's shocked question of "What have you *done*?" he retorted, "Just what you should have done, and didn't when you had the chance. Cut corners. Employed shock tactics. Infiltrated enemy lines. Stormed the pass—"

"But it's not fair! She is in bed—she can't walk out on

him if she wants to. You have put her at a cru
disadvantage!"

"And when, can you tell me," he countered, "wa
Agathe ever at a disadvantage for long? She has ouste
me; she routed my father on his peace mission; she is qui
capable of getting rid of Dinand by freezing him out. But i
she hasn't done it within minutes, I've an idea she won'
He has a good case and I'm backing him to make her lis
ten." He turned again to the nurse. "Twenty minutes, hal
an hour, and you can make an excuse to go in. Thoug
sooner, of course, if you hear sounds of active battle."

She looked doubtful. "I thought you said they were ol
friends, monsieur?"

"So they are. So they were . . . once. The very best, i
fact. You understand me, nurse?"

She smiled conspiratorially. "I think so, monsieur.
shall give them a full half hour."

"And so shall we . . . and more. If Mademoiselle Jure
asks for her niece, tell her, will you, that she is with me
And if my father wants to know why we are not at lunch
eon, say that we are both otherwise occupied—rathe
pressingly—and we shall be with him for dinner." Orso'
hand, compellingly beneath Maria's elbow, gave her n
choice but to go with him downstairs.

In the hall they were met by the junior maid with
lunch hamper that he took from her after inspecting an
apparently approving the contents.

"Where are we going?" asked Maria, hanging back.

"On a picnic for two. At random . . . does it really matte
where?"

"I shouldn't leave Aunt Agathe, and I haven't even got
handbag."

He made a gesture of mock resignation. "Habit die
hard . . . you have to quibble, don't you? Agathe couldn't b
in better hands. But fetch your handbag if you must."

When she rejoined him in the car it seemed that he was driving merely at random through gentle countryside and nestling villages where the noon silence and desertion were almost complete. For her part she sat beside him, content to trust whatever promise lay in his purposeful kidnapping. They had to "talk"—and soon, he had said. And alone, her instinct knew he had implied. Her memory ran back over the things she had to treasure—his calling her "little one," his "Wait for me," the tenderness of his kiss on parting from her to go out to the fire. So little really. But enough for her woman's awareness to hope on, to cherish, to long to answer whatever they had seemed to ask. But she could wait. Suspended in her vacuum of not knowing yet sensing, she could afford to wait.

As he drove, they talked. Impersonally—of Agathe and Marcel Dinand; of Gian's news for his father.

Of the latter Maria asked, "How will Monsieur Laurent take it ?"

"Badly at first. He had plans for Gian, as all Corsican parents have. But I think he'll be generous enough to concede defeat. He's not a typical diehard father, and it's to be hoped I can make it up to him," Orso said.

Of Marcel Dinand's chances with Agathe he claimed to be sanguine. "He is a determined type and, as you pointed out, she can't get away from him. She can only argue."

"Or refuse to listen to him."

"To someone who insists on talking? Or better still, *acts* in a way no woman can misunderstand? She may not take him today or tomorrow, but the fact of his years of devotion can't fail to intrigue her and I think he'll have his way in the end." Orso paused, adding, "If he carries her off to Bonifacio, that will leave you without anchorage at the Maas, won't it?"

"But I don't feel nearly as sure as you are that she will accept Monsieur Dinand. Because she told me this morn-

ing she plans to give me the property now, so that I can
help her to develop it. Possibly as a bee farm, she suggested."

"A *bee farm*?" Orso echoed. "Honey? To sell to whom,
did she say?"

"Why, isn't there a market for it?"

"Only locally, and then probably only by barter. We
can't compete with the French honeys of, say, Narbonne
and the Maritime Alps. And so—how did you react to this
pipe dream?"

"I said I couldn't possibly accept the Maas from her."

"As a revolt against bees, or for any other reason?"

"Simply because I felt she shouldn't hand it over to me
during her lifetime. I didn't want her to leave it to me, either, as you know."

"Do I not!" He grimaced. "I remember your trouncing
me soundly for suggesting you should abet her in keeping
it in the family. Anyway, I've an idea you can't win. I happened to tell Dinand that she had willed the property to
you and he was delighted. And he could be even better
pleased if he hasn't to take it on, like an old man of the sea,
as part of the price of getting Agathe."

"But her will won't stand if she marries him."

"No. Though, if that is what she has in mind, a deed of
gift could. Incidentally—" Orso looked straight ahead as
he went on "—at the last interview I had with Chantal Garson, she had the impudence to suggest that you, knowing
the invalidity of wills made before marriage, had engi-
neered Agathe's refusal to see Dinand."

Maria said quietly, "She accused me of it, too."

Orso glanced around quickly. "She did? When?"

"At your father's party. Before she . . . ." Maria broke off
uncomfortably, then hesitated. "I—I don't understand
about Chantal. About what happened. I thought you . . . ."

But if she expected Orso to enlighten her about his relations with Chantal, she was to be disappointed. He was driving the car at a dawdling pace along a road that seemed to spring a surprise at every one of its many turns—here, a far glimpse of the sea; there, an olive grove, a string of ambling wild goats, a field white with mushrooms, a group of tumbled prehistoric stones, an avenue of chestnuts arching navelike across the road. He explained, "I'm looking for water, sun and shade for you, a view—a place to remember.... Ah, here we have it, I think. Will you come?"

He helped her out of the car and across a low stone wall toward the music of a stream, which seethed and creamed about the rocks that forded it roughly. A few meters above where Orso and Maria came upon it, a moss-grown bridge spanned it; about at the same distance below, it eddied and foamed, throwing crystal spume high as it dropped over a steep rock shelf and gradually smoothed as it widened into a miniature lake. Beyond, the high banks that bordered the narrows of the stream flattened out, giving a vista of open country and a fan of sky.

Orso chose a spot where a fine tree dappled shade onto the carpet of dry bracken beneath it. He knelt, pushing the picnic basket into deeper shade, and put up a hand to draw Maria down beside him.

"Will this do?" he asked.

"Lovely." She settled her back into the natural armchair afforded by the base of the tree trunk, and clasped her hands around her knees.

"Hungry? Thirsty?"

"Not yet. I want to look at the view."

"So do I." But knowing his eyes were fixed upon her, she felt her color rise. She sought for something to say.

"You didn't happen on this place by chance? You were looking for it?" she asked.

"It is one of the headstreams of the Tavignano, which you saw at Corte." He knelt up beside her. "You are making small talk. You don't really want to know *how* I came to bring you here. You are pretending you don't know why!" he accused her.

"I'm not pretending...." Her voice was a mere thread of a whisper.

He shook his head at her. "You couldn't agree with me for once, could you? But if you are not pretending, then you know?"

"No...."

She hadn't been pretending. She had known his purpose. But when he gathered her to him it was her own surrender, her own hunger for his touch, his searching lips, which took her unawares. She clung to him, making herself his, as he ruffled her hair, kissed her brow, her eyelids, each cheek and finally her mouth in a passionate assertion and question, which her straining need of him answered in urgent, leaping rapture.

Presently he held her back from him, smiling down at her.

"So I can...after all?" he queried.

"Can...what?"

"Make you 'feel like a woman.' Do you remember?"

She nodded. "You had already. You did that night. You always could."

"Then be one for me. *Only* for me. But why didn't you tell me? Show me?"

"I thought I had. But you called it just a trick. Besides, I dared not let you know. There was Chantal...."

"Ah, of course, Chantal." He sat beside her, holding her hand, smoothing its back with a gentle thumb. "How much do you know about her?"

"As much as Gian knew, and told me when I first met her at your house. But this morning your father told me that even Gian had never known that it was you who broke off the engagement match with her."

Orso nodded. "True, though I don't remember just when I realized she wasn't either the girl or the wife for me, and said so. I was young, but old enough. And of course she never forgave me, though we kept the secret well."

"But you... when she came back, a widow, you encouraged her, took her about. Gian said...."

His dark eyes, mischief in them, glanced up. "And did nothing strike you about the timing of all that? That *she* had come back from America only shortly before *you* appeared on the scene? No? Well, having fallen in love with you almost on sight—though not quite, don't flatter yourself—you were far too aloof and detached.... Now, where was I? Yes, well...I argued that a little visible dalliance with Chantal wouldn't do you any harm. So I indulged it and father innocently helped, hoping, as I think he did until her viperish exhibition at his party, that she and I would marry after all."

Maria murmured, "If it was just an act, you did it pretty thoroughly. I ought to tell you... I once read part of a letter of hers to you. It was in the pocket of the parka you lent me, and it read as if she wanted to make up a lovers' quarrel."

"But I do quarrel pretty emphatically with people ... hadn't you noticed?"

"Yes."

He laughed. "I asked for that! However, though I don't even remember this occasion, one could always trust Chantal to turn a mere difference into a highly charged scene, to be followed by dramatic apologies and forgiveness. When you returned my parka I guessed you might have found her note, but I wasn't very concerned."

"You wanted to make me jealous?"

"You seemed to resent me so much I couldn't hope jealousy for love had ever entered your head. But yes, I did want you to believe I was valued elsewhere while I was doing my best to persuade you to stay around long enough to learn to appreciate me yourself!"

As he put his arm around her and she leaned back against the hollow of his shoulder, Maria said, "No one would have guessed. Even Gian said you and your father had marriage plans for him and me. And Chantal claimed—though I hated believing her—that you hoped the Manoir would get possession of the Maas land through a match between Gian and me."

"And you took her lies in silence instead of confronting me with them to deny?"

"I—I was afraid. You *were* going out of your way to persuade me to stay here, and supposing you couldn't deny the lies, I...didn't want to know."

"Any more, possibly, than I wanted to hear from your own lips that you were falling for Gian. I didn't want to know for certain, either!" Orso drew her closer and laughed softly. "A couple of moral cowards, aren't we? Tell me, when did I first put over the message that I wanted you, *only* you—in love?"

"I think—when you kissed me—was it only last night—after you had asked me, not ordered me, to stay behind when you went to the fire."

"Because, though the danger of your going with me wasn't great, at that moment I was as afraid for Agathe as you were. I wouldn't admit it to you, but if it were possible that she had fired the *maquis* in vendetta against us, I could gauge the anger of my men if they had caught her, and I wouldn't have you witness that."

"And instead, bless her, she was trying to put it out!" Maria laughed shakily. "One thing is certain—when she hears about you and me, she won't be making me a gift of the Maas."

Orso scorned, "Who cares? Though I shouldn't be too sure, if I were you. When she changes her name to Dinand, she'll have to have some way of keeping it in the family."

"We don't know she is going to change her name."

"She'd better—after all the trouble we have gone to for her!" he threatened.

"And Gian? And your father?"

"Gian will see us as an extra escape route for his conscience. And for father you are all he has ever wanted in a bride for me—of good family, of Corsican blood, and modest and generous and honest, as he knows now Chantal never was. Even your name—there has always been a Maria in our family. Shall we make doubly sure, *mignonne*, by calling our first daughter after you?"

"Oh, Orso, it's so strange . . . wonderful that you love me!" She turned her face shyly against the silk of his shirt. "Tell me, when did you first . . . ?"

"I've told you—not at first sight. I thought you were a headstrong, foolhardy little baggage."

She giggled happily. "You've thought and said as much often since! But seriously, when?"

"I don't know when I first loved you. But the night you accused me of treating you like a dropped parcel . . . ."

"That was the night you kissed me. In—in a punishment kind of way."

"Yes, well . . . my temper was up. I remembered what the *signadore* who told our fortunes had said to you and to me, and I resolved that I was going to be your 'dark man' and you were going to be 'the wrong girl' I was going to leap ahead of myself and kiss . . . and kiss . . . one day, or I'd know the reason why!"

"Meaning," she murmured, "that I was the wrong girl for you once?"

"Only while I thought you saw me as the wrong man for you." His finger and thumb on her chin turned her face up to his. "Want me to go on telling you and showing you just how right you are now?"

"I still can't believe it. But...please!"

He didn't hurry over it. With the passing of time the cool shade shifted from the picnic basket, leaving it exposed to full sun. But neither of them noticed or cared that the recherché food might spoil or the wine lose its chill. While they kissed and touched and talked lovers' nonsense and laughed, their need was a different kind of hunger and thirst.

THE HABIT OF LOVE

The Habit
of Love

Joyce Dingwell

Brit was the brown moth of the family; Cara the beautiful butterfly. Brit had long been accustomed to the fact that sacrifices had to be made for her talented sister.

So when the unexpected legacy came to Brit, she planned to share it. But Cara had never shared anything—and she walked off with everything, leaving Brit penniless.

It was then that Link Wayland revealed his investment in her family and demanded repayment from Brit. "I've come to the stage where marriage is advisable," he said. "I need a wife."

Brit had no recourse but to agree. But could there ever be happiness with a man who rode roughshod over everyone?

CHAPTER ONE

"Mifmif, ith nearly time!"

Small Helena was considered sophisticated enough by her proud parents to attend Brit's posture classes, but she was still young enough to be bothered by s's. Obviously, and Brit smiled ruefully and secretly as she superintended her weaving line of girls, posture bothered her, too.

"Mifmif," Helena began again, one eye on the wall clock that apparently she could read, because, noted Brit, it was nearly time.

"Yes, dear," Brit conceded. "One more sequence, class. The wind, girls, rustling through the leaves."

They all loved this one, mainly, Brit suspected, because it was the last before their release, but she could be wrong there, for the wind entailed action, and all young things want action.

Brit looked around at the different winds. Plump Marcia, a good solid wind, one that would bang doors and scatter papers. Lenore, a delicate wind, scarcely a breeze, you could say. Jeanette—

"Time, Mifmif," called Helena triumphantly, and the lesson was over. Out they ran, the St. Hilda day girls to their homes, the St. Hilda boarders to their school home. St. Hilda's posture class was finished for today.

How much had they absorbed? Brit shrugged as she gathered her things and prepared to leave, too. It had worried her at first, since she was a born worrier, but Miss Asquith, the Principal, had merely smiled.

"My dear, their parents do not ask for results, all they

want is for their child to be availed of everything that is
offered. Speak to Miss Pidcock—" Miss Pidcock was the
music mistress "—and she'll tell you that quite often a girl
doesn't turn up for her lesson at all, but so long as Miss
Pidcock can drum "Moon Moths" into them, or "Winter
Sleigh Ride," the parents are content. We are strictly a social school, so salve your conscience."

Brit had salved it, but she never had succeeded in really
enjoying her post apart from the fact that it paid satisfactory money. She would have liked to have achieved results.
She was fond of children, and wanted to teach them something, not just provide another social extra. But posture to
these girls was premature, she strongly suspected; sixes to
twelves needed unhindered action, not discipline and re-
straint. Still, it paid money. And money was what
they—*Cara*—must have.

It was half dark by the time Brit finished her daily
school report and left north end St. Hilda's behind her
When she reached their western suburban flat it would be
night. She wished for once, if just for once, that Cara
would put on their outside light. On winter evenings like
this you looked for a light. But Cara would be curled up by
the electric fire, painting her fingernails, or her toes, or forgetting, as ever, to start their evening meal. Then if Brit
said anything to her about the light, she would retort, and
rightly: "But you always go on about money, Brittie."

Brit was aware that she often did. She was well paid, but
the pay had to stretch for two, it had to include Cara. Cara
was at ballet school, an expensive, exclusive school. One
day, Cara always promised, everything would be repaid,
but until she was ready, or until someone discovered
her....

Besides—with a sweet little Cara smile—remember how
mummy and daddy had believed in giving her a chance?

Giving Cara a chance. If Brit had wanted to forget that.

certainly Cara would not have given Brit the chance. Not that Brit did want to forget. She was as blindly proud and as blindly devoted to her younger sister as her parents had been to their baby daughter.

Brit had been a disappointment to her parents; she had known that from the age of six. A much wiser six than Helena, Brit thought now, buttoning her coat collar from Sydney's sharp August wind. She could remember it all as clearly as though it had been said last week, not all those years ago.

"Willis—" Willis had been her father "—you're wasting your time on this one," mother had said.

Her father had sighed and agreed: "Yes, Edith." Edith was her mother. "I did hope you might pass on your gift."

Brit had known what the "gift" was. Her mother had been a dancer. She had married Willis Smith after his successful *Hinterland* ballet, a music sequence that had swept all the Australian states but still never graduated from Australia; also a success Willis Smith had never repeated. He was working on one then, he was always working on one, but how, he had said irascibly to his wife, could he hope to achieve anything with no one to help him? For Edith had lost her gift with maternity and his daughter Brit obviously had no gift. The child moved nicely, stood well, but there was nothing else there. Willis Smith had said all that to his wife, and small Brit had heard.

She had stood listening at the other side of the door. Then she had listened to her mother telling her father there would be another baby, and because he was so pleased about it, about what it might mean, Brit had been pleased, too, had loved the baby even before it arrived.

And when Cara had arrived she had adored her. She had not needed her parents' frequent injunctions later, when Cara had shown definite talent right from an infant, to do everything humanly possible to give Cara her chance.

Only—and Brit stepped into the appropriate bus—th chance seemed to be taking a long time. Brit was twenty five now. Cara was nineteen. A lovely butterfly of nine teen, not, as her father had said quite fondly of his elde girl, a brown moth.

"You're our little brown moth." He had patted Brit head.

Sometimes Brit had felt like protesting. Around twenty two she had definitely felt like that, for twenty-two i dreaming time, time for bright wings and long flight. Cer tainly no brown moth phase. But her mother had died, an she could see how bereft her father was. Also, her father sister had come to live with them, and Aunt Truda ha supported her brother in his beliefs. Once Brit remembere Aunt Truda saying loudly and with asperity: "There's onl room in a family for one shining light." She had meant i of course, against *her*, Brit had miserably deduced. She re membered, too, how she had shrunk sensitively away.

Then father had died. Then, several months ago now Aunt Truda.

"I suppose," Cara had said faintly when the family in come had been diminished to only one source, "I'd bette do something." She had looked appealingly at Brit, an when Cara did that....

"You have to finish first, darling," Brit had assured he "You have to have your chance."

Giving Cara her chance.

The bus was approaching the stop nearest to the fla Brit pulled the cord and got out. It was only a hundre yards to the apartment, but every step of the way sh thought eargerly: *If only the light is on saying "Come i You're home."* She would have loved a welcoming light. I only Cara had started dinner.

Then she reached Lockwood Court and her heart lifte John's car was in the parking lot. So John was visitin them. Why, it was as good as a light, Brit thought gladly, definitely better than chops being grilled.

She was actually singing as she ran up the stairs.

Cara was toasting herself, as Brit had expected, but because John was there she was not finger or toe painting. Instead she was looking over some ballet music he had brought along. John Ferris was following the same road Willis Smith had, though so far he had gained not even one success. Still, he was young, only a little older than Brit. Brit glanced at the sheets that Cara studied and saw that John had progressed with them since last time. That was good. She smiled across at the tall, fair young man.

He smiled back . . . and Brit, being a woman, even though a rather naive one, knew there was something special in that smile. Also that it was for her. She was glad, because she felt something rather special for John.

A little irritably as she watched the quick exchange, Cara complained: "Must have been an easy day for you, Brit, you seem fresh as a daisy. Oh, lord, have I had a grind and a bore!"

Brit looked at her sister with loving sympathy. That glance from John helped her do it, because, she thought, *I can well afford it. In John, I am—and will be—rich.*

"Stopping for dinner?" she asked the man.

"Will it stretch that far?" he grinned.

"If Cara will halve her chop."

"Why me? I've been on my toes for hours."

And I have been, thought Brit, *on my feet, on my senses, on my discretion, tact and best behavior (for social St. Hilda's demanded that) all day.*

"I was joking, of course," she said. "There's plenty."

There wasn't, but Brit ate at school, so she didn't need two hot meals.

Over the dinner, John explained his new sequence. He was calling his ballet *Southern Cross.* Cara got up and did

some spontaneous interpretation for him. She kicked off
her shoes and took up a scarf, but that was the extent of
her props, and it was enough. She had definite talent.

There was silence as she twisted and wreathed. She was
moonlight seeking the stars of the cross, thought Brit, and
she looked a little secretly to see if John, too, was feeling
that.

He obviously did feel it. He was rapt. But, evidently
sensing her glance, he looked at Brit, and his eyes were
warm ... *and for her.*

"It has to be Europe." John said later as he rolled up the
music. "There's nothing happening here."

"I feel that, too," Cara came in plaintively.

"But, darling," remonstrated Brit, "but, Cara, it has to
be here for you. I mean—well, it just has to be, and you
know it." She said it a little anxiously. One never knew
with Cara.

"I could go," pouted her younger sister. "Other girls go.
Live in a garret, all that." But she said it vaguely, without
conviction. She had no conviction, and neither had Brit.
Cara would starve in an attic, Brit knew, unless, as was
quite likely, someone saw her (for you had only to see her)
and came to her rescue.

"Ballet is improving here," Brit offered a little weakly.

"Improvement!" disparaged Cara.

"I feel it will arrive in a grand manner," came in John,
"and quite soon. But with my ballet, I'll have to start on
the bottom rung. So I must try Europe first." He got up.
"Thanks for the meal, Brit, thanks for the listening ear."

"Thanking me for the dancing feet?" put in Cara.

"You know I always do that," John smiled, but it was
not the smile he gave Brit, and Cara knew that.

When he had gone Cara said pettishly: "His ballet is no
good."

"I thought it had promise."

"But you wouldn't know, would you?"

"Not like you, darling," placated Brit. She knew that Cara, lovely, spoiled Cara, had seen those personal looks, so she felt she could forgive her resentment.

Cara was regarding her sister speculatively. Always she had rejoiced in being the family glittering light, but wasn't there something quietly attractive, *enduringly* attractive, in Brit's less-than-prettiness? Brit—sweet maiden in Greek—and indubitably that was Brit. Sweet. Cara stirred a little impatiently. Some men found sweetness more attractive than beauty. Obviously John had. She had seen his glowing eyes, a glow for her sister.

She stared at Brit covertly. Once she had been pleased at her own suave maturity, even at six years the junior, over her sister. She had been more polished, more sophisticated, she knew, more the finished article. Now Brit's youngness—young at near twenty-six!—vaguely irritated her. Why, she looked almost girlish.

"Some of your pupils have rubbed off on you," she said a little spitefully.

"Then I hope it's not Helena," giggled Brit. She added: "She calls me Mifmif."

"How do you stand the little pigs?"

"They're not really, they're just not ready for moods and what-have-yous yet. Still, I don't mind admitting I'm not that keen, either, but—"

"But it's good money." Cara came in quickly with that. She didn't want Brit to descend the financial ladder by changing to some less lucrative job.

Finance reminded her of something.

"Mail," she said. "Two bills. Money, money. What a pest it is!"

Brit nodded, and sighed slightly. She took up the letters and opened the first. A bill, as Cara had said. Then, a little absently, she opened the next letter.

It was from a firm of solicitors called ... but that didn't

matter. What they said was what mattered. Most of all what they enclosed.

They enclosed a letter from the girl's aunt. Dead Aunt Truda. But the letter was for one girl only—for Brit.

"My dear Brit. . . ." How strange, how moving, thought Brit, to read a letter written by a hand that would write no more. . . .

> By the time this is received by you I shall have left you. I have given strict orders to my solicitors that on no account are you to receive this until I have gone, and until all my concerns have been wound up.

Concerns? Aunt Truda? But Aunt Truda had been poor; she had had to come to them because of that, because living by herself was too expensive. Perhaps, though, the old lady had been sentimental over some trinkets she possessed, for Brit felt sure she would have possessed no more than that. Probably a print, or an ornament. Some such.

> I was not what you could have called a wealthy woman, Brit, but I was far more comfortable than your father thought. I started with a little but had the good fortune of excellent help and profitable advice. However, I kept it to myself. Unkind of me, I suppose, not to have helped Willis more, but I did pay my way and helping my brother only meant helping someone else, and frankly, Brit, that someone else has had more than her share of help. *You* have had nothing.

I, Aunt Truda? But you yourself once said, and said it with firmness, with asperity: "There's only room in a family for one shining light." Didn't you mean that there was only room for Cara, that everything should be for Cara? You couldn't have meant. . . .

Cara can and should be able to look after herself. She has talent, and certainly nothing has been spared to encourage that talent.

But everything was spared when it came to you, and that is why I am writing this now. I have left a bequest with my lawyers to pay you the sum of—

Brit read that sum again. Read it a third time.

I would like to make a stipulation as to how you deal with this money, but my solicitors tell me that at your responsible age this is not advised.

But I can suggest, and the solicitors agree with me, that an annuity would be a good thing.

However, I do see that trying to control other lives, young lives, is not an old lady's prerogative, so I leave you this money as a gift. You are absolutely free to do what you like with it.

By the time you read this all death duties and claims have been settled. The sum is entirely yours.

Just collect your legacy, Brit, and try to think kindly of me, which I am sure you often felt like *not* thinking in the past.

Goodbye, sweet girl. At least Willis named you well in that.

Your Aunt Truda.

Brit put the letter down. She was still staring straight ahead, not wholly absorbing the words she had read, definitely not for one moment believing them, as Cara took the letter up.

CHAPTER TWO

CARA'S FIRST IMPRESSION was incredulity, the same as it had been with Brit. The same as with Brit, she read the amount, then read it again.

"That cunning old duck!" she gasped.

"Cara!" scolded Brit.

"She was. Oh, I know she paid her way, but to be sitting on all that. What a fox!"

"*Cara!*" exclaimed Brit again.

"Sorry, darling. No—sorry, heiress. For you are, aren't you? It's quite a lump."

"It's—well, it's a satisfactory sum."

"It's riches. Why did the old meanie leave me out?"

"You read the letter, Cara. Evidently Aunt Truda was of the opinion that, well...."

"But that's unfair! It wasn't like that at all. It was a different matter with me."

Cara looked at Brit as only Cara could look, and Brit said at once: "Of course, pet. I agree that Aunt Truda had her own peculiar ideas."

"With the result that you gain and I...." Tears choked Cara, and she did not finish.

"With the result," came in Brit warmly, "that *we* gain, that the family gains. I mean, Cara, Aunt Truda could have left her nest egg anywhere. Even to an outsider."

"Yes." Cara dabbed her eyes and put away the handkerchief. She looked slightly more cheerful. "Yes, she could." But presently, caught up in envy again, she repeated: "Rich!"

"Not really."

"Well, I could do a lot of things with it."

"Like?" asked Brit.

"Like—like buying my own small car so I could whiz around looking for openings."

"An agent can do that for you."

"An agent can't look like me, and you must admit that looks help sell."

"Yes," agreed Brit. With a face like Cara's you had to agree with that. She asked, in the hope of placating Cara: "What else would you buy?"

"Clothes. Gorgeous clothes. Not the ones you run up.... Oh, sorry, Brit, but you understand."

"I understand."

"Clothes," repeated Cara, "that demand you get noticed."

"You always look nice, Cara."

"Nice!" Cara sniffed. She must have decided she was overdoing things, though, for she asked dutifully: "And you, Brit? What are you planning?"

"First of all, goodbye to St. Hilda's."

"Is that wise? After all, it's—"

"It's good pay, but I won't need that anymore."

"No, *you* won't," Cara said pointedly.

"Darling, don't be touchy. You're in this, too, of course you are, but St. Hilda's was killing me; I hated it right from the first day dad—and Link Wayland—why, yes, it was *him*, remember?—got the post for me. They thought they were doing me a great service, dad keeping the family tradition alive in a way, Link Wayland believing I could do with extra money, I suppose, but neither considering how I felt."

"Link," mused Cara, momentarily diverted. "I haven't seen him in years."

"Not since he left the suburb and its local editing for the city rounds. I've heard, though, that he's done extremely

well," Brit said carelessly. She had not liked Link Wayland. She had not cared for the long enigmatical looks he
always had given her. It had been all she could do to thank
him when he secured her the St. Hilda job.

When the Willis Smiths had settled in Winfield, Link
Wayland had called on the family to do a story on the
once Australian-known composer of the *Hinterland* ballet
for his *Winfield Times*. He had reported graciously on Willis Smith, and father, Brit remembered, had been very
pleased about it, had predicted a fine future for the young
journalist.

Whether her father had been perspicacious or merely
flattered, he had still been right about Link Wayland. The
man had advanced from paper to paper, and, Brit had
heard, now controlled a whole suburban series of his own.
But she had heard, too, he still took a personal and intimate interest in them all, visited them and advised them,
though she had learned this from Aunt Truda, who had
mutual friends with Link, and not personally or intimately
herself. After Link Wayland had left Winfield she had seen
him rarely.

The last time they had spoken was the time her father
had to remind her to thank Link Wayland for getting her
the posture job at St. Hilda's. Mr. Smith had been gratified
that his daughter was not taking on something ordinary,
gratified that the money was so good.

Brit had been twenty-one then. . . . Good heavens, had
she been "posturing" for almost five years?

Father had said promptingly: "Brit, dear, Mr. Wayland
really worked on the St. Hilda trustees for you."

"I'm sure he did." Brit had tried to hide a hard frustration in her voice. She must have, from father, but she had
not been so sure of Link Wayland. The man, slightly more
mature than twenty-one generally favors, had given her
one of those long probing looks.

"Well—" a little chidingly from father —"*well*, Brit?"

"Well, thank you, Mr. Wayland. It was wonderful of you, Mr. Wayland. I can never repay you, Mr. Wayland," Brit fairly had burst out.

The dark, almost Indian-bronze six-footer, the man who should have been riding a horse, roughriding it, not writing a news story, had looked back at Brit with deliberate calculation.

"Just as well you're a dancer, Miss Smith, for you certainly would never make a writer. Far too many effusions. A simple word or two goes as far, and believe me, much more effectively."

"I'm not a dancer," Brit had said stiffly.

"She has very nice posture," father had come in, not understanding Brit, not understanding the way Link Wayland was talking. "She'll be a great benefit to the girls."

"Aged six to twelve," Brit had said, "teaching six to twelve how to stand."

"Perhaps you don't want this job." It had been said so quietly, so cunningly, that Mr. Smith had not heard.

But Brit had.

"I want the job." She had known she had gone too far. She had said thank you again, shaken Mr. Wayland's hand, escaped and left father telling the journalist of other highlights that had happened to him in the hope that they, too, might find publication.

After that they had not conversed again. Brit had seen Link Wayland sometimes in Winfield—an Indian-red man like he was had to be seen—but she had not acknowledged him.

Aunt Truda had mentioned him often. She had said that Mr. Wayland, whom she met frequently at friends' homes, had asked about Brit.

"A very nice gentleman," Aunt Truda had said warmly.

Brit had left it at that.

"Yes," she repeated to Cara now, "it was Link Wayland who really got me into St. Hilda's."

"Link," mused Cara, still diverted.

Brit, watching her, knew what she was thinking. Link Wayland was—or had been—the kind of man to appeal to a girl. He had that authoritative, almost dominant way about him that thrills young things. *Yet I, too, was young, or youngish,* Brit recalled, *and I disliked him.*

"Strong white teeth against a burnished skin," remembered Cara. "Quite a dish."

She came back to the subject of Brit.

"If you leave St. Hilda's, what?" she asked.

"I don't know. It's all too early yet."

"Europe?"

"No. A holiday, perhaps, but, Cara, I . . . I mean we . . . well, there's no actual riches entailed."

"*One* could do Europe." Cara's voice was thoughtful.

"And two could go to bed and sleep on it. Yes, Cara, I insist. How otherwise will you perform tomorrow at class?"

"Class!" But Cara did allow herself to be persuaded.

Soon she was breathing evenly in the next bedroom. Cara never allowed herself to carry over any cares. Brit recalled father telling Cara once: "Cara means dear, not care. And dear you are, baby, especially—" with the Willis over-humor "—to our pockets. You're a very costly little girl."

She had always been costly, and Brit supposed that in all fairness one couldn't expect her to change now. She had been reared expensively and now the expensive bud was ready to blossom. It would be a very lovely flower. Brit's eyes as she lay in her bed in her own bedroom grew heavy. She did not expect to sleep, not after all her excitement, but she could feel oblivion approaching. A very lovely blossom, she repeated drowsily, a flower that must have its chance. Giving Cara her chance. Brit slept. . . .

She awoke to dawn thinly buttering the windowsill with pale yellow. Her first thought was: *I'm free!*

But she had to go to school to establish her freedom, perhaps in fairness give St. Hilda's a week to find a replacement.

She was brewing the coffee as Cara came into the kitchen.

"Was it a dream?" Cara took the slice of toast that Brit had just buttered for herself.

"No dream. I give my notice today."

"St. Hilda's, St. Hilda's, you can't ever get away from it, can you?"

"But I *am*," Brit grinned.

Cara was not in a smiling mood. "It's all right for you, going in and saying 'Count me out,' " she complained.

"I didn't intend those words."

"You know what I mean."

"Yes, I do, dear, but Cara, your school is nice."

"It's a bore," snapped Cara.

"Until you're ready—"

"Actually, Brit, I think I'm ready now. I believe Madame thinks so, too. She asked me if I would come to superintend a class. Me! A class!"

Brit said nothing.

"Lucky you, sauntering down, sauntering home, filling in time," Cara went on.

"I have no doubt I'll be expected to work all the week," Brit assured her.

"With your means you can tell them where to go."

"But I wouldn't."

"No, *you* wouldn't, not ever. Brit: Sweet Maiden," sneered Cara.

"You're Cara, meaning dear."

"I must be, no one has bought me." Cara yawned and got up. "Don't spend all your fortune today."

"I wish you wouldn't keep on saying you and your," sighed Brit.

"Well, it's not I and mine."

"It will be."

Cara actually paused a contemplative moment. "You *are* sweet," she admitted reluctantly. She added: "I don't know how you do it."

Brit laughed. "Thanks, pet. For that nice admission, I'll promise I won't spend. I couldn't, anyway, I have to collect first."

"According to Aunt Truda's letter the check is ready."

"If my resignation is accepted at once I'll go in this afternoon then."

The resignation was not. Miss Asquith looked at Brit and looked at the same time at a loss. A complete loss. Hadn't she ever heard of legacies?

"This is rather awkward," she murmured.

"I'm aware of that, Miss Asquith, and I'm willing to help you for a while."

"You mean with classes?" Miss Asquith said rather vaguely.

What else could there be, Brit thought. She waited for the principal to recover herself.

"Just carry on until I find out, won't you, dear?" she appealed.

Find out what, wondered Brit. But she agreed.

She found herself quite enjoying her posture periods that morning; she permitted a lot more windy movements than usual. Helena, who was present again, smiled: "Mifmif, ith nith today."

"Thank you, Helena."

"*You're* nith," alloted Helena, "but breaving ithn't, not breaving to one, two, free."

"Thank you, Helena," Brit said again.

It was late shopping night, and on the way home Brit bought a bottle of champagne for celebrating. When she reached the flat, she saw John's car, and wondered if Cara had broken the news.

When she opened the door it was to Cara and John sitting close together as they studied a page of the atlas. John got to his feet and came across to Brit and held out his hand.

"Congrats and all that," he grinned.

Somehow it came distastefully to Brit. She wanted him to smile, to look disbelieving, to run his hand through his hair in that surprised boyish way of his. She had always found that a very endearing gesture.

But John just stood very straight...and somehow aloof.

"A windfall, Brit."

"Yes." Odd when you are full of words, words waiting to tumble out, how sometimes only monosyllables will emerge.

"I came to tell you—" began John, and Brit thought: *John is finding a reason to visit us, visit me; before he just came because he wanted to.* "—To tell you I'll be pushing off quite soon," John finished. "If I can place *Southern Cross* overseas I can be assured it will move favorably here."

"Yes." Again that was all Brit could find to say.

"And you?" John asked her.

"I?"

"I suppose you'll be changing your address." He glanced around the small apartment.

"I suppose." Two words this time, not one.

"Well, I must push off."

"Dinner?" She was back to one word again.

"I have an appointment." No "Will it stretch that far?" accompanied by that grin of his.

They looked awkwardly away from each other. Brit knew that she, anyhow, was avoiding John's eyes.

"I'll see you again," John said.

"Yes, do that," nodded Brit.

Cara said nothing. She was nail-painting and her attention was on the current color she was brushing on, a bright fuchsia. But Brit knew she would be missing nothing.

She did miss nothing. As soon as the door closed on John, she said: "The way people avoid the word goodbye."

"What do you mean?"

"You won't see John again."

"Of course I—we'll see each other."

"I should have added not until after Europe," Cara amended. "Perhaps he might turn up later if he becomes rich and successful."

"He would come poor and unsuccessful."

"Oh, no, Brit. John's proud. He's one of those old-fashioned men who like their women dependent on them, looking to them for help, not heiressing it all over them."

"I didn't!" exclaimed Brit indignantly.

"I know, my pet, but it still remains a fact that you have vastly more than John, doesn't it?"

"At present."

"A very expansive present. It even extends into the dim future. And it could be very dim for John, the same—" a pathetic break in Cara's voice "—as it could be for me."

"Cara!"

"Oh, I know you say we, you say family, but Brit, it does make a difference, doesn't it? It must, for John saw it, and you must admit that. I see it, too." Without another word, Cara wheeled around and ran to her room. Brit heard the door shut and then the key turn. Oh, no, she thought, not Cara, too. Not Cara as well as John.

That night Brit did *not* sleep.

But in the morning Cara was herself again, yet not herself really; there was a self-effacement about her young sister, that, had Brit earnestly considered it, had never been displayed before. But all Brit felt was a relief that Cara, anyhow, was friendly.

"This is your toast, Brit," Cara called as she passed

across what she always took first for herself. "Brit, why did you let me drink all the coffee?"

Then: "Well, into class, though what they think they can do with poor clumsy little me I don't know."

Confused, unsure of herself, of what she heard, still obsessed with the subject of John, Brit went to her school, to her posture lessons. But first of all to a word from Miss Asquith.

"I've found out," the principal said.

"If I'm to last out the week or if I can leave at once?" helped Brit, for Miss Asquith seemed a little awkward, a little uncertain, not at all the self-sufficient woman she always was.

"Last out the week?" Miss Asquith said it, Brit thought, in the same vague way as yesterday she had said: "You mean the class?" As though somehow it was not the point under discussion. That it was not connected. Brit wondered what else there could be.

"I've found out from Mr. Wayland," said Miss Asquith.

"Mr. Wayland? But how does he come into it? But of course, he must be a school trustee." Brit said it more to herself. She knew little about Link Wayland. Probably he was married now and had a daughter booked for St. Hilda's—parents booked daughters well ahead at this exclusive school. He might even have a daughter here now. That was how little she knew about Link Wayland. He could have been married that time he had got her the posture post, she hadn't known or cared to find out. But if he had been married he could easily have a child here. She tried to think of any little girl with the surname Wayland.

"Yes." Miss Asquith's voice was a little faint, but Brit did not hear the faintness. "A kind of trustee."

Brit had always thought that trustees were trustees, that no kind-ofs came into it. But evidently she was wrong, and the "kind-of" trustee that Link Wayland was had proved necessary for what Miss Asquith now had to announce.

"You can leave," said Miss Asquith.

"Thank you—or should I say thank you, Mr. Way
land?"

It was then, Brit thought in retrospect, that Miss Asquit
said a rather odd thing. She said, very seriously, ver
meaningfully: "Yes. Yes, you should indeed."

It was odd going out of the big St. Hilda gates in th
middle of the morning. As she passed through, Brit me
Helena also passing through, but through from the stree
side.

"I had to go to the dentith," the child offered, evidentl
considering that Brit required an excuse.

"Did you, dear?"

"Really I'm not late at all."

"It wouldn't matter if you were," said Brit. "I'm leav
ing."

"No more lethonth?"

"No."

"Oh, beaut!"

Brit smiled.

"If only Mif Pidcock would leave, too, and Mif Brow
and Mif—" Helena stopped abruptly. "But I liked you,
she assured Brit, "I juth didn't like breaving, and now I'
never going to breave any more."

"Goodbye, darling," laughed Brit . . . but she wasn't fa
from tears.

She phoned, made an appointment and went to the so
licitors.

Murgatroyd and Mason were very cooperative. The
had the check ready and repeated to Brit what Aunt Trud
had said in her letter, the advice about the wisdom of goo
annuities.

Brit nodded.

"But," the partners went on, "you are a responsib
adult and can choose for yourself entirely."

Again Brit nodded. Ever since last night—and John—she had felt an almost unbearable heaviness somewhere in her. Even with the check in her hand—freedom—or so she had thought, in the hollow of her hand, she could not lose that deep depression.

"You're a fortunate young woman," Mr. Murgatroyd was saying. "It's not often that someone of your age comes into such a welcome windfall."

Welcome? Brit bit her lip. John walking out as he had last night. Cara, definitely on edge, wary, watching, waiting.

"Yes, a very handy sum." Mr. Mason was adding his piece.

"But still money." Brit was not aware that she said this aloud, said it rather desperately, until she saw the two men smiling sympathetically on her.

"Has it been so onerous already?" they asked.

Mr. Murgatroyd, the senior partner, began to talk again about investment. "Some reliable source," he said, "that will assure you a safe, steady income, that will support you."

"You're an attractive young woman," took up Mr. Mason with a courtly bow, "but sometimes even attractive young women don't—well...." He looked at Brit in apology.

"Don't marry." Brit helped him out. She wondered what he would say if she told him that she knew she wouldn't marry, that she had known it last night. It wasn't as if there had been anything definite between herself and John; there had not been, but there had been a warmth, a quiet feeling that one day....

It had gone when John had crossed a room to put out his hand and say: "Congrats and all that."

Money. Money meant freedom. But did it have to mean a hollowness inside you as well?

As she went home Brit remembered the celebration champagne she had taken home last night, then forgotten to open. No, she hadn't forgotten, there had simply been nobody with whom to celebrate. You don't rejoice, you can't rejoice, on your own, and after John had left, Cara had run to her room.

As she reached the flat she saw that there was no car, no car, anyway, that belonged to John. But when she reached the hall, the light was on.

"Come in," called Cara sweetly. "You're home."

Chops were grilling.

"Guess what, I told Madame I'd take a class. I announced it this afternoon," Cara said over dinner.

"But, Cara," began Brit, "now that there's no need to—"

"There is need. It's your money. You must use it. Travel, get yourself a nicer apartment, spend. Yes, Brittie, you must."

"But last night you said—"

"I regret last night."

"And I," said Brit in sudden passion, "regret everything. *Everything!*" Choked up, she rose from the table and ran to her room.

Brit always had had a sense of humor, and even in her emotional shutting of her bedroom door a moment afterward, even in her burst of tears, she could not help herself from half crying, half giggling: "Now it's my turn to slam doors, stage a performance—what a perfect sister act we would make!"

But the act hadn't even started, Brit knew happily. The relieving tears stopped at last, she reached her decision. It was her money, Aunt Truda had said so, even if she had accompanied it with advice. It was still hers to do with as she pleased.

And it was not, and Brit felt herself smiling, really smiling, for the first time since John's leaving, going to be prudently invested in any annuity.

It was going to be invested in . . . well, life, one could say.
Assuredly, she knew, it was to be invested in love.

Brit did sleep that night.

CHAPTER THREE

IN THE MORNING Cara was the same wistful, sweet, self-effacing figure.

"Brittie, don't do that again," she begged. "Not ever, ever again."

"What, Cara?"

"Don't shut the door on me."

"You did it with me," Brit pointed out.

"I," admitted Cara frankly, "am irresponsible. I'm spoiled rotten, Brit, thanks to mother, father, you. What I am, you've made me."

"And made a lovely job." Though she didn't quite understand this Cara, the change was refreshing, and anyway, Cara *was* a lovely job.

Her sister went off to classes without her usual whine. Brit watched her go, a reed-slender girl with titian hair hanging shining to her slim waist. She had amber eyes to tone with the hair, a faintly tawny touch to her perfect skin. A scintillating golden girl.

I, mused Brit, *am surely the brown moth.*

Cara even had made an attempt to do the breakfast dishes, but Brit had stopped that. She picked up a saucepan and looked at herself in it now. Brown hair, brown eyes, the same skin tone as Cara but with none of the golden glow. Sallow, Brit supposed. Her features were inelegantly blunter, her proportions sturdier, though that might have been because she was not as tall as Cara. However, and she felt it with a rather wry satisfaction, since all it seemed to have gained her was a posture class, she stood and moved quite well.

She put the saucepan down. The apartment seemed very quiet. It was the first time, Brit realized, she had been in it on a working day. She wondered how it felt to do nothing, that is nothing except housework. Not that she intended to be idle permanently. The legacy was not that big, and besides, she would get bored. If she was married with a family, then it would be a different story. She fell to planning, as she always had since she was a child, for she had always loved children, her small beloved four. Two boys like . . . well, like John. Brit felt her cheeks grow warm. Then a couple of little Helenas, maddening though they might be, for she felt she could not have coped with more Caras.

Yes, little Helenas, not up to pronouncing s's; Helenas she would teach to walk beautifully, but in play, never in lessons.

I'm wasting time, Brit told herself, and she tidied up the apartment. To her amazement Cara had made her bed.

Now into Sydney, but not to Murgatroyd and Mason to tell them she would take their advice, that she would put Aunt Truda's money into an annuity, but to much more interesting assignments. Like travel agencies. Like boutiques.

It was late afternoon before Brit realized it, and, because she seemed to have accumulated so many parcels, she took a taxi home instead of the bus.

Cara was just walking up the apartment drive, and her eyes widened at Brit alighting from a cab. If she resented her sister returning from town in comfort while she fought for a seat, there was no sign in the welcome she gave Brit.

"Darling, how sensible of you!" Her shining gold eyes were looking at the parcels.

"Wait till you see what I've bought," Brit said mysteriously.

"Yes." Now, if Brit had listened, there was not quite so much affability in Cara's voice. However, she sat on the floor beside Brit as Brit opened bag after bag.

"But, Brittie," Cara said after a long pause, "this isn't your size." She was looking at a gold creation, definitely—and everyone would know it at once—a creation for Cara. "Darling," she said sympathetically to Brit, "you must have forgotten—you're a twelve, not—"

"I might forget that," smiled Brit, "but I'd never forget what you are." That was true. Brit had made all Cara's clothes, made them tastefully, though scarcely ever satisfactorily, that is, satisfactorily for her sister.

But you would not have suspected that now. Cara's large gold eyes positively glittered.

"You mean...oh, you can't mean...but Brit, but Brittie dearest, you always made the cutest things." As she spoke Cara held up the garment and shivered with pleasure.

It was good to watch her. Brit brought out more parcels, laughed as Cara positively pounced on them with shrill little squeals of rapture. She was every inch a girl, Brit thought.

"But everything is for me, just everything! Darling, you haven't bought yourself one article."

Only that article called love, Brit knew. She felt happy again. John had gone, but he would come back. He had been dismayed at her changed circumstances and she had let him go dismayed. Next time she would be wiser. As for Cara, she would make no such mistake with her.

"Earrings," she said happily. "They're not junk, Cara. Perhaps not as precious as they could be, but...."

"Oh, Brit! Oh, *Brit!*"

After that came the pleasure that Brit had kept for last. Nothing actual this time, but the prospect of actuality. The prospect of a trip abroad—for two.

"You mean—" gasped Cara.

"Both of us. You could take extra lessons in Europe, get a final finishing touch. I would be home in the garret waiting to feed you." Brit smiled. In her heart she thought: *And somewhere there'll be John, striving after his career, needing to be fed—and loved—too. Oh, I'm glad I've decided to follow this path. To receive love you must give it. Annuities!*

There were actually tears in Cara's eyes, for once she was beyond words. She put her arms around Brit, something she seldom did, and for a few moments just remained there.

"Why?" she asked at last.

"Why what, Cara?"

"It doesn't matter," said Cara, and began turning over the brochures.

"It mustn't be all work or you'll be a dull girl," laughed Brit. "We must see all the renowned places between your lessons." See John in some of those places, Brit dreamed. The Opera House in Vienna, perhaps, John with them in one of the white and golden boxes. The Rhine, and John half-closing his eyes as they sailed past the Lorelei, hearing errant tunes that could be adapted to movement, that *he* would adapt. San Marino curling up a hill. Budapest.

"Oh, yes," said Cara.

She turned over the travel folders with delight, exclaiming at some of the luxuries that were offered.

"I'm afraid, Cara, that for the two of us it would need to be tourist," Brit put in.

"Of course." Cara turned over the page, but she turned it more slowly, almost with calculation.

They had not thought about dinner, but eventually hunger did nudge them.

"I never bought anything," said Brit with shock, for she never had done such a thing in her life. "I tell you what, Cara, we'll eat out."

"In Winfield?"

"You could have said that once," Brit reminded her, "but what about that new restaurant that's opened?"

"The Rembrandt? But, Brit, it's not Winfield, even

though it's in Winfield. It's Sydney. It's big city. What I really mean is it's out of town dining, not just a suburban offering."

"Who wants a suburban offering?" grinned Brit. She felt a little intoxicated, and yet the celebration champagne she had bought yesterday was still tightly corked. She told Cara about the champagne and they giggled together.

"We'll keep it for some future occasion," Brit said. "Tonight we'll have the champagne poured for us."

"I'm wearing the gold. Why not? The Rembrandt is that sort of place."

"Why not, except I won't match you."

"Oh, Brit, you should have fixed yourself up as well."

"Too ashamed to have me tag along?"

"You idiot, you always look nice." Cara, with the knowledge that tonight she would look beautiful, said it generously, so generously indeed that when Brit put on her long black skirt and the demure white lace blouse she almost persuaded herself she was pretty.

But when Cara came out....

"It has to be a taxi," Brit barely breathed. Looking at Cara, she was beyond any other words. She crossed to the phone.

But what she forgot, and surprisingly Cara forgot, too, for Cara was knowledgeable about such things, was the necessity of booking a table. The Rembrandt, as Cara had said, was not just a suburban offering, it was a *cordon bleu* establishment. And there were no tables left. The manager said it proudly, if, looking at Cara, a little regretfully. Every night there were press cameras here, reporters on the lookout for a known face, or a pretty face, and this girl in shining gold....

Cara was near tears in her disappointment. Brit, knowing her young sister, knew she was still young enough in her lack of self-control to stamp her foot and insist on entry. But for that knowledge, she would not have accepted the offer that came with a soft-footed, smooth-voiced waiter. The waiter whispered in the maitre d'hotel's ear, and the next moment it was a different story. They were being guided across the darkened, candlelit room, placed at undoubtedly the best table in the room, a table closest to the floor show, the very good orchestra, undoubtedly under the personal attention of the head waiter.

But still Brit would have refused, but for Cara, and Cara's temper, though she did not know which would have been worse, an outburst by Cara or....

Or sitting opposite to Link Wayland, as, with much deference, Cara and Brit were being seated now.

Unlike Brit, it was some time before Cara realized with whom they were seated. Brit had known it at once, known it with intense distaste.

But Cara, dazzled for a few moments, took longer. Then at last she withdrew her glance from the many admiring glances being directed at her, and looked instead to the man who could have been a North American Indian with his bronzed skin, a man with teeth very white in contrast. A tall, broad man. Cara remembered him rather thrillingly, she had always liked dominant men.

"Why, it's Link! Link Wayland," she claimed.

"It's the child," Link Wayland said admiringly, and the admiration as well as what he chose to call her delighted Cara. Of late she had wondered if she had been maturing; beside Brit she seemed quite the adult, not a teenager, but then Brit, of course, was positively immature. But Link Wayland's "child" now pleased her. She pouted prettily.

"Oh, no, I've grown up."

"And very beautifully," Link said.

"It's such a coincidence," Cara prattled. "We were talking about you."

His brows, two thick black wings, rose; it gave him, Cara decided, a rather devilish look, something, too, she liked in men.

"It wasn't awful," she laughed, "well, only a little. Brit was blaming you for St. Hilda's."

"Ah, Brit." For the first time Link Wayland turned to the older sister. "Brit," he said again, and his eyes probed Brit's.

"How do you do, Mr. Wayland," Brit acknowledged.

The waiter was pouring wine. There was no time for a second raising of brows, as Brit knew Link Wayland would raise his brows at her formality.

She waited until the wine had been served, then raised her glass with Cara's and the man's. A toast was said.

Someone caught Link Wayland's eye across the room. Link smiled and nodded back, and the next moment the young man joined them. It wasn't long before he and Cara were dancing.

"That's what she wanted," Brit said softly, fondly, but to herself, she thought.

"And what Cara wants..." Link said suavely, and left it at that. He was fixing himself a cigarette. For a sophisticated man in a sophisticated nightclub he did it in an inappropriate manner. He actually rolled the tobacco first in his almost tobacco-brown hand. He had always rolled his own, Brit remembered, remembering, too, how, if reluctantly, it had fascinated her. Her father had had a silver cigarette case which he opened and shut with sharp precision, none of the lazy deliberation of the smoker who first molded the brown weed and then carefully enclosed it. She recalled the whisper of the paper and heard the same whisper now. She saw Link Wayland put the cigarette in his mouth, light it, the scratch of the ignition making a near-inaudible little sound. Then, against her will, almost as though compelled, she raised her glance to the eyes, Link Wayland's dark, probing, calculating yet incalculable eyes.

"Seen enough?" he asked.

She knew she flushed vividly by the sudden warmth in her cheeks. She tried to gaze back at the man, to return his cool stare with hers, but it was hard. Those dark enigmatical eyes made her want to look away. She held out as long as she could then pretended intrigue in the color of the wine. It was a dark wine, dark as deep red apples.

In a slightly amused voice he informed her of the house and vintage. His tone implied that he saw through her insinuated interest.

He smoked for a few moments, the blue weave from his cigarette spiralled around him in the candlelit gloom.

"I haven't seen you around Winfield of late," he said presently.

"I've been around," she replied sparsely. As he did not comment, she said meaningfully: "I am—was—a teacher at St. Hilda's." That "was" came out gladly.

The dark brows raised, but that was all . . . for the moment.

"You must be like a little gray mouse that sits in its hole."

"A brown moth, was my father's description."

"Yes—Willis Smith. What a work that *Hinterland* was!"

"He died . . . but you would know that."

"Yes, I did a piece on him," Link told her.

She had read it, and it had made her proud, but she wouldn't tell this man.

"My aunt died, too. I believe you knew her."

"I did indeed." Now his voice was warm.

There was silence for a while. Cara and the young man who had claimed her swung past, and Link Wayland said: "She certainly is a gorgeous creature." He switched his glance quickly from sister to sister. "Has it been worth it?"

"Has what been worth it?"

"Not what. Has Cara been worth all the sacrifices?"

"I don't know what you're talking about," said Brit flatly.

"Giving Cara her chance," he said laconically, flicking the ash off his cigarette.

She looked at him in dismay—how did he know that family phrase? But of course, Aunt Truda.

"Yes," she said firmly, "she has."

"Yet you still grumble."

"Grumble?"

"St. Hilda's, which obviously you've never liked."

"No."

"Then why in hell didn't you tell me?"

"Tell you? Oh, I forgot, you're a trustee or something. Or you have a daughter there."

"I have not."

"Then booked there."

He said flatly: "I'm a bachelor, Brit."

"But St. Hilda's—" she began.

"Is in Winfield. It was in Winfield that I climbed my first rung to success, so I felt I had to show some allegiance. If you ask at the hospital you will learn that I also take an interest there."

"A kind of debt?" Brit interpreted.

"A glad debt," he nodded. "From Winfield I kept on climbing. Indeed I've climbed so high you must listen one day while I tell you all about it."

"Oh, I know you've acquired a suburban paper monopoly," Brit nodded. "I've heard that most of your fantastic prosperity is because of the personal interest you still take in every paper. No doubt that's why you're here tonight."

"No," he said blandly. "I came in the express hope of running into you."

She smiled perfunctorily at the smooth lie, then smiled brightly at Cara and the young man who were returning to the table.

For a while the conversation was general. Mark Gilmour, Cara's escort, said something about a new project of Link Wayland's, an overseas newspaper consolidation. Across the candlelight Link nodded at Brit and she knew he was indicating that this was the rung he had reached now. She took no notice, but Cara's eyes were wide.

Photographers were moving around the Rembrandt. Tomorrow's social pages would read: "Seen at the Candle Room"..."Dining out last night"....

With a small, rather lopsided smile Link Wayland nodded to Mark, and the young man took Cara off to be posed by every attendant cameraman.

"She'll love that," said Brit. "Thank you."

"You, I rather gather, would not like it, so there's no need for your own personal thanks."

"No, I wouldn't. Also, I'm not particularly good at thanks. Remember when you got me my St. Hilda's post?"

"I'll never forget it," he assured her.

"It was good money, though." Brit had to admit that, and this time he did pick her up on that past tense.

"Was?"

"I've left," she told him.

"Of course. You inherited."

"How would you know?"

"I spoke often to your aunt," Link explained.

"Yes, she told me. She quite admired you."

"Unlike her niece," he said dryly.

"Does a highly successful man also have to be highly liked?"

"It helps." Another few moments of attention to his cigarette, then: "Are you doing what your aunt advised, putting the money into an annuity?"

"My aunt never actually advised that, she only suggested it."

"Are you?"

"It's none of your business."

"Are you?" he insisted.

"Look here, Mr. Wayland—"

"*Are you?*"

"No."

"Then you're not only immature and naive, you're a fool."

"It's my money," she retorted crossly.

"I'm not so sure about that."

"Then whose—oh, I see. You're thinking of Aunt Truda saving it for me." A pause. "I think of that, too. Do please believe I'm not that heartless."

"Heartlessness is the last thing I would accuse you of Just—just crass stupidity."

"Aunt Truda wanted my happiness, and having an annuity would never have returned me that."

"How do you know without giving it a try?"

"I know," was all Brit could think to say.

Cara was finishing her different poses. Mark was stepping forward to take her arm and return her to the table.

"Have you done anything final yet?" Link Wayland' voice snapped urgently across the candlelight at Brit.

"No, though what it has to do with you—"

"Then don't," he said, all the old dominant authority she so well remembered emphasizing both words. "Don't do you hear? Don't, until you talk with me."

"Mr. Wayland—"

"Link, for heaven's sake. Surely you've known me tha long."

"That's why it's Mr. Wayland," she said coldly.

"My God, young Brit, you're as irritating as you ever were!" He glanced away from her. "They're coming There'll be no more opportunity tonight."

"Any night."

"Day will do."

"Any day."

"Just hold your horses," he said finally, for there was no time for any more.

Cara, her golden eyes gleaming, came back on Mark's arm. Brit saw to it that there was no other chance to talk.

Cara babbled excitedly all the way home. Mark was a dear, beautifully polished, but he counted for nothing really, not compared to Link. Goodness, Brit, how Link had succeeded. He must be rich. He must be quite fabulously rich. When you were rich, you could do anything, get everyone to jump to your call. Why, she might have sat all night and not have been noticed, whereas at a nod from Link—

"You would have been noticed regardless, Cara," Brit assured her, but Cara's thrill over her new dresses, over the prospect of going overseas, was not now so acute.

"To be that rich!" she sighed.

They went to bed on that note, Cara to sigh enviously before sleep took her, Brit to toss uneasily for many hours before she slipped into an unrefreshing oblivion. . . . Thank goodness there was no St. Hilda's in the morning.

"Just hold your horses." Brit heard Link Wayland's low voice in the silent bedroom. "Don't do anything final."

Then: "Don't do anything until you talk with me."

And: "Don't do anything."

She heard: "Don't."

If she had needed decision, that decided Brit.

She told Cara the next morning to cancel the class she had announced she was taking for Madame, but it appeared the class hadn't started yet. Cara said it vaguely as though she had forgotten all about it. Brit shrugged. It didn't matter. All that mattered was that there was nothing to stop Cara going into Sydney, choosing a route, a date, a manner of travel.

"You'll know better than I do, darling," Brit told her after Cara had nodded delightedly.

"You could come, too," Cara invited perfunctorily.

Brit could, but somewhere, unadmitted, unacknowledged, only quietly anticipated . . . *hoped for* . . . was th thought that John might call in.

Cara returned home that evening piled with literature with tentative bookings, with departure times.

John did not come.

CHAPTER FOUR

JOHN CALLED at the end of the week. It was the longest week Brit could remember. She supposed this was because she was not working now, that she had time to fill in so that the hours passed more sluggishly. Yet with an exciting journey in view surely this should not have been the case. What, then? But there was no need for self-examination. Brit had to admit miserably that it was because of the manner in which she had parted with John.

When she saw his car pull into the apartment drive that evening she felt a rush of joy. She watched John leap from his old sports car, then come around to the other side to help Cara climb out. He must have picked her sister up on her way home. The pair did not look across to the apartment, they were talking animatedly together, and for a few seconds Brit just stood looking down on them. Her two dearest possessions, she thought, though John was not that, not her possession, not yet, perhaps never, though something sweet—if elusive—told her....

When the couple came in, Brit learned the reason for the animation. John had received an overseas cable asking him to present his work personally to a European house.

"It might mean nothing—" the young composer grinned boyishly, it probably won't, but this company is a good one, a prestigious one, an international one, and just to be asked is something, and...well...." He grinned again.

Brit was running out for the champagne. "I had it ready before," she said a little breathlessly, "only we didn't get around to it. But this time...." She handed John the bottle to open.

"No, Brit, *next* time." He said it softly, only for Brit, as he poured then held up his glass to her glass. That was all he said, but it was enough.

Apart from those few quick words for her, it seemed that John could not stop talking about his own good luck. His fare had been paid, he said, and he would be accommodated over there while he showed what he had to sell. Then after that—he gave a little shrug. It could be all it might amount to, he added cautiously, but....

"But the La Salle Company," murmured Cara thoughtfully, "La Salle is just—well ...." She spread her graceful hands, her expressive dancer's hands. She looked very impressed.

In the excitement of John's imminent departure, the thrilling reason for it, it was quite a while before Brit realized that she and Cara had not babbled out their news.

"John—" she began laughingly, "John—a coincidence you'll never believe—"

"Brit!" Cara's voice cut in as conclusively as a sharp knife. "No, don't jump, sweetie," she added apologetically, "it was just a reminder that the percolator is going mad out there."

Brit had started no coffee, but she hurried after Cara to the tiny kitchen.

"Cara—"

"It's nothing, Brit, except I thought what fun to surprise Johnny instead."

"You mean—over there?"

"Yes."

"But how would we know where to find him?"

"The La Salle Company!" Cara demeaned her sister.

"I suppose there would be no trouble, and yes, it would be pleasant." Brit saw the three of them meeting up in Europe, John's eyes holding hers as they had held them only a few moments ago, warmly, with promise. With the background of romantic Europe after this dingy little apartment room....

"You think of everything," Brit laughed. "I promise you—not a word."

To make her sudden absence from the room convincing, she did brew coffee.

John did not stop long, he had lots to do.

"When you two go overseas .... When are you going, incidentally?... You'll understand the rush," he told them.

That was an awkward moment, but when John did not press for a firm answer, instead talked excitedly on, the moment passed.

The moment passed, too, of his leaving them. A kiss for Cara, but only a hand-press for Brit. Yet in the tight feel of those fingers....

Cara was silent after John left, silent, anyway, for Cara.

"Everything all right, darling?" Brit asked. She had had so much to do with Cara, she almost could have stated how many more or how many fewer words her sister spoke from day to day. Now Cara was speaking very few.

"Oh, yes. I've a bit of a headache, that's all. I've had a frightful lot of running around."

"Tomorrow I'll help you. I'll come, too." She could, now that John....

"Oh, no, Brit, no need for that."

But there was no need now for Brit to wait on a phone call, look through a window to the parking lot. She had seen John.

"No trouble, Cara," she assured her sister.

"It will be for me if you suddenly feel off color, Brit. As you will, and take my word for it, for you had your shots the day after I did, and I feel rotten now."

"You don't have to react that way," demurred Brit. "Some people don't."

"The clinic said it was the only way they could judge

that the vaccine had taken." Cara sounded tired and irritable, and Brit supposed her sister could be right.

There was a lot still to be done in the apartment; what things they were taking had to be packed, the landlord had to be told they were leaving, tradesmen informed, telephone, post office, papers....

"Well, if you can manage, Cara."

Cara looked covertly at Brit. "I've done it all along, so I think it might be better if I finished it now."

"Thanks, pet. If we had any sense we would have dealt locally and there would have been no need for town."

"I'll survive," shrugged Cara. "Tomorrow I'll do a lot of things. Money among them. We'll need oceans of travelers' checks."

"I thought of having the bank transfer a sum to London."

"Making it necessary for us to go to London every time we run out? That doesn't make sense."

"I suppose not," Brit agreed. "Then what?"

"Travelers' checks, as I said. As a matter of fact, Brit, that was what I wanted to talk to you about, only John came in with me."

"Yes?"

"It would be much better, the agent advised, for only one of us to carry the checks. It's easier negotiation here and handier over there."

"But what if you wanted something and I wasn't around?"

Cara did not reply at once, and when she did speak her voice was carefully careless, if a voice could be that. It was careless enough, anyway, for Brit not to put any undue importance on what she said.

"Oh, I'll carry them, sweetie, in my name, seeing as I'm doing the rest of the business. I'll get them fixed up tomorrow."

She told Brit the amount she thought, and Brit agreed that it sounded reasonable.

"The rest of my—our money?" Brit asked.

"Leave that to me, too. You were right about having a sum transferred, but not to London, I think. You give me a blank check tomorrow and I'll ask the consultant. He's very helpful and will advise us on the best course."

It was getting late and it had been a long day. Also Cara could be right about the vaccine, Brit conceded, for she did feel a little depleted.

"Thank you, Cara, you're doing well.... Did your reaction feel like I suspect I'm beginning to feel now?"

"I told you so," pounced Cara. "You go right to bed, and stop there. Only, pet, in case you get like I did, or nearly did, give me that blank check now. Then you can stay in tomorrow."

Brit did, then went to bed. Her arm was throbbing and she felt a slight nausea. But her spirits were high, as high, anyway, as spirits could be when you felt less than fit.

"... No, Brit, *next* time," she heard John say again. She saw his eyes, warm with hers.

She felt better in the morning, and got up relieved that she was to be spared a reaction after all. But although she came out to the kitchen no later than usual, Cara had already left. Bless her, smiled Brit fondly, she's really keen over this trip. She had never known Cara away so promptly before.

As she did more packing she smiled over yesterday, and how she had waited for the phone, but today....

The phone rang. Brit picked it up and a voice, a woman's controlled, obviously secretarial voice, asked: "Miss Smith? Miss Brit Smith?"

"Speaking."

"One moment, please." There was the usual office background, then distantly but distinctly a timber that Brit recognized immediately. Link Wayland's.

Before she realized what she was doing she put the phone down.

It was a foolish thing to have done—she knew that at once. Link Wayland would only be scornfully amused at her childish action, he would have his secretary dial the number again.

He did, or at least Brit presumed the ring was his, but, although she knew she would not be deceiving him, that he was too shrewd for any subterfuges she might make, Brit continued her juvenile behavior. She let it ring.

Intermittently throughout the morning the peal shrilled through the small apartment. Then it stopped persisting, and Brit heaved a sigh of relief.

She did not know what nudged her to look out of the window at the same time as the big black car swept up to the parking area, but she was thankful she did. A quick glimpse of the driver assured her that Link Wayland had not given up, but then that man never gave up, never had, never would, and she should have remembered it. Oh, how she hated him, Brit thought.

She watched him get out, heard him slam the door with more force than was necessary, then for a few moments she just looked at him, something she had never done with Link Wayland, always she had glanced quickly away. Once more the thought came to her that a man like him seemed out of place here; he was essentially a western, not an eastern Australian, a man of the outdoors, something to do with horses, somewhere that he could ride free, untrammeled and, she thought with dislike, roughshod. A roughrider.

He was pausing a moment to roll one of his cigarettes. She could not hear the dry whisper of the tobacco up here, but she could see the smoothing movement of the long brown fingers. Then she saw him lick the edges of the paper together. That gave her an odd feeling, something she never had encountered before, not with John, or any man, something she could not have given a name to, have tried to define. Disturbed, not knowing why or how, she withdrew from the window. Then, surreptitiously, she drew the curtains.

She was shaking a little, and was annoyed with herself for it, as she checked the door. She had barely driven home the bolt when the knock came—definite, imperative, an open-at-once sharpness.

Brit stood there.

He knocked again—louder. One thing, he could not disturb anyone, get the landlord to give him a key, for the entire apartment population including the landlord worked, and were absent during the day. She was alone in the block. The only fear was that Cara might arrive home, but, glancing at the clock, at this time that was unlikely.

"Open up, Brit, I know you're there!" he called irritably. It was not just a guess, the certainty of his voice assured Brit of that; he *knew* she stood on the other side, and how did he know? How could he?

"You're a young idiot, it's only for your own good. Can't you see that if I wanted to get in—for myself—I'd take no notice of locks, I'd kick the door in." For myself? What did he mean by that?

A minute went by.

"All right, be a fool and reap the harvest!" He said it in cold anger. She heard him descend the steps, heard the car start.

She was back at the window now, peeping down at him. Just as he turned the corner of the drive, he leaned out and raised an arm up to her. Yet he couldn't possibly see her, she knew that. With reddened cheeks she came back into the room.

"Be a fool and reap the harvest." She heard his coldly angry voice saying that again.

But most of all she wondered about that "...if I wanted to get in for myself...."

For myself? For Link Wayland's self? But what...? But how...?

She brewed tea, did some more packing, dreaded the phone ringing, wished Cara would get back.

Later, much later than the other times she had gone into Sydney, Cara did. The girl looked a little pale, slightly drawn, so evidently she had had a difficult day, too. Cara threw her things down, glanced across at Brit, then heaved a large sigh.

"Bad day?" asked Brit.

"Disappointing. I mean, after getting all emotionally ready—"

"For what?"

"Overseas. Well, *I* did, anyway. I've just been living from day to day for it, and now—"

"And now?"

"Now we have a few more days to wait. We're put back for a while, Brit. There's been a run of bookings, or a strike, or something. Anyway, we won't be going for another week."

Another week. Seven days of listening for a phone call . . . watching through a window. "Oh, no!" cried Brit desperately. She saw Cara looking at her curiously, so she proffered: "I'm emotionally ready, too."

"Are you? But you seemed...well, as though it wasn't so important to you." Cara looked a little disturbed, but only a little, and the look didn't last long.

"No. Only I wanted to get away when we planned, not at some future time."

"It can't be helped," Cara snapped at her; her nerves must be equally on edge.

"No, it can't. Sorry, darling. I suppose it's just anticlimax."

"I suppose so." Cara moved restlessly around the room, picking up things, putting them down again. "I think I'll go to bed," she said.

"This early?"

"I was up early."

"Yes, why so early, Cara?"

"Lots to be done. Oh, by the way, I fixed up your money, believing we'd be in a rush. But that can wait till tomorrow for your checking, can't it?"

"Yes, dear." Suddenly Brit felt as tired as Cara said she was. She told Cara to go to bed and she would bring in a tray, but when she did the girl was already asleep.

Brit stood looking down at her, at the fan of lashes on her cheeks, rather pale cheeks tonight for Cara, who usually had a pretty high color. Poor little girl, she was disappointed as well. Only Brit's feeling was not really disappointment, and she knew it, it was the feeling of walls closing in on her, Wayland walls. Link Wayland himself was a wall of a man.

"Don't do anything until you talk to me."

"You're a young idiot, it's only for your own good."

"All right, be a fool and reap the harvest."

Brit took up the tray and went out again. She knew she would not sleep, so she found a book and read, read until the small hours. She was nearly drugged with sleep when at last she permitted herself to put out the light.

She wakened to bright daylight, no mere buttering of an early sun, and to the hands of her bedroom clock showing nine.

Nine! She supposed Cara had looked in a dozen times and decided against waking her.

But Cara had not looked in to make that decision, Cara had decided last night. Brit knew this as she read the letter propped against the toast rack. No toast had been made, Brit noted vaguely, the teapot had not been used. Wherever Cara had gone, she had gone in a hurry, no time for even a quick breakfast.

Dear Brit, excuse the hurried scrawl. I lied to you about the delay in our booking, there wasn't any delay, just the same as there wasn't any booking. Except for me—us, I should say. For John and for me. We're a poor pair, no doubt about that, only we must *both* make good, not only one of us, Brit, and the way we see it, three will make it harder to achieve than two. I think that you, even though you're hurt at first, will see it that way, too, in the end. We're leaving together on an early plane. When John presents his ballet composition, I'm going to interpret it for him. Perhaps both of us will be accepted then.

I'm sorry about the money—you see, Brit, I'm afraid it's *all* the money, all your money, but think of it as an investment, for I'm sure we'll make the top. Then you won't be merely comfortable, you'll be rich.

Also, just in case you're concerned conventionally, and you're just the old-fashioned sort who would be, we're getting married as soon as we land at—well, wherever we do land. John has a ton of promise, so I know I'm doing the right thing, and John feels exactly the same about me. We'll make a good pair.

On the financial side, if it helps any, all those lovely dresses you bought for me can be returned. The ones I haven't worn yet, I mean. Simeon of Gowns by Simeon is very cooperative, or so I've heard. I'd love to take them with me, but John made a stipulation about traveling light.

That's all, Brit. Do please forgive.

Your Cara.

A long minute went by before Brit put the letter down.

CHAPTER FIVE

THE JANITOR CAME BREEZING up the stairs, then he began sweeping along the silent corridor, whistling as he worked, audibly grumbling at something that annoyed him now and then. He did this chore regularly at ten o'clock every day, so Brit knew dully that she had been sitting there for an hour.

Some time later she heard the postman inserting letters in the different boxes. He came around noon . . . but it couldn't be that time, she couldn't have remained there staring straight ahead for all that long.

She looked up at the clock and saw it was half-past eleven. She went out to their box. Somewhere in her muddled mind she thought there would be a letter from Cara saying it was all a joke. She could almost read the words: "Ha ha, caught you this time!"

There was no letter, but there was a circular advertising a round-the-world sea trip, one of the firms they had written to when they had first decided on going overseas.

Brit took it inside, sat down and opened it. It was ridiculous looking at it now, but it was something to do.

"See Florence," it said. "See Cologne." "See . . . ." "See . . . ." "See . . . ." She would be seeing nothing, but Cara would. And John. Cara *with* John.

That was the numbing pain. The other part, the financial part, had not occurred to Brit yet. Only Cara and John.

"We're getting married as soon as we land."

It wasn't true, it couldn't be true. It just didn't make sense. People didn't marry because, as Cara had put it, they felt they were doing the right thing, because their partner had promise, because the other partner felt the same in return, simply a "promise," they married because they loved each other, because they had looked across a room at each other—and known.

Or had only *one* known, had only *she* known, wondered Brit. Had she imagined that warmth in John's eyes, had she heard something that was not really there when John had said: "No, Brit, *next* time."

He had said it as he had held up his champagne, and Brit had taken it to mean—had taken it to mean wedding champagne, arms linked as two people looked deeply at each other.

"Oh, no," Brit said, and she got up and walked around the room.

She understood now why Cara had cut her short when she had started to announce their journey to John on the night he had announced his journey. He and Cara would already have discussed their plans, and Cara would have feared that John, always a little transparent, Brit remembered achingly, might have revealed what there was between them. What there was . . . . Yet she, Brit, had never seen it. But she remembered painfully once saying to John that Cara was so lovely it was a wonder he had not fallen in love with her. He had replied carelessly, or carelessly she had thought, that: "I expect every man is a little in love with the world's Caras."

He must have been much more than a little to have joined forces with her sister, departed with her. That sort of thing was not done on the spur of the moment. It took time. It took deliberation.

Twelve o'clock chimed, and mechanically Brit made a pot of tea. She supposed she had better have something to eat; if you didn't eat you could die. How long would it take to die? She did not know, she only knew that it had not taken long for a dream to die.

The tea revived her slightly. It still could be a joke, she thought, a sick joke, one of Cara's silly kind of jokes. *Before I do . . . well, whatever I'm going to have to do,* she thought, *I'd better check.* She crossed to the phone.

The Tressider Tourist House, where Cara had been making the bookings, or so Brit had believed, said quite bluntly: "Miss Smith canceled all the reservations yesterday." The clerk sounded annoyed.

"Yesterday?"

"It put us to considerable trouble. On some of the bookings we couldn't refund the lot; after all, she canceled without notice."

So at least, sighed Brit, Cara had booked at some time. Her note—among other things—had said: ". . . there wasn't any booking." Her sister must have meant that there wasn't any—*not now*—for Brit.

"I see," she said over the phone. "Did—did she explain why?"

"Only that circumstances had cropped up, that instead of the attractive stopovers we'd planned they would go express."

"She said they?"

"Yes." The voice sounded surprised now, a little curious. "Who did you say was speaking?"

"It doesn't matter." Brit put down the phone.

The paper was still outside the door. Brit brought it inside, put it on the table and turned to Flight Departures. There were three lines announcing morning schedules. She took up the phone and dialed the first company. No, they had no Miss Smith on their list. "A—Mr. Ferris?"

"No Mr. Ferris."

"Thank you."

It was the same with Apollo Air, but Glamis . . . .

"A Miss Smith? Yes. Several indeed. There's a Miss Cara Smith. Would that be—"

"Yes, that would be the right one."

"The other name again?"

"Ferris."

"John Ferris?"

"Yes."

"He is also on our papers."

"Thank you," said Brit. She cradled the receiver again.

So it wasn't a sick joke. There was to be no: "Ha ha
caught you this time!" It was true. *True.*

She put her head in her hands. She longed for releasing
tears. She longed and even tried, but none came. She sa
there dry eyed for the rest of the afternoon. She sat til
steps started up the stairs and down the halls. The tenant
were coming home again. It was the end of the day.

Darkness stole into the room, it was time for lights; in a
dozen apartments people were cooking their evening
meals. What time was it where Cara and John were? Tim
changed in different countries, Brit thought vaguely, i
could be hours forward, or hours backward. What did i
matter, anyway? What did anything matter?

Eventually she brewed more tea, forced herself to eat a
slice of bread, then went again to her room.

She steeled herself to look into Cara's room. The bed
was rumpled and unmade, drawers open, wardrobe open
The new dresses hung in the wardrobe, as her sister had
written. She had said: "If it helps, all those lovely dresse
you bought for me can be returned." But trust could not b
returned. Nor John. Gowns by Simeon! Did her siste
think they could help?

Brit still did not receive the impact of money, or rathe
the lack of money. It was not until hours later, still lying
wide-eyed in the dark room, that at last the fact did occur
She put it aside. Cara might be selfish, mercenary, but sh
would never leave her sister without something. Undoubt
edly she would have helped herself to a lion's share—
something Brit deserved, she thought wryly, presenting the

girl with a blank check like that, but she would leave her an amount at least to start her off again. Start off where? Brit shivered a little though it was rather warm tonight. Start where? *Where?* She could do nothing, she was completely untrained—that is, apart from posture—and who, aside from St. Hilda's, would be interested in posture? *And St. Hilda's was out.* She knew fiercely that she never wanted to go back there. Not because of the lessons, though she had disliked them, and never because of the children, since she had loved them, but because of Link Wayland. Link had got her the post; to Brit he was the job. So she couldn't go there again. Thinking of Link made her think of something else, one of the many things that Link had said that night. He had looked across the table at the Rembrandt and warned her: "Don't do anything final until you talk with me. Do you hear?"

What had Link known...or thought?

She actually slept; she did not know how, but she did. She got up at dawn to an empty house .... Had Cara and John reached their destination yet...? She went and made herself breakfast. It was the breakfast that really awakened Brit's sensibilities. There was only an inch of milk, understandable when she had not shopped yesterday, only a crust of bread ... but it was food. She made toast of the crust, made it thoughtfully. *I must find out how I stand*, she thought at last.

The check she had given her sister had been a blank check, negotiable by anyone, no name given. Her check from the solicitors had been in her name, but she had had it altered so that Cara could work on it. Cara had said she had taken out "oceans" of travelers' checks, that she would transfer the rest. Then everything would be quite all right; there would be a substantial "rest" not transferred, otherwise Cara would not have said as she had the night before: "I fixed up your money, believing we'd be in a rush. But

that can wait till tomorrow for your checking, can't it?
Cara herself had suggested the checking. So the mone
would be there.

In a way, Brit thought wryly, she deserved to los
it—imagine not putting some away, as Aunt Truda had ad
vised. But they had been departing from Australia, aban
doning it for years, as far as they knew perhaps forever. S
what was the use of leaving money here?

She waited till bank opening time, then phoned the ban
that had issued the bank check. No, Miss Smith had take
out no travelers' checks here, but she had spoken of doin
so, and as she had seemed in a hurry they had recom
mended an express firm. They required notice themselve
so they had sent Miss Smith to . . . . They said the name
and Brit thanked them. She phoned at once.

Yes, Miss C. Smith had bought checks, she had take
out . . . . They told Brit the amount.

It didn't make sense at first. It was beyond belief. Car
couldn't take out that much money, it would leave nothin
to transfer. It would leave—well, it would leave nothing a
all.

Brit asked the amount again, giving her credentials, say
ing it was important to know. The clerk repeated th
figure, and Brit found she had heard correctly. Cara ha
transacted the entire amount.

Now Brit did not sit still and stare ahead, she checke
little things she would never have thought of doing befor
Like the rent for tomorrow, when it became due. It wa
gone. Like the telephone box. It was empty. Her purse hel
a few coins, and as a last thought Cara must have decide
to leave her something bigger, for a dollar was left intact.

And that was all. *All*.

No—another letter was left. A brief one.

I had to have my taxi fare, but you'll be richly repaid, and meanwhile you can go back to St. Hilda's. You did quite well there. One day you'll be glad you gave me my chance.   C.

Giving Cara her chance. Brit looked at the dollar, looked at the letter. No, never St. Hilda's, she determined; even in her desperation she was adamant about that.

But the next day she was obliged to give St. Hilda's another thought. Her father had certainly seen to it that she could do nothing, that is nothing except what personally had gratified him. Theatrical stuff. Not that a posture class was really that, but at least it was not like dressmaking, which Brit could not have done, anyway. Or typing. Any of these occupations. What, then, could she do? If she had even the rudiments of commerce, of selling, of doing any of the many things girls did these days, Brit would not have been so concerned now. *Why,* she thought, *I couldn't even turn my hand—it should be foot,* she thought a little hysterically—*to teaching dancing, since, because of my obvious lack of talent, I was never taught myself.* Physical education? No, you had to know something about that, as well.

She supposed she could clean, but cleaning nowadays was extremely competitive; you had to take along with you all sorts of expensive aids. Day-care work, too, demanded a more specialized education than Brit had had. There were factories, but mostly you started as a junior, and knew all about your machine by the time you reached her age. A nurse's aide? You had to have a first aid certificate at least. *I have nothing,* Brit sighed.

The next day she faced up to the fact that she must go and ask St. Hilda's to give her back her job. She did not want to, but she had exhausted everything; she only knew about standing straight, breathing correctly while you did, and who else but St. Hilda's would buy that?

So she went.

It seemed ironical that the first one she saw at the school was Helena. Helena with one sock dangling as ever and a smudge—as ever—on her small nose.

"Helth belth, Mifmif," Helena said. She must have remembered she was not to say hell's bells because she added hopefully: "You're not here anymore."

"I may be," Brit told her.

"Good gwief!"

"Don't you want me?" smiled Brit.

"I like you, Mifmif, but not all that breaving."

"Perhaps I won't be accepted."

"Yeth," said Helena brightly.

Miss Asquith was silent as Brit poured out a story of changed circumstances, changed plans. She listened gravely to Brit's request.

"It is rather difficult. We dropped the posture class, you see—I mean, what was the purpose when—"

"Couldn't I start it again?"

"It was never really in great demand, not like the dancing, and eurythmics."

"Miss Asquith, isn't there anything at all? I—I simply must get something."

Miss Asquith looked at Brit reproachfully. "You really have been quite foolish, haven't you? You should never burn your bridges, you should have remembered that."

"Yes, I have been foolish," Brit sighed.

"I'm afraid that I personally can't help you," said Miss Asquith.

"The school?"

"I am the school. But—"

"Yes? Yes, Miss Asquith?"

"Please wait here. I shall make a phone call."

Brit nodded bleakly. "Anything will do," she appealed as the headmistress went out.

The school bell rang. Brit heard the classes being marshaled into lines. She heard the singing class trilling scales, the French class reciting verbs.

Miss Asquith was a long time. She was so long Brit began to think she had forgotten her.

Later she heard a car pull up outside. She heard Miss Asquith's voice.... So the Principal was still there. She was talking to whomever had come in the car. Brit listened closely, but she could not catch any words. Then the door was opening. Miss Asquith was returning.

And with her a man who was the last person in the world Brit wished to see. Not now. Not ever.

"Well, then...." Link Wayland drawled.

Miss Asquith went out and Link Wayland found himself a chair.

"So Cara's chance cost more than you bargained for," he began.

"I didn't bargain," Brit said. "You don't bargain on love."

A long moment went past, then: "No," Link agreed. He looked steadily across at Brit and although his dark eyes probed and calculated as ever, there was a certain gentleness there. The gentleness undid her. To her dismay Brit began to cry.

They were the broken little sobs of a child, and Link Wayland thought that she looked only a child hunched up there in the big chair, the tears streaming unwiped down her cheeks. He took out a handkerchief, unfolded, shook, then leaned over and quietly began mopping up.

The first kindness she had received for over twenty-four hours—it seemed twenty-four years—was the final straw for Brit. Instead of just a flow of tears, there was a deluge.

The next moment she was on her feet. He was leading her outside, leading her to his big car parked strategically near the door. He put her in the car, pulled down a blind.

It was a very luxurious car, Brit noted abstractedly, with many blinds, many accessories.

"I'll tell Miss Asquith." He was gone, then back in minutes. Without a word he started the engine, and they went out of the St. Hilda gates.

He drove, still without speaking, until they reached a fairly secluded park. He stopped the car near trees, took out his makings, then advised: "You can cry as much and as loud as you like now, only the birds to hear."

But Brit listened to his tobacco processes instead, to the whisper of the weed in his palm, to the crackle of the paper, finally to the ignition of the match.

"I'm all dried out," she admitted.

"Good. Tears are a release, but they don't provide a solution. Feel up to accounting to me now?"

"I feel all right, but I see no reason why I should account to you. I went to Miss Asquith for help, not to—"

"Not to the man who got you there in the first place?"

"I'd forgotten that," she said dully. "I'd forgotten you had a say in the school."

"No say," he corrected.

"But—"

"Only a say in you." He looked at her narrowly through a blue weave of smoke.

"A say in me?" she echoed.

"That's it. You see, Brit, and you may as well know this now since it seems you certainly will later, I carved out that job for you."

"Carved it out?"

"Inaugurated it, established it, thought it up. . . . Oh, find your own word."

"I think the word is prevailed. I think you prevailed upon the board to start me."

"Yes."

"You must have influenced them."

"Not at all."

"Then you must have a persuasive tongue."

"Rather a persuasive pocket," he amended, and, as she stared horrified at him: "Yes, I paid for you."

"You—you—" she stammered.

"Every payday I provided that sum you got handed to you in your salary envelope."

"*You* did!"

"Yes."

"But why, why?"

"Your father had asked me if I knew of anything suitable for you, meaning, I knew at once, something suitable to him." Link Wayland smiled slightly. "He said it had to be something—"

"Something acceptable to the composer of ballet music," said Brit tightly.

"Yes," Link said.

"But I still don't understand. Why should you have done it just because father asked it?"

"Good question," he awarded.

"Is there an answer to it?"

"Yes, there is. I wanted you under my eye.... Well, not too far away from that eye, anyway. You see, even then—" Link Wayland flicked the ash off his cigarette "—I'd decided it would be you."

"Me?"

"As a journalist I must correct you there, Brit; you should say I."

"You had decided it would be I?" she complied desperately.

"Yes."

"For what?"

"For marriage."

"With whom?"

"Mine is the opposite answer this time; I say me, not I."

"Are we having a grammar lesson?" she demanded crossly.

"If you like."

"I don't like. I want a reply. A marriage—my marriage—with whom?"

"With me. I just said so. Your marriage with me."

He put down the cigarette and waited for Brit's reaction.

CHAPTER SIX

WHEN BRIT DID NOT SPEAK, when she just stared dumbfounded at Link Wayland, the journalist drawled: "Now you're going to say 'You're mad!' "

Brit still did not speak, for she *had* been going to say that.

"Mad," Link continued blithely, "and I, according to romance fiction, which incidentally I also have tackled, since, as a determined writer, I've been through the entire gamut, from advertisements to articles to what-have-you—"

"According to romance fiction?" Brit reminded him.

"I answer: 'Yes. Mad for you.' "

"Only—" Brit smiled narrowly "—you're not."

"Only I'm not."

"Then?"

"Then?" he inquired maddeningly, thick brows rising.

"Then why have you done all this?"

"I eventually came to a stage in my career," Link told Brit leisurely, "when marriage became strongly advisable."

"I can't imagine a man like you ever finding it that."

"It is surprising—" he shrugged "—but it's still a fact. I needed—indeed had to have—a wife. I could have done with one in my provincial days, actually, helping me write up the hospital balls, telling me the correct name of the blue in the matron of honor's gown. I could have done with one when I became a city man."

"And now what are you becoming?" she asked thinly.

"If I were not modest I would say an international

figure. But I am modest—" he looked wryly at her and awaited a scornful comment, which Brit did not offer "—so I'll reply that I'm becoming a South American figure."

"South American?"

"I'm negotiating with a paper complex in Brazil," he explained.

"How will you manage the Spanish?" Brit asked coolly.

He smiled as coolly back at her. "*Portuguese.*"

"Is it?"

"Yes."

"Well, it's the same," she argued.

"Oh, no."

She felt very ignorant, very immature. She could think of nothing to say.

"I must have my wife beside me when I go to Rio," he began again. "It's expected there that a successful man is accompanied by his successful wife."

"I wouldn't be successful," signed Brit.

"Oh, yes, you would."

"But I've never been."

"You would," he persisted. "You would have succeeded in getting me."

"Haven't you got it the wrong way around?"

"You mean it should be I got you? Well, Brit, have I?"

"No."

There was silence for a few moments. Now Brit could hear the park birds.

"We'll start at the beginning," Link Wayland said. And he proceeded to do so.

"I always knew what I wanted," he told Brit, "right from a kid. My granny reared me, my parents had split up, and gran used to say: 'Link decides what it's to be, then goes after it' "

"Don't tell me you saw me and felt that," she taunted.

"Believe it or not, I did."

"But—but why? I'm not—"

"Not your sister Cara? I didn't want your sister Cara. I wanted you. You suited, still suit, me in every way."

"What way?"

"I like your quiet looks; as a writer I've always gone in for understatement, for the finer, more subtle style. I loathe flamboyance. I like your naiveté—when I require sophistication I can provide it for myself. I like your way of standing, of walking—"

"The posture mistress."

He ignored that. "I knew how important it was socially to have a wife who stood like a poppy," he continued blandly, "more important than anything else really. To the South American particularly carriage is an estimable thing."

"I should think there would be many straight-standing *señoritas,*" Brit interrupted rudely.

"*Senhoritas,*" he corrected. "A faint intake of breath after the first syllable." He paused. "Ah, but I will have my senhora beside me."

"You *are* mad!" she exclaimed.

"No, I just have a neatly pigeonholed mind."

"And now you're looking into the particular pigeonhole marked Matrimony?"

"Yes." He decided on another cigarette and went through the usual process. "Well, what do you say, Brit?"

"No, of course."

"Of course doesn't come into it. Nor, after we discuss all this, does No. We're going to be married. Were my granny here she would tell you the futility of fighting."

"Link decides what it's to be, then goes after it," murmured Brit. She asked curiously: "Is your name Lincoln?"

"Link. A vain idea of my mother's that I would join up the marriage again. I didn't. However, the name is a constant reminder that *my* marriage will not be like that one.

When we marry, Brit, it's really going to be a link, a link in a long chain of years."

"I'm not marrying you," she declared.

"Then," he asked, "what are you going to do? We haven't got down to basic facts yet, but we will now. You're broke, aren't you?"

It was useless to lie to this man, so Brit said simply: "Yes."

"How much did she get away with?"

"Everything."

"Everything? Good lord, how in heaven could she do that?"

Brit told him in a low, unemotional voice; she seemed to have no emotion left.

"You gave her a blank check for the lot? Are you quite crazy?"

"I suppose I am," she sighed.

"Didn't you have any suspicion?"

"Of my sister?"

"Your sister *Cara*."

"I had love." Brit had said it before and it had silenced him. But it didn't now.

"You utter idiot," he told her. "You stupid little fool." He was quiet a while, then he ordered her to tell him the exact details of Cara's duplicity.

"You say it all happened several days ago? What have you been doing since then?"

"The first day I think I just sat. After that I did check to see if it was all true."

"You just sat, you said." He took her up quickly on that. "Was the money that much of a blow?" He was looking at her keenly now.

"No," she had to admit.

"Then?"

"My sister was the blow."

He nodded thoughtfully, but she could see he was unsatisfied. His sharp journalist's mind was seeking something. Presently she knew what he was after.

"Women don't go to pieces over women," he said extractingly. "Who else was in this affair?"

"What do you mean?"

"Whom. Whom do I mean." He was correcting her grammatically again. He asked: "Did Cara leave the time-honored letter?"

"Yes."

He held out his hand.

"It's none of your business!" Brit snapped.

But the hand still remained stretched, and after a moment Brit opened her bag and gave him her sister's note. *What does it matter,* she thought dully, *I can't be any lower than I am now.*

She watched him read it, watched his dark face grow even darker, his lips tighten. Then he came to the part that had been Brit's real blow. John.

"John," Link Wayland said. He read it through again, then, without asking her, he tore it across. "It's all it's worth," he said when she went to object. "Now tell me about John."

"He's a composer. Something like father was." Wayland looked unimpressed. "He submitted his ballet *Southern Cross* to a European house and they wrote that they wanted to see him."

"With your sister?"

"No. Cara just went, too."

"But with John's connivance?"

"You've read the letter," Brit said sharply.

"Yes, I have. But—" closely "—*have you?*"

"What do you mean?"

"Have you read the finality of it?" he asked. "Accepted the finality? Accepted the oldest writing of all on streets, walls, trunks of trees...accepted 'J loves C?' "

"He doesn't."

"Oh, I know it's not put that way, I know it's expressed as doing 'the right thing,' but boiled down it still comes to what *you* wanted with this fellow John, and—" a shrug "—will never get."

"You're cruel!" she burst out.

"I'm kind, actually, because I'm honest. You've lost him, Brit."

"I never had him."

"Then what are you whining about?"

"You'd never understand," she answered brokenly, "you only understand words. It doesn't have to be words, you see."

"That could be," Link Wayland said surprisingly. "I'm not what you would call an experienced man." He looked at her. "I suppose that amuses you."

"Why should it?"

"A man of the world! A man who's made a success!"

"I think you've been too busy becoming that success to find time for anything else," she told him.

"You mean love," he said bluntly. "You're right. But I'm a good student. Can it be taught, do you think? Not 'French Without Tears' but 'Love Without Words?' "

"You have a tag for everything," she said. "You have an answer."

"It's *your* answer that I want now," he told her significantly.

"It's no," said Brit.

"You don't like me?"

"I don't like you."

"Apart from that?"

"Apart from what?" she said in disbelief. What else could there be, if you didn't actually love someone, other than liking them? What made this man tick?

"Apart from not liking me could you—"

"No."

"Then—" a sigh "—we'll begin again."

"Mr. Wayland, you're wasting your time."

He ignored her. He started down another road. "What," he asked, "are you going to do?"

"Find a job."

"At what?"

"I don't know. There must be something, though."

He shrugged discouragingly at that. "Is there nothing at all to salvage?" he asked. "Oh, I know she took the lot, but you must have had a bank balance, you've been well paid throughout the years, Brit." A short laugh. "*I* know that."

"Yes." Brit's nails dug into her palms. "You know that."

"Well?"

"There's nothing. Cara's ballet school was expensive. Cara was—"

"Expensive." He nodded wryly. "Go on, please."

"Cara even took her taxi fare." From my purse, Brit could have added, but she didn't. "I owe the landlord," she admitted.

"Are you eating?"

"Only what remains in the house—Mr. Wayland, you're hurting me!" For Link Wayland had leaned across and grabbed her hand, grabbed it roughly.

"I could shake a little fool like you till . . . " he said hoarsely. "I could . . . ." He left it at that.

"Well, it's over. I can't alter it. Neither—" Brit looked at him with finality, or at least she strove for finality "—can you."

"You mean it's the end of the book. The last period. Full stop. Oh, no, my Brit, you don't get away like that. How, for instance, do you intend to pay me back?"

"Pay you back?" She reddened. She had forgotten all those years of good salary that he had given her through St. Hilda's. "But I did work," she reminded him a little tremulously.

"Yet *I* received nothing from it," he reminded her in his turn. "Anyway, passing that over, what about your Aunt Truda?"

"Aunt Truda? But her money had nothing to do with you—she had her own means."

"Some," he agreed blandly, "that I helped her expand. Expand considerably." He gave a narrow smile.

"You mean you advised her regarding investments?" Brit interpreted.

He did not answer. Intentionally, she sensed. She looked up at him; she kept on looking. Oh, no, she was protesting inside her, not that, too!

"You didn't give Aunt Truda all that money?" she begged him.

"No, I did not give Aunt Truda the money; I gave it to you. She knew what I had in mind, so she agreed. She was very fond of you, Brit."

"The—the money Aunt Truda left me was your money?" Brit said again, hollowly.

"Not all of it."

"But most of it?" she persisted.

"Don't let it worry you," he advised.

She thought that over a minute, then said: "But it must be worrying you, that fact that I've lost you the money."

"I haven't lost. Well—not yet."

"But Cara has it. Or—" knowing Cara "—she had it."

"I still haven't lost." He looked meaningfully at her. "I've explained myself," he reminded her. "I couldn't be more explicit if I burned midnight oil over it. *You* were my investment, Brit."

"Then the investment has failed," she told him. "I'll try to pay back my salary; also, in time, any money you paid Aunt Truda."

"And then," he came in quietly, almost indifferently, "your father's debts?"

"My . . . ." She stared at him dumbfounded, yet not this time in disbelief. For she had often wondered how they had lived so comfortably.

"Yes, your father." He was silent a while. "I'm sorry this has come out. I never intended it to. It wouldn't have had you only been reasonable."

"Reasonable!" she echoed.

"Brit, I decided on you all those years ago. I've never regretted the decision and I don't now. When you marry me I'll hand you an unconditional receipt, I'll pull no more strings."

"I can't marry you!" she insisted desperately.

"Then I must think of something else. Perhaps find Cara."

"Cara is married to John." Brit did not realize that she was actually saying this without pain, but she was.

"Good lord," Link said, "not for that, you idiot, I told you before that Cara meant nothing as far as I was concerned. No, Brit, I would simply tell Cara the truth."

"That wouldn't help you."

"It could impede her," he said shrewdly, shrewd because he anticipated the sudden dismay in Brit's startled face.

"Oh, no," she cried, "that's not fair—after all, she's young, she didn't know, she had no idea. . . ." Her voice trailed off. He just wasn't listening.

"Yes," he proceeded coldly, "I would spoil the chance, or at least hinder the chance, that you, your father, your mother, and heaven knows who else have always been at pains to afford her.

"Giving Cara her chance," he said harshly. "No, my dear Brit, no more."

There was a long silence, and during that quiet Brit rallied her forces.

"But, Link." She said his name unthinkingly. "It could ruin Cara. She's an artist, and temperamental, emotional.

If she was on the threshold of something big it could be th finish for her."

"Keep on," Link advised, "the tears are starting."

"I know she's spoiled, but that's not her fault. Righ from a baby she was doted on, so how could she be an different now?"

"Brit, you have to give me something better than that, he smiled blandly.

"She's my sister."

"Still something better."

"I love her."

"And," Link included sharply, "*John?*"

"I think so," Brit said honestly, "though there never wa anything."

"Nor will be now, yet you can still plead for Cara?"

"Yes, I am pleading for her: I can't have her told. She' my sister, my baby sister. It's nothing to do with Cara."

"Except that she's put you into this position."

"I still love her," Brit insisted.

"Love!" he said in disgust.

"Yet it exists. I know you can't understand that, can' believe it, but it does."

"Then," Link said, "prove love to me. Prove your lov for your sister." He looked hard at Brit. "You know what mean."

"Marriage?"

"Yes."

"With you?"

He nodded.

"What sort of return would you be getting?" she asked.

"Leave that to me."

"You know that I don't care for you."

He shrugged.

"I could never love you."

He shrugged again.

"I—I even dislike you."

"Hate is your next step," he advised.

"All right, I hate you. So what?"

"So I still say marriage. But note that I don't 'offer' it, Brit, I *say* it."

"And if I don't, then you go to Cara and John, jeopardize whatever they've achieved?"

"That's a little dramatic, surely."

"But true. John is very honorable ... oh, yes—" flushing "—he is. He would pay you back every penny."

"How?"

"His music. And that would involve Cara. The marriage could split up. Marriages do when want comes in."

"Thus it would be advantageous for you," he suggested slyly. "I mean John would be back in the fold again."

"He was never in the fold," she sighed.

"You know what I mean."

"Yes, I know, and the answer is no. I would never want it like that with John."

"Very well then, you know what to do."

Another silence enfolded them. Distantly a car roared, but mostly the only noise was the sound of the birds.

"What—what sort of marriage?" Brit asked nervously.

"Are there varieties?"

"You should know, you said your parents—"

"Not one like that," he came in harshly. "Also," he went on, "never a marriage of convenience—as an author I've always had my tongue in my cheek when it came to that. No two people in the world, no man and woman, can live together without *living*.... You're following me, Brit?"

"Yes."

"We'll live. We'll be man and wife."

"I think you mean live but not love?"

"Yes, you do follow me. I'll demand a full life, a man-and-wife life. I'll want children. In return you will be cared for, you will be more than ordinarily comfortable, and your damned sister allowed to keep her chance."

"Live but not love," Brit repeated.

He did not speak for a while, then he said carelessly, as though it did not matter one way or other to him: "One of us, or both of us, can always change our mind."

"You mean live *and* love."

"You're coming along nicely," he smiled. "I might even make a copy girl of you."

"Can I have time to think, Link?" she begged.

"There isn't anything to think, is there?"

"But can I?"

He considered a moment, then said: "Yes. But first of all you're going to get something inside you. You're going to leave your apartment and stay at a good hotel, some-where where the meals will be brought to you, somewhere where you're not depending on yourself."

"Yes, Link." She said it docilely; she could not believe she said it like that.

He evidently could not believe it either. He gave her a sharp, suspicious look, found nothing there, then without warning turned on the car, reversed into the road again, and drove back to town.

He left Brit at the flat with the direction to be ready by the time he returned from his office.

"I can't have an answer by then," she protested.

"I meant be ready to change your address, Brit. Your packing seen to, all that. However, as regards the other, I'll expect an answer in the morning."

"You don't give me long."

"That's Wayland. Riding roughshod was your descrip-tion once, I seem to think."

"I'm sorry," Brit whispered.

"I quite like it," he assured her. "I've never wanted to be an indefinite man."

"Link decides what it's to be, then goes after it."

"Exactly. You know—" consideringly "—you're a great deal like my gran."

"She had brown hair? She was a brown moth?"

"She was . . . ." But Brit did not hear the rest. Link Wayland had started the big car again; he was maneuvering it away, whatever he called was lost in the turn of the engine.

All Brit did hear was a reminding: "One hour only."

She watched him go.

CHAPTER SEVEN

BRIT DID LITTLE in that hour. She was still gazing blankly at the clothes hanging in the wardrobe, clothes that all had to be folded and packed, and to which she had crossed dutifully at once—then never touched—when she heard Link returning. Goodness, had an hour gone already?

She said so aloud, and he shrugged: "If the rest of it goes so quickly you need have nothing to worry about." He looked impatiently at the negligible onslaught she had made, and stepping forward he bundled all the dresses up in one swoop.

"Some of them are Cara's," Brit protested.

"Oh, so she did leave something? You can sort them out at the hotel."

"What about our cups and saucers, our pots and pans?" she asked.

"Leave them to the next tenant. Are you ready?"

"You *are* a roughrider," she said, but it was said rather enviously. It must be wonderful to make clear decisions on things, then act on them.

"I'm beginning to believe that." He went in front of her down the stairs so that she could pick up the garments he would be sure to drop since he carried so many.

The hotel he had chosen was in a quiet part of the city. As soon as he established Brit, he left her.

"I've ordered dinner to be brought up, breakfast in the morning. After that—"

"Decision?" she asked.

"Decision," he nodded. "Goodbye, Brit, until tomorrow." He stood looking at her a moment longer than was necessary. Then he wheeled around and went along the corridor to the elevator.

But Brit sat on at the window that she had crossed to, sat staring down at the traffic. Decision. She had to make her decision. Yet what decision could she come to other than the one he had forced on her? She could never let Cara down, not now, not ever; she had got too much into the habit of love.

The unalterable fact that Link Wayland would do exactly what he had warned her he would do was very clear in her mind. He was a roughrider who thought nothing of anybody or anything, only of his own purpose, and he was essentially a man of his word. If she persisted, she had no second thoughts on what would happen. Cara would be contacted, John would be told, the pound of flesh extracted. Two lives ruined.

The habit of love. Brit kept coming back to that phrase. *I've got into the habit of love,* she thought, *a habit that has lasted nineteen years, ever since father woke me up one morning and said: "You have a little sister, Brit, a very beautiful little sister. We don't know yet, of course, but her small hands and shells of feet are so slender and graceful one can almost tell now that she's going to be something special. My little brown moth, you and mummy and I will always have to give our beautiful girl her chance."*

Giving Cara her chance. Yes, the habit of love, Brit accepted; it's too hard to break. *Cara has been abominable, but how much of it has been her fault? How much ours? We—I—made her what she is, and now I—I alone this time—reap the harvest.* "Be a fool," Link had called from the other side of a door that morning, she recalled, "and reap the harvest."

Link had seen what she could not see—he had suspected Cara's duplicity. But then he was an onlooker, he was not involved, he had not learned that habit of love. According to Mr. Link Wayland, he never would. Live but not love, he had stated. He had said that that would be their pattern. Then Brit remembered something else that man had said. "No two people, no man and woman, can live together without *living*.... You are following me, Brit?"

Brit gave a little shiver.

But she was woman enough to know that he spoke a basic truth; she knew that the elemental facts of life were the strongest facts in all existence. She knew, too, she really would not want it any other way. Life was beautiful, and life was to be *lived*. Only—a little sadly—she had always thought of it more as the end of a lane, a sweet conclusion that you finally reached because coming at last to it was the only natural, only loving thing that you wanted, that you asked for. That you then received.

"Oh, John!" she whispered brokenly.

Dinner came up ... then she realized that once more she had had no effect on the clothes that Link had thrown carelessly on the bed. Her own clothes were intermingled with Cara's. Many more of Cara's than hers. But they could wait till the morning. Tonight was for decision.

Later, lying in bed, the clothes tossed on the floor, staring through the window at a segment of navy blue sky, Brit knew she had come to her decision. Link had not left her any alternative, but even if he had she knew she would not have availed herself of it. Marrying Link Wayland would be advantageous, to say the least, and any advantage she gained would find its way in the end to Cara. That habit of love, she sighed, resigning herself for a night of wakefulness.

The next thing she knew was the sun finding its way by some miracle around soaring city buildings to poke yellow fingers over the bedroom sill. She had slept after all, it was yesterday's tomorrow. Link, she half smiled, who scorned effusion, would have said: "Use today, not yesterday's tomorrow, don't hedge." Well, today then, within hours, he would be here to ask her. There was a tap on the door. The maid, Brit thought, with breakfast. She got up, pulled on a robe, and opened up.

It was breakfast, but not brought by any maid. Link Wayland carried it in. Brit saw that the tray had been set for two.

"They were a little surprised, too—" he laughed at Brit's surprised eyes "—but rather delighted really. That fellow who started 'Love makes the world go round' really began something."

"How does love come into it?" she asked. "You're only saving the maid a few steps."

"So unromantic, Brit! Does that portend—no, don't tell me yet. Never tell a man his fate before a cup of brew. Pour, please, Brit. Of course the staff believed love came into it. You're the sugar in my coffee and all that."

"But you're only interested in life, not love," she reminded him.

"Two lumps, please," he directed. "And love, my child, is for velvet nights, not bustling days." He glanced meaningfully at the traffic now beginning to roar below. Brit, flushing, looked, too. But not for long.

"Link—" she began determinedly.

"Not before bacon and eggs."

"Don't—don't you want to hear?"

"I want to have something under my belt when I do."

"But it's all right. It's yes."

"Wise girl!" He never even looked at her. "I hate eating from a tray, it's awkward. Butter my toast, will you, Brit."

Brit leaned over to do so . . . then she laughed. "This must be the oddest acceptance in all the world!" She found herself actually giggling.

He put down his knife and fork. "Laughing suits you," he grinned. "Keep it up."

He looked years younger himself, almost a boy. "It suits you, too," said Brit.

"Then we both must laugh and laugh."

They laughed until the meal was over, and then Brit asked: "When?"

"The wedding?"

"Yes."

"Oh, some time . . . . I can't tell you exactly yet; you see I wasn't sure myself, so . . . ." He was reaching for his makings.

"But you must have been fairly sure; you knew how I felt about Cara."

"Yes, your sister was my winning card, wasn't she?" He looked at Brit curiously. "Tell me, Brit, how does one get like that?"

"Like what?"

"Like all that much loving?"

"The habit of love." She said it abstractedly, but he picked it up sharply.

"The habit of love," he repeated. "But don't habits breed monotony?"

"I think it would depend on the receiver of the love, but I don't know really." Brit suddenly found she did not want to talk about it. "You must give me some idea, Link," she insisted.

"About the wedding date?"

"Yes."

"Why?"

"Well—I want to be ready."

"Physically, emotionally or—"

"Don't be ridiculous!" she snapped. "At least I don't want it to be in a negligée. Like now."

"I don't mind," he assured her. He added impudently: "In fact it could save time." When she did not comment he told her: "Not to worry, Brit, unless you're one of those girls who must have a white wedding, all the bridal fal-lals."

"No, I'm not."

"Good. I'm not the man to demand it. I covered too many such weddings in my cadet days to require the same myself. So no fuss. Suit you, Brit?"

"It suits me, but all the same—"

"I'll just bowl along and take you to the preacher when I get around to it. Which won't be this morning."

"I should hope not!" she exclaimed.

He gave her a quick look. "It would be," he assured her, "if I didn't have two board meetings to attend." He got up, hesitated a moment, then touched Brit's brown head with a light hand.

"Sort out your things. Take a stroll in the park. But don't go getting any new decision ideas, and don't go run-ning away, or—"

"Or?" she dared ask.

"Or I'll drag you back by the hair. Which you'll proba-bly like, anyway. Women, so my romantic publisher told me years ago, like dominant men."

"I won't get any other ideas, Link—I can't, can I?"

"You mean Cara?"

"Who else?"

"Who else?" He was preoccupied a moment, then shrugged. He went to the door, then abruptly he wheeled back again. He came right up to her, only a breath away. "All the same, Brit, I must extract a promise," he said.

"What?" she asked, confused.

"Your solemn promise on what we've agreed."

"I've told you yes."

"*Your solemn promise,* Brit," he repeated.

"You're ridiculous!" she said crossly.

"I want it." His dark eyes fairly bored into hers. She went as though to withdraw, but he put out a hand and held her. The grasp was iron-tight and it hurt.

"Link—"

"Promise me, solemnly promise me, or by heaven—"

"I promise you." She stepped back at last, and stood rubbing the painful spot where he had put the pressure. He must be mad! He was mad. She opened her mouth to tell him so, but he had gone.

The maid came and removed the trays. She looked at the bed and Brit knew she wanted to fix it, fix the room. Brit told the girl she was going out.

She strolled downtown, looking into shop windows. One of the boutiques was a bridal one, and that reminded Brit that she was going to be married. Some time, she remembered from Link, when there were no board meetings. That obviously ruled out that flowing white dress she was looking at, and anyway, Link did not want one of those weddings, he had told her so.

What kind, then? Although he might decree it to be quiet and unobtrusive, there probably would be a few people there, editors, newspaper owners, influential and important people of the kind Link certainly would know. Womanlike, Brit thought at once: *What shall I wear?*

As well as getting into the habit of love, Brit had got into the habit of making do for her own wardrobe. She had few clothes; she had had no need at St. Hilda's. When Aunt Truda's legacy had come—no, not Aunt Truda's, *his, Link's*—it had been her pleasure to buy for Cara, not herself. *I've nothing suitable,* Brit thought now.

She began walking again, slowly, thoughtfully. She was thinking: "I also have no money to buy anything."

Link, and thank heaven for this, at least had spared her a final humility by not offering her any. Probably he had thought she would have some, even if a very little, somewhere. She had none.

She wandered back to the hotel. The maid had finished the room. She had even hung up the dresses that had been tumbled down. Cara's dresses. Her own. Some of Cara's not even worn yet. As she looked at them Brit recalled Cara's letter. After the other things, it had said:

> On the financial side, if it helps any, all those lovely dresses you bought for me can be returned. The ones I haven't worn yet, I mean. Simeon of Gowns by Simeon is very cooperative, or so I've heard....

Yes, the firm was cooperative, Brit remembered, for she had bought Cara's dresses herself, and the assistant had assured her that they could be returned. She took them out and looked them over. Perhaps Simeon's would exchange them for something for herself. Cara's dresses were not her type of dresses; also Cara was taller, had different measurements. As she thought this, Brit was encasing the dresses in their individual boutique bags.

She went out of the hotel again.

Simeon was not in the fashionable part of Sydney, in fact the small arcade that Brit entered was definitely shabby. But Simeon, she knew, had no need to go to the people; the people—smart women, discerning women—went to him. He was one of the few prestigious Sydney couturiers, few since Australia had not climbed the world's fashion ladder as yet, but, it was said, and Brit had read it, that Simeon should go far. Go international.

If the arcade was not prepossessing, Simeon's house was a cool, tasteful retreat. Its decor was quite perfect, Brit thought, with its cool silvers and serene aquas. It was one of those boutiques where you could browse to your heart's delight, and Brit did now.

Something for a wedding. *My wedding.* How unbelievable that sounded! She tried the opposite corner to the corner from which she had chosen Cara's dresses. There seemed to be no one in attendance, so until help came Brit put her bags on a lounge, and began looking through the dresses that were moving slightly in the breeze from the silent fan above the long brass rail.

She liked them all. This Simeon, she thought, had a very gracious line to his designs. This soft amber silk. This dull blue brocade.

"No." The voice came from so close beside her that Brit actually jumped.

At once the man apologized . . . . It was a man, not a woman assistant, a man of average height, less than average build, somehow not robust; a man with quietly smiling bramble brown eyes. John, thought Brit with a small sharp pain, had eyes that color.

"I'm sorry you didn't hear me beside you. I wouldn't have wanted to startle you." He smiled again.

"You said no?" Brit felt at home with this man at once and made her answer to him a question.

"It's not your dress." He touched the dull blue brocade.

"I know. I'm in the brown category. I should wear the autumn colors."

"Not necessarily. Blue could be quite wonderful on you, but a more vibrant blue, Miss . . . ?" He looked at her inquiringly.

"Miss Smith. I was here quite recently purchasing clothes for my sister."

"Yes, I remember Miss Smith on the accounts." That made them both smile.

Brit laughed: " A Smith among many other Smiths," and he laughed with her.

"Now it's your turn?" he inquired.

"Yes and no. I mean, I'm not buying afresh. I'm returning my sister's dresses and hoping I can substitute something for myself."

"Why not?"

"Aren't you disappointed? I mean, you must prefer new sales."

"Miss Smith, I'm happy in what I do, but most of my happiness is in other people's happiness. If your sister is not satisfied with the dresses—"

"But she was. She loved them. Could anyone—" sincerely "—help but be delighted with them?" He gave her a pleased look, and Brit finished: "But she had to go away."

"These are the returned items, Miss Smith?"

"Yes, Mr. . . . ?"

"I am Simeon." He bowed slightly. "There is another name, of course, quite as everyday as yours. I'm quite fond of it, I like ordinary things, but I found that my clients prefer the unusual. So—" he shrugged "—Simeon."

"It is a good name for a salon, and it's a beautiful salon." Brit paused. "If your assistant is here perhaps she could tell me if I'm in my right size section."

"Today she's not here at all. She has the flu. Also her assistant and her assistant's assistant have it. No doubt the infection ran the whole gamut."

"You escaped?"

"So far," he nodded.

"So you're by yourself?"

"Yes. Would you care to help?" He laughed.

Brit laughed back. "I wouldn't be much good, I'm afraid, but so long as you don't mind me helping myself now."

"When I'm here to do it?" he reproached. He gave her a long calculating look. "I know the size," he said, "and the type."

"You're very astute," she commented.

"It's my trade."

He was veering Brit to another corner, his fingers under her elbow were impersonal and yet somehow involved. At the rack he paused and looked at her again.

"These are all the correct sizes, but you haven't said what kind of dress you want."

A little uncomfortable, Brit said: "Is that necessary?"

"You wouldn't wear a sun dress to a dinner party."

"I'm going—to a wedding," she told him.

"Morning? Afternoon? Four o'clock? Five?"

"I don't know, I mean—"

He smiled gently at her uncertainty, but he did not press her.

"Friend of the groom? Of the bride? Very close or mere acquaintance?"

Brit said hesitantly, yet knowing she could hedge around no longer: "I'm the bride."

He nodded slightly and smiled again. He had a nice smile, Brit thought, a smile that touched his eyes as well as his lips. There was warmth in it.

"Not formal?"

"I—well, you see . . . ." Brit bit her lip. "As a matter of fact," she admitted with a rush, "I don't know myself. Now—" a little challengingly "—laugh."

"Why should I? I find it quite enchanting. Why should a bride worry about such trivia as formality and the like when there are the important things to be remembered?"

"Like?" Brit half whispered it. There was something intrinsic about this man that made it easy for her to speak at once on a subject she would not have spoken to others in years.

"Like seeing his face—or her face," he said eloquently, "every time you look around. Like lighting a candle in your heart every time you say his—or her—name. Oh yes—" a self-effacing laugh "—I would have liked to have been a poet. But I didn't have that art. So instead . . . ." He extended his hands.

"Your gowns are poems," she told him.

"Thank you." A pause. "So the dress is for your wedding?"

"Yes."

"Then it must be something very special."

"No," Brit said. She was as surprised by the single word as he was. He half turned to select a gown, but at once he turned around again. He looked at her.

"I'm sorry, Miss Smith," he said gently.

"I'm sorry I said it," Brit returned.

They both shifted the dresses along the rack.

"This should suit you," he advised at length. It was a pale primrose chiffon he offered, barely primrose, almost only a buttered cream.

"Yes, I like it."

"Will you try it on?" He nodded to one of the cubicles.

"Yes."

As Brit pulled the curtain he called: "Will you let me see it on you?"

"Yes," Brit said again.

The dress fitted perfectly; nothing needed to be altered. She came out to where he waited. He studied her a long time, then he asked her to walk.

"Yes." There was a half sigh with the affirmative. "Yes, it's you."

"Thank you for finding it for me." She smiled.

"Thanking you for making of it what I had in mind."

"Do I?"

"Oh, yes, yes!" He spoke sincerely.

Brit went back and changed. She tidied her hair, put on a trace of lipstick and came out with the dress to be wrapped.

"You still have more to choose—or would you prefer a refund?" he asked.

"I would like more dresses, but not today. Can I choose again?"

"Please," he said.

He put the gown into a box marked Simeon.

"Why," he said unexpectedly, yet somehow without intruding, although such a question should intrude, "is the gown not to be special?"

"It's not a special marriage," she shrugged.

"A pity." There was silence a while, and then he asked still intimately yet never intruding: "Why does a lovely gi not marry specially?"

"I'm not lovely," she protested.

"You're beautiful, Miss Smith, you're just what I . . . . He smiled ruefully and shrugged. "I'm very rude," he tol her presently. "It would be your right in your turn to as me why I'm designing dresses when I could do othe things." He shrugged again. "Many people do."

"And what do you say to them?"

Now he laughed. "The truth, I'm afraid. That I can't d other things."

"You mean poetry?"

"And active things. Men's things. Unhappily, I'm nc strong. But I like my work and when I see a dress I'v dreamed up come to life on someone like you, then I lov it. I loved it just now."

"Then that's good."

"Yet not good enough, for it doesn't happen ofte enough. Why," he repeated, "does a girl like you—"

"I could say money," she suggested.

"But it wouldn't be true," he suggested back to her.

"Yes, it is . . . in a way."

"Then find your money elsewhere."

"Like you—can I say Simeon?"

He nodded.

"Like you, Simeon, I can't find it elsewhere."

"That I could never believe, not with your grace. Wha were you, a ballerina?"

"Not even in the corps de ballet. No, I taught posture."

"I can believe that. You move like a wind throug trees—why are you laughing?"

"I taught that to the class." Brit laughed again . . . but sh was not far from tears.

"And that's all your gracefulness got you?"

"Yes."

"But modeling, surely. A model is extremely well paid."

"I don't think I'd be right."

He was looking at her with professional estimation. "Perhaps not for every house," he said. "The trend now is for staccato action, the graceful sweep is out. But you would be ideal for some of the more serious haute couture. You would be ideal for mine."

She looked at him with interest, and he nodded.

"Gowns need a certain person," he said. "For my gowns you would be the right person."

"Well," she said a little wistfully, "even though I can't do it, it's flattering to know I could have. Thank you, Simeon."

"Are you sure you can't?" he came in carefully.

"Very sure." She smiled. "Are you sure in your turn you did want me?" She tried to make it flippant, but he answered her gravely, sincerely.

"Quite sure. I would pay you a salary of...."

Brit, who had opened her mouth to stop him, stood with her mouth still parted, nothing said. Then: "That's a lot of money," she said doubtfully.

"To speak in the jargon they do now," he said rather boyishly, "you're a lot of girl. By that I mean you have everything—everything, anyway, I would want."

"You're not serious," she protested.

"I have never been more serious in my life. I've been looking for someone, Miss Smith. This is not a sudden urge. It has to be the right person, the person you are. I could tell it at once. I offer you that salary now. I even offer you a future partnership. I could do with you. More than that, I want you." He waited a moment. "It's early yet; I've taken you by surprise, but if you would think about it—"

"I can't!" Brit said with a half sob. "I can't." She turned blindly and went for the door.

He came after her. "Your gown," he told her, and handed her the box. "Also don't forget the other credits on your returns. And if you can bring yourself to it, do consider what I've said, will you?"

"Why," asked Brit in sudden desperation, "have you said it too late?"

"But many married women, indeed most married women, have a career."

"Yes."

"Also, you're not yet married."

"No."

"Then—"

"Please," said Brit, and this time she did leave the salon. She even started to run.

She heard his voice as she went along the arcade.

"Consider it," he called in a low yet reaching tone. "Consider what I've said."

Brit emerged from the arcade and the city hum drowned out the voice.

Now the shops could not divert her; she kept on thinking of the salary he had just offered, the possiblities it opened up for her. She kept thinking what she could have done with her life instead of....

"It's not too late." She did not realize she had said that aloud until she saw someone looking curiously at her.

She went back to the hotel, and with every step her resolve began to build. *This is my chance,* she thought, *Simeon is my chance—why, he even spoke of a future partnership; I could do even better than that very attractive salary he promised. I could save, save very quickly. I could pay back Link Wayland, add the interest he would no doubt expect. I could buy my way out of this—this nightmare. I could....*

And that, she knew, was what she was going to do. Marriage was final—well, to her it was final. Link Wayland had let it be known how he felt, too. "Not," he had said harshly, "marriage like that of my parents."

She did not like the man. More than that she knew that she nearly hated him. He was all the things she loathed in his sex: dominating, authoritative...a roughrider.

No one could make her do anything; he couldn't—the only pull he had on her was money, money to stop him from dealing instead with Cara; and she now had, or could have, money.

She had reached the hotel by now, and she ran up the steps. When she got to her room it was to find the door unlocked and half open. She went questioningly in...perhaps the maid still had not finished. Link sat on the bed.

"Where on earth have you been?" he complained. "I've waited almost an hour."

"Was I to be kept a prisoner here?" she snapped.

"I expected you to go out—I said so—but not for this long."

"Was I wanted, then?"

"Yes."

"Is it Cara? She's got in touch? She's—"

"No, not your sister, your fiancé."

"Fiancé?" echoed Brit.

"Yes. Link Wayland, the roughrider. Remember?"

"Why did you want me?" she asked, disappointed.

"For our marriage," he came back, "in—" he looked at his watch "—exactly half an hour."

"It's not true!" she gasped.

"It is."

"You're joking!"

"It's arranged for less than half an hour. A second has elapsed. Just you, me, the minister, someone pulled off the street for a witness. Also, of course, the background of a church."

"People aren't married like that—I mean, they don't run in for a few minutes the same as they would run into a shop for a pound of butter or—or for a length of cotton."

"We're booked in twenty-five minutes," he told her firmly.

"No!"

"I'm sorry you want something more formal, Brit, but this has to be it."

She looked at him wretchedly—nervously, as well, nervous because of what she had to say, yet still she faced up, for it had to be said.

"I don't want anything at all, neither formality nor lack of it. Link—Link, I've changed my mind."

"The hell you have!" he came back.

"I'm serious, Link."

"What do you think I was when I made you give me that promise? Brit, I meant every word."

"You can't make me!"

"I'll make you all right."

"You won't be out of pocket, either." She ignored his threat. "I'll even repay you much more."

"Who's the Midas you have got hold of since leaving here?" He was lighting one of his cigarettes, eyeing her through the blue weave of smoke.

"You wouldn't know him, so the name doesn't matter. He's a gentleman." She heard him laugh. "He will employ me, and—and it's not just employment, it's a chance, too, a very remarkable chance. The money is wonderful. I could start repaying you at once. Then there's the offer of a partnership. There's—"

"What about *our* partnership?" Link Wayland broke in.

"We would never be partners," Brit cried, "surely you can see that? It's so much better to face it now, not wait until—"

"There'll be no waiting." He said it definitely, the voice allowed no argument. "We're being married *now*, Brit; you gave me your promise and by heaven you're keeping to it."

"What if I . . . ." But she stopped. She had to. He had

stepped forward and put his big dark hand across her mouth.

"I'm marrying you now. If you won't walk out of the hotel to the church, which incidentally is just around the corner, I'll carry you. If you won't answer the minister I'll—"

"Yes?"

He did not answer that, but his dark eyes bored into hers. "You promised me and you're not going back on it," he said instead.

"What satisfaction will you get out of knowing I came unwillingly?"

"It doesn't matter one iota to me so long as you come. And you are coming." He put his hand under her arm and began impelling her to the door.

"I could scream," she warned.

"You'd only scream once."

"Kick."

"You could, but I think you're a lady," he said.

"You could be wrong there."

"I'll try you out."

He guided her down the passage, pressed the elevator button . . . and it was as he said, she thought wearily, with hopeless resignation, she *was* a lady. Either that or she could not go through the embarrassment, the humility, of a scene.

"Do you, Brit . . ." she heard in a daze. The church was small and brown.

She answered: "I do."

"Do you, Link . . . ."

"I do."

The disinterested witness wandered off again. The minister shook both their hands, then led them to the door.

They came back to the hotel room. And there Link Wayland took Brit in his arms and held her as she never had been held before. Eyes to eyes, lips to lips. Breath-close. Almost thought-close. He kissed her, quietly at first, and then longer, more fiercely. Hungrily. He lifted her up, held her aloft a moment, then carried her to the bed.

"John," he said scornfully. "The nice gentleman. Ghosts, both of them—wraiths, dreams. I'm a man. Your man."

She turned away from him, she resisted, withdrew... and then all at once she was not turning away, not resisting, withdrawing any longer. They *were* ghosts, wraiths, dreams; she knew it in a bemused but strangely positive kind of way. This was a man.

But her man?

Sensibility had returned to her. She sat up. Yet she did not look at him.

"Well?" he challenged her. "You always said I was a tough customer."

"I said you never considered people, that you rode roughshod over them."

"A roughrider," he agreed. He said it almost with disinterest. "So what?"

"So I hate you."

"Why do you keep on saying that? The first thing a journalist learns is never to repeat himself in the writing game. I take back what I said about making you a copy girl."

"I wish I could take back...." Sobs prevented her from finishing.

"But you can't. We're married, Brit. You're my wife. *My wife.*" He was still lying back as he called it, and though she did not turn to look at him she knew he watched her.

Yes, I'm married, she knew dully; *married to this man. I've given Cara her chance . . . but what chance has this marriage?*

What chance have I?

CHAPTER EIGHT

THEY STAYED ON at the hotel. Link told Brit he had an apartment but that he would want it redecorated now that he had a wife.

"What is right for a bachelor is not right for a married man," he said. "That will be something for you to do."

"Yes, I want something," Brit agreed.

He had looked at her quickly, had started to say something, then evidently changed his mind.

They had gone out to visit Miss Asquith, visit St. Hilda's, and the Principal had assembled all the school and introduced Mrs. Wayland, once their own Miss Smith.

At the outskirts of the throng of Brit's congratulatory former colleagues, a small girl with a knickered leg dangling had stood waiting to catch Brit's eye. Catch Link's eye, too, it appeared, for Link greeted Helena by name.

"Helena of Troy," he hailed.

"I live in Braefield. Pleath Mifmif—"

"Mrs. Wayland now, Helena of Troy," Link directed grandly. But of course the name of Wayland must be grand.

"Mithmith Wayland, I'm marrying an Indian, too," announced Helena.

"Are you, darling? When?" asked Brit.

"I haven't met him, but I like Indianth." Helena looked admiringly at Link, no doubt very large to a small girl, looked at his swarthy brownish red skin.

"Will you call your little girl Moonlight on the Water?" asked Helena eagerly. "That wath in a TV movie. I think ith luverly."

Brit, hiding her laughter, had said diplomatically: "We'll see." She hadn't dared look at Link for some minutes, and then when at last she did she found that he was laughing, too.

But not at the Indian part—it appeared he was used to that—but at Brit's face.

"So serious," he grinned.

"You didn't mind?"

"Lord no. But I thought you did."

"Being married to an Indian?"

"Having a daughter so soon."

"Oh!" said Brit flatly.

"I myself have no objection, because I would prefer a daughter. I have a special corner for girls. Keep that in mind, Brit."

She had not answered him. Part of her silence had been wonder, wonder that this big tough man would not demand sons. The other part had been the assured way he spoke, as though a family was not just a possibility but a looked-for conclusion. Yet he did not appear father material.

Link had said they would not bother doing up the apartment yet, not until they came back.

"From South America?"

"I'll be going there alone, Brit; it seems it will only be a quick visit, so too wearying for you. Later on we'll go and take our time over it. Rio is a dream place and can't be hurried. Then once I get you into Brasilia you'll never want to leave all those gems."

"Are there?"

"Yes. Glorious gems. That reminds me, I never bought you an engagement ring, did I? What stone do you want?"

"Isn't it rather unusual getting an engagement ring after a wedding ring?"

"Isn't unusual the kind of marriage we have? Ruby or emerald?"

"Surprise me," she challenged.

"I will."

Presently he said: "Will you be all right while I'm gone?"

"Of course."

"It was rather a foolish question," he admitted, "but one, I gather, that's expected of abandoning husbands."

"I wouldn't know." She shrugged.

"I'll feel better about deserting you if you're left in the hotel—that way I'll know you'll eat."

"Meals three times a day. Am I to be regimented, too, when it comes to going out?"

"I leave that to you—" he shrugged "—to your discretion."

"Discretion?"

"You're a married woman now," he reminded her.

"I didn't think you would be a conventional man. Journalists aren't, are they?"

"They're the same as anyone else; like in any other group, it takes all sorts. So—" a long look at Brit "—I'll leave it to you." He waited a moment. "When I come back," he resumed, "if you're a good girl you'll be rewarded."

"If I'm discreet, you mean."

He grinned. "How would I know? Would you tell me? No, you'll be rewarded, anyway, by a honeymoon."

"A honeymoon?" she echoed.

"We never had one—remember I was, and I still am, too busy. But in two weeks' time—"

"Is that how long you'll be away?"

"Yes. In two weeks' time we'll fly to Hawaii. Would you like that?"

"Hawaii...oh, yes. But why?"

"Why a honeymoon or why Hawaii?"

"Both, I expect."

"Because I've never had a honeymoon and I'd rather like to find out what it's all about, and because Hawaii is my idea of perhaps the loveliest place in the world. So in two weeks, Brit."

He flew out the next day.

At first Brit felt a lightness and a relief. It was wonderful not to look across the room to find his dark eyes watching her, revealing nothing of his own thoughts, simply weighing up and estimating her. It was like old times, even better, really, for all she was expected to do was to sit at the hotel dinner table and be fussed over, no more coming home after a day's work again. And not just fussed over, either, but quite lavishly spoiled. Brit decided that the staff must have been previously very well rewarded.

They all liked her, however, or seemed to, and they commiserated with her often for being a temporary widow. They tried to cheer her up, jolly her out of the loneliness they mistakenly attributed to her. Then one morning, to Brit's utter surprise—and disgust—she knew they were right.

She was lonely. She missed him. She could not stand Link Wayland but in some ironical way she missed him.

Brit had few friends. Her life prior to this new strange life had been taken up by Cara. Entirely by Cara. There were teachers she had liked at St. Hilda's, but now there was a barrier, she knew. She could not go back and claim them. They still worked; she had her leisure. She had sensed that difference the day Link had taken her to visit Miss Asquith; she had known that she no longer belonged. Also, she thought with a rather lopsided smile, she had felt their faint envy, not because of her obvious comfort but because of—Link. Yes, because of Link. She had noticed them looking at Link, at the big masculinity of him. Unlike Brit, unmistakably they had seen no roughrider in him, only someone they obviously found most attractive. Brit wondered a little over it; she certainly did not find Link that. Yet she might be the exception. Even small Helena had sighed over the Indian.

No, St. Hilda's was out.

It was no use sitting waiting for a letter from Cara, she knew her Cara—probably the two notes she had scribbled when she had left were the longest she had written in her life. In the beginning Brit had worried about it, then Link had very sensibly pointed out that no news was good news, that nothing could have happened to her sister without them finding out. Because she had no address she could not fill in time writing to Cara. John, as she had expected, had sent no word, so even though she supposed she could have contacted the La Salle Company, she would not do so. Link had sent her a postcard, but that was all; obviously he expected no reply from his wife.

Brit struck up a friendship with Clare, the maid, but Clare had her work to do.

Eventually Brit did what she had known—but not dared think—all along she would do, what it was inevitable that she do, though she would never have admitted it. She went to Simeon.

The assistants at Gowns by Simeon were back after their flu attack, helpful girls who found exactly what Brit sought, made the transaction of substituting Cara's rejected dresses with dresses for herself a simple one. Brit found herself wishing it was not all so easy, otherwise they would have had to consult Simeon.

Then, almost as though he had seen her enter, though he couldn't have, not behind his paneled office door, the couturier came into the salon.

"Why, Mrs. Wayland!" he greeted.

Brit flushed. He had known her before as Miss Smith, and her marriage to Link Wayland had had no publicity. They had not even announced it in the appropriate section of the papers.

"Simeon," she acknowledged.

She took the hand he extended, then found it was not just to shake her hand but to guide her into his sanctum.

"While Miss Malling is wrapping your dress you can surely spare me a few minutes," he appealed. "By the way, you were suited, Mrs. Wayland?"

"As much as if you'd been choosing yourself—you train your girls to think like yourself." As she was speaking Brit was looking curiously around her, at the large sketching blocks, at the random figures imposed on the blocks.

"This is where the magic begins?" she asked.

"Or the mistakes are concocted."

"I don't think you make any mistakes, Simeon."

"No, I've been fortunate."

Brit had taken up a rough sketch. The girl in the picture was caught in a gust of wind and the wind was lifting the edge of a swirling skirt. "You spoke about wanting to be a poet," she said, "but you never said you were an artist."

"I'm not," he assured her.

"This picture—"

"Is to demonstrate the correct fluid use of silk jersey." He shrugged. "No, that's the full extent of my talent, I'm afraid."

"But with training—"

He shook his head, shook it with finality. "Art, unlike writing, requires certain physical capability. To be brief, in front of a canvas I would be required to stand. I don't think you've noticed, Mrs. Wayland, or if you have, you have generously let it pass over, but I'm something of a cripple."

She had not noticed, but she did now. There was a difficulty with his left foot. He moved for her and she saw that he limped slightly.

"It's barely more than a hesitancy," she assured him.

"Thank you, I like to think that, too. I have no trouble

with it, except, as I said, the trouble of accepting my inadequacy when it entails restriction in what I want to do."

"Polio?" Brit inquired.

"Yes. I was six."

"I'm sorry."

"You are, aren't you?" He smiled at her.

"How did you know I was Mrs. Wayland?" she asked
then.

"I made it my business. It was easy enough—your husband is a very well-known person."

"How did you know I was here? There's no glass in the
door."

"I can't answer that as promptly. I simply knew." He
said it diffidently.

Someone else had known, if not diffidently, recalled Brit.
Link had stood on the other side of a locked door and
shouted: "Open up, Brit, I know you're there." Then he
had called: "If I wanted to get in for myself, I'd take no
notice of locks, I'd kick the door in."

The roughrider. So different, so very different from Simeon.

"Your husband is in South America. Oh, no—" a smile
"—I didn't 'sense' that, I read the item in a paper."

"Yes, he's gone on business," Brit told him.

"You must be lonely."

"No. No, of course not. I mean—well, I suppose I am,
Simeon." She gave a rueful little moue.

"Nothing to do?"

"No."

"Then—" tentatively "—could you do something for
me?"

"For you?"

He glanced down at his sketching blocks. "I'm working
from imagination."

"And doing very well," she smiled.

"But how much better if I had a model."

"Your girls—"

"They're kept busy. Anyway, they're not the type I want for this consignment of material." He brought out a bolt of the fluid jersey he had mentally used for the wind girl's frock.

"It's beautiful." Brit touched the supple silk appreciatively.

"It's you," he said. "So will you help me?"

"I—well...."

"Please." He smiled.

Brit looked around her, looked at the interesting things Gowns by Simeon had to offer. She had been bored these last few days. No one to talk to. Nowhere to go. Nothing, as this man had said, to do. It would be fun, she thought. I would be a welcome diversion. Yet still she hesitated.

Then her eyes finished roving the room and rested on Simeon. He looked steadily back at her, and he waited.

"Yes," she agreed.

She stayed the rest of the day. Simeon would make quick sketches, then she would leave him to work on them and go out and talk to the girls. She got on well with the girls. Once she actually made a sale, and twice she modeled a gown and they made sales.

At closing time she went into the office again.

"Hilary has been saying how helpful you've been." Hilary Malling was the senior assistant. "Brit, we haven't discussed rates." Earlier in the afternoon they had agreed on her being Brit. After all, if she called him Simeon....

"Oh, no," Brit protested, "I don't want to be paid."

"I can't have you otherwise."

She could see that he meant it, could see he would be bitterly disappointed to let her go, but that he still would. He would be a proud man, she knew. She would be disappointed, too. This day, after her recent days of boredom, had been sheer delight.

"Then dresses," she laughed. "This one, perhaps?"

"The whole salon," he urged.

"You silly man!"

"You...." But he did not go on.

"Stupid girl?" she suggested flippantly, suddenly feeling a need for flippancy, anything but Simeon's quiet seriousness. "Oaf? Idiot? My husband calls me these names." *My husband.* Brit thought with surprise that this perhaps was the first time she had said that.

"Oh, no," refused Simeon.

In the end they agreed upon several dresses to be chosen at the end of the week, or before Link returned and when Brit gave up the temporary post.

"Though," objected Simeon, "with remuneration how can it be called a post?"

"I've looked at the price tags on several dresses I have my eye on, and they would take me weeks of salary. What time tomorrow, Simeon?"

He glanced at her, surprised. "You come when you wish, of course, but note—" eagerly "—I'm not saying *if* you wish."

"I'll be here," she promised.

Brit was. She was there early and she stayed late. For the week she went to Simeon's she was not back at the hotel for one dinner. Lunches, of course, were always taken at the salon.

But at night Simeon took her to a variety of places. She found his taste in quiet restaurants was her taste. He had a dislike for show, for gilt, loud orchestras and long menus. He preferred simple bills of fare with a few, but very carefully prepared, offerings.

"We match," Brit said one evening.

"I've been thinking the same. We're the right blue with the right pink."

"The right contrast of textures," Brit laughed ... and as the laugh was dying away, she was looking at Simeon looking at her with his gentle bramble colored eyes. John, too had bramble eyes.

"Brit—" Simeon began.

"Yes, Simeon?"

"I'm going to Hawaii."

She stared at that. Until he said it she had completel forgotten about her approaching "honeymoon."

"I wish you could be there, too," he went on. "I plan t present a new idea I've dreamed up against one of thos fabulous Hawaiian backgrounds. For Hawaii is truly fabulous. Have you been to that enchanted island?"

"No, but—"

"I wish you could come now. Be my model. I know jus where I would place you, the colors I would use, the style."

"I can't come, you know that, but—" a little laug "—I'm coming."

He looked at her in question, and she said: "It happen that we're going, Simeon. It's unbelievable, I mean the co incidence is, but Link and I are leaving soon after he re turns."

"You and your husband," Simeon said slowly.

"Of course."

There was a moment's silence, then Simeon smiled "That will be wonderful. I can see you there. I can mee your husband."

"Yes, you can meet Link."

"He might even be enthusiastic about my sketchin you." Simeon's voice was so hopeful that some of the hop splashed over on Brit.

"He might," she cooperated.

But once away from the candle glow of the intimate res taurant, away from Simeon's eager face across the table Brit saw things in a different light. Especially when Link card came.

Am finishing my South American business here in
Santiago. Will leave tomorrow at noon. This should
bring me home by Thursday noon. A dutiful wife
would meet her husband at the terminal. Anyway,
Brit, I'll certainly expect that. The location of the sce-
nic side of this card is the Andes, of course. I'll take
you there one day. Till I see you—Link.

Thursday. Thursday was the day after tomorrow. In two
days' time Link would be back.

Brit did not know how she felt about Link's return. Her
loneliness in the first few days of his absence had surprised
her, but after she had seen Simeon she had not felt lonely
any more. She was aware of a confusion now, an unsure-
ness, yet in all the uncertainty one positive thing stood out
for Brit. Link must not know that she had been attending
the salon. There had been nothing wrong in it, an ordinary
man would have been pleased for her diversion, even for
her rewards for her service, but Link Wayland was never
ordinary. She did not want to deceive Link, deception got
you nowhere; at some time or other you were discovered
and then it became much worse. But for all that knowledge
and her uneasy conscience, Brit still knew the salon visits
were something she must keep to herself and Simeon. At
least for some time yet.

She determined to confide in Simeon the next day. He
would be hurt at her appeal, even shocked, perhaps not
agreeable, but she must try to paint the picture truly, make
him see it her way.

However, Brit had no such opportunity, for Simeon was
not there, he was down with the flu.

"It's funny how it sweeps right through," said Hilary
Malling. "I hope you don't get it."

"I feel fine now." Brit was wondering whether she could
discover Simeon's address, call at his home and tell him.

"Then I hope you'll help us," appealed Hilary. "With Simeon away it makes so much more to do."

What could Brit say? Anyway, she told herself, it would have been foolish to have gone to Simeon's place even if she knew where it was.

They were very busy that day, there was no opportunity for doubts and self-questionings. Hilary thanked Brit warmly, was saddened when she knew her temporary service was over.

"You've been manna from heaven," she told her as Brit left.

There was no postcard from Link. Brit had not expected one; he would have started on his return trip by now. There was still no letter from Cara. No word from John.

Brit sat in the hotel room and wondered about Simeon. She decided at last to phone his home, talk with him, and she picked up the directory to find his home number. Then she smiled to herself. An ordinary name. Simeon had told her at their first meeting, but he had not said what it was. Well, perhaps it was better this way. She put the directory down.

She did not sleep well that night. She looked in the mirror in the morning and she hoped the signs did not show. If they did Link would be certain to notice them.

She took a taxi to Kingsford Smith, then waited outside the Customs terminal. She had timed her arrival neatly but still knew she could have a long wait; Customs was always unpredictable.

She was surprised when the door opened almost at once and Link came out. Yet should she ever be surprised with that man? Undoubtedly he knew someone who could hurry him through first. Yes, that would be Link.

If his prompt appearance had surprised her it was nothing to her surprise at his greeting. Patently oblivious of an audience, he came over to Brit and lifted her up in his arms. She was embarrassed, but one glance at that dark, Indian-red face told her that he was not.

"Why the coyness?" he teased. "I'm your husband, remember?" He kissed her. Then he held her at arm's length. "Good," he said, well satisfied, "you're a bit washed out. You've been pining for me. I didn't want to come back and find you bounding with health." He glanced around the terminal. "It almost seems a waste of time going back to the hotel seeing as we leave again tomorrow."

"Tomorrow?" she exclaimed.

"Hawaii." He said it with the usual impatience he adopted if someone did not keep up with his mercurial train of thought.

"But tomorrow.... You'll be too tired."

"I?" He laughed ... and Brit knew she had been ridiculous. This man would never be tired.

In the taxi he handed her the small parcel.

"Shall I open it now?" she asked.

"You'll wear it now. Can't have you going around without an engagement ring."

"What is it?"

"Open it up, Brit."

She did, wondering what he had chosen. He would select, she decided, something that to him was her. A warm ruby? A cool emerald? A quietly glowing pearl? The velvet box had been unfolded from its tissue now and Brit unsnapped the catch. She looked down at the ring, a ring with a stone she did not know but very beautifully set in tiny diamonds. She admired the setting, but it was the stone that fascinated her. "What is it?" she begged.

"An Alexandrite. You like it?"

"Oh, yes!"

"I do as well, even though it's a two-timer."

"What?"

He had put the ring on her finger by this time and now he slanted her hand to a darker section of the cab. Instantly the stone that merely had fascinated Brit before deeply enthralled her. It had changed its color to a lustrous purple. . . . No, it was a deeply shining green. . . . No, it was. . . .

"It's wonderful!" she exclaimed.

"It's a wonderful cheat. I chose it because it's you, Brit, you with your different faces for different people."

A little unevenly, she asked: "Which color am I, then?"

"To whom? To John?"

"To you?"

Abruptly he pulled her hand back to the brighter light. "There's no luminosity for me yet," he answered her.

When they arrived at the hotel, Brit went ahead with the porter who carried Link's bags while Link waited a few moments to speak with the proprietor. As they stepped into the elevator she could hear Link talking about Buenos Aires, of his impressions.

But the pair must have spoken of other things after she had ascended, for when Link came into the suite some time later his face was thunderous. She wondered why—but wondered only briefly.

"Now I know why you look so peaky," Link stormed. "Once again you haven't been eating."

"I have been," she assured him.

"Don't lie to me, Brit. Mr. Devon tells me you haven't been here for lunch or for dinner for almost a week. Lunch I can allow for. You could have it in a park. In some arcade."

Brit gave an involuntary start at that, but he did not notice.

"But dinner is the meal of the day," he went on, "and you chose not to eat it, even though I left strict instructions that you should. Why, Brit?"

"I didn't feel like it," she evaded. "I—I wasn't hungry."

"Why?"

"I've just told you, Link. I wasn't hungry."

"No, not that, girl, but why weren't you hungry? Could—could it have been that you didn't feel like food because I wasn't here with you?" He said it a little roughly. If Brit had looked at him she would have seen another kind of hunger, not a hunger for food, in his lean dark face.

"Yes," she agreed. She would have agreed to anything to save a scene, for she sensed now that the fact of Simeon would create a scene.

"Brit." Link was pulling her to him, his lips were pressing down on hers, pressing down as they never had before, not at the air terminal, not even on their wedding night. "Brit, my girl, my girl. It's been awful away from you, it's never going to happen again. Not ever again." Now the lips were in the crook of her throat. How luminously brown his skin was, she thought, surprised.

She felt him leave her to lock the door. She heard him draw the curtains.

"Not ever again," Link said.

He came back to her.

CHAPTER NINE

HAWAII WAS A RED HIBISCUS. Hawaii was brown bodies gleaming in the sunlight as they skimmed in canoes over sapphire water. Hawaii was purple mountains, fold upon fold of purple mountains looking down on freeways, soaring apartments, green palm trees and yellow sand. Hawaii was a touch of silk.

As she had had this last impression, Brit, of course, had thought at once of Simeon, Simeon who might be here, too, and who would think of Hawaii as silk, just as she did.

She and Link had reveled in it for a week now. Ten hours after leaving Sydney they had had their first glimpse together, since Link had seen it all before, of the fabulous islands. Looking down, they had seen Kahului, and then Pearl Harbor on Oahu.

After they had skimmed in they had joined other passengers and entered a quaint bus. There was a procession of buses, all joined together, and they had moved off in a single file. Leis had been placed around their necks; pink carnations today, the pretty hostess had said, tomorrow perhaps white oleander, or wild yellow orchids. When Link and Brit had reached their hotel their room had been massed with flowers and ferns.

They had both been weary enough to rest until evening, and then they had strolled out to see the shops, every conceivable type of shop, parking areas serving them with space for thousands of cars.

After dinner, eaten by a tinkling fountain that filled in the listening space with its own silver music, when the guitar players paused, a dinner at which Brit was introduced to the famous coconut pie, they drove to a point above the city to look down on the old Iolani Palace, the brilliantly lit hotels fringing Waikiki Beach. Link paid off the taxi and they walked back under banyan trees so thick that the navy blue night sky was only etched here and there between the dense leaves. There was a heavy honey smell in the air. Frangipanni, said Link, or jasmine.

He had his arm linked in hers, and Brit let it stay there. She could barely see her way ahead, and anyway, it was that hand-holding kind of night.

"A lovers' night," Link told her.

Later in the hotel room, the doors flung wide open to the small patio to frame a moon, stars and a corner of rustling palm, Brit could almost have believed that. She fell asleep in Link's arms.

They went sailing in Kailua Bay. They drove around the island to Waimea where the big waves break, some thirty feet high, and here they watched the surfers.

That night they did not return to their hotel, but stayed in an old Hawaiian inn that had enchanted Brit. It was cool and green and quiet, deep in milky frangipanni and crimson poinciana, with a ceiling of woven bark and a grass matting floor. Fountains played in enormous shells.

Link bought Brit a muumuu and insisted she wear it. Also a hibiscus on the correct side of her head.

"Because you're married now."

If she had forgotten she would have remembered again on that velvet evening. Just outside their room a bird sang in a bamboo, and suddenly Brit knew she was trapped deep, trapped in something else as well as all this beauty; she felt herself enfolded, she felt a moment grow into timelessness. She knew a strange, sweet, inexplicable joy. And when she wakened she was still in strong yet tender arms.

"Good morning. Have a happy day," Link smiled. He added: "That's the authentic Hawaiian greeting."

She nodded, suddenly blissfully happy, though not understanding it. "Good morning," she said. "Have a happy day."

When Link said later that he had business to do, that for the next few days she must amuse herself, she looked at him in reproach before she realized it.

"Do you have to?" she asked.

"I always have to. How else can I buy you coconut pies, you little nong?"

Nong was not one of the words she had told Simeon about. Simeon! He seemed a long time ago now.

"All the same I appreciate your concern," Link grinned. "It makes you sound like a wife. Wives, I'm told, always complain when they don't receive full attention." He took out his wallet and handed her a roll of notes. "Go shopping," he smiled.

They returned to Waikiki Beach Hotel, and Brit enjoyed herself poking into small antique shops, eating at different national restaurants, buying souvenirs and swimming in the deliciously warm water. She learned to string flowers into leis. She was shown how to float with snorkel and goggles, the only way to experience a new exotic water world. She ventured into native markets, native eating houses.

While Link negotiated for more coconut pie wherewithal for his missus, or so he said, Brit looked beyond the reef to Molokai (the Friendly Isle) and Lanai (the Isle of Pineapples).

Link was home most evenings and once when he was late Brit surprised herself with her unease. What had happened to him? The cars here moved at a terrific speed—had something happened to Link?

When he came in she actually started to run across to him, then stopped herself. He gave her a long probing look, then said: "No note of excuse, I'm afraid, but a reason. I met a Sydneysider. I'll tell you over dinner. Put on a

muumuu and wear your hibiscus to prove you belong to
me—we're going to Lobster House."

Lobster House had the background of lovely Mariner
Bay. There were flares on the wharf and they lit up yachts,
launches, cruisers and fishing boats, all rocking gently now
at anchor.

The restaurant was in the form of an old boat, decks,
both upper and lower, simulated cargo in casks and crates,
many riggings and ropes. The table Link selected had its
own porthole and was lit by a red lantern. The menu was
seafood, crab, lobster, many varieties of fish. The ever-
present pineapple was served with each dish.

Brit smiled over the doggy bag she was handed for
uneaten food. Doggy bags, Link explained, were just that,
though he wondered if doggies ever received them. "More
likely they're used for that hunger that attacks you in the
middle of the night."

"I'm always asleep in the middle of the night."

"Yes, little one, I know that." He smiled, and she wondered if he did know, if he had watched her while she slept.

He ordered coffee and two daiquiris to have with it, because the seafood left a salty taste in the mouth.

"Rum," he interpreted to Brit of the daiquiris, "with
fresh Hawaiian lime." She tasted hers and proclaimed it
delicious.

After he had rolled a cigarette, he said: "I met this Sydneysider. Funny that, Brit, however international you are
you still instinctively turn to your own."

"Was he your own? It was a male, I'm presuming?"

"Yes. Male."

"Then was he? I mean, so many people you meet are
never your own."

"You'll like this fellow. Come to think of it"— looking
across at Brit "—he's your type."

"What's that?"

"Quiet. I could almost say gentle. But a real man for all that. But never—" seriously, no smile at all "—a roughrider."

"You don't forget that, do you?" she said.

"Tell me when *you* do."

"Is this man you encountered in your line of business?"

"No. We met over a coffee break I was grabbing. He was grabbing one, too. Like us, he's over here for a few weeks."

"But, unlike you, only on vacation?" she said meaningfully.

"The nagging wife again!" But Link grinned as he said it. "No," he went on, "as a matter of fact, he, too, is sandwiching in some business. But he has more spare time than I have, and seeing as he's by himself, I thought it would be good if he spent that time with you."

Brit looked irritated. "You might think that, but I mightn't. I'd sooner be alone."

"I'd sooner you have someone with you. This island is idyllic, but even idyllic paradises can have a flaw."

"I'm perfectly safe," she insisted.

"So far." Link drank some more of his lime rum. "Don't be pigheaded, Brit, a woman is better anywhere with a man."

"Including a maternity ward?" she flung.

"If you like," he agreed calmly. "Just let me know before and I'll arrange it."

"You're impossible!"

He hunched his shoulders carelessly, then went on, "The two of you could visit some of the other islands—Kauai, Molokai, Lanai, Maui. I'm proposing this because I have to flip over to Los Angeles. I know I said I never would, but something has cropped up. Now don't put on your wifely look."

"I won't, I'll keep in mind you have to buy my coconut pies."

"You'll remember more than that, Brit," he said, "and that's a promise, not a threat." He smiled at her flushing cheeks.

"I can go with a serene mind," he said presently, "if you agree to be friendly with this fellow."

"The fellow may not want to be friendly with me," she pointed out.

A wind had sprung up and the gentle sway of the craft at the end of the wharf had augmented to a busy rock. The lighted flares moved up and down. A lighthouse somewhere sent a beam on a passing ship. Years ago missionaries sailed here, thought Brit; how had they felt when they had come from their cold north to the warmth of the islands? Like: "Good morning. Have a happy day," said with both arms outstretched as did the Hawaiians?

Link now was draining his daiquiri. He said: "I believe he will, though. I'm sure Sim will."

Sim. Sim? Brit sat very still a moment.

"Simon, I expect." She listened to her own voice, a cool, rather aloof voice.

"No, as a matter of fact. Something much less usual, though still an old name. His name's Simeon."

"Oh." Brit said no more.

"He's in the rag trade, though rags are the last thing you would call his creations. I'd bet on that without even seeing them."

"Why?"

"He's elegant. I really mean he's never rags."

"I wouldn't think he'd be your type," she commented.

"I wouldn't think so, either, but we clicked at once."

"And you mentioned me?"

"You came in all the time. Talk about husband-obsessed wives, I'm one wife-obsessed husband!" he laughed.

"*I'm* not laughing," Brit pointed out. "Can't you see you're embarrassing me?"

"How? By talking about you? I like talking about you."

"By making arrangements for me." Brit added: "With this person."

"You'll like this person."

"Because you like him?"

"That seems as good a reason as any to me."

"Then not to me. I might take an instant dislike to him." Brit gulped when she said that. *How,* she thought, *how can I go on like this?*

"Well," Link said with sudden indifference, "you're seeing him whether you like it or not, you're going out with him whether you like it or not."

"Then what if I do like it?" she flung suddenly. "What if I like it—a lot?"

"Then that at least will be something, won't it? So far, Brit, you've been anything but a red hibiscus, more a cool rose."

"With thorns?"

"With thorns," he concurred. As she sat fuming, he went on: "I fly out in the morning. I'll be in L.A. till the end of the week. If it interests you at all I reckon this takeover I'm intending will assure you of crates of coconut pies."

"Meanwhile I entertain Mr. Simeon." She said that deliberately. It needn't be Simeon, though the coincidence seemed too strong a one.

"Simeon White." White was Simeon's name then, that is if it was him.

"I don't think I'll do it," she said.

"You'll damn well do it, Brit; you'll damn well do what you're told."

"Told by you?"

"Yes."

"And if I don't?"

Link caught the waiter's eye and signaled for the bill. They started to the door—then the waiter came running after them with Brit's doggy bag. She left it to Link to take and went on to the threshold of the make-believe old boat, finding no magic now in the rigging, the portholes, the gangplanks.

She looked back and saw that Link and the Hawaiian were talking together . . . and smiling. The Hawaiian gave her a quick glance, smiled again and said something to Link, then Link answered. He was laughing to himself as he joined Brit.

"I told him I would probably consume the contents of the doggy bag myself tonight as we'd had a quarrel."

"You what?"

"But he had an answer to that—fortunately in Hawaiian."

"You understand Hawaiian?" she asked.

"I've been here a number of times," Link reminded her.

"What did he say?" Brit demanded. "I mean the Hawaiian part?"

"Literally, you want?"

She looked at him and waited.

"Then," interpreted Link, "it was: 'Ah, friend, but all quarrels are sweet in the dark of the night.'"

She started walking quickly, but he hurried and caught up to her. "So," he finished, "we won't need our doggy bag." A liquid-eyed ragamuffin was sidling along the wharf. Link gave a whistle and sent the bag through the air. The small boy caught it deftly and raced off.

"Now—" and Link turned to Brit "—we'll see if our Hawaiian was right." He nodded to a taxi and gave the name of the hotel. Inside the cab he finished: "We'll see if all quarrels are sweet in the dark of the night."

IT WAS MORNING, and Link had left. Brit must have been asleep when he had gone, for she had heard nothing. She would not have known now but for the empty place in the bed and the quick note: "Good morning. Have a happy day." Link had added: "Also have a good breakfast."

That at least made her smile, for breakfasts here were
unbelievably large. They started, in Brit's case, with guava
juice, went on to pancakes and maple syrup, sliced turkey
eggs, fresh crumbly bread and a long pot of coffee. Have a
good breakfast, he had said!

She sat on at the patio table. She did not know quite
what to do. Link had let her know last night that he had
meant what he had said about Simeon White. She was to
meet him—or at least he was to meet her. She was to go
out with him.

Once again she had dared: "If I don't?" at Link, and
Link had silenced her with his lips.

But he had found a moment to warn: "Then I'll thrash
you, my darling, just as I'll thrash that Benjamin."

"Who's Benjamin?"

"He was our waiter at the Lobster House, the one who
advised me that all quarrels are sweet in the night. Yet
shall I judge him too promptly? Too soon? Stop quarreling
with me, Brit." He had drawn her inevitably to him.

Now she drank more breakfast coffee. Perhaps if she
went out as soon as she was finished she would miss Simeon; no one moved around early in this Hawaii. It
seemed inevitable that she meet him eventually, but the
longer she put it off....

She drained the coffee, then tried to get up. But she
found herself sitting on. Sitting on. She tried again, still sat.
I must go, she willed herself, *I must. Link will be mad with
me, but it's much better to avoid something, or at least to post-
pone something, until....*

Then she saw it was too late. She saw Simeon moving
among a thicket of palms only some fifty yards away,
stopping, as Simeon would, to unfold a leaf, to look into its
green hollow.

There could still be time if she moved at once, if she
went down to the beach. Simeon would inquire at the desk,

but if she wasn't in the hotel then—then she just couldn't be found.

But he had seen her. He was hurrying, almost running, across the perfect green lawn.

Brit had left the table to go to him. They met under a bank of brilliant creeper; he had come down some twisting steps beneath fern and bamboo and had crossed to the sun-drenched wall.

"Brit!"

"Simeon!"

"It's a dream!" he exclaimed.

"It's true," she smiled.

"It's a dream that I'm here...and so are you."

CHAPTER TEN

BRIT AND SIMEON went over to the terrace table. Th
waiter had cleared away the remains of Brit's breakfas
and now the tall Hawaiian came across and smiled at S
meon.

"Good morning. Have a happy day. Coffee, perhaps?"

"Coffee." Simeon smiled back at the man.

When he had gone the two under the gaily striped un
brella simply looked at each other.

"It's a dream," Simeon said again.

"It's true," Brit repeated herself.

Seats under other umbrellas were filling up aroun
them, so Simeon guided their conversation into less pe
sonal channels. He looked around him, looked at the shim
mering quality of the morning. A very good morning; suc
good mornings had to be happy days. Simeon said so, ad
ing: "I want to capture it; I want to put sunshine, blu
water and green palms into the swing of a dress. Does tha
sound ridiculous to you?"

"No, Simeon," Brit assured him.

"If I had been Gauguin in Tahiti I would have sough
out a special kind of pink. I'm not Gauguin, I'm Simeo
White taking a working vacation in Hawaii and wanting t
express myself in—well, in a rag." He looked ruefully an
humbly at Brit.

"No, never a rag," Brit refused, and she remembere
that Link had refused that, too.

Simeon said gratefully: "You believe in me, don't you?"

"Oh, yes."

The coffee came and they sipped it silently for a while.

Then: "Why, Simeon?" Brit asked. She knew he would understand what she meant.

"Why didn't I say to your husband: 'I know your wife, Mr. Wayland, she modeled for me last week, we dined together, we—'"

"Yes, Simeon. Why?"

"I don't know," he replied.

A long moment went past. Then: "I simply don't know, Brit," Simeon said again. "I just liked him—he's quite terrific, but then you'll be aware of that, of course."

"No, I don't believe so."

"Then wake up, Brit," Simeon advised.

"This is still not telling me why you started an intrigue, Simeon."

"Did I? I suppose I did in a way. But I just couldn't say it somehow. I couldn't, Brit."

"Yet *why*?" Brit still persisted. "There was nothing to tell. I mean, it could sound like something, but really it was nothing, nothing at all."

"*I* know that," nodded Simeon, "*you* know that, but Link—"

"Oh, so you two are on first-name terms," she observed.

"Yes—" he nodded "—we took to each other at once."

"And you think Link would not know it?" she probed, returning to their discussion.

He shrugged. "That could be. It could happen like that. And—well, I just liked him too much, Brit."

"Yes, you said so before."

"I like him so much," continued Simeon after a short pause, "I wouldn't want him hurt."

"He couldn't be, he's not the type, he's—he's a roughrider."

"Oh, no, my dear," Simeon protested.

"You don't know him—I do. Anyway, Simeon, what was there to tell?"

"Nothing, as you said."

"Then—"

"Nothing apparent. Only—"

"Yes?"

"Only that I love you, Brit.'" Simeon had lowered his voice, but he still spoke clearly and she heard every syllable. "Only," he continued still in the low but distinct voice, "if I told him anything, anything at all, I know that love would have to show. It must show, Brit."

"But, Simeon—"

"I'm sorry. That's how it is."

She looked at him incredulously. "Simeon, I can't believe you."

"I love you, Brit," Simeon said again.

They finished the coffee; they walked side by side down to the beach. They were amused—or they would have been amused if they had not been preoccupied—with the grass matting to walk on right to the water's edge. "So different from the beaches of Australia," Brit said absently.

"Yes," nodded Simeon just as absently, "sand between the toes is an expected thing there."

They sat on a rock and watched the bathers. There were no large waves at Waikiki, the sea swirled softly up and withdrew again in a long blue sigh.

"You don't really love me," Brit endeavored rather weakly. "I was just the first one to do justice to your new fabric."

He leaned across and pressed her hand as it cupped and then trickled out sand. "We'll leave it at that, then. Thank you for the reason, Brit. Now what do we do this week?"

"What do we do?"

"Link has asked me among other things to take you interisland. He has been there himself and is particularly anxious that you go as well."

"Haven't you been before?"

"No. I've only ever visited this island, this Oahu. The

tourists' island, you could say. Apart from Honolulu I really know very little, yet that little was sufficient to lure me back. I barely even know Waikiki."

"Then I'll show you that," she offered eagerly.

"I hoped you would. Then when we finish we can see Maui and Hawaii, Hawaii that gave the group of islands its name. We'll be seeing them for the first time at the same time. I like that. Do you?"

"Yes," said Brit, cupping more sand. She wondered if all this was really happening.

FIRST OF ALL it was Brit's turn to show Simeon what she had discovered here. Although he had been a visitor before she had, he had not, as he had confessed, seen much.

"Then what did you do with yourself?" Brit teased. "Daydream?"

"As well as sketch. And I hope now to sketch you. With—" quickly "—a view to a new design. I told your husband so and he approved."

"Did he?" said Brit, a little surprised. "What did you say?"

"I didn't actually say, I showed. I handed him my sketchbook and at once he offered your services."

"Yes, Link is very good at doing things with other people."

"You sound bitter. Don't be bitter, Brit, it's not you."

"I know," she rebelled, "I'm Greek for sweet; I'm a sweet maiden."

"You are indeed." His smile dissolved her rancor.

They decided to start their explorations that afternoon. They began by doing all the little shops, Simeon being particularly interested in the silk-screening the islanders presented so enchantingly. It seemed sacrilege, Brit sighed once, to come out after fingering material with the feel of petals as well as the design of petals to eat at an authentic

Japanese restaurant where they cooked their own steak and onions at the table and dipped it in the sauce of their choice, but that was Hawaii and particularly Honolulu.

They inspected the coral, the fish reserved in a bay enclosed by the reef, then decided at last it was time to see the other side of the Hawaiian Islands. It was not the Hawaiian face that most tourists see, and Brit felt excited as she boarded the interisland plane with Simeon. Link had recommended Maui and Hawaii as real Pacific islands, undisturbed much by the visitor and the busy trend of city life.

It was not far across, and because they had not come to see a town, any kind of town, they made at once for the mountains, passing pineapple fields on the way tended by Japanese planters wearing large coolie hats. There were also cowboys on horses, but their driver said that here they were called paniolis.

Simeon had his heart set on seeing the crater Haleakala, a dormant volcano.

"Its name means House of the Sun," he told Brit dreamily. "Legend has it that the sun was once imprisoned there."

The volcano was some ten thousand feet and around the six thousand mark the trees became sparse and the bushes stunted; it seemed unbelievable after all the previous lushness. But it did not last long, for the simple reason that two thousand feet higher they could see nothing; they were part of a cloud. The driver pushed on, Brit could not have said how he did it, and then they were above the cloud and could look around again.

It was magnificent. It was clear up here, though halfway down clouds still hung to the mountainside. The driver showed them the distant island of Hawaii, the largest of the group so that it had given its name to them. He told them that unlike Haleakala, or House of the Sun, there the volcanoes did not sleep.

Brit stood a little behind Simeon as they looked down on Haleakala. What did Simeon see in the House of the Sun, she wondered. She only saw internal fire, rising and subsiding. But Simeon seemed fascinated. Instinctively he put out his hands.

"I thought I'd lost you," Brit laughed on their way down again.

"I felt at peace. Crazy, isn't it? I felt—I felt strong, Brit." He gave a quick, rather embarrassed laugh. "According to our brochure we now see three-hundred-year-old drawings. We sit under a hundred-year-old banyan tree."

Brit peered ahead. "I would like a cup of tea at that five-hundred-year-old edifice—or is it only four hundred and fifty?"

"It's the disused jail, so you won't have tea there, only ghosts."

But, as Brit presently declared, they were nice ghosts.

"No baddies, I think, Simeon, just roistering sailors or peace-disturbing natives."

"Now who's crazy?" he laughed.

They had found a tea place on a small bay; the water lapped rhythmically as Brit took up the pot and poured. The smiling girl had brought freshly sliced lime instead of milk. The tea was deliciously refreshing.

It was halfway to sunset. The mountains were putting on their purple cloaks but the sky was pink, red and bright orange. It was timeless, somehow. Although they sat alone there, Brit had the sensation that they were part of a large company of Hawaiians long gone, Hawaiians who, too, had listened to the silver lap of the water, looked at the purple, pink, red and orange.

They walked together back to the small inn that had been provided, companionably quiet, needing no words. Their hands brushed.

The next day they left Maui for the island of Hawaii, the

still-volcanic island. As they approached it they could see the volcanoes. Mauna Kea and Mauna Loa, Brit read from the interisland plane tourist brochure.

It had been arranged—by Link, who had done it all before—that they take the old road along the Honokao coast. There were a few other tourists in their group, and although they were all now on a friendly basis, Brit and Simeon were pleased when they were seated in a small car to themselves.

They rimmed tiny coves with dancing blue water, palm tree gullies and pineapple plantations. Guavas were there for the taking, and several times the driver paused and smiled as Brit tumbled eagerly out to eat the small, red, luscious fruit. She always chose guava juice at breakfast at Waikiki, and now she enjoyed the cherrylike globes that provided the luscious nectar.

Bamboos encroached on them now, waterfalls splayed above them. The island of Hawaii proved totally different to Brit; it had a strangely arresting beauty, not at all like its pretty sister isles. For instance Mauna Kea, which rose over thirteen thousand feet out of lush jungle, showed a powder puff of snow. Snow in the tropics, she marveled.

The party was to stop overnight in yet another Hawaiian inn. This pleased Brit, for although she reveled in the American-type luxury of the Waikiki hotel, these woven bark refuges, with their cool, their quiet, always a fountain playing in a huge clam, delighted her.

This inn did not even serve its meals at conventional tables, but always spread what was offered on long benches under trees.

What was offered at the evening meal astounded the party. Pig that had been marinated in shoyu and ginger awaited them, freshwater shrimps, mussels and fish. Mostly the fish was raw, but delicately and exotically presented. There was liver, poi, huge baskets of papaya, ba-

nanas, melons and berries, and rush flagons of a very fruity
wine.

It was a heady wine, and when the guitars began to sing
it did not take much persuasion for Brit to join the other
ladies in their group in a lesson in the hula. As Brit learned
all about the gentle swinging of the hips, the movement of
the hands and fingers, the ripple of the arms, she smiled at
Simeon watching her, swaying as the other onlookers did
to the intoxicating rhythm.

While the guitars rested, or rather by the sense of rising
excitement while they got ready for a star turn, Simeon led
her to a tiny cascade at the side of the inn. It was a paper
moon and tinsel kind of night, almost too unreal. Brit said
this as she leaned against a pandanus and caught her
breath again. The hula was very exhausting.

Simeon seemed a little abstracted. When he spoke it was
seriously, not with a smile as Brit had, not in tinsel strain
to match the tinsel night.

"It's all so timeless," he said. "I feel I'm in the past, the
present and the future all at once. If anything happened to
me it could have happened yesterday, today or tomorrow."

"Oh, Simeon, don't talk like that!" she begged.

"I'm not unhappy. Don't think it, Brit. This last week
has been the happiest week of my life. You've done it." He
touched—barely touched—her hand.

Presently he said: "I have no one, you know, Brit, no
brothers, sisters, no relations at all."

"Sometimes," Brit tried to banter, and thinking to herself as she spoke that she spoke a near-truth, as regarded
Cara, anyway, "one is better off that way."

"Why I said that, about my being alone, was to explain
to you what I've done."

"What's that, Simeon?"

"An impertinence in its way, I suppose, but—"

"Come," called a honeyed Hawaiian voice. "Come!" A
guitar twanged a summons as well.

In pairs, the group returned to the circle. Lines of lovely dusky girls were waiting for the music. When it came, Brit had to smile to herself at her hula attempt compared to their art.

Then she was not smiling. She was watching enthralled as a quite huge, quite elderly Hawaiian woman came into the center of the dancers, and then began the swaying movements. Never had Brit seen such beauty, such grace, such tender feeling. Simeon had spoken of timelessness, and this, she thought, was the essence of time itself. She clasped Simeon's hand as she watched the story of Hawaii, the culture of Hawaii, the soul of Hawaii, unfold.

When it had finished, no one seemed to want to talk. Even the guitars whispered into silence. When Brit said "Good night, Simeon," he nodded his understanding and left as well.

It was only a moment before sleep that Brit recalled Simeon's: "Why I said that, about my being alone, was to explain to you what I've done."

What had Simeon done, she thought drowsily. A great pandanus leaf disengaged itself from its parent tree and fell on the roof of the grass hut. Brit did not hear. She was asleep.

THE VOLCANO KILAUEA was throwing molten lava into the air. It only erupted yearly, at the most twice a year, and then briefly. This time it was a little more restless, their guide had said, and had overflowed the crater so that at night a glittering red snake ran into the sea. No, he smiled to nervous tourists, it was safe.

When the explosion occurred, many of the tourists gravely doubted this. It happened late in the afternoon on the day before their return to Honolulu. Some of them were out in small boats, some of them were beachcombing. Brit and Simeon were sitting under a tree.

At the sound all eyes turned at once to Kilauea. A fountain of fire was rising skyward; it subsided, then it rose again; there were a few rockets of crimson spray.

The guide went from group to group assuring each that it was nothing; the goddess was simply a little annoyed, simply showing off, but that was all.

And it would have been all—save for the minor earthquake the eruption aggravated. Or did the earthquake aggravate the eruption? Even scientists later could not agree which came first.

One moment Brit was saying to Simeon of the crater flare: "It's scary, but it's beautiful in a way," and the next moment she was looking horrified at the scene before her. It was all aslant. The little bay was crooked. The banks around the bay bent. There was a rumbling beneath them in the ground. Brit saw some vines collapse, spilling orange petals over grass that all at once had gaping cracks in it. She saw the path to the inn heave up then down like a mythical dragon.

She did not see the tree under which they sat uproot, and all she felt when it happened was a soft flurry of leaves over her face.

But Simeon did not know about the leaves; he only knew the bruising tree trunk bursting down on him. When Brit parted the branches, moved away the twigs, he seemed all right, just a tiny wound in the side of his head. It was an unimportant-looking wound, only an inch or so of congealing blood.

"Simeon!" she cried.

He did not answer.

"Simeon...*Simeon*!" she screamed.

He opened his lids, and Brit, horrified, could see that his gaze was blurring, his lips stiffening, his eyes beginning to glaze. "Oh, no!" she cried.

He was trying to say something, and she leaned over to

hear him. There were only two words she could decipher. They were " .... for you."

Then Simeon died.

CHAPTER ELEVEN

BRIT WAITED on the island of Hawaii until Link flew over. The rest of the party had hurried away, even though the area had been declared quite safe. There had only been one victim of the phenomenon—an earthquake at the same time as an eruption had been termed a phenomenon—and that was a sad misfortune, the authorities regretted. Had the pair not sat under that particular tree....

One victim—Simeon. Simeon White of Australia. No dependants. No one at all. Brit had answered all this to the officials.

"We have had word from your husband, Mrs. Wayland," they said gently. "You are to remain here until he crosses over, then he will take you back himself. Please don't worry. Nothing more will happen. You are quite safe."

Yes, she was safe. She was also alive. But Simeon....

"Why?" she asked herself "Why—" It was the first thing she asked Link.

"I don't know, darling." In her numbness Brit did not hear that darling. "I'm as upset as you are. Even though I wasn't here, and not part of the tragedy, I still feel I'm in it as well. Also—" a painful pause "—I feel responsible that he came here at all."

"Why did he?" she asked dully. "I mean, why did you tell him?"

Link hunched his shoulders. "I wanted you to see the islands and it seemed a good opportunity for you to see them with him. My God, when I think that I might have been sending you to your death as well...."

Common sense prompted Brit to tell Link not to think that way. Simeon had been keen to come; he would probably have come, anyway.

"I suppose so." Link was still distressed. Presently he asked: "How did you find him as a man?"

"Oh—he was nice."

"I told you so. I knew you two would click."

"Perhaps if we hadn't—" Her voice broke.

Now it was Link's turn to tell Brit to be sensible. After he had repeated several times that it might have happened wherever Simeon was, whoever he had accompanied, he asked: "They said—the report said—you two were sitting under a tree?"

"We'd seen everything. It was the last day; some of the group were boating; some were combing the beach. We were just sitting and talking."

"Yes, he was an easy guy to talk to. Did you find that, too?"

Brit nodded.

"What happened then?"

"The crater was erupting; it does so once or twice a year. Then suddenly there was this explosion, though the scientists say now the quake happened first."

"It's hard to establish," said Link, nodding. "The quake was actually subterranean, some miles away, and only this island received any effect. What else, Brit?"

"Everything aslant," she described, "everything bent or the wrong way around. The path to the inn looked like the Loch Ness monster."

"Yes?"

"Then—then the tree was uprooted, I expect. I never saw it, I only felt leaves on my face."

"Poor Simeon got the trunk on his chest and head."

"Link, don't—please don't!" she begged.

Link was silent a moment. "Had you got to know him very well?" he asked.

Brit paused, then said: "No."

"A pity. He would have been a good friend. Did he speak before he died?"

Again Brit paused. Then she said: "No."

She could not have said why she spoke these lies. Unless, she thought, it was the tightness in her, the soreness in her heart. She wanted no probing finger on that sore heart. Not yet.

"We'll go home," Link said.

"You mean fly back to Honolulu?"

"Home. Sydney. You can occupy yourself fixing up our flat. I'm sorry, Brit, that it turned out like this. I'm not making much of a success of your honeymoon, am I? Away half the time. Having this happen."

"You didn't make it happen."

"No," he said bleakly.

She wanted to comfort him, to say something to take that strained look away from his face. But she was too saddened herself, and—she had to admit it—she simply did not know how to reach Link. *I don't understand him,* she realized. *I don't even know how to approach him. He is my husband, but I don't know.*

They flew out the next day. At Brit's suggestion they went straight to the flat. She felt her hotel days were finished. Besides, the place had too many ghosts of Simeon. For over a week she had come busily and happily down the hotel steps to walk to the arcade to Simeon's. For over a week she had returned from Simeon's. She wanted to get away from the place.

"It's rough," warned Link of the apartment. "To suit," he added obliquely, "a roughrider."

"I'll tell you when I see it," she said.

When she saw it, Brit was surprised.

It was decorated in the usual down-to-earth tans and browns that men went in for, but there were some surprising touches. A French walnut bureau, for instance. A Georgian dropside table. A soft pink marble washstand.

Also—a photograph.

Brit stood before it and stared in disbelief. It had started out as one of Cara and herself taken years ago. It had been taken, Brit estimated, just around the time of her acceptance by St. Hilda's. Cara had been a schoolgirl, and that was probably why she had been cut off. Only Brit remained—a brown moth of a Brit, very little different, she thought ruefully, from what she was now. She wondered why on earth Link had kept it. She shrugged and began looking around again.

There was a study positively bursting with books. That, she knew wisely, must be left strictly alone. There was a large dining-cum-lounge room, a small compact kitchen. There was only one bedroom.

She had reached the bedroom now, tan and brown as the rest of the apartment, and was mentally adding some soft yellow, perhaps some nasturtium to provide the color that a woman must have, when he spoke from the doorway. She had not heard him knock to be let in, but she presumed that when he had deposited her here while he checked up on the office he had taken a key. Anyway, he stood there.

"Do you think it will do until we can find something larger?" he asked. "Perhaps build our own place?"

"It's an excellent bachelor apartment," she conceded, "but a little confined for more than one."

"Not when you're in love," he said tauntingly. "Even a single bed is ample when love sleeps there as well."

Aware of her reddened cheeks, she remarked: "Most flats are now two-bedroom units."

"One room is enough." Again he said it tauntingly, and she knew he was laughing at her.

"Go ahead with any redecoration, any color alteration," he tossed. "Although we won't be here long we might as well be as happy as any wall wash will give us."

"I like the color. I like the autumn shades."

"Good. Everything else suit you?"

"Not," Brit said, "the out-of-date photograph."

"Which one?"

"Are there more?"

"No. Only you. So you don't like it?"

"No."

"All the same it remains, Mrs. Wayland."

"Why?"

"It's a long story. I'll tell you one day. But meanwhile don't dare lay a finger on it. Understand?"

"I think I do. I think it's there to remind you what I was like when you bought me."

"Go on."

"Though why," she said desperately, "why you ever bought me is beyond understanding."

"That's another story I'll tell you one day."

"One thing," Brit sighed. "I haven't altered. I'm still father's brown moth."

"Your father—" he shrugged "—was a fool."

She turned angrily on him, but he spoke before she could.

"No, he wasn't a fool. He was too shrewd for a fool."

"Can my family be left out of this?"

"All your family can," he came back.

That brought Cara into Brit's mind, Cara who had still not written.

"She'll be all right," Link said irritably when she spoke of Cara aloud.

"It's weeks. You'd think she would have scribbled a note. Or—" a biting of Brit's lip "—that John would."

She was turned away from Link, but even turned away

she felt, if she did not see, his sharp whirl around. But h
said nothing.

"Go ahead," he directed her again. "Do anything yo
want to. Buy anything."

"As you buy anything that catches your interest?"

"Meaning?"

"Nothing."

"*Meaning,* Brit?" He started walking toward her.

Suddenly angry, not knowing why she should be, sh
flung: "Well, you bought me, didn't you? That photo—"

"What about it?"

"It's a record, isn't it, a record of the first day of you
purchase."

"Actually," he came in coldly, "I had seen you befor
that. But yes, you're right, I had told the school board jus
around that time."

"Why?"

"Because a school board has to be referred to, o
course."

"You know what I mean," she insisted.

"I do. You mean why did I pick you? Good lord, don
you think I often ask that myself?"

"Link—"

"I ask myself why in hell did I look a second tim
at—at—"

"At a nincompoop, an idiot, an oaf, a nong—"

"Brit," he said with maddening triumph, "you *do* liste
to me!"

"You—you . . . ." She could say no more. She flung her
self angrily into the next room, expecting him, with hi
taunting tongue, to follow.

He didn't. He went out. She heard the door shut.

And with it, as often happened, and it dismayed her, sh
knew a curious disappointment, an anticlimax to some
thing that hadn't happened . . . and she wished had.

She wished had? *Oh, heavens,* Brit thought, *I can't, I don't, I mustn't feel like that for that man.*

Yet "that man" was her husband. If she felt any unreality about it during the day, Brit felt none at night. On their wedding evening he had said: "John. The nice gentleman. Ghosts, all of them."

And, remembered Brit, they had been. There had been no man between herself and Link. She shivered a little and made herself concentrate on the room.

She had not gone to the arcade salon. Why should she? There had only been Simeon really to take her there. She had liked the girls, but that was all it had been, just a liking.

She was a little surprised then when Hilary Malling phoned her.

"Mrs. Wayland, we thought you'd be around."

"Why?" Brit started to ask, then stopped herself. It sounded a little insensitive.

"It would be very hard," she said instead. "As it must be for you."

"For all of us. He was a fine person. We all loved Simeon."

"Yes."

"Please, won't you come? After all, you should take an interest."

Should I, thought Brit. *But why? I liked Simeon, I liked him very much, but why should I . . . .*

"We, the girls and I, would like to see you. Later when some of the shock is over, do come around."

"Yes," Brit heard herself say. She put down the phone.

She absorbed herself in the redecoration, putting more into it than she felt actually, for after all it was only a place of bricks and mortar, but at least it was something to do.

She finished the sole bedroom— "One room is enough," he had said—then went to the lounge. She was pleased with the result, so pleased that she determined to tackle the study. She knew that a study was sacrosanct, but she still felt she could make something more of it than the brown enclosure it was now. If she was careful not to move a book, disarray a paper, Link might not mind her adding a touch here and there. If it came alive, as she pictured it coming alive, he might even appreciate her work. And suddenly Brit knew she wanted Link's appreciation. She wanted his praise. She wanted to glow in that praise.

I am that fool, nincompoop, oaf, she thought in surprise.

She changed the carpet to a warmer color. She added a big black leather chair. The straight-hanging curtains were exchanged for tie-backs to let in more natural light. As a last thought she bought and placed a silver calendar on the desk.

Placing it into position, Brit disarranged Link's large green blotter. She straightened it to how he had had it before, then saw that the movement had disengaged a letter that evidently had been pushed under the leather flap.

She put the letter back.

Brit had gone on to something else—in fact it all could have been a movie double-take—when the significance of the name of the addressee on the letter came to her.

Miss B. Smith. For several moments that meant nothing; she had become accustomed now to Mrs. Wayland. Then—Miss B. Smith. She was—had been—that.

She went back and took the letter out. It was addressed to the flat, their old flat, so it must be hers. But how was it that she never had received it?

Then she remembered how Link had established her in the hotel. It must have come after her departure, and the landlord either sent it on or Link collected it himself. But if he had, why hadn't he given it to her?

She looked at the date. It had arrived before her marriage with Link, barely arrived, but it had still come before.

Had Link forgotten it? At a time like that you were likely to forget anything; but if so had he kept on forgetting afterward? He was an extremely cool man, he had everything in control always; she thought it unlikely that Link would forget.

In her absorption she did not hear him come in. She had been expecting him, and had looked forward to his pleased surprise, for the room did look nice.

But all he did was stand at the door and look at Brit looking at the letter.

"Been snooping?"

"I have not."

"Anyway, you've found it, haven't you?"

"Found what?"

"Found what you hold in your hand."

"Had it been lost?" she asked.

"Not lost, concealed. I never expected you to come in here."

"I know. I know studies are personal places—"

"Then why in hell did you intrude?"

She could have understood it if she had not been on the right side. Holding a letter addressed to yourself, a letter that never had been passed on, must make hers the right side.

"Did you forget to give me this?" she asked.

"No."

"You mean—you withheld it deliberately?"

"Yes."

"How dared you? Just how dared you, Link?"

"It came shortly before our marriage. I was letting nothing get in the way of that marriage. I didn't know what was in the letter, I didn't know who had written it, but I wasn't taking a chance."

"You're abominable!" she burst out.

"Yes," he agreed. "Well," he went on after a moment, "aren't you going to open John's letter?"

"I wouldn't know whose letter it was." He smiled thinly, and she said a little wildly: "I've never had a letter from John."

"Only written to him."

"Nor that, either, though it's no business of yours."

"It was no business," Link said. "It is now."

"Whoever wrote this letter—" Brit was turning the letter over "—wrote it before it was your business." She looked at the man. "Why have I only got the letter now?"

"I forgot it," he admitted.

"In the past weeks, perhaps, but when you actually received it?"

"Then," he admitted coolly, "I simply withheld it."

"You *what*?"

"I withheld it. I thought it might be John's, and I wanted nothing to upset my plans, I wanted no man standing between my bride and me. After that—" he shrugged "—I really forgot." He added: "You can believe that or not."

"I believe nothing from you," she cried. She looked down again at the letter, the letter with that telltale date. She looked at the stamp. It had been posted at....

"Open it," Link said. "Don't tease yourself."

"It's waited this long, it can wait longer."

"Open it, Brit."

"I'll open it when I please, and I don't please now."

"You'll damn well get this thing over. Either that or I'll open it for you myself. Read it out."

"You dare!"

"I mean it, Brit. Open it, I say."

She saw his angry eyes, his hard lips; she saw his half step forward. She opened the letter.

"Is it from—" he asked.

"Yes. John."

She said it dully. She was reading the letter, reading at first with joy, then with frustration, then with anger but anger at Link, never John. John had written:

My dear, my very, very dear, my darling, darling Brit. Can you forgive me for not being in touch at once? But I wanted to be sure of what I could offer you before I spoke out, before I told you what I've never told you—but have felt. I think, I pray, we both have felt.

When only Cara met me on the plane when I had expected you and Cara—yes, that's so, that's what she'd told me—I was nearly out of my mind. But it was too late. We'd left by then. Later Cara admitted to me what she had written to you ... that crazy marriage story. She did it, she said, to make sure you would make no move to stop her, but I really think she meant it so you would make no move to retrieve, or try to retrieve, any of the money. I was dumbfounded, Brit, so much so I could think of nothing, do nothing. When later I did regain my senses I knew how wonderful it would be if I could tell you of my success when I wrote about Cara's deception, tell you that any monetary loss you had sustained was now inconsequential.

Well, dear Brit, I *am* telling you, telling you that *Southern Cross* has been accepted, that I am on the upgrade at last .... But telling you most of all that I love you. Brit, I love you. As soon as I can I'm coming. Coming home to my girl.

Always—Your John.

CHAPTER TWELVE

BRIT COULD NOT HAVE said how long she stood there looking at the letter, John's letter; she could not have said how
long she still would have stood had Link not called to her.

"Are you sharing it?" he asked harshly, and the roughness stiffened her.

"No," she said.

"I could take it from you; you know that."

"Oh, I know it—" bitterly "—you can take anything you
want. You have the means to buy it, and if it's beyond
cost, you have the brute strength."

"Wouldn't strength do without the brute?"

"No," she said tonelessly.

He was rolling his cigarette, that old ritual once more.
She turned away as he licked the edges of the paper together, for some reason she could never bear to watch Link do
that.

"It's all right," he said cursorily. "I've finished." Brit
flushed vividly. Why did this man always know, she
thought.

"I suppose a gentleman would withdraw quietly," Link
said. "Leave you to read it again. Only—" a pause "—I'm
not a gentleman. Tell me what it contains, Brit."

"I won't."

"In that case I'll have the letter." He actually began to
cross to her.

"No," she said. Then she relented: "If I tell you, will
that do?"

"You mean cut the love and kisses?"

"John might not be a writer, but he's not as banal as that."

"Give me the general trend." His voice was harsh again.

"It was all a lie about John and Cara," Brit reported dully. "Cara had told John we both would be on his plane, supposedly surprising him. He had expected us."

"Why should Cara do that?"

"It would make the marriage part more convincing to me, I expect, two on a plane together."

"You mean—" a pause "—that that's the lie you're talking about?"

"Yes."

"That he didn't intend marrying her?"

"No."

"But he did intend marrying you?"

"In time. If he made a success."

"And this letter says he has?"

"Yes."

The silence was a long one this time. When Link spoke it was about Cara once more. "Why did that archdemoness tell such a story?"

"She needed the money, I suppose, *all* the money. By involving John in the way she did, she knew I would be too wretched to do anything."

"I see. A bright little button, that sister of yours."

"Oh, Cara's bright," Brit said.

"The thing that bugs me is why your swain didn't get in touch at once. Why didn't he come back? At least why didn't he cable?"

"He wanted to be a success. He was only thinking of me."

"Well, take it like that if you want to, but in my book it suggests a laggard lover."

"John is not!" she said hotly.

"Laggard is one who loiters behind the others, or—" significantly "—the other. Singular. You could say a come-late. My dear Brit, your John was a come-late."

"Yes. You saw to that," said Brit.

"I saw to it because I had made my plans and there was a chance the letter could delay them."

"Delay!" she said in contempt. As though John's letter would only "delay." Why, it would have put an *end* to it all.

"I think you're trying to tell me that it would be something stronger than delay," Link came in. "In which case I'm glad I did what I did."

She looked at him curiously ... and, though she was unaware of it, a little piteously. Why was this man always so brutal? He had had a bad childhood, but surely he had stepped away from that now. He wanted something better for himself than his parents had had, he had said so, but you don't reap a harvest from hard dry ground. Link, she almost called out, take off your armor, or at least show me a chink in the metal. Yet what did she want even with a softer Link? She had nothing for him. It was John; it always had been John. Simeon she had liked very much; she had wanted somehow to protect him, but John—what did it matter then how hard was this man?

"That's all you have to tell, then?" He said it almost disinterestedly. "No plans for the future. That is—" a thin smile "—on the laggard lover's part?"

"There was a plan. He was coming home to marry me."

"Too bad." It was almost drawled. Picking up a sheaf of papers, Link went casually out.

Suddenly Brit wanted to run after him, face him, tell him what she thought of him. Slap that unsmiling-smiling face.

Only, she knew, she would be slapped back.

She began mechanically on the room again, and as she worked, she worked, too, on a reply to John.

"...John, if only you had written earlier..."

"...John, why didn't you tell me at once?"

But when she wrote that night all Brit said was:

I'm married to Link Wayland, John. Can you tell me
about Cara? Should you meet her tell her to write. Tell
her the episode is over.

She had added: "You and I are over, too." Then she had
signed it simply: "Brit."

Link commended her work on the apartment. "You certainly have a touch. Though of course the unlimited re-
sources helped. Do you think you could have done as well
on John's stint?"

"It's not a stint!" she snapped.

"It is also not Wayland weight."

"Wayland, Wayland, Wayland!"

"Yes, Mrs. Wayland." Link smiled. "Tell me," he said,
"if I'd delivered the letter in time would you have—"

She had turned fully on him. "Yes, Link, I would."

"Would have waited for John or would have gone
through with it?"

"I would never have gone through with it." She said it
coolly and deliberately and unmistakably, and she wondered how she could speak like that when inside of her
there was a hot turmoil, no cool deliberation at all.

The next day he told her to have a divan put in his
study. He said: "I can't sleep with ghosts."

"But you're the one who said there would be no one between," she reminded him, wondering why she did.

"Put it this way—" the dry whisper of the tobacco in his
big palm again "—I'm older and wiser."

"Link, I'm not a child, I'm aware that as a wife it's my
duty—"

"My God, Brit, you know how to be cruel, don't you?
Duty." He stood looking down at her for a long moment.
Then: "Get that divan put in," he ordered.

A week went past. Two weeks. A letter came from John.

It was nostalgic, it was wistful, longing, regretful. Whether it had acceptance or not, Brit could not have told. She read it again and again, but she still did not know, yet John must have accepted, she decided, for he asked nothing more of her. The excitement of his success was helping him, she thought. He said that he would stay on a while yet in Europe. The company had asked him to, and he had declined before, but now .... He hoped Brit was happy, then left it at that. Then he said:

> Cara has gone to England to try her luck there. She's good, Brit, but there are dozens as good. Many better. I'm sorry if that upsets you, but it's well for someone to know the truth. To be frank I don't think Cara was cut out for a dancer, there are more than dreams in her pretty little head. At a rough guess I would say business would be her forte. Your father should have taught her bookkeeping instead.

Brit left the letter around. She wanted Link to ask her about it. She wanted to tell him that everything was finished .... She wanted to tell him quite desperately. But he didn't ask, so Brit did not tell.

She went out to see the girls at Simeon's and was surprised at the way they greeted her, just as if they had expected her to come, as though she belonged there. Hilary Malling even asked her advice over an order. When she left they wanted to know when she would be there again. Brit was puzzled, but she did not think much about it. *Then.*

But she thought about it that night.

Link was busy, had been busy for a week. He had told Brit that while the rush was on he would be eating in town. He was also sleeping more nights than not in the city hotel suite that he kept for himself or for overseas visitors, for most mornings Brit found the study bed had not been disturbed.

Brit had become used to it. In Link's present mood she had preferred it. When she reached the apartment tonight and saw his car and realized he was there, she felt first of all a swift gladness that she would not be alone, but a nervous uneasiness followed at once. The car was untidily parked, not the way Link usually did things. He must have been in a hurry to run up the stairs, she thought.

She went up the stairs herself. She unlocked the door and went into the apartment. Link was standing at the bar he had had installed, and he had a stiff whiskey in his hand. When he looked across at her she knew by the careless way he held the glass that there had been glasses before this one.

"Home from business, eh?" he greeted her.

She looked at him, confused.

"Home from Brit's, late Simeon's," he went on. "Or will you keep the old name?"

She still stared at him, then, when he did not enlighten her, she said: "Yes, I have been to see the girls."

"Your girls."

"Simeon's," she corrected.

"Now Brit's. Or—" he repeated his prior question "—will you keep the old name?"

"Link, what on earth are you talking about?"

Link said deliberately: "I'm talking about your little concern, Brit, your arcade boutique—salon—whatever you choose to call it."

"It's not mine. Simply because I go out to see Hilary and—"

"It *is* yours," he said harshly. "Don't lie to me, Mrs. Wayland. You know as well as I know—*now*—what Simeon did with his worldly goods."

"You're mad!" she gasped.

"Yes, mad to have believed you when you put up that pretense of not wanting to meet him over in Hawaii. 'I'd sooner be alone,' you said when I told you that you were to have a companion while I flew over to L.A. 'I'm perfectly safe.' Then: 'I might take a dislike to him.' " Link gave a short ugly laugh. He poured himself another whiskey.

"Then when I returned from Los Angeles and asked you how you found him it was: 'Oh—he was nice,' in an uninterested tone of voice. Tell me—" putting down the whiskey and crossing to take Brit's wrist in a hurting grip "—whom was the uninterest for? Me? To put me off the scent? Or that poor wretch now that you'd got what you wanted out of him?"

She tugged her wrist away. Leaning up, she caught him a blow across his cheek, but only a single blow. He grabbed her arm away and warned: "Do that again Brit, and by heaven you'll have it done to you."

"You shouldn't have said that," she muttered.

"But you did pretend uninterest, you did give the impression you had never met him. Admit it, Brit."

She was silent a moment, then she said in a low voice: "Yes, I did that."

"V to M?" he asked. "No, not view to matrimony, it was too late for that, but view to money, more of."

"No."

"Then why, for heaven's sake? Don't tell me you fell in love with him?"

"I liked him very much."

"I said love."

"Why shouldn't I love him?" she demanded.

"He is—was—not your type. He was a very good person, I would say, no devious undercurrents like Mrs. Wayland."

"Don't call me that!"

"But I can hardly call you Miss Smith," he reminded her brutally. "Not—now." His eyes flicked remindingly at her.

She started to turn away, then turned back. This was something that had to be cleared up now.

"Link," she appealed, "will you please tell me? It may seem that I know, but I assure you I don't."

"It takes a lot of believing, Brit," he answered seriously.

"Then believe."

He was silent a moment. "Even if I do believe you," he said presently, "even if you knew nothing of the bequest, as you assert, you still can't deny your lies and evasions."

"You mean giving you the impression that I hadn't met Simeon?"

"I mean that. Why, Brit?"

Why? There had been nothing to hide and yet she had not told him. But Simeon, too, had withheld from Link the fact that he had already met Link's wife. "I like him so much," Simeon had said, "that I wouldn't want him hurt."

But Brit could not say that because she did not like Link. No . . . *no* . . . and the sudden realization came so sharply, so poignantly that instinctively she put out her hand to the back of a chair to steady herself. . . . *I don't like Link.*

I love him.

"Brit, are you all right?" Link's voice seemed to come from a distance. She saw him looking anxiously at her. "Damned if I don't have to believe you when you say you knew nothing about Simeon's will," he went on, "for you certainly seem surprised enough. But you still have to answer for your pretence to me. For heaven's sake tell me, Brit, tell me why you made me think you didn't know the man."

Why? Why again? But this time Brit knew the answer, an answer that was too unbelievable . . . and yet it was true. She had pretended to Link not because she had been afraid of losing him. Because even then, though she hadn't known it, she had loved him. Loved Link Wayland! Loved the roughrider!

"Don't stand there concocting more lies." His voice came in angrily. "My God, Brit, have you no conscience at all?"

It was a splash of cold water. Brit felt herself recovering. She looked at Link. He didn't love her; he possessed her. Never once in their union had he said "I love you" because he was not interested in love, only in possession. He would not be interested now.

She heard herself say coolly: "I'd like confirmation of all this."

"Guthrie and Fenton are the law men. By some coincidence they act for me, too."

"But aren't wills a private affair?" Her voice was cold. She felt herself shivering, yet not from any chill but from what she had just discovered about herself. She looked at him obliquely, knowing he would put a different interpretation on that chilly note. He would deduce from it that she was questioning his prior knowledge of the affair.

He did deduce just that. He said: "Yes. Private. But then so is marriage. Guthrie and Fenton naturally thought that being your husband I was entitled to know."

"Before I knew?"

"They're an old-fashioned firm." Link shrugged. "They still believe the male is the head of the house."

"Can I see the will?" she asked.

"You'll have to see it," he said brusquely. "You'll have to sign a lot of papers, have to prove that you're indeed that legatee. But if it's so urgent right now I think I can tell you what you will read. I would say it would be: '... to my friend, Brit Wayland, I give, devise and bequeath....'"

He did not finish, or if he did Brit did not hear him. She had run from the room, from the apartment, from the building. She did not stop until she reached the street.

BRIT WALKED FOR MILES. She walked until it was dark. " . . . to my friend, Brit Wayland, I give, devise and bequeath...." She heard Link taunting her with it again. Simeon's will. Simeon's last wish. ". . . to Brit Wayland, I give, devise and bequeath...." And Link firmly believed if she had not exactly contrived this, then at least she had done nothing to avoid it.

Like failing, for instance, to tell Link in Hawaii that she knew Simeon already. Like merely telling Link after the tragedy that Simeon was nice.

Link was right; everything he had said of her had been true. Except the motive. Except the feeling. For the feeling she had had for Simeon had only been a gentle one; there had been nothing there apart from that. She truly believed there had been nothing, either, on Simeon's side, for all that he had said he loved her. Only a very deep gratefulness for her friendship. So deep, it now turned out, that he had made her his legatee. *Oh, Simeon,* Brit grieved, *you were too young to die yet.*

Little things came back to her as she walked along the darkling streets. People were coming home from work, as she had once. Those days seemed a million years ago now. So much had happened since. She recalled Simeon standing at the crater Haleakala, House of the Sun. She had been nervous, but Simeon had been engrossed. He had said: "I felt at peace. I felt strong, Brit." Simeon, who obviously had not been strong.

Then later, on that beautiful tinsel Hawaiian night, he had told her he had no one. When she lightly answered that sometimes one was better off, he had replied: "That was to explain to you what I've done."

Finally, when he had been dying, he had looked up and said two words. "For you." He had meant what he had willed to her.

Oh, Simeon, Simeon! Brit began to cry.

Because, even in an uncaring, homebound throng, tea
are noticed, Brit went home, too. She was relieved to se
Link's car gone.

She did not go out the next day. Link did not come.
was the same the day after, except that a check arrive
from her husband, presumably to feed and clothe her, sh
thought with rising anger. How dared Link, how dared h
treat her like this without letting her speak first? Oh, ye
he had heard her out, but had he *listened?* Did that rough
rider of a man ever listen to any other voice but his own?

The third day the letter from the solicitors arrived.
told Brit what Link Wayland already had told her, that sh
had inherited Simeon's. She was asked to come to the
office.

She left it several days and during those days anothe
check arrived from Link. What did he think she did wit
his wretched money? Eat it? Make paper dolls out of i
Even the first check was untouched as yet.

She phoned and made an appointment with Guthri
and Fenton. The firm, as Link had said, proved an ol
fashioned one.

Brit, on edge, still not believing what had happened, sai
pointedly: "Mr. Wayland acquainted me with all this b
fore you did."

Old Mr. Guthrie smiled paternally and answered: "A
he is your husband, my dear, we thought that would b
right."

It wasn't right, Brit felt like retorting, like wiping tha
kind of look off Mr. Guthrie's amiable married face. Be
cause, she would have liked to say, not all marriages ar
kind and amiable. Ours isn't. But the senior partner wa
reading what Link already had told her. "I give, devise an
bequeath...."

She barely listened. She barely listened when Mr. Guth
rie told her that the bequest was the salon only, that an

moneys had been otherwise accounted for. He advised Brit very strongly to go to the salon, spend some time there.

"For," he finished cautiously, "every business has two economic sides, Mrs. Wayland, the side to the customer and the side to the owner. Not always is the owner's side what the customer, or public, might think."

Brit nodded. She signed papers. Finally she got up, shook Mr. Guthrie's hand and left.

It was a week since she had seen Link. She wondered what he would do if she suddenly turned up at his office.

She didn't, of course; she went home, and there awaited a third check.

It was just too much. Brit collected the others and put them all under a paperweight in his study. At some time or other, she figured, he must come and see them. But he would not see her. She would not be here.

She packed her bag. She was recalling a small rooming house not far from Simeon's. She had walked past it a dozen times, and its vacancy notice was clear in her mind. It would do for a while.

She left no note. She simply walked out. But before she shut the door behind her, she looked around. Their first home, you could almost say, only a small one, but....

"One room is enough," Link had said. "Even a single bed is ample when love sleeps there as well."

Love?

Brit closed the door.

CHAPTER THIRTEEN

THE ROOM WAS DRAB. The apartment Brit and Cara had shared had been anything but a luxury one, but at least they had had their possessions strewn around—Cara's absurd dolls that she collected, Brit's favorite prints. This place was nothing.

But Brit considered she was lucky to have obtained so easily a corner to sleep in, though probably the drabness had seen to that. As soon as she had unpacked, she went down and bought a cheap meal, cheap because after she had paid the proprietor, who had insisted on payment in advance, there had been very little left. Little, anyway, when you had to consider all the tomorrows.

Brit smiled rather crookedly when she thought of those big checks waiting in Link's study. They would have paid for her room here for several months. For her meals, and not cheap ones. As to any other money—well, she simply hadn't handled any. Link had bought everything for her, bought too much; she had needed nothing. But when it came to actual money .... All she possessed now were a few American dollars left over from Hawaii that she had changed into Australian currency. That was all. Well, not to worry, she was the owner of Simeon's now, and tomorrow she must present herself there as the owner, not as she had presented herself before, as someone simply visiting the girls. She felt herself withdrawing nervously at the thought. What would they think of her? They had been Simeon's old and trusted employees; she was someone who had just come in at the end. Yet were they unaware? She recalled the way that they had greeted her, as though they had expected her to come. Hilary had said: ". . . after all, you should take an interest." It had puzzled her.

But she understood now . . . though if that made her wiser it did not make her happier. It had been all right, her thoughts ran wretchedly on, when she hadn't known what Simeon had done, but now that she was aware of her position, it was an ordeal. She wished desperately she did not have to go on.

Still, short of having the solicitors sell the place, she must comply, and certainly she must if she intended to carry on, and Brit did intend that. *What else*, she thought, *do I have?* She wished she could feel enthusiastic over it. It would be wonderful to hide oneself in work, forget everything else like career women seemed to do. *Only,* knew Brit, *a career woman I am not. Any interest I have in the executive side will have to be forced. I am what father always said: a brown moth.*

She went to sleep at last on the rather uncomfortable bed on that discouraging note.

She timed her arrival for midmorning. If she had turned up earlier, she thought sensitively, it could have looked as though she had come to claim what now belonged to her.

She had awakened hours ago, but had lain in the narrow bed staring at the drab room until she estimated the shop where she had bought her cheap dinner last night would be open for breakfast. She had washed in a discouraging bathroom along the passage, dressed, then gone downstairs. The proprietor had asked whether she would be staying another night, and when she said yes, he reminded her that all rooms must be paid for in advance. After she had paid, Brit decided that breakfast must be very meager since there were more breakfasts for other mornings to be bought.

She had sat over tea and toast for as long as she could,

then spent several hours in the park. A family on the next bench sat eating from a bag of buns, and Brit thought rue-fully that she could have eaten a bun, too. For an heiress—she was that, she supposed, in a way—she was in a decidedly bad monetary position. *Yet if I have a bun,* she thought, not far from hysterical laughter, *I'll have to buy that much less lunch.*

She looked at her watch, and decided she could now walk around to the arcade.

With every step she grew more nervous. She could see Hilary Malling looking a little scornfully at her. All the girls darting her slightly contemptuous looks. And why not? In their books she was a newcomer, a Johnny-come-lately, female version, someone who had maneuvered her way into Simeon's life, a life that had stopped soon after. Very convenient for the one to whom he had slanted his will, they would think.

"Mrs. Wayland . . . Brit!" There was no doubting the warmth in Hilary Malling's voice as she came out of the arcade to greet Brit even before Brit entered the boutique. The rest of the staff smiled welcomingly at her. Hilary made coffee at once, and they drank it in the room where Simeon had dreamed up his designs.

"Thank heaven you've come," the head assistant said. "This ship badly needs a helmsman." She smiled and cor-rected, "Helmswoman."

"But I'm not. I mean . . . . Oh, Hilary, I didn't know any-thing about any of this. Can—can you believe that?"

"About the salon? Of course you didn't. But I did, and I believe the girls guessed."

"But how? But why?"

"It's simple really. Simeon wanted you to have it. Just as simple as that."

"But why?" Brit asked again.

Hilary poured more coffee, took her time in creaming and sugaring it.

"Didn't the solicitor explain anything?" she asked.

"Only that I inherited the salon. Oh—" remembering "—he did say that Simeon's money had been accounted for."

"Exactly. Simeon wasn't rich, Brit, very far from it, but he did have a comfortable, if decidedly less than large, amount. Which—" looking quizzically at Brit "—he divided entirely among the staff."

"Oh, I'm glad to hear that," Brit said wholeheartedly.

Hilary heaved a sigh of relief. "Then I—we—are certainly glad to hear you say that. So many legatees could be resentful, could wonder why they hadn't received that very necessary cash."

"Necessary?" queried Brit.

"It is necessary—" nodded Hillary "—because business-wise this salon is by no means a gold mine. Never was. It was entirely because of Simeon." Her face grew soft. "We have a lot of outstanding debts, Brit."

"Tell me everything, Hilary," Brit begged.

"All of us here started with Simeon," Hilary complied. "Every one of us stayed. We also would have continued to stay. Simeon was that kind of person."

"Yes, he was," agreed Brit.

"Simeon was exceptional. His gift had to be recognized, and it was. But being recognized doesn't always bring in the money, Brit; also Simeon would never just make do, he had to have the best. To be a financially successful house you have to be careful here and there. In a lining, perhaps, or a button, or a cheaper thread. But never Simeon. Also, many of his designs were beautiful but not—well, not called-for. He would not bow to demand, he only followed his instincts, and they were exceptional but not always acceptable. When you go through Simeon's desk you'll find dozens of glorious sketches, dresses that elegant countesses would buy, but where in Australia—" Hilary made a rueful moue "—do you meet elegant countesses?"

"I see what you mean."

"There is a wonderful business here . . . but not exactly the kind of business Simeon dreamed of. There have to be practicalities as well as dreams. And that, I'm afraid, will be your job, Brit."

"Yet why me?" Brit looked at the older woman with frank eyes. "I don't know how you and the girls consider me, Hilary, but never at any time were Simeon and I—were we—I mean—" She flushed and broke off.

Hilary leaned over and took Brit's hand. "We know just how Simeon felt about you, Brit. Remember we'd all been together right from the concept; we knew each other like brother and sister. Remember, too, that Simeon left *us*, not *you*, his money. But he left you what he *loved*, Brit—the salon. He left it because he loved you."

"But I didn't—"

"We know that, too. Simeon knew. He knew how you felt about your husband."

Brit bit her lip. If Simeon had known, then it must have been remarkable intuition, for she herself had not known. Not then. Why, she remembered, she had even told Simeon on that first day in his boutique that it was not a "special" wedding. He had understood what she had meant.

"I still can't understand," Brit said presently. "There must have been something else."

"There was. Simeon was not strong. But I suppose you sensed that?"

"Yes, I did."

"If it hadn't happened like it has, then it would have happened fairly soon in some other way. He knew it. We did. And he had no relations."

"He had his good friends," said Brit. "He had them in his employees."

"But not one of them with capital," Hilary insinuated.

"Simeon knew you had that. He believed that if—when—it came to it, when he had to go, you could carry on. Employ the staff he already employed." Hilary gave a small sigh. "He never stopped thinking of people. He remembered us."

"No, he was everything dear," agreed Brit wretchedly. "But he was also very wrong."

Hilary looked questioningly at her.

"You see, I have no money," Brit explained.

"But—"

"My husband has it, yes, but that's not me."

"I've met Mr. Wayland," said Hilary. "He seemed to me to be the kind of person who would like to have a finger in all kinds of pies. I know from the papers it's not just the news world with him."

"He would like it. But it would have to be his finger only in the pie. Oh—" impatiently "—why talk in circles? The fact is, Hilary, I've left him. I don't want his money, I hate his money. I also—" deliberately "—don't want him."

"Brit—Mrs. Wayland...." Hilary began.

"I would sooner Brit, and if you're going to say: 'Are you sure?' then yes, I am sure. So—" a shrug "—I just have to make this work by myself, don't I?"

"Yes," Hilary Malling agreed. But there was a small doubt in her voice. Presently she said: "I'll leave you to go through Simeon's things."

Brit cried a little over Simeon's dreams, for that was what she called the piles of scraps of sketches pushed in his office pigeonholes. A girl reaching to pluck a blossom from a tree and the folds of her dress following her fluid movement. A girl on a hilltop with a wind blowing silken skirts so that the skirts became part of the wind itself. Oh, yes, Simeon had had a rare talent.

She was still sitting absorbed when Hilary brought in a lunch tray. The older woman's eyes fell on the picture that

Brit was studying now, for all Simeon's designs were that—they were more artistry than pattern. This time Simeon's model held a basket of oranges, and the lines of the frock were equally softly rounded as the globes of golden fruit.

Hilary half sighed. Brit looked up at her. Now she knew she understood. "Too beautiful?" she asked.

"Yes. That is if a thing can be that. You see, Brit, to keep this place going there had to be less of the fine seams and more of the—the—well, you know what I mean."

"Yes, I know," Brit said regretfully, putting away Simeon's last design. When Hilary had gone, she closed the desk. Closed up Simeon's dreams, she thought.

"Goodbye, my dear," she said softly.

BRIT FOUND CHEAPER LODGINGS. The room she had obtained when she had left Link had been poor enough, but it had functioned on a daily basis. Her new room was weekly, so more moderate still. It also gave Brit more scope to add a personal touch or two, make it a little less barren. Though very little, she thought ruefully, surveying it on the weekend after a day's toil on it. With nothing to work on, or work with, all she could hope to do with it was to make it not so much of a cell.

She had not heard from Link, but she had not expected to. She had read in the paper that he was making a flying visit to London. Probably he had gone without returning to the flat. If he had called he would have thought that she was out, or refusing to answer. He would not have seen the untouched checks. She supposed there would be more checks again poked under the door by the mailman. She had not stopped the mail.

She could have done with those checks now. She thought that rather desperately when the accounts came in.

"The trouble is," Hilary said tactfully when shown the accounts, "you're buying the wrong way." She added: "As Simeon did."

"Well, if Simeon did it—"

"Simeon did it because he hadn't the right kind of money to buy any other way."

"Neither have I."

"No," agreed Hilary significantly. "You see," the head assistant went on after a pause, "to buy more reasonably you must buy bigger."

"We're not doing well enough for that," said Brit.

This was true. Although people came and looked wistfully at the lovely things, because of the more expensive buying the goods were more expensive. It seemed a vicious circle.

"If only we could get a loan. It would be paid back in no time. There would be no risk," Hilary said once again.

"I can't," Brit answered in the same way as she had before.

At the end of the month when Brit went through the books as thoroughly as her rather less-than-financial brain could help her, she could see that for all her efforts, and she *had* tried—Hilary and all the girls had assured her of that—that Simeon's was not advancing. That a few more months of this could only end in one thing—closure.

The next day Link phoned.

"Miss Smith?" His voice came carelessly over the wire—but Brit's heart was not careless; it thumped with almost painful deliberation.

"Brit Wayland here." She knew he had said Smith intentionally and she made of it a prop to brace herself.

"I've just returned from New York." he told her, ignoring her correction.

"The paper said London."

"Oh, so you read me up?"

"I just happened to see the item."

"I went to the apartment for the first time since I walked out—you walked out, too, apparently—that last day. I found the checks. What gives, Brit?"

"You don't," she came crisply back. She commended herself mentally on that.

"Doing all right with Simeon's, then?" he asked.

"Thank you, yes," she lied.

A pause at the other end, then: "Well, I will say you're not like many girls—most, I would guess. Even if they have enough there's always room for more. Money, I mean."

"I have plenty," she assured him.

"Simeon did you well, eh?"

"I need nothing," she said firmly.

"You mean—nothing from me?"

"Did you have anything else to say?"

"Yes. I was wondering if you forbid me sending you money if you also forbid me sending—something else?"

"I have everything—I told you."

"Anyway, it's being sent, Brit, whether you forbid it or not. It comes with my best wishes. Do what you like with it, it's yours." Link finished: "With my blessing."

"Link?" Brit called, puzzled, but his phone was down. What had he meant, she wondered.

As Brit was closing up that evening, John came in.

THE STAFF HAD GONE. If she could not promise them any future Brit had at least been determined that they enjoyed good conditions now. She always insisted that they got away promptly. If any stragglers came in, she attended to them. Why not? She had only a single room to go home to.

Brit stood looking stupidly at John for a long minute. In the end it was John who came forward to take her hand in his.

"Brit!"

"I thought you were in Europe, John," she whispered.

"I flew in last night."

"Didn't things—" Brit paused sensitively "—didn't they come out as you planned?"

"More than I planned. I'm signed to do the theme music for a new thing they're starting. Something quite fresh, a new concept. I'm very excited about it, Brit."

"That's wonderful. It's good to get what you want."

There was a slight silence. Then John said meaningfully: "Not entirely what I want."

"Oh, John!" she half laughed, half cried. But the cry was not for John.

"I came back here to wind up my affairs," John said. "It looks like I may be indefinitely in Europe. Who knows? I may even be there for the rest of my life. One thing may lead to another. So—" a hunch of his shoulders "—I'm shutting the door here."

"And another door opening?"

"Yes. Brit—" tentatively "—I wish we could go through that new door together."

"It's too late," she said flatly.

"It seems it... but *is* it? I met your husband. He's quite a guy, isn't he?" Simeon had said that ...."But would a man send another man, as Link Wayland did, to his wife? Because he did just that." John looked bewildered. "He sent me to you, Brit. Can you explain that to me?"

"Where did you meet?" she asked.

"I didn't know where to find you, so I went to Wayland's office. He was very decent to me; undoubtedly he's a very decent fellow, and that's what got me."

"What, John?"

"He practically forced me to come here," he explained.

"But you expressed a wish to see me?"

"Of course. But I thought he might suggest drinks together, all three of us, not—well—"

"What did Link say? I mean, how much did he tell you?"

John looked at her frankly. "That things hadn't turned out, Brit. Then he said...." He paused.

"Yes?"

"He said to me: 'It's your turn now.' "

She was silent a moment. Link had said that!

"Then you came, John," she half whispered.

"Yes."

There was a long quiet in the boutique now. Shopping hours were over, only window gazers meandered through the arcade. The city traffic was becoming less busy, more muted. Brit looked at John across the room, but John, uncertain, still bemused, idly fingered a length of material and avoided Brit's gaze.

Presently he looked up again and said: "It's not what I came back for, Brit, this breakup of a marriage, I mean, and you must understand that."

"You mean you didn't really come back for me?"

"No. How could I? I came back, as I said, to wind up my affairs here. When I called to see Wayland it was because I didn't want you to think I'd come and gone again without seeing you." John let go the material and walked the narrow length of the boutique. "But now it's different," he said.

"Different?" she queried.

"You're not the married woman I thought you were."

"I am married, John."

"But not *the* married woman I believed. Brit, I would never have spoken like this had I thought for one moment that.... But it's not like that, is it? Anyway, Wayland has told me practically so himself. Besides, he's there, you're here. You don't even have the same address. So—"

"So, John?"

"So," said John quietly, "come with me, my dear."

She did not answer at once. As unthinkingly as he had fingered the material, she picked up a dress, put it back on a hanger, did it all again.

"Why?" she asked at last.

"Because I love you. Because I believe you love me."

"I don't think so. I mean, there was never anything *certain,* was there? We, never spoke about it, never told each other. Why—" a slight note of hysteria "—we never even kissed."

"We looked across a room and knew. At least—" eagerly "—I knew."

"I believed I did, too—then. But—"

"Things don't change, Brit."

"Sometimes they do."

"You mean you love someone else?"

"I didn't say that."

"But you meant it?"

"Oh, John, John," was all Brit said. She went across to him and for the very first time he kissed her. When he had finished he gave her a little half push away.

"That wasn't for me, was it?"

When she did not reply he went on: "Not to worry—about me, I mean. I have my plate more than full. Too full, actually—" a slight laugh "—for a loving wife as well. If it had happened, then I would have been apprehensive. A man can't have everything. As it is, I'm a lucky fellow. Shall we leave it at that?"

"You're dear, John," she said softly.

"But not dear enough," he teased ruefully. "All right, Brit, the subject is closed. Unless you want me to report to Link Wayland and tell him it was no good."

"No," she said decisively, too decisively, "don't do that." He gave her a quick shrewd look, but he dropped the topic.

"You haven't asked me about your sister," he said instead.

"You told me in your letter. You said she went to England. I wish—" a little troubled "—Cara would write."

"Probably thought she'd see you before any letter ar
rived."

"What? What are you talking about, John?"

"Cara. She didn't go to England after all. I thought sh
had, then she turned up again. She'd changed her mind
Or—" ruefully "—the money had run out."

"She borrowed from you," Brit said wretchedly. Wa
there nothing Cara would not do?

"I didn't mind; she's your sister, and I knew I wouldn*
be seeing her again...well, not for a long time."

"With you both in Europe?"

"Both of us in Australia at the moment, though I won*
be here long."

Brit did not hear that, she was hearing only,"Both of u
in Australia."

"You mean Cara is back?" she demanded.

"Back, and, believe it or not, hanging back. I do believ*
for once that girl is ashamed."

"Where is she? Where is she, John?"

"As a matter of fact, at the end of the arcade. I made he
wait there, though it didn't take much making; she didn*
want to come any more than I wanted her. Brit...Brit!"

But Brit did not hear. She was running—racing dow*
the empty passage, calling her sister's name. She had n*
reason to run to her, but the heart has no reasoning, it sim
ply loves.

"Cara!" she called, and Cara, standing waiting as Joh*
had said, turned and ran to her.

CHAPTER FOURTEEN

CARA'S GENTLE HUMILITY lasted for exactly a month, and when the month was up Brit was almost glad. Quiet, chastened docility sat incongruously on Cara. The subdued mouse instead of the paradise bird was not her sister.

Tears had flowed. Cara had confessed everything, called herself every wretched creature in the universe, hung her head, thrown herself on Brit's mercy. That she meant it had been apparent when she even had not objected, vocally, anyway, to sharing Brit's mediocre lodging. After an involuntary "Oh—" she had not said a word. She had even offered to make supper.

Over coffee she had asked tentatively about Link.

"When I heard through John," she said, "I thought how well you'd done for yourself. I mean—" at a look in Brit's face "—I thought, I hope dear Brit is happy."

That, Brit knew, Cara had *not* thought, or if she had it had been an afterthought. But it was no use trying to turn your back on Cara. Or close your heart. You could not, Brit knew, dictate to a heart.

"I'm sorry it didn't turn out." Cara glanced quickly around the mean little room.

"Well, let's not talk about it. Let's talk about you, darling."

"I didn't make it, Brit. To the top, I mean. Even halfway. Oh, I wasn't a flop, but—well . . . ." Cara shrugged.

"John said there's a lot of competition."

"Yes. And all of them ready to starve and grovel until they get their foot on the ladder. Brit, I just couldn't; I'm not made that way. Anyhow—" a slight sigh "—dancing a bore."

"But, Cara—"

"It was daddy who insisted on it. Frankly I never liked that much. I think the only part I did like was dressing up I adore dressing." Cara fiddled with her coffee spoor "What's this about you owning a boutique?"

Brit cut short a sigh. She was not in a mood to relate to Cara, but she knew she must tell her some time. So sh told.

Cara's eyes grew wide. "A rich husband and a legacy a well!"

"Link and I have separated, and the legacy is a lovel but uneconomical dress salon that I have not a hope o making prosper."

"Can I see it, Brit?"

"Of course. Only . . . ." Brit had been going to say "Onl don't get any ideas of taking over, for I'm wiser now." Sh didn't say it, though, for the simple reason that Car couldn't take it over, not successfully. She had even les money than Brit, and Gowns by Simeon had to have cap tal.

"I'll come with you tomorrow, Brit," Cara said eagerly.

"It would be better for you to look for a job."

"Can't I work for you?"

"Cara, I have no money," Brit pointed out.

"I'd work for nothing in a dress shop."

"You still have to eat." Brit reminded her. "But don let's discuss it now. You'll understand better when I sho you Simeon's tomorrow."

But Cara did not understand. She said so. She said: " can't understand anyone letting a place like this go." Sh looked around her and her eyes were starry.

"It's not paying, Cara."

"Make it."

"That's easier said than done."

"*I* could do it." Cara's voice trembled a little with excitement, but for all the slight shake there was a firm confidence there. A *knowledge,* you could say.

That was the first day.

Three weeks later, however hard Brit tried to turn away from the fact, deny it, refuse it, she still had to admit that Cara wasn't just efficient at business, she was excellent. She was even inspired. Discreetly at first, and then more boldly, Cara had stepped in and taken over a dozen things that Brit had been handling—or mishandling.

Ordering, for instance. Simeon's had never sold only their own dresses, they had bought from outside sources as well. Now Cara edged herself into the buying, ordered, then sold. Sold within days, hours.

"She has a talent," Hilary said once to Brit during the second week.

Astonishingly—astonishing to Brit—Cara understood the books. She frowned over the clumsy balances Brit reached, and said: "It's not good, yet not devastatingly bad, either. With decent capital...." She glanced obliquely at her sister.

"No, Cara." Brit knew what Cara was thinking, or at least of whom Cara was thinking.

"No," she said again.

Cara had left it at that... *then.*

Though the staff did not actually like Cara—no girls ever liked her sister; Cara had had, Brit recalled, very few school friends—they still respected her get-up-and-go. Frankly, that get-up-and-go astounded Brit; Cara always had been a flower. Now she could not get to work fast enough.

It worried Brit. She was glad to see the boutique prosper—for even in several weeks it had prospered—but she did not know how long she could let Cara attend the salon, receiving for her services only her meals and a dress if it appealed to her. However, Cara seemed completely satisfied—to Brit's eyes, anyhow. It took Hilary Malling to open those eyes.

"Brit." It was exactly a month now since Cara had returned. She was emerging from her chrysalis of contrition—Brit had seen the signs. She knew from Hilary Malling's voice that she was going to speak about her sister. She sighed. Cara could be very sharp if things did not suit her. She hoped she had not snapped at one of the girls. Now that her humility was gone that could be so.

She was not aware that she had said this aloud until Hilary said: "Oh, no, they admire your sister tremendously. She's not you—" an apologetic smile "—but perhaps that's better so far as they're concerned." Brit looked inquiringly at Hilary, and the senior assistant wasted no time.

"You're not a businesswoman, Brit."

"I'm afraid that's true," Brit admitted.

"Your sister, however, was born for trade."

"Cara was born to be a dancer."

"I don't think so. She doesn't think so, either."

"Oh, I know she's got it into her head that she doesn't like dancing, but dancing *is* Cara."

"It might have been, I don't know. . . . But I do know that dancing is not Miss Smith—*now.*"

"Then," breathed Brit, "what is?" But she knew she need not have asked. She knew the answer when it came would be one word and a proper name. It was.

Hilary replied: "Simeon's."

"It can't be. For one thing my sister is not—well, dependable," Brit admitted wretchedly.

"You mean she *was* not. Perhaps that was because she was the wrong peg in the wrong hole. Now it's different."

"For how long?"

"Does it matter? I mean so long as you can get Simeon's on its feet sufficiently even to sell it."

"I don't want to sell it," Brit said firmly.

"You want to keep on mismanaging it? Oh, I'm sorry, my dear, don't take this personally, but as the head of a concern you're about as good as dear Simeon was himself. Anyway, I didn't really mean that. About selling, Brit. All of the staff are very anxious that the salon remains. As you know, apart from sentimental interest, they all happen to be dependent on their jobs. I mentioned this before."

"Yes, you did.... But, Hilary, how can I help?"

Hilary Malling took a deep breath.

"You could let Cara take over," she said presently in a cautious voice.

"I don't mind doing that," Brit admitted. "I know I'm no good at it. But it doesn't solve the problem, does it? The problem of money, money that I don't happen to have."

"Mr. Wayland has it."

"No!"

"Then, Brit, you'll be closing the salon and putting a staff of worthwhile people—you know yourself they're that—out of work."

"No." Brit said it again, said it of Link.

"Think it over," said Hilary. "Perhaps you could make a business deal of it."

"That's all it would be," Brit came in quickly.

"You could offer Mr. Wayland an attractive profit," Hilary went on with it, ignoring Brit's interruption.

"I couldn't."

"Think it over," Hilary urged again.

Cara—the old Cara once more—tackled Brit that afternoon.

"Brit, I want to take over the reins of the boutique. I can make a go of it, a wonderful go of it. Brit, I *know* I can!"

"Yes, Cara, I've seen your talent," Brit said a little wearily.

"You have to have a hard streak, Brit, and you haven't. You'd never make it prosper in a hundred years."

"Perhaps, Cara, but money comes into it as well as talent, and I've told you all along that money is what I have *not* got."

Now Cara said what Hilary had, only Cara said "he," not "Mr. Wayland."

"He has it."

"So?"

"So you're his wife. Look, Brit, I don't know what went wrong between you two, but I still think he's pretty rotten to have left you high and dry like this."

"He didn't. He doesn't know. He thinks I have plenty." Brit stopped at the astounded look on Cara's face.

"You mean you pretended that—"

"Yes."

Cara was dumbfounded. After a long pause all she could manage to say was: "Oh, Brit!" She recovered, though. She said triumphantly: "Then I'll tell him."

"Cara, you're not to, Cara, you mustn't!"

"I'll tell him, Brit. If you don't go to him and offer him a profit in Simeon's if he will invest I'll tell Link. Look—" Cara took out papers "—I've written everything down. You might not understand the figures, but that tycoon will. It's my bet he'll invest very deeply."

"He won't be asked to," Brit insisted.

"He will, though. If you don't ask him, I shall. Then as I do it I'll tell him how you've been living from hand to mouth, not on the fat of the land as you let him think. You'll feel, and be, a complete fool, Brit."

"No!"

"You have no choice."

"No," Brit repeated.

"Do I go—or you?" Cara asked warningly. "I'm deadly earnest, Brit. Which of us? I mean that."

Some time later—Cara still waiting relentlessly by Brit's side—Brit said miserably: "I suppose I will." She closed the subject by turning definitely away.

But when Cara had skipped triumphantly off, Brit sat on looking into space, looking wretchedly, dismally, futilely, dreading what lay ahead. *What,* she thought distastefully, *can I say to Link? How long can I put the asking off?*

However, Cara was not one to let the grass grow. "You must do it at once," she said, coming in soon after to report a difficult but very lucrative sale. "As a matter of fact, Brit, I took the liberty of phoning your husband, telling him you wanted a word with him."

"Oh, Cara!"

"Well, it had to be personal, hadn't it? You could never hope to achieve anything over a phone."

"You should have left it to me."

"And never get it done! I told Link you had to see him, then asked where and when, and he said at his city hotel room would be the best, and to come around nine tonight." Cara looked at Brit curiously. "He didn't say which hotel—would you know it?"

Would she know it? Brit sat for a very still moment remembering her wedding night—Link holding her in his arms as she never had been held before, eyes to eyes, lips to lips. Breath-close. Thought-close. Link saying of John and Simeon: "Ghosts. Dreams. I'm a man—your man."

"Yes, I know it," Brit said.

"Nine, then. And please darling, put on one of our new dresses."

"Our" already! Brit had to smile.

But when Cara went out again, she did not smile. She was withdrawing with every fiber of her being from the approaching interview. She was dreading Link's dark extracting eyes, Link's thinned lips.

She did not want a scene, recriminations, reproaches, explanations, appeals. What did she want, she thought dully. And then it came clearly, shiningly clearly, to her. . . . She wanted to hear Link saying as he had said that time in Ha-

waii, that bright dawn after that night in the Hawaiian inn:
"Good morning. Have a happy day." Warm. Smiling. Both
arms outstretched. The authentic Hawaiian greeting.

But could morning ever be good again? Could there be a
happy day?

Cara opened the door. "This dress, I think. And, Brit,
for heaven's sake, *smile!*"

THE HOTEL PROPRIETOR smiled at Brit as she came up to
the desk.

"Nice to see you again, Mrs. Wayland. Mr. Wayland
has been telling us how busy you've been, yet how successful. Well, your gain has been our loss. We've missed seeing
you." He turned and took down a key. "The same room.
Shall Harry take up your bags?"

"No bags," Brit said. She went to the elevator.

The seventh floor. She remembered watching the number in the indicator as the figures flashed on, then flashed
off again. At the seventh the door opened and Brit went
down the corridor to the suite of rooms right at the end.
This was classified in the hotel list of accommodation as
the honeymoon unit, or so Link once had told her. She put
the key in the lock and went in.

She had half expected Link to be there; it would be one
of those deliberately surprising things he would do. But
the suite was empty. She took off her coat, put it on a chair,
carefully kept her gaze from the large bed—Link had insisted on a king-sized bed, had even had the hotel regimen
upset until one had been installed—then she went and sat
in her old position at the window. To wait.

How often had she waited here, very reluctant, all of her
protesting; yet somewhere in that reluctance and that
protestation....

She looked down on the busy street far below. *I wish it
was another scene,* she thought, *I wish it was pink dawn in*

Hawaii and I was waking in a room fragrant with honeyed hibiscus and Link was smiling at me and saying: "Good evening, Brit."

Link stood at the door.

She looked at him hungrily; she had not seen him for over a month. In case he saw the eagerness, immediately she turned her eyes away. He always had had a talent for knowing what she thought. He must not know now.

"You're thinner, Link."

He came in casually, pulled out another chair and sat back to front in it, arms around the top rail. He faced Brit.

"Pining for you," he proffered teasingly. When she did not respond, he said: "Well, what's this all about?"

"Cara didn't tell you?"

"Only asked the time and the place. So your little sister is back?"

"Yes."

"Thrown it in?"

"Well—"

"I hardly think she made the top in that short time." His voice was laconic. "Even," he added, "if your friend John did."

"John went over practically assured of success."

"And got it. Though why is he back here?"

"He's not—not now. He left at once," Brit told him.

"Left at once?" Link stared at her. "Yet you . . . . Oh, I see. You're following. But before you go, in dutiful sisterly fashion you want Cara settled. Oh, yes, Cara told me how much she liked the business. The pieces are falling into a pattern. The penny is dropping. How much do you want, Brit?"

"You've reached a wrong conclusion."

"How much?" he repeated.

"Well, if you want it that way, here's the prospectus."

Brit handed Link Cara's sheet of paper. What had Cara

said? "You might not understand the figures, but that tycoon will."

He accepted the sheet and took his time scrutinizing it.

"I see." He put it down.

"Well?"

"Promising. Quite promising." A pause. "But where do I come in?"

"I—we thought you might like to invest," faltered Brit.

"Is that necessary? I mean, with the money Simeon left you—"

"Simeon left me only the boutique, a very beautiful but unprofitable boutique. I think—Hilary and the others think that Simeon hoped that someone with capital could save it."

"Name of Wayland," Link grinned, but it was a thin, unamused grin.

"Yes."

There was silence for a while, then Link said: "You really meant that about inheriting no money?"

"There wasn't a great deal. Simeon wasn't rich, but what he had to pass on went to his staff. They're loyal and devoted."

"I see. Then what have you been living on? You've never touched one of my checks."

"I'm alive."

"Answer me, Brit!"

"I'm breathing, aren't I?" She said it a little apprehensively; she could see that old rage beginning to burn in his eyes.

"You were starving, but you wouldn't come to me."

"Don't be melodramatic. I wasn't starving, I was simply having to make ends meet."

"But you wouldn't come?"

"No."

"How you must hate me." He said it in an almost matter-of-fact voice, as though it was unimportant to him.

"And why the appeal now?" he asked presently. He was taking out his makings, and she realized how much she had missed that ritual.

"I'm giving the business to my sister," she explained.

"Giving Cara her chance."

"I think—I feel sure—it will be right this time; she has exceptional talent—also, surprisingly, she has a good business head."

"Not like you."

"No," Brit agreed.

"That's very true. Cara would have taken all that offered." Link was still spreading tobacco, rolling it up, thinning it again. "She wouldn't have slummed it in some down-at-heel dump."

"It's clean and respectable."

"However," he went on, "perhaps I'm underrating your business acumen; perhaps the smaller things are discarded but the bigger issues carefully attended."

"What do you mean?"

"I mean *John* could have settled Cara; he's in the big money now, he told me. But that big money is for you, I should say for both of you, so *I* am called upon for sister Cara. I'd like to say no, Brit, not on your life, Brit, but actually I can't. I'm responsible for you until we are legally separated, until you remarry, so I have to fork out whether I like it or not. So I will. How you use the cash once I pass it over is not my concern, but the law does expect me ostensibly to keep you."

"I don't need your ostensible keep, I'm just offering you a favorable proposition."

"It appears like that, but actually yours is a case of: 'John can take care of me but not my sister as well; Wayland's my lawful husband, why should he get off scot-free?' "

"You are," said Brit in a low taut voice, "a very cruel man."

The tobacco was still in the large palm, the strong fingers were still flattening and rolling it.

"You should be the last to say that," Link drawled. "You've been afforded every material comfort. It's not my fault you've been on iron rations the last few weeks."

"Cruelty comes in other forms," she reminded him. "You say cruel things."

"Like?"

"Like believing I would do that. Go away with John, yet expect you to help me out with Cara."

"Isn't it what you're doing?"

"I told you, Link. John has left."

"And once you have Cara accounted for, you're following."

"I am not following," she insisted.

He was packing the tobacco into the paper now, putting the weed in neatly, tapping each end to get rid of any surplus shreds.

"Why?" he asked.

"I'm just not going."

"He didn't ask you?"

"He asked me, but I'm not going. Link, *I am not going.* Can't you understand that?"

"No," Link said. He waited a moment, then he reminded her: "You loved the fellow. You never denied it."

"There was nothing between us."

"Yet you loved him."

"I thought I did. When he came back—"

"You had had the taste of something better?"

"Must it always come back to money?" she sighed.

"I was not," Link said, "speaking of money." His dark eyes flicked narrowly at her, and once more she remembered fierce arms around her, a voice saying: "Ghosts. Dreams. I am your man."

His tongue was darting out to lick the paper edges together, and she turned away.

"You never liked that, did you?" There was banter in Link's lazy voice.

"You notice things," she commented.

"I've noticed them ever since I first saw you, Brit, and decided what was to be done."

She had heard that story before, but never the reason behind it.

"Why was it to be me?" she asked.

"You stood there a little behind the family group. Remember, Brit, I'd come to interview your father. I saw you like I knew I'd been—lonely, not wanted, hungry."

"I wasn't!" she said indignantly.

"Oh, yes, you were, don't you think I know the symptoms? I've had them all myself. I did have a good granny, but she died, and that made it all the worse. But you had no one, you poor little mutt."

"So it was pity?"

"Oh, no—" firmly "—it was never pity. If it had been that I needn't have gone through the ritual, need I? Marriage and the rest."

"Then it was . . . ." But she could not finish. How could she ask this hard man if, apart from physical satisfaction, she had ever meant anything to him, anything at all?

"Finish it, Brit," he drawled.

"It would be a waste of time, Link. I've only ever been a possession to you, something you put money out on, so naturally couldn't let go."

"You think that, do you?"

"What else can I think? Have you ever given me any real tenderness? Have you ever said that you love me?"

"And have it thrown back at me, if not in actual words, then in John, in Simeon?"

"I've told you and told you," she said in despair.

"But you haven't told me what you want me to tell you. Be fair, Brit. You have to come halfway as well."

She said simply: "I love you." She waited for his reaction.

It was disappointing. "Interesting," he said. "And when did this remarkable state of affairs first occur to you?"

"I think it was in that Hawaiian hotel, the first inn I ever saw with a fountain singing out of a big shell. You woke me up—" she knew her cheeks were burning "—and said: 'Good morning. Have a happy day.'"

"Which you proceeded to have soon after with Simeon."

"Link!" She almost shouted it. "Link, do you have to go on like this?"

"Yes, because I'm tired of being hurt, Brit. I'm tired of giving and not receiving, of kissing and not being the kissed. It would be pleasant to believe you, pleasant to have all this over, but I'm still not sure, what's more I'm not even sure if you're worth it, girl."

"What do you want me to do?" she half cried. When he did not answer, she said: "Because I'll do it, Link."

He stood up.

"I'm going out. I'm going to walk the city. No—" as she went to rise as well "—you're not coming, too. Go to bed, Brit. Or sit here and look out. But don't try to follow me. I have to find myself. Know myself. I've been a roughrider. . . . Oh, yes, you were right. I believed I had only to ride hard and long and the world was mine."

"It is yours," she said eagerly, "and you weren't a roughrider."

"I was, and I got what I went after. But now I don't know if I want it. . . . Either that, or maybe it's come too late."

"No, Link," she appealed. She put out her hand, but he turned away.

"I want to know myself," he said again.

"Then know me, too," she pleaded . . . but she called only to the door.

She heard his footsteps along the passage. She heard the elevator descending. Then there was nothing, nothing for hours, for Brit sat on there for all those hours, sat on so long that dawn came in, a rather yellow dawn, the dawns big cities put on, the sun rays mixed with dust and tinged gray with commerce. Oh, for a pink Hawaiian break of day!

Then she heard the elevator. The steps. The turning of the door handle. He had come to say .... Oh, what had he come to say?

He stood there a long, long moment looking at her, and all at once she recognized in the look, as well as a possession, a pride, an authority, a mastery—for Link would always have these; they were Link—a very tender love.

When he came to her, Brit knew intrinsically, as well as passion there would be a great gentleness. A lover's gentleness. She waited for that...and for him.

And across the room he saw her waiting, and he outstretched both arms as he said with a promise as well as a greeting: "Good morning, Mrs. Wayland. Have a happy day."

THE EXTRAORDINARY ENGAGEMENT

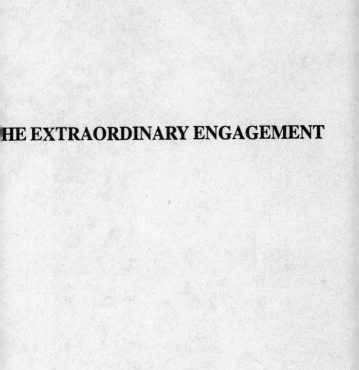

The
Extraordinary
Engagement
Marjorie Lewty

"It's not dishonest to marry where money is, it's just plain common sense." With these words Liz learned that the man she'd flown across the ocean to marry had found a better bargain. It was ironic that a series of bizarre events should place her in a similar situation.

A plane crash and a case of mistaken identity had landed her in the home of millionaire J. B. Rockington, who, blind and dying, thought Liz was his estranged granddaughter. To give the old man peace of mind she agreed to play out the role, becoming engaged to his protégé, Brett Denton.

The advantages were obvious; but falling in love with Brett soon made Liz's position impossible.

CHAPTER ONE

LIZ HARTLEY OPENED HER EYES and blinked down through the rectangular window of the plane. She must have dropped off to sleep, for it seemed no time at all since they took off from Rome, and now she saw the English Channel coming up in the distance, a steel gray ribbon in the pale evening light.

Waking suddenly, off guard, she thought, *Terry*, and inside she felt warm and soft and dreamy as she always did when she thought of him. Then memory stabbed with cutting sharpness, and she winced with the raw pain of it, her eyes filling with tears so that the wide countryside below blurred and glistened.

It was over. Terry hadn't wanted to marry her after all, and she was flying back to England to John and Dorothy who would both rather enjoy saying, "I told you so."

The stewardess came along the aisle and the girl in the next seat to Liz looked up and said wearily, "How m-much longer before we get in?"

The perky navy blue cap bobbed. "We're due at Elmdon at eighteen-twenty, madam."

"Thanks."

Liz glanced sideways with quick sympathy for a fellow sufferer. Mostly you forgot about a stammer, but when you were tired or worried it was apt to get on top of you and make everything worse, as she knew only too well herself.

This girl looked both tired and worried. Liz had hardly glanced at her when they both joined the plane in Rome; she'd been too drowned in her own misery. They had

merely smiled vaguely in each other's direction as they settled down, and then Liz put her head back and closed her
eyes in an effort to shut out the world; and that had been
that.

But now she really saw the girl next to her and she
thought, *She's unhappy, too, that makes a pair of us.* She
saw other things, too. She saw that the girl was beautiful.
Not just pretty but really beautiful; with smudgy violet
eyes, gorgeous fine skin and silky dark hair. Rich, too, for
her sage green suit had undoubtedly come from a designer
department, and the stole thrown over her knee was mink.
Beautiful, and rich, and unhappy.

And I'm ordinary-looking, and poor, and unhappy, Liz
thought; *it doesn't make any difference really.*

For the first time since Terry walked out of her hotel
room in Cape Town, many hours ago, Liz's mouth quirked
into something like a grin, and she looked almost like her
normal cheerful self again.

The man with graying hair on the other side of the aisle
cast a glance toward the two girls—not for the first time on
the journey—and he thought, *The one in green's gorgeous,
but give me the other one every time; the one next to the window, the lively one.* She could be good fun, he'd be willing
to bet. That quirky little smile was quite something. He
liked the way her hair curved into her neck, and her legs
were long and slim. . . . He sighed and turned back to the
Financial Times.

The plane hit an air pocket and Liz found her companion's mink stole sliding onto her lap.

Her fingers touched it appreciatively before she handed
it back with a smile. "Um—lovely!"

"Oh! Oh, yes, thanks very much."

The other girl's voice was vaguely surprised, as if she'd
been recalled from some faraway place. Evidently she
didn't at all want to start a conversation.

That was all right with Liz, but it might have been a help to talk to a stranger. Now that they were nearly at Elmdon the black misery was beginning to weigh heavily inside her again.

They must be almost across the Channel now. It was getting dark quickly and lights twinkled out from the English coast. To keep her mind safely busy Liz tried to draw up a balance sheet for herself. On the credit side: youth, health, reasonable looks, excellent secretarial qualifications. On the debit side: no job, very little money, no family to turn to except her stepbrother, John, fifteen years her senior. John had disliked Terry and has disapproved very vocally when she gave up her job and went out to join him in South Africa.

Well, this time John had been right and Terry had proved to be all he said, hadn't he? She winced inwardly as she remembered how John had described Terry, and how angry she had been. Weak, unreliable, only out for himself. But it was true, wasn't it? It was this Terry she must remember now, not the tall man with sun-streaked fair hair who had strolled into the office and sent her whole world into a spin—was it only five months ago?

For a split second she saw it all again vividly: herself looking up from her typewriter, the winter sun shining palely through the dusty window. And he had smiled down at her and said....

Stop it! she shrieked silently at herself, for the pain felt physically there, in her heart and lungs and throat. *Remember the end, if you like, but not the beginning.*

Remember how Terry had come into her hotel room on Monday evening with her return plane tickets. Remember how he'd looked then, embarrassed, guilty.

His eyes had avoided hers as he said, "I've managed to fix it. That's one useful thing about working for a travel agency. There's a cancellation on a scheduled flight leaving here at sixteen hundred hours tomorrow. You'll have to change planes at Rome and pick up a charter flight returning to Elmdon. A bit clumsy, but the best I could do on the spur of the moment. Think you can cope?"

"Of course." He couldn't wait to rush her back home, could he?

"I've sent off a cable to your stepbrother, saying you should be with him in Birmingham by Wednesday evening."

She took the folder with the tickets in it. "Thank you. I'll send you a check for this as soon as I get home."

She wondered how much longer her self-control would hold out. It would be hateful and humiliating if she broke down while he was here.

"Oh, forget about that," he said with strained joviality. "Let me look after it. After all...."

"No," she cut in.

He looked at her and flushed. "Don't be bitter, Liz. I thought we could cope with this situation like modern, civilized people. I thought I'd explained and said how sorry I am...."

"You have explained. You cabled me to stop flying out, but I'd left my place and the cable never reached me. I got here expecting that we'd be making plans for our wedding, but you told me you'd changed your mind and decided to marry someone else, the daughter of your managing director. That was how it was, surely?"

He flung away from her. "Oh, good lord, Liz, you make it sound...I mean, there was more to it than that."

She was shaking inside, but there was something else she must say somehow. She tightened her mouth. "Terry, tell me one thing, you owe me that. This girl, do you really love her? More than you said you loved me?"

They stood staring at each other in the small hotel room. Everything was tidy and impersonal; the gray carpet, the stiff rose design on the curtains, the clean folded towel hanging on the washbasin, Liz's unpacked suitcase. She'd pictured so often this moment of arrival, with Terry's arms around her, holding her close while they planned happily for their future together. And now....

At first she thought he wasn't going to reply. He was looking strangely at her. Then he laughed without humor. "Love! Women talk a lot about love and romance and men play along with them. But we're not little tin gods, you know, Liz. We have to be practical and consider our position in the world. It's not dishonest to marry where the money is, it's just plain common sense."

Everything in her revolted against his words. She stared at him as if she'd never known him and she felt that something in her was dying.

"Love's a luxury," he went on moodily, "like the icing on the cake. I don't believe there's a man alive who'd pass up a chance like I've got. If it helps any, Liz, I'll tell you that I still want you. I want you like hell. But—" he spread out his hands in a gesture of helplessness "—but I'm going to marry Frank Carter's daughter and that's how it is. Can't you see it my way? You're modern and intelligent...."

It was incredible. He was asking her to forgive him as if he were a little boy. He held out his arms. "Let's part friends, can't we?"

She shook her head slowly. "You want everything, d-don't you?" Then, abruptly, she turned her back on him. "Please go now."

She hadn't wanted to see him again, but his reflection was there in the mirror across the room.

His hands dropped slackly to his sides. "That's it then, Liz, if that's how you want it."

He moved and the reflection disappeared. A moment later she heard the click of the door as it closed behind him.

She stood quite still until the whine of the descending elevator died away, her nails biting into the palms of her hands. At least she'd kept her pride; she hadn't stormed or wept or pleaded. It wasn't much of a consolation, but it was something.

Minutes later the phone rang and the reception clerk said, "The gentleman asked me to tell you that he has ordered a taxi to take you to the airport tomorrow afternoon."

"Thank you," whispered Liz, and put the receiver carefully back in its cradle. That was when she began to cry....

It felt as if the plane was losing height. The girl in the green suit was gathering bag and gloves together. The man with graying hair drained his brandy glass and turned to his companion with a grin. "The wife's meeting me with the car. I don't have to drive."

Liz wondered if John would be at Elmdon when the plane got in. Probably not. He disliked snap decisions and even the pleasure of having been proved right would hardly outweigh his irritation at Liz's sudden arrival to disturb his routine.

She decided that if he wasn't there she would stay the night at a Birmingham hotel. Tomorrow she would feel more resigned to eating humble pie. She would have to ask for a loan to refund Terry her plane fare. Until she had repaid that debt she would feel humiliated.

The stewardess appeared at the front of the cabin. "Ladies and gentlemen, may I have your attention, please." She smiled calmly. "I have a message for you from the captain. He asks me to say that a slight difficulty has cropped up and it may be another quarter of an hour or so before we land at Elmdon. Would anyone care for drinks while we wait?"

Liz ordered coffee. The girl next to her had something in a glass. There was a buzz of conversation around the cabin, followed by a silence as everyone seemed to be listening to the sound of the engines.

Liz said to her neighbor, "What do you suppose is the matter?"

The girl in the green suit shrugged and smiled faintly. "I haven't a clue." She didn't sound even remotely interested.

The gray-haired man leaned across to the two girls and said very heartily, "We'll be okay. These fellows are marvelous, they can do anything with a plane."

Time slipped by. It was quite dark outside the windows now. The stewardess moved around among the passengers, serving drinks, joking with the children.

A man's voice came over the address system. "This is your captain speaking. I shall be putting the plane down in three minutes. Please check that your seat belts are adjusted correctly. The landing may be a little rough, but everything is under control. Thank you."

It's an emergency, thought Liz, and wondered why she didn't feel frightened. Perhaps because the crew seemed so calm.

They were losing height now. For a few strained moments everyone was very still, waiting. Liz was conscious of holding her breath.

Then there was a bump, a rise, another bump more brutal than the first, then another accompanied by a crunching, tearing sound, violent, somehow outrageous.

Just before the lights went out Liz saw the whole cabin heave up drunkenly above her and it seemed as if a gust of cold air cut her face like a knife.

The last thing she remembered was the thought, *John will be so cross about this if he's waiting for me.*

LIZ FELT DAMP AND NUMB and something was scratching her cheek. She opened her eyes and saw the sky, quite dark above, but glowing around the edges of her vision. For an eternity she lay there, drifting backward and forward between consciousness and unconsciousness, but finally she was fully awake and knowing what had happened.

Cautiously she tested arms and legs. They seemed to work. She could lift her head, too; it made her neck ache, but she could do it. She tried to lever herself up a few inches, but her hands sank into muddy earth and she flopped back. She touched her face and found that that, too, was covered with mud.

After a while she tried again. And again. Finally, after what seemed hours, she managed to struggle into a sitting position and found that she was in a newly plowed field, spiked with stubble. Some way away, she couldn't tell how far, there was the plane. She could see lights, hear voices. One wing stuck up crookedly against the glow in the sky.

Somehow she must get to the plane, where there were lights and people. She managed to drag herself to her feet, slipping and floundering in the muddy earth, her eyes doggedly fixed on the plane across the field. One step forward and she was down in a heap again, sobbing with frustration.

Presently she tried again, this time crawling on hands and knees. The stubble scratched her legs and her neck hurt badly, but she was making a little progress now.

She struggled on, half laughing, half crying, with painful slowness. Time had stopped meaning anything at all, but at some point there was somebody near her in the field.

She tried to look up, but her neck hurt and she giggled absurdly from her all fours position down there. "Hullo, whoever you are. I'm here. D-do I look like a wallowing hippo...hippopotamus?"

Golly, that had been a tricky word to get around! She was down flat on the ground again, laughing helplessly, weakly, the tears running down her cheeks. She could taste salt mingled with mud on her lips.

Someone was kneeling beside her and a man's voice said, "Elizabeth, it's you. Thank God!"

So John had come to meet her after all. It must be John, because nobody else ever called her Elizabeth. She wished she could see his face and then she would know if he was angry. He didn't sound angry, but she was sure he must be. He was an angry sort of person. It used to frighten her when she was a little girl, before she learned that you had to stand up to people like John.

But now she couldn't stop laughing. "So s-sorry," she spluttered. "What a very... und-dignified arrival...." The laughter rose shrilly, out of control.

John's hand was on her shoulder, quite gently. "Stop it, Elizabeth, pull yourself together. Try to tell me... can you move your limbs? Any acute pain anywhere?"

He spoke quietly, but there was a quality in his voice that made her stop laughing. She drew in a breath and said, "Not too bad."

"That's fine, that's a good girl." He was humoring her now. "Just relax, I'm going to carry you to the car. Tell me if I hurt you."

She'd never imagined John had such strength. As he stumbled over the muddy ground she leaned her whole body against him and it was like leaning against a rock.

"You're very—" she began. Then everything blacked out again.

Next time she opened her eyes she was wrapped up in the front seat of a car, her head supported by something soft. She moved her eyes carefully and could see John's left hand on the wheel and the panel of the dashboard. The needle flickered around seventy. *Well!* she thought hazily, John must have bought a new car, the old Austin couldn't have risen to that. Anyway, he never drove faster than fifty-five. He must be breaking his own rules to get her home quickly. Perhaps she had misjudged John. Perhaps he was kinder than she'd known.

She moved and he said quickly, "Are you awake, Elizabeth? All right?"

"Yes, thank you." She eased one arm up carefully to rub her neck. "Things are beginning to make sense again at last."

"I'm glad of that. I took a risk in bringing you away with me, but I was afraid they'd want to cart you off to hospital and it seemed more important to get you back home as quickly as possible. Actually you've been asleep for quite a time. We're nearly there."

She smiled to herself in the darkness. "In the circumstances I shouldn't have thought you'd have been so eager to get me back. You're being very forgiving."

"Don't let's talk about that now, Elizabeth. It's J.B. who matters now. He's very ill indeed, you know. Worse than when I phoned you in Rome. He's asking for you all the time."

Liz closed her eyes and her mind seemed to revolve slowly. Of course! Why hadn't she thought of it before?

Cautiously, because her neck hurt when she moved it, she tipped back her head until she could see the face of the man beside her, faintly lit by the reflected glow from the headlights. Her breath caught in her throat. No wonder she had imagined that John had changed both his car and himself. She got an impression of strong, clear-cut features and thick dark hair. Whoever this man was, he certainly wasn't her stepbrother John.

The car swung around between high stone pillars into a curving driveway. In the headlights' beam the banks of rhododendrons in full bloom looked like huge crimson faces. Liz had a moment of shocked fear. She was alone with this stranger, somewhere in the heart of the country.

The car crunched to a halt in front of an imposing stone portico and the man who wasn't John came around and opened the door on her side. "You stay right where you are, Elizabeth. I'll find Farthingale and we'll carry you upstairs."

"Wait a minute!" She turned her face, caked with mud, so that the light from the house fell on it. "I've only this second realized what's happened and it's completely crazy. Who, exactly, do you imagine I am?"

He bent down to the car window and stared in for a long, incredulous moment. Then he burst out, "What in the name of—what is this? Why didn't you tell me you weren't Elizabeth?"

"Probably because I am Elizabeth. If it comes to that, why didn't you tell me you weren't my brother John?"

He straightened up and she watched that sink in. It didn't take long. "All right then," he said, "so there's been some sort of mix-up. We'll have to straighten it out later, but now I've got to get straight back to Elmdon. You must stay here and I'll get them to look after you. Now, don't move, whatever you do."

He took the steps to the front door in two strides, and almost immediately, it seemed to Liz, he was back, accompanied by a middle-aged man in chauffeur's uniform and an elderly woman in a plain gray dress, who came toward the car.

"You leave the young lady with me, Mr. Brett, you'll want to hurry back. There, miss, this is a proper mix-up, isn't it?" Her forehead was crisscrossed with worry lines. "Let me help you out. Easy now."

The dark-haired man was back in the driving seat almost before Liz was out of the car. He lowered the window and said crisply, "Farthingale, get the address and phone number of this young lady's relatives. Try to contact them and explain what happened; bring them here if that seems best. You'd better phone the police in Birmingham, too, in case inquiries come in to them. I'll deal with things at the airport. Mrs. Jackson, you know how to cope with your

side of things. Call Dr. Winter and ask him to come over
as soon as he can."

His brief, abstracted nod included them all vaguely but
his eyes were on the way ahead and a moment later the big
car had disappeared with a swish around the corner of the
driveway.

Liz wanted to giggle again. She felt she knew his type already: a man who expected to give orders and have them
obeyed on the dot. She wondered how he would react if
anyone challenged his authority. It might be fun to find
out. Fun, but slightly dangerous, too.

Tonight, however, she was in no mood to challenge anyone. With hazy content she noted that the bedroom into
which they helped her was large and luxurious, that the
nightdress produced by Mrs. Jackson—who was dour and
silent, though kind enough—was a flimsy dream, and the
bed itself as soft as a cloud to her aching limbs.

After a time a doctor came, examined her gently and
asked a lot of questions. When he had gone Mrs. Jackson
came back with two tablets and a glass of hot milk. Then
Liz floated away into sleep.

WHEN SHE AWOKE AGAIN Liz felt comparatively normal
except for an aching neck and shoulder.

She lay quiet, her eyes taking in the room. Chinks of
sunlight crept in around the edges of the blue brocade curtains that hung stiffly to the floor. The carpet was blue,
too; it looked as soft and silky as a kitten's fur. The built-in
furniture was of pale burnished wood. Silver and crystal
gleamed from the dressing table. A beautiful room; expensive, luxurious, feminine. Did it, Liz wondered, belong to
her unknown namesake? And what relation was the other
Elizabeth to the man who had brought her here?

She moved sideways in the bed to catch her reflection in
the dressing-table mirror. Her face was now perfectly

clean, Mrs. Jackson must have washed it last night when Liz was asleep. What else had happened while she slept? Had the dark-haired man come back and stood by her bed, looking down at her, perhaps wondering who she was?

The thought disturbed her oddly and she pushed it away. What next, she wondered. She looked around for her clothes, but they were nowhere to be seen. No doubt they were being cleaned and pressed by a squad of chambermaids, she thought with a grin. A silk tasseled rope hung beside the bed and she wondered if this was intended for use or as an ornament. For use, probably. Feeling like an aristocrat at the Court of the Sun King, Liz gave the silk rope a tentative pull.

After a short interval there was a tap at the door and Mrs. Jackson came in. She pulled back the heavy curtains, letting in a flood of sunlight.

"Good morning, miss, how do you feel this morning?"

Liz smiled at her. "Oh, I feel fine, thanks, but very bewildered. Won't you put me in the picture, please? I don't even know where I am."

Mrs. Jackson came and stood at a respectful distance from the bed. This morning she wore a dark blue dress with an old-fashioned gold locket on a chain around her neck. She was well past middle-age and her furrowed face wore a look of permanently harassed efficiency.

"The house is called Heronswood, miss. I'm housekeeper here."

"Heronswood...that's where? Warwickshire?"

"Yes, miss. Not far from Kenilworth."

She turned to the built-in wardrobe, which ran the whole length of the room, and took out a fleecy white bed jacket. When she had helped Liz into this she said, "I'll send your breakfast up now, miss."

Liz glanced at the highly compressed lips in the thin,

lined face. Not much information would be forthcomin
from Mrs. Jackson, that was sure. Oh, well, what did
matter? She would be leaving soon.

"Do you know if they managed to get in touch with m
brother at the address in Solihull?"

The housekeeper shook her head. "I haven't heard, miss
I didn't see Farthingale when he came back last night, an
he doesn't live in the house."

"I see. Would you tell me the time, please? My watc
seems to be missing, like everything else, I'm afraid." Sh
wondered if her suitcase had been rescued from the plane.

"Just turned half-past eleven, miss. Mr. Brett telephone
earlier from Birmingham to say that he would be back her
by midday and he gave orders that you were on no ac
count to get up until he had seen you."

A gleam came into Liz's eyes. *So, he gave orders to he*
did he? He would.

"Yes, well, thank you for giving me the message, Mrs
Jackson. And...."

"Yes, miss?" The housekeeper turned, on her way to th
door.

"I just wanted to say thank you for what you did for m
last night. You were very kind. And for lending me thes
lovely things." Liz made a gesture toward the filmy night
dress and the bed jacket of cuddly soft wool.

For a moment Mrs. Jackson's look rested on her. The
her lips compressed tightly and without a word she wen
out of the room.

Liz stared after her. She had thought the housekeepe
stiff and taciturn, but in that moment she had seen some
thing that changed her impression altogether. She had see
that the tightened lips were shaking uncontrollably and th
faded eyes were brimming over with tears.

She lay back and stared at the ceiling. How strange i
was to be pitchforked into the middle of other people's lif

stories, she thought. How impossible to get any idea of what it was all about. But she was sorry to have upset the housekeeper, who had been kind.

A few minutes later there was another knock at the door and a very small maid came in bearing a large tray. She wore an old-fashioned housemaid's uniform, even down to the starched white cap on her wispy red hair, and she beamed at Liz shyly. "I'm Ethel. I've brought your breakfast and Mrs. Jackson hopes it's to your liking."

Liz looked at the tray: delicate rose-sprigged china on a lacy cloth, a silver coffeepot sending out the most wonderful aroma, scrambled eggs, toast, marmalade, pats of yellow butter. She felt suddenly weak with hunger.

She sat up and took the tray on her knee. "Thank you, Ethel. And please tell Mrs. Jackson that it looks wonderful and I'm sure I shall enjoy it very much."

Ethel grinned widely and departed, and Liz proceeded to make the most of her gracious living. After this it would be cheap and nasty lodgings or a bed-sitter until she could build up her funds again, for even if John and Dorothy invited her to stay with them in Solihull, she didn't think she could bear it.

When she had eaten every last morsel of food and drained the coffeepot she lay back and relaxed. What a silent house it was! In the morning one would expect to hear at the very least the whirr of a vacuum cleaner, but there hadn't been a sound outside the door since the moment she wakened.

As if to contradict her, somewhere a clock struck twelve with a mellow chime, and almost immediately there was a tap on the door.

"Come in," she called, and the man she now knew as Mr. Brett came into the room. There was a chair near the window and he walked across and sat down with his back to the light, facing her.

"Good morning." His tone was quite formal. "I hope you're feeling not too much the worse for last night's happenings."

"Thank you, I feel very much better this morning."

She looked at him curiously. He was younger than she had taken him for last night. She had guessed him at about John's age, but perhaps that was because of his decisive manner. She thought now that he must be about thirty or a bit over. Last night she'd got an impression of an almost fastidious good grooming and it was still evident today. But in spite of the clean shirt and general air of having just bathed, you wouldn't call him immaculate. His thick dark hair was brushed aside carelessly and his cheek had been bleeding from an encounter with a shaver,

She realized that she was staring, and looked away quickly. "I'm very grateful to you for letting me stay here and to Mrs. Jackson for looking after me, but I mustn't trouble you any further. Perhaps if you'd ask someone to bring my clothes I could leave as soon as convenient."

He shook his head, dismissing her prim little speech as if it were of no possible importance. "Oh, no, that wouldn't do at all. I had a word with Dr. Winter on the phone and he tells me that you should definitely rest up for today and he'll look in and see you again this evening."

"Oh, I'm sure there's no need for that. I feel perfectly fit this morning. It's very kind of you, but—"

He went on just as if she hadn't spoken. "I've told Mrs. Jackson that you'll stay in bed for the present. She'll enjoy looking after you."

Liz seethed inwardly. He reminded her of John in the calm way he assumed that she would do what he told her. He was even more arrogant than John.

But she knew from experience that it was useless to meet arrogance with anger, so she looked at him very calmly and said, "It was kind of you to give me hospitality last night, but I must really insist on leaving now."

"And I," he said in the tone of a man at the end of his patience, "must really insist on your staying."

She sat up very straight in the big bed. "Mr. Brett," she said with what she hoped was dignity, "what makes you think you can give me orders?"

"Oh, for heaven's sake, girl, can't you see my position? I was responsible for bringing you here. All right, it was a mistake, but it was still my responsibility. I might have done untold harm. I might have killed you, moving you as I did. If it hadn't seemed so urgent to get you here I'd never have taken the risk. I'd have waited for a doctor ... an ambulance."

It was odd how everything that had happened last night had for the moment left Liz's mind, but now it all came back.

"What happened?" she asked. "What did you find when you got back?"

He got up and walked to the window, with his back to her. "It was ... bad. The plane took a gash in its side when it came down and the middle section was pretty well wrecked. That was how you came to be where you were, I suppose. Did you realize you still had your safety belt on and part of the seat it was locked to?"

She shook her head silently.

"It may have been lucky for you it broke away," he said. "It's inexplicable how these things happen. There are a lot of people in hospital."

"And the ... the other Elizabeth? The one you mistook me for?"

He didn't move. "She is among them."

"Oh! Oh, I'm so very s-sorry."

He turned around slowly. "That's it. That's what put me on the wrong trail last night. You and she, your voices are almost identical. And she has the same funny little stammer."

Funny little stammer! She'd never thought it amusing.

She wanted to hear more about the other Elizabeth, but he changed the subject. "I'm afraid we've been unsuccessful in getting in touch with your people. There was no reply from the phone number you gave Farthingale. And this morning he drove over to Solihull, but found the house apparently closed up."

"Oh," said Liz blankly. She hadn't thought of the possibility that John and Dorothy might be away. "Then my brother couldn't have got my cable. He won't know I'm back in England."

This was a blow indeed. John, though he would certainly have delivered a protracted lecture, wouldn't have refused to help her. Where could she go if he was away from home? London, where she had made friends in her last job, was too far; Cornwall, where she'd looked after her stepfather until he died, even farther. All her worldly possessions were on a boat on the way to South Africa. And her bank account was drained to the dregs.

Perhaps her thoughts were mirrored in her face, for her visitor said, "Well then, if there isn't anyone expecting you, there can be no reason why you shouldn't stay here for today, can there? And I must insist that you do, I'm afraid."

If he hadn't added that final maddening word of command Liz would probably have given in gracefully. As it was it touched off every instinct that had grown up inside her through the years. She felt the hot blood rushing into her cheeks as she blurted out, "Look, Mr. Brett, I must explain to you that I object very strongly to being ordered around, whether for my own good or to allay your pangs of conscience. Please let me have my clothes at once."

He had walked across the room and now had one hand on the door handle. Just for a second she thought his mouth was going to twitch into a smile, but that must have been a delusion.

"I simply haven't time to stay and argue with you now,"

he said. "If you insist on behaving like an obstinate child, I'll just have to treat you like one. And, by the way, the name is Denton, Brett Denton."

He went out of the room and closed the door behind him and, with amazement mounting almost to panic, Liz heard the key turn in the lock.

CHAPTER TWO

LIZ STARED WIDE-EYED at the closed door. How dared he lock her in? How dared he? Angry tears burned behind her eyelids.

But living with John had taught her one important lesson: that wallowing in resentment without taking action is a strong poison. And that the very best antidote is to find something in the situation to laugh at, if it's humanly possible.

"So I'm an obstinate child, am I?" she said aloud, and made a satisfyingly childish grimace toward the door. Then she threw back the covers and slipped out of bed.

For a moment the room rocked around her. She waited until it had steadied itself, then she went across to the window and looked out. Below, the smooth lawns sloped away to end in a high, curving beech hedge and above this the jagged ruin of Kenilworth Castle stood out against the sky, in the distance. There were flowering shrubs and low-growing trees and neat rose beds. It all looked as if it had been there for a long, long time.

A very, very desirable property, this, thought Liz with a grin. *The kind of place that only a rich man can afford to keep up.* She wondered if it belonged to Mr. Brett Denton.

With an effort she pushed up the heavy sash window and peered out, pulling the woolly bed jacket around her shoulders. *Oh, yes, a lovely house; a lovely country house of rosy brick with a dignified flat façade and rows of long, rectangular windows.*

She leaned out farther and noticed something that made

her heart begin to beat very fast. Just below the level of the first-floor windows the builders, or the prospective owner, must have become tired of classical simplicity and decided to add some discreet ornament. A narrow stone balcony, not much wider than a ledge and with a low balustrade of decorative stone forms, ran the whole length of the house.

Liz stared at the balcony for some time and then found that a plan had formulated itself without her actually thinking it all out. If she could find some clothes she would make her way along the balcony. With any luck one of the other first-floor windows would be unlocked. Then, hey, presto, downstairs and out of the house without being noticed by anyone. The police at Kenilworth would surely help her to get to John's home. He would probably be back by now. If not, she would enlist the help of the people next door.

As a plan of action, it was all a bit hazy, and she'd have to be very careful how she crept downstairs, but it was better to try it than to stay here, locked in her room like a naughty child.

She rummaged in the wardrobe and found, among the expensive dresses and suits, a pair of navy slacks and a white sweater. The dressing-table drawers contained nylon underwear. In a cupboard she found a pair of sandals.

Five minutes later she was pushing up the window of the next bedroom.

The room she saw was much the same size as the one in which she had slept, but very differently furnished. Hers had been light and modern; this was dark and Victorian. Heavy rosewood dressing chests; a massive writing desk; chairs of moss-green velvet. The bed was covered by a thick white quilt and half-hidden by a Chinese screen embroidered with scarlet dragons.

Holding her breath, Liz climbed over the sill and tiptoed across the room. Her feet made no sound on the shaggy, whitish carpet, so when, suddenly, what seemed to be a hump on the floor uncurled itself and jumped up she let out a smothered shriek.

The hump transformed itself immediately into a white Persian cat, and at the same moment a voice from behind her, thin as a reed sound, said, "Who ... who is there? Is it you, nurse?"

Liz turned around to see an old man lying in the bed, propped high against the pillows. He was lying very still and she saw that the screen had hidden him from her as she came into the room. His hair was pure white and his face, although fallen away in illness, was the most wonderful face she'd ever seen. It reminded her of one of those marvelous portraits by Rembrandt in the National Gallery: a face full of humanity, compassion, generosity.

She didn't hesitate. She went up to the bed and said gently, "I'm t-terribly sorry if you were asleep ...." *That absurd stammer again!* "I just wanted t-to ...."

An electrifying change had come over the old man's face. It was as if he'd taken some vital draft which had poured new life into him.

"Elizabeth, you're here! Brett told me you would come, but I daren't let myself believe it. Oh, my dear, dear child ...."

His faded blue eyes, fixed on some point beyond her shoulder, were brimming with tears. He was, she realized now, quite blind.

"B-but I'm not ..." she faltered.

"Don't say anything now, my dearest. Not another word. All that is over and done with." His hands went out, groping for hers. "I only wish I could see you, Elizabeth. Did they tell you I was blind? So silly of me, isn't it?" The thin voice went on and on and she was powerless to stop it. "I was never really ill before, was I? Only a stubborn old man who wanted his own way. But you forgave me and came back. Don't leave me again, Elizabeth. Stay . . . please...."

The voice quavered, stopped. She responded as she would have done to a frightened child. She sat on the edge of the bed, holding the frail hand between her own warm fingers.

His head went back against the pillow; he looked deeply exhausted. "Now I can...rest...." It was a mere breath.

His eyelids were closed. He seemed to be asleep.

Liz sat there, holding his hands and thinking hard. Some of the pieces of the puzzle were fitting into place. There was the girl who had sat next to her on the plane, the beautiful girl with the smudgy violet eyes. She had stammered, too. And there was that thing Brett Denton had said in the car last night, which she'd forgotten until now, something about "J.B. being ill and asking for you all the time."

And now the other Elizabeth was in hospital while she, Liz, seemed to be acting as a kind of stand-in. What exactly would happen next?

It was almost like an answer to that question when the door opened and a uniformed nurse appeared. Behind her was Brett Denton.

The nurse reacted predictably to seeing a stranger sitting beside her patient. Her plump, pleasant face registered amazement and professional disapproval, and she took a couple of steps forward, looking rather as if Liz were a burglar she'd caught tucking the silver away into a bag.

But Brett's hand shot out and restrained her. "It's all right, nurse, no harm done. I'll explain later." He walked up to the bed and looked down. "He's really sleeping at last, praise be."

His look moved to Liz, still holding the old man's thin fingers in her hands, and she braced herself against the anger that must come. But she saw no anger, only an immense naked fatigue.

"Shall we go, Elizabeth?" he said, and she disengaged her hands gently and followed him out of the room.

In the wide, carpeted corridor they faced each other. Liz was aware that her heart was thumping most uncomfortably in her throat.

She said quickly, without much hope of self-justification, "I'm sorry about this, but I couldn't just stay locked in there like a prisoner." She gestured toward the closed door of the next room.

He brushed her words away irritably and his eyes narrowed, looking down at her. It was absurd, of course, but she had an impression that he was assessing her as a man appointing a candidate for some responsible job.

Finally he said, "Look, this is going to sound very strange, I know, but you must make up your mind about it quickly ... and about me. There's no time to explain anything now because I have to get straight back to the hospital. I can only tell you that what I ask is vitally important, and you'll have to take the whole thing on trust. Me, too. What I'm asking is this: will you stay here until I come back? Just stay, without asking any questions? Will you ... please?"

Her mind fluttered a warning. All this had nothing to do with her. It wasn't her fault that he had brought her here. She could walk out of the house now and he couldn't possibly stop her.

"But why should I—" she began.

"Please," he cut in. "Just yes or no."

She looked up at him, saw the drawn lines beside his mouth, heard the urgency in his voice. She knew that she herself was hardly registering with him at all, as a person. She was just a last straw added to some burden that she knew nothing about.

Suddenly and illogically she wanted to help him. "All right," she said, "I'll stay."

He let out his breath. "Ah, that's a relief. Thank you." He looked around him vaguely and added, "Just—make yourself at home."

Then he turned and strode away along the corridor and turned the corner out of sight, and she knew that he had already forgotten all about her.

Perhaps it was because the conventional little phrase seemed so out of place in the circumstances, or perhaps it was a relaxation of tension, but Liz found herself smiling as she unlocked the bedroom door and went back inside again.

THE CHIMING CLOCK STRUCK the hour six times before Brett Denton came back.

As soon as he came into the room Liz sensed a change in him. It was as if a taut spring had snapped.

She was sitting in a chair by the window and he pulled up another chair and sank into it.

What she had been expecting she didn't know, but the ordinariness of his words gave her a small shock of surprise. "Have they been looking after you?"

"Oh, yes, wonderfully, thank you. Mrs. Jackson sent me up a lovely lunch and I've just been lazy."

He glanced at her and away again. "Good."

The silence that followed spread out like a pool. At first she thought he had forgotten all about her. Then she realized that he was searching for the words to say to her.

Finally he turned his head. "I owe you all manner of apologies, don't I? Will you take them as said? I'm not awfully good at apologizing."

No, she thought, *you wouldn't be. Not with that mouth and that jaw.* "Certainly," she said stiffly.

His brows lifted. "What a prickly child you are . . . Elizabeth. Do they call you Elizabeth, by the way?"

"Everyone calls me Liz. Only John, my stepbrother, ever uses my full name, and he's...."

"Yes?"

What could she say about John? "He's always seemed rather formal," she said. "Perhaps I only imagine it, because he's a lot older than I am. Nearly fifteen years."

"You live with him?"

"No, not now. I did for a while, after my stepfather died. Then when I began to work I moved to London."

"And yesterday you were on your way back to your job after a holiday, I expect?"

"No, I've left my job. I was . . . ." She broke off, seeing the gleam in his eye and realizing that she was being deliberately quizzed. "Does it matter?" She lifted her chin.

"It may well matter quite a lot," he said slowly and very gravely.

There was a heaviness in his voice that deflated her small bubble of resentment, and she waited for him to tell her what he meant.

But he didn't go on. He turned away and stared down into the garden, leaning forward with his chin propped on his hand.

He seemed to have forgotten all about her and she sat back in her chair and took a really good look at him for the first time. He was certainly a man you wouldn't forget, once you'd met him. She noticed the carved line of the cheekbone with the brown skin stretched tightly over it, the hard mouth, the brooding dark eyes, the almost black hair. *Nothing of the Anglo-Saxon about him,* she thought. He might have come from some southern land where the sun shines harshly, where men are still masters and their women submit without question. Not, in fact, her type of man in the least.

So vivid was her impression of him that when he swung around and said, "Then you're free at the moment to please yourself what you do?" she replied involuntarily.

"Yes, quite free."

Too late she saw the trap she'd fallen into and added, flustered, "That is, of course, my brother is expecting me."

He shook his head. "You can't have it both ways, you know. You said yourself that he couldn't have received your cable if he's away from home."

"Look," she began furiously, "I don't have to—"

"Of course you don't," he interrupted. "Now just keep calm for a minute, will you, and we'll try to straighten all this out."

He pulled his chair around and sat looking directly at her. "I'll do my best to give you the facts. Stop me if I leave anything out." He rubbed his forehead, between his eyebrows. "By the way, do you believe in fate?"

"Fate? You mean things happening because...."

"Because they have to happen. Yes."

"I don't know," she said. "I suppose in a way, I do."

He nodded. "I suppose, in a way, I do, too—now. Just look at this. Firstly, I brought you here by mistake and because of an odd coincidence. You know about all that. Secondly, when I found out the truth I wanted to be quite sure that I'd done you no harm by my action. I'm afraid I was a little...hasty...in my way of going about it at times, but I've already said I'm sorry about that. Of course I meant you to be free to leave as soon as the doctor thought it wise. But now, things are different."

Something in his voice touched off a wriggle of fear inside Liz. Her eyes opened wide. "You mean ... you're going to try to s-stop me?"

"Oh, for Pete's sake, girl, what do you take me for? No, I feel that when you know the facts you may feel it's your responsibility to stay."

"What do you mean, my responsibility?"

"Exactly that. Nobody asked you to walk into a private room. Or—when once there—to mislead a blind old man into believing you were another girl. That's what happened, isn't it?"

"That's not fair. I d-didn't mean to, but he seemed so ill...I couldn't..." she stammered, distressed.

"All right, you needn't spell it out, I can guess very well how it happened. You had me fooled, too, remember?"

"I...had you fooled...."

He lifted a hand wearily. "All right, let it go. I chose the wrong word. Let's just say I was mistaken, will that do?"

Liz said nothing.

He rubbed his forehead again. "Where was I? Oh, yes, the facts. Well, the man you saw in the next room is J.B. Rockington—"

"Rockington?" Liz couldn't help interrupting. "The J.B. Rockington?"

He nodded briefly. "There's only one, isn't there? J.B. Rockington, master builder."

And millionaire, Liz added to herself. She had a quick picture in her mind of towering office buildings going up, schools, supermarkets, blocks of apartments. And always, prominent among the steel girders and concrete mixers, there would be that ubiquitous shiny red board with the one word in bold black letters: ROCKINGTON.

"J.B. is my employer," Brett Denton went on, "but there's much more to it than that, from my point of view. He's my friend and benefactor, as well. He means a very great deal to me. I'm sorry if this all sounds somewhat extravagant, but it's an important part of the situation. For me the most important part."

"Go on," she said.

"Well, J.B. brought up his granddaughter, the other Elizabeth, from the time she was a baby. His son died in the war and his son's wife, Elizabeth's mother, soon afterward. J.B. adored Elizabeth; you could almost say he lived for her. Then, about a year ago, they disagreed seriously for the first time—about a man. He was an actor...films mostly. J.B. disapproved and said so. Finally everything blew up, there was a bad quarrel and she left home. J.B. took it badly. He would never talk about her and all her photographs were put away. But I'm sure he believed she would come back. Her room was kept ready for her—all her clothes—you see...." He glanced around.

"This is her room?" Liz said. "And she was coming back?"

He nodded. "Only because I managed to trace her in Italy and ask her to. Yesterday she phoned me to say she was returning by plane. The next part of the story you know already."

His eyes held hers, very dark and grave. "Do you see now what I'm getting at? Do you appreciate the position you've put yourself—and all of us—in by going into that room and acting as you did?"

She shivered. "Not...exactly."

"Then I'll have to spell it out for you. A very sick old man has been holding onto life, kept going by the hope of being reconciled with the one person he cares for most in all the world. The girl comes back to him. He hears her voice, touches her hand. In his weakness he never questions that she is the girl he is waiting for, that she loves him and wants to bury the past as much as he does. He is still going to die but now he's happy. What is going to happen to him if she disappears again now, without explanation?"

Liz drew a slow breath. "You mean, you think I should go on pretending to be his granddaughter—the other Elizabeth? But he would know eventually. He wouldn't go on accepting me."

"I think he would. He's already accepted you and it's always the first step that's the important one. It isn't as if he were in normal health. He's a very sick man—completely blind—with not very long to live."

She pressed her hand against her mouth. To be old and blind, to know that you are dying and that there is a pain-

ful rift between you and the one you care most for. Ther
couldn't be anything much worse than that, could there?

But she said, "I don't know if I could do it. But
wouldn't be for long, would it? Only until the other Eliz
beth is better, then it could all be explained."

His mouth went hard again and for the first time she ap
preciated to the full the enormous control he was imposin
on himself.

"The other Elizabeth died this afternoon in the opera
ing theater," he said.

She shrank back. "Oh, no—oh, how dreadful—I can
believe it. . . ."

He said curtly, "I'm afraid you'll have to believe it."

There was a tap on the door and the round, pleasar
face of the nurse appeared. "Mr. Rockington is awake an
seems rested and a little stronger. He's asking to see hi
granddaughter."

She stood there waiting composedly for Liz to get up
Brett was on his feet, too, beside her chair. She had t
make up her mind now, this instant, no time to consider.

Inside her something seemed to be smiling ruefully
*Mind? What has your mind got to do with it? This is a time t
feel, not to think.*

"Elizabeth?" Brett said quietly, holding out his hand t
her.

Things happen because they have to happen.

"Of course I'll come," she said, and put her hand int
his.

He smiled and pulled her to her feet. He hadn't doubte
for a moment, had he, that she would fall in with his plans

At the doorway of the next bedroom Liz stopped an
said in a low voice, "What do I call him?"

"Call him J.B. Elizabeth always did. Everyone calls hir
J.B."

She nodded. "Will you stay?"

"Better not. Just plunge in at the deep end, you'll manage." He gripped her hand hard. For a pep talk, she thought, he hadn't much to offer.

"But there's so much I don't know."

He drew in a deep breath. It might have registered exasperation or not, she just didn't know. "He's been ill for some time, you know, and his mind isn't absolutely clear. I really don't believe he'll want to talk much. It will be enough to have you here. Be gentle with him, that's all that matters. If anything crops up that you can't understand, just play it by ear for the present. I'll put you in the picture at the first possible moment, I promise you. I've got to go out now, but I'll see you when I get back tonight, then I can brief you properly."

"I'll do my best," she said, and went slowly across the room to the bed.

The nurse said brightly, "Here's your granddaughter to see you, Mr. Rockington." She pulled up a small cane-backed chair to the bed. "Only a few minutes, I'm afraid," she said to Liz, and went out of the room and closed the door.

"Elizabeth, are you there, my dear? I was afraid I'd dreamed it all." It was true, his voice did sound stronger.

"I'm here, J.B. It really is me," she said, and she leaned forward to kiss him.

Liz had never known her own father, or either of her grandfathers. Her mother had remarried when Liz was a child, but her stepfather had been a cold, remote man who had had no warmth or affection to give her. At the touch of J.B.'s dry old cheek under her lips and the love in his face she felt her eyes fill with tears.

His hands searched her face. "My dearest child, you're crying. You mustn't cry for me, you know. That won't do at all. I've had a long inning and now that you've come home I don't mind how soon I retire to the bull pen." He smiled. "One mustn't hog the pitching, you know."

"Don't talk about retiring," Liz said with a smile and a lump in her throat.

He closed his eyes and was quiet. But presently he spoke again. "Elizabeth...are you still here?"

"Yes, I'm here." She took his hands.

"There's something . . . ." He broke off. "Is there anybody else here?"

"No, we're quite alone."

He drew in his breath. "Will you tell me, my dear, did you marry...that man?"

She smiled. At least she could tell the truth now. "No, I didn't marry him. I found out that he wasn't—that I didn't love him after all."

He nodded slowly, "I'm glad. Sorry . . . you were hurt. But glad you're still...free. You know...what I've always hoped for you, don't you, child?"

"Do I?" she said gently. *You'll have to play it by ear,* Brett had told her.

"I think you do. You and Brett—it's always been my dearest hope. But he was proud as a boy and the man is just as proud. You know...why he would never ask you, don't you, Elizabeth?"

She squeezed his hand and that seemed to satisfy him. A little smile hovered around his mouth and she guessed he was back in the past where she couldn't follow.

The nurse appeared at her side, unpinned her watch and took the old man's wrist between her fingers.

Liz stood up. "Goodbye, J.B. I'll come again soon to see you," she whispered, but she didn't think he heard her as she went softly out of the room.

Back in her own room Liz sat for a long time looking out of the window. Suddenly she felt exhausted, physically and mentally. So much had happened in less than a week. Could it have only been last Friday that she set out for London Airport on her way to South Africa and Terry?

She'd been so deliriously happy. "Deliriously" was the right word, she thought now. Being in love, as she'd been in love with Terry, was a kind of delirium, a kind of madness.

She stared down at the garden. The lilac and laburnum had turned to a shadowy gray now. Fluffy mist began to gather low in the rose beds. The white Persian cat, which had disturbed her this morning, stalked across the lawn and disappeared into the bushes. In the distance the shell of Kenilworth Castle stood out starkly against the pale sky.

It all looked so calm and she was so tired. She didn't want to think anymore, or to feel. She put her head back against the cushion of her chair and slept.

She was awakened by a touch on her shoulder. She blinked against a sudden flood of light and saw Brett Denton standing beside her chair. There was another man with him who was vaguely familiar, a youngish man in a gray suit with smooth fair hair and gold-rimmed spectacles. Yes, of course, the doctor who had examined her last night.

Brett said, "I've brought Dr. Winter to have another look at you."

The young doctor slipped into the chair beside her and Brett turned to the door. "I'll leave you to it, then, Colin. I'll see you downstairs when you've finished."

When the door had closed the doctor turned to Liz. "Well, how are you feeling today, generally?"

"Much better, thank you. I've been fine all day up to now, but I felt a bit tired and I must have dropped off to sleep." She sat up and smoothed the navy slacks over her knees.

"I'm not surprised you felt tired after what's been going on," the doctor said drily. "I've been hearing all about it from Brett."

"All about—you mean...."

"Yes, all about this crazy idea of his, too."

"Do you think it's crazy?" she said eagerly. Surely if the doctor put his foot down Brett would have to give up his plan, and that would let her out. But then what about J.B.?

"From a professional point of view? Or because I'm a friend of the family?"

"Well, both, I suppose. Are they different?"

"No, I don't think they are. From both angles. J.B.'s health comes first every time."

"And you think it will do him good—believing that Elizabeth has come back?"

"I think it has done him good already. His heart is stronger tonight than it's been for some time. Happiness, as they say, is a powerful medicine." He spoke in a pleasant, quiet voice, reassuringly relaxed.

"Yes," said Liz, and frowned.

"But you're still bothered?"

"A little," she said. "It's all happened so suddenly and I don't know whether it's right to deceive him. I suppose, really, I feel guilty about it."

He shook his head at her. "Don't," he advised. "Feeling guilty is a luxury nobody can afford. It's really only another name for feeling sorry for ourselves and that's pretty stupid, too, though we all do it at times."

"Then you think I did right to agree?"

He smiled. "It's too late at night for making moral judgments. Let's say I think you were very plucky and very human about it, and I told Brett so."

She felt her cheeks go warm. "Oh, I don't know about that. It was my fault that it all happened. If I hadn't been trespassing...."

"Yes, I heard about that, too. And why. I certainly wouldn't feel bad about any of it. Brett can be very high-handed when he feels like it, and he had a lot on his mind this morning."

She nodded slowly. "I realize that now, but I didn't

know then. There's so much I don't know." She rubbed her forehead confusedly.

There was one question she wanted to ask and she wondered if Dr. Winter knew the answer. And whether he would tell her if he did.

But before she could think of a way to ask it he said, "And now, suppose we take another look at those bruises of yours."

Ten minutes later he was packing his instruments away into their leather case. Liz sat up in bed and pulled the borrowed sweater back over her head.

"Going on very well," Dr. Winter said. "You've been lucky."

She swung her legs over the side of the bed. "Yes," she said soberly, "I've been lucky."

He picked up his case. "I come in every day to see Mr. Rockington, so I'll see you again before I sign you off finally. In any case I'll be in touch with Brett."

He stood smiling down at her as she sat on the edge of the bed, with its heavy cover of pale blue satin. She was a lovely girl, he thought, slim and young and enchanting, with deep-set gray eyes that looked back at you honestly and candidly, and a perfect skin, warmed now by a faint glow of pink. There was something oddly touching about the way she held her head back so that her pale fawn-colored hair curved in at her neck.

Colin Winter felt suddenly uneasy about the way Denton seemed to be making use of her. He understood the pressures, of course, and how it had all happened. Still, it seemed a downright shame to mix up a vulnerable young girl like this in such a grim situation. He liked what he knew of Brett Denton and had found him dependable—he'd been almost too much of a stickler for duty and fair play at school—but all the same he intended to keep an eye on how things went here, and maybe when Liz was no longer his patient....

He blinked suddenly as she spoke. "You know Mr. Denton well?"

"Fairly well. We were at the same school. We lost touch after that, but we met up again recently." He looked seriously at her and added, "If you're feeling worried I can set your mind at rest about one thing. So far as one man can judge another I'd say Brett Denton is a man of the greatest personal integrity."

And that, he thought with a wry grin, was absolutely as far as he was prepared to go in singing another man's praises to this girl.

Liz saw the grin and found the young doctor easy and sympathetic. Perhaps she could ask him. . . .

"Dr. Winter, there's something I'd like to ask you. . . . "

"Fire ahead," he said encouragingly.

"It's just that . . . ." She stopped. No, she couldn't do it. The question seemed too outrageously personal altogether. Even if he knew the answer, which he probably didn't, she couldn't explain why it seemed so important to her.

Hastily she searched her brain for a substitute.

"I wanted to ask you about . . . about Mr. Rockington. Mr. Denton seems to believe that he won't recover, but I wondered—" She bit her lip. "I know doctors don't talk about their patients. Do you mind my asking?"

He gave her a reassuring glance. "Of course I don't mind. In the circumstances you've every reason to ask, and I've every reason to give you as straight an answer as I can. Barring miracles he can't live more than a few weeks at most. That's the opinion of the top men I've had out to look at him. He may rally a little or he may not. All we can do is to make things as easy as possible for him."

Liz nodded. It wasn't an answer to the question she had intended to ask, but it was just as important. Perhaps, she thought, even more important, for it seemed to clear away the last remaining feeling of doubt and guilt from her mind.

"I see," said Liz. "Thank you for telling me."

AFTER THE DOCTOR HAD GONE Liz waited for Brett. What had he said this morning? "I'll see you when I get back tonight and then I can brief you properly." She would be happier when she knew more about the situation. The feeling of having been thrust onto the stage as a last-minute understudy, knowing nothing of the play or the other actors, was frightening.

The little maid brought up her supper on a tray—fresh salmon and salad and a strawberry mousse. Liz wanted to ask her what Brett was doing, but decided not to. He would come in his own good time.

It was quite dark now and she ate her supper by the light of a table lamp. Outside the long window the gardens had settled for the night. Stars were bright in the darkness of the summer sky. From somewhere at the front of the house came the sound of a car engine starting, revving up, fading away. That would be Dr. Winter leaving.

The door of the next room opened and closed softly several times. Quiet voices sounded in the corridor, probably the night nurse taking over.

Half an hour later the little maid came back for the tray, bringing a copy of a glossy county magazine. "Mrs. Jackson thought you might like something to read, miss."

When she had gone Liz tried to read, but the photographs of weddings and hunt balls and point-to-point meetings meant nothing to her. She threw down the magazine and began to pace up and down the room. *Why didn't Brett Denton come?*

Time crawled, marked by the chimes of the clock outside somewhere. Half-past eight. Nine o'clock. Half-past nine. Ten o'clock. At about three minutes past ten Ethel knocked and came in, bearing biscuits and Ovaltine.

She placed the tray carefully on the low table by the

window. "I'll draw the curtains for you, miss, or the midges'll get in. My mum says they always bite something awful when they get into a room of an evening." She closed the window and drew the blue brocade curtains. "Mrs. Jackson's gone to bed, Miss Elizabeth. Her arthritis is something cruel tonight. Is there anything else I can do for you?"

Liz smiled at the child hovering by the door, pink cheeked and wispy haired and obviously eager to please. "No, thank you, Ethel, you've looked after me beautifully."

The pink turned to a gratified crimson. "Thank you ever so, miss. Good night, then."

"Good night, Ethel."

With the curtains drawn the room had taken on a claustrophobic atmosphere. After the little maid had gone Liz waited a moment or two and then opened them again. Better to be bitten by midges than to have this horrid suffocating feeling in her throat.

She drank the Ovaltine, jibbed at the crumbly biscuits which, she was sure, would choke her and tried to reason herself out of it. She had always considered herself a fairly practical person, not much given to attacks of the jitters. It must be the result of the accident and all that had happened since.

But she was uneasily aware that her palms were damp and her breathing uneven. This was quite absurd and something must be done about it. Whatever mad thing she'd undertaken, she had no intention of letting the situation make her neurotic. The very least that Brett Denton could do was to keep his promise, and clear things up for her. Probably he was having his supper and had forgotten all about her.

She opened the door and walked softly along the corridor, turned the corner and found herself looking down into a large, square hall with several doors opening off it. It was all spacious and had the elegance of a past age, with polished wood everywhere and a great copper urn full of delphiniums on the refectory table in the middle of the hall. It was the kind of place that Liz had only encountered previously when she had paid her gate-money to be conducted around one of the smaller "stately homes."

But she wasn't in any mood, just now, to appreciate her surroundings. She went carefully down the stairs, her feet in their rubber-soled sandals making no sound on the bare oak. One of the doors leading off the hall was standing ajar and she went across and looked inside. It was a smallish room, furnished as a study; a comfortable room with a red carpet, book-lined walls, leather chairs and a massive desk.

On the desk there was a tray laid out for supper. It hadn't been touched. Beside the desk sat Brett Denton, holding in his hands a silver-framed photograph, and even from across the room Liz could not mistake the face of the girl who had sat next to her in the plane.

Brett was turned three-quarters away from the door and Liz couldn't see his face, but everything about him—the droop of his head, the weariness of the hunched shoulders, the tenseness of the hands that held the photograph—everything gave her the answer to the question she hadn't had the courage to ask Dr. Winter.

It wasn't only J.B. who loved Elizabeth. Brett had loved her, too. Still did, in spite of the fact that she had run away to marry another man, in spite of the fact that she was dead.

She would never know the whole story, she thought. She was a stranger, an outsider. But neither could she intrude on his private grief just because she had let herself get jittery in an empty silent room. Very quietly she turned away and made her way back to her bedroom.

The strange thing was that as she closed the door she no

longer had any sense of being shut in. Her jitters had entirely disappeared. Seeing Brett Denton as she'd just seen him had given her confidence to go on. He wasn't hard and rather ruthless, as she'd been inclined to think. He was just a man who could suffer, who had feelings.

Nothing was any different really, but it seemed to be. It wasn't even necessary to fret and wonder if she was doing the right thing. She knew now that she would play her part to the best of her ability, for as long as was necessary.

With a feeling of having shed a huge load from her back Liz undressed, slid into bed, and was almost immediately asleep.

CHAPTER THREE

ETHEL HAD JUST LEFT Liz's breakfast tray the following morning when there was a knock on the door.

"Come in," she called, and Brett appeared in the doorway.

He walked a short way into the room and stopped, a leather briefcase tucked under one arm, the other hanging loose, relaxed. Most people, Liz thought, would walk to something—a table, a chair. Not so Brett Denton. He needed nothing at all to prop him up. His dark brown hair was brushed smoothly, his tie firmly knotted over a crisply laundered shirt. He looked very much in command of himself.

Liz remembered her own night of loss and despair such a short time ago and wondered how much willpower he had had to use to achieve the transformation from the hunched, desolate figure she'd seen in the study last night. A small rush of fellow feeling made her smile at him.

His answering smile was a token only. "Good morning," he said. "How are you feeling?"

"Fine, thanks. Much better."

"Good. Sorry about last night, but by the time I was free it was pretty late and I thought you'd be asleep."

He hitched the briefcase up and glanced at his wristwatch. "The trouble is that I'm afraid I'll have to ask you to wait until this afternoon. I've got a conference this morning in Birmingham. Do you think you can go on holding the fort? I'll try to get back about three unless something cataclysmic turns up. Then we can get things sorted out. That suit you?"

"I'll be ready, Mr. Denton," she said, and recognized her office voice.

His mouth twisted. "Perhaps you'd better get used to calling me Brett. We more or less grew up together."

"I'll be ready...Brett."

"That's better," he said with the half smile that wasn't really a smile at all. "Well, until then do just as you wish. Mrs. Jackson and Farthingale understand the true position, of course, but the other servants and the nurses will accept you as J.B.'s granddaughter. None of them ever saw the real Elizabeth. Have a stroll around the garden if you like...it's worth seeing."

"Yes," said Liz, "I'd like that. But there's just one thing...."

"Yes?"

"I'm afraid I haven't any clothes to wear. I suppose my own things were pretty well ruined when I was deposited in the field. I had to...to borrow the slacks and sweater I wore yesterday from—" she nodded toward the wardrobe "—from there. I'm sorry about that, but I had no choice." She looked inquiringly and ruefully at him.

His mouth tightened. She guessed that the prospect of seeing another girl walking around in Elizabeth's clothes was one that he didn't relish. Neither did she, for that matter, she thought sadly.

He looked at the wardrobe and said, "Can you fix yourself up adequately for the moment with what's in there?"

"Oh, yes, it was just that I didn't know—"

"Then that's the best thing to do," he cut in. "In fact it's the only thing to do until there's an opportunity for you to get out and buy some clothes for yourself."

"All right," said Liz in a very small voice.

He turned to go, then seemed to change his mind and came back toward the bed. "It's rotten for you, but try not to mind too much," he said.

Perhaps, she thought when he'd gone, *perhaps he is human after all*. She hoped so. If they were going to work together in this crazy scheme (as Dr. Winter had called it) they would have to trust each other. But it would be so much easier if she could manage to like him, as well.

She'd have to work on it, she decided.

She was draining the pot of its last drop of coffee when Ethel came up for the tray, half an hour later. The little maid looked very young and fresh this morning, hair brushed tidily, pink cheeks scrubbed.

"Oh, you haven't quite finished, miss. I don't want to hurry you, I'll come back. It was just that I was going to start me washing up."

"No, don't go, Ethel, you can have the tray in two minutes. I can't bear to waste any of Mrs. Jackson's coffee, it's very good."

"I'll tell her, miss, she'll be pleased." The child wriggled her thin shoulders under the blue print dress, which looked about two sizes too large for her. "And how are you feeling this morning, miss? You're looking better, if I may say so. Got a bit of color in your cheeks, as me mum would say. You looked proper peaky yesterday."

Liz smiled. "Yes, I was feeling rather peaky, but I'm much better this morning. You won't have to run up and down with the tray anymore. I shall come downstairs."

"Ooh, that'll be nice. It'll make the house a bit more lively to have you about the place. It's that quiet—" she lowered her voice with a glance toward the direction of the next bedroom "—what with the poor old gentleman so ill and the nurses shushing you all the time. And Mrs. Jackson's a very nice lady, but she don't talk much, if you know what I mean," she added forlornly.

"Have you many brothers and sisters?" Liz asked.

Ethel brightened. "Six. Four girls and two boys, and I'm the eldest, and the first one to go out to work and send home some of my wages. I could've gone to Woolworth's or into the clothing factory, but me mum said it'd be nicer for me in service. But I don't know as I'll stick it long."

"There aren't any other young people employed in the house?"

Ethel pulled a lugubrious face. "All as old as the hills. There's Mrs. Jackson and there's Mrs. Boot, who comes in three mornings to do the heavy work. There's Farthingale, who drives Mr. Brett's car and there's Ames, the gardener. He's about a hundred."

"No one else?"

"Not a soul." Suddenly she clucked her tongue. "There, now, I've got a head like a sieve, as me mum would say. Of course there's that Miss Johnson, but she's away now."

"Miss Johnson?"

"She's the old master's sec ... secretary. She's been staying here since the old master was took ill, and now she works with Mr. Brett sometimes in the study, but she went off on holiday last week. And good riddance to bad rubbish," she added with an old-fashioned look toward Liz. Suddenly she clapped a hand to her mouth. "Oh, dear, I shouldn't be gossiping like this. Mrs. Jackson 'ud skin me alive." She cast a wary eye at the door.

Liz smiled at her. "Never mind, you can say I kept you. As a matter of fact there is something you could tell me. Do you know what happened to the clothes I was wearing when—you know—when they brought me here after the plane accident?"

"Oh, yes, miss, that pretty blue dress and coat. They was all muddy and Mrs. Jackson sent me to the cleaners in Kenilworth with them. They'll be ready tomorrow and I'll go and get them for you."

"I see. Thank you very much for taking them, Ethel." She glanced toward the big wardrobe. "I'll have to find something else to wear then."

Ethel ran eagerly across the room and pushed open the sliding doors. "Ooh, miss, you've got such lovely things in here, haven't you? I couldn't help just looking at them when I come up to do the room. Mrs. Jackson told me to light the electric heater and open all the drawers and cupboards, to keep everything aired for when you came home again."

Very carefully she pushed the dresses and suits along the rail. "This one is my favorite." She pointed to a cherry-red dinner dress in dull satin with glittering sequins encrusted around the halter neckline.

"Yes, it's very . . . pretty." Liz looked away quickly. "Now, I've quite finished with the tray, Ethel, if you'd like to take it down."

"Oh, yes, miss, thank you." Ethel was remembering her training now. Carefully she lifted the tray from the bed and balanced it on one arm. "Would there be anything more, miss?"

"No, thank you. Except to tell Mrs. Jackson that I'll be coming downstairs later on. Will you do that?"

"Yes, miss. And . . . ." Her cheeks were pinker than ever, her eyes large and solemn.

"Yes?"

"I'm ever so glad you've come back home, Miss Elizabeth," said the little maid shyly.

THE GARDENS WERE JUST AS BEAUTIFUL as she had expected, Liz thought, as she wandered out an hour later. She had bathed, and washed the residue of mud out of her hair, and was wearing the simplest dress she could find, a green cotton shirtwaist with a silver buckle on the belt. It looked as if it had never been worn before, and that was what Liz hoped, especially as no flicker of recognition had come into Mrs. Jackson's face when Liz arrived downstairs.

If Mrs. Jackson hadn't seen Elizabeth wearing the dress,

then Brett probably hadn't either. It would be better if h
didn't think of Elizabeth every time he looked at her.

She strolled across the grass, still glittering with dew in
the morning sunshine. The bank of shrubs flanking th
lawn was starred with yellow and pink and purple. Th
scent of lilac and mayflower hung in the air. Liz took deep
appreciative sniffs, then turned around to get a view of th
house itself.

Oh, but it was lovely, a dream of a house, its classica
beauty of line softened by the mass of foliage that trailec
around the lower windows: wisteria, magnolia, anothe
that she thought was jasmine. The mellow bricks wer
crimson red against the silver birches that flanked th
house on either side. It was a fairly large house and yet i
had a gentle quality as if it were content to blend into th
surroundings of gardens and trees.

And Elizabeth had left everything and walked awa
from a home like this! How she must have loved the man
whoever he was.

She wandered across the lawn, through an archway cu
in the beech hedge, and found herself looking at a kitchen
garden. Liz knew a bit about kitchen gardens. Nobod
could live with brother John and not pick up a smattering.

Every day when John came home from the bank h
changed out of his business suit, put on the green garden
er's apron with the large pockets, which Dorothy had giver
him for his birthday, and went out to do battle with any in
vading weeds, flies, fungi, or other pests that were fool
hardy enough to show themselves among the neat rows o
growing plants. John's scarlet runners won prizes at th
local show and his asparagus bed was the envy of hi
neighbors. He hadn't much time left over to grow flowers
but Dorothy's display of bedding plants stood up smartl
to attention, every bit as well disciplined as her husband'
vegetable rows. Liz sometimes wondered what would hap

pen to those two if they had children, but she never came up with an answer.

The kitchen garden she was looking at now was not in the least like John's. Tidy was the last word you'd have called it. It was lush and extravagant and at a first glance there seemed to be as many weeds as plants. Peas flopped heavily to earth, scarlet runners had reached the top of their poles and were twirling wildly outwards, looking for support in vain. Carrots, onions, cabbage, vied with groundsel and chickweed for survival.

The fruit bushes had the best of it, perhaps because they'd been longer in residence. Enormous spiky goose-berry bushes skirted the paths, heavy with great green globes. Raspberries, strawberries, currants—everywhere fruit was swelling, ripening. Peaches and apricots hung from the walls enclosing the garden.

Liz wandered along the center path. What bliss to be here in about a month's time when the fruit was ripe. Her mouth watered at the very thought. Those raspber-ries—umm, gorgeous!

She bent down to prop up one of the canes that was ly-ing on the ground and came face to face, through the bushes, with an old man who was doing the same thing on the other side of the row.

This must be Ames, who was, Ethel had said, about a hundred. She might have been right, Liz thought. His skin was like creased brown paper and he stared at her with eyes as bright and pinpointed as a bird's. Come to that, he was rather like a bird: he looked as if he might be going to flap his wings and hustle her off his territory.

"Hullo," said Liz. "I didn't see anyone there. I hope you don't mind my coming in. I'm Mr. Rockington's grand-daughter, and you must be Ames?" Liz Hartley would probably have said "Mr. Ames," but Elizabeth Rockington never.

The gardener grunted and straightened as far as he could, which still left a good-sized lump on his back. "Ah," he wheezed. "They said as you was comin' home."

My goodness, but he was old, and no mistake. Not exactly a hundred, but she could see Ethel's point. "You don't look after all this place yourself, do you?" she asked.

There was a pause to let the question sink in, then he said, "Ah, I 'ave to, since the lad went. You can't get lads now, they all go to the car works. Big money they get in the works. When they're not on strike," he added with a dry cackle.

"Too true," said Liz. "Well, I think you do marvels, with no help. The lawns are beautiful, and the roses and everything."

He pulled out a grimy handkerchief and passed it over his forehead. "I try to keep the front tidy for the master. But the fruit and veges are more than I can properly manage now. I'm not as young as I was," he pointed out.

Liz walked round to his side of the raspberry canes. "P'raps I could lend a hand with the weeding. I always—"

She stopped herself. *Careful now*, she'd nearly said that she always helped her stepbrother when she had time. Had the old man noticed anything? He looked as if his awareness began and ended with his garden, but you never could tell.

"I always used to help when I was at home before," she finished lamely.

He was three or four inches shorter than she was, because of the hump on his back. When he peered up at her with his bird-bright eyes she was glad she'd covered up. Ames might be a hundred years old, but he was nobody's fool.

"Ah," he said, "that would be in Masterman's time. He was here before me."

"You haven't worked here long, then?"

"Two years, give or take a month," he told her, and turned back to the raspberry canes.

"Ames, are you here?" A pretty, clear voice came from somewhere and Liz turned to see a girl in an ivory pantsuit at the far end of the kitchen garden. She was smallish and slender, with pale silky hair and a smooth tanned skin. She held a small dumpy boy of about two in a baggy blue playsuit firmly by the hand.

"Ames, I'm leaving Timmy with you for a bit. Keep an eye on him, will you?"

The old man scowled and grunted something unintelligible without looking up. At the same moment the girl saw Liz and, loosing the child's hand, came running down the path.

"Why, hullo, you must be Elizabeth. Brett told me you were expected. I'm Clare Jessing and I live over in the cottage. I expect Brett's told you about me." She held out a smooth brown arm in greeting.

Liz took the extended hand, smiling. This was it, then. This was where she began to be Elizabeth Rockington in real earnest. And who exactly was Clare Jessing? Nanny? Au pair? Timmy's mother? A friend of Brett Denton, evidently. A close friend from the way she'd spoken his name. Liz waited for clues.

The girl tossed back her hair in a graceful movement and said, "This is fun, meeting you. I was just going to make coffee, you simply must come and have some with me. It would be doing me a kindness to have someone to talk to, I haven't seen another soul but Timmy for two whole days. I'm simply marooned here. I haven't a car and Brett's been too busy to drive me anywhere. I get so bored." She sighed, then brightened up. "Never mind, now you're here I'll be okay."

She linked her arm with Liz's, as if they'd been friends all their lives, and was leading her back along the path. It was going to be difficult to refuse, and she didn't want to seem standoffish to a friend of the family. All the same she wished this encounter had happened after her briefing from Brett and not before.

Timmy, released, was staggering up and down the rows of vegetables on unsteady feet. As Liz hesitated he tripped over a root and fell flat on his face just behind her. He set up a terrible howl and Liz moved to pick him up, but the other girl stopped her.

"It's all right, he's not hurt. He'll begin to play up for attention if you notice him," said Clare carelessly. "Come on."

Liz wasn't so sure he wasn't hurt, and she would have liked to stay and make sure, but the fair girl was urging her on. Also, she was getting the impression that Timmy was Clare's son, in which case she had no right to interfere. So she allowed herself to be led through a wooden gate at the far end of the kitchen garden, and was relieved to hear the howls tail off and stop.

"See?" Clare turned to her with mischievously sparkling eyes. She had clear blue eyes with long curving lashes that gave her smile a pretty, provocative quality. In fact she was an extremely attractive girl altogether. If Timmy were indeed her child, then what was her husband doing allowing Brett Denton to drive her around, Liz wondered.

"We'll go in the back way, if you don't mind, it's quicker," Clare said. "I expect you remember the cottage, but you won't have seen it since the old gardener left—what was his name—Masterman. He had it for years, and then when he died it was empty, for the old boy you saw just now lives out with his daughter. Anyway, J.B. decided to have it all done up and modernized. Lucky for me, as it happened, because when I had my bit of bad luck he was a darling and said I could move in until I got myself sorted out. Do sit down while I make the coffee."

She had led the way into a small, bright, very untidy kitchen. Liz pushed a pile of magazines aside on the window seat and sat down, wondering what the bit of bad luck could be. Did it tie up with not having a husband? Could any girl refer to losing a husband as a "bit of bad luck"?

Apparently Clare could. "Do you know about Jack?" She spooned coffee powder into two mugs. "I hope you don't mind instant?"

"No, of course not. And I'm afraid I don't know. I've rather lost touch, being abroad."

"Yes, well, Jack was only at Rockington's about a year, so you wouldn't have heard about the accident. He was one of J.B.'s bright young men. One of the whiz kids. You get on pretty quickly at Rockington's if you're bright and go-ahead, and Jack was." Her mouth drooped. "We had some marvelous times together, Jack and I."

She topped up the mugs with milk, handed one to Liz and sat down at the table, her blue eyes suddenly bleak and hard.

Liz was silent, guessing at some tragedy, so it came as more than a slight shock when Clare turned to her with deliberation and resentment that she didn't bother to hide, and said, "You'd think that a man earning four thousand a year would take out life insurance for his wife, wouldn't you?"

Liz blinked. "I s-suppose you would."

"Well, Jack didn't. He bought a super car, and after he was killed in it all I got was the insurance on the car, believe it or not. We'd got a gorgeous house in Knowle, but it was practically all on mortgage, so of course it had to go. Even the furniture wasn't paid for. And there was I, with a baby to look after, and when all the bills and everything were paid up there was practically nothing left. If it hadn't been for J.B. letting us come and live here I don't know what I'd have done."

Liz tried to think of something to say, but there didn't seem to be anything, except that she was sorry, so she said it.

Clare shrugged under the ivory silk tunic. "Oh, I'll get by, I expect. I'm glad you've come though, it'll be nice to have someone to talk to."

While they drank their coffee she chattered on about the house in Knowle and the holiday they'd had in Majorca and how she missed going up to London to see the new fashions, and how cut off she was at Heronswood.

Liz had a kind heart and was as prepared as the next girl to listen to someone else's moans, but enough was enough. After ten minutes she got to her feet. "I must be getting back now in case J.B. asks for me."

Clare got up, too, with a movement that suggested that she might have been a model; a quick, graceful, spontaneous flick from pose to pose while the cameras clicked. "Must you, what a shame! I've enjoyed our talk. You must come again, Elizabeth, and do call me Clare, won't you? I feel like one of the family, living so near. I suppose you plan to stay on until the old man dies?"

Liz stared at her. "Yes," she said coolly.

"Good, then we'll be able to arrange a get-together. We'll find another man and all have a night out. Brett and I usually go to the Black Swan in Kenilworth for dinner, but I've heard there's a super new place opened just outside Stratford where they have a floor show. We could try that."

Liz went out of the back door and turned to say thank you for the coffee.

"Not a bit. Drop in whenever you feel like it, you'll always find me at home—unfortunately." She pulled a wry face in the direction of Timmy who was some distance away, amusing himself by throwing stones in the direction of the white Persian cat who was sitting under the hedge well out of range.

As she walked back to the house the way she had come, Liz thought that a little of Clare Jessing would go a long, long way.

And yet she had no right to be critical. It was hard luck, ghastly hard luck, on any young woman to be left alone with a child and very little money. Had she loved her husband at all, or only the goodies he'd provided? And what had he been like, Jack Jessing, J.B.'s whiz kid? Had he been proud of his success, of his beautiful wife, his luxury house, his glossy car? Everything going his way and then—all over in a flash, just like that. Liz sighed and walked up the steps to the paved terrace and into the house.

As she reached the hall the day nurse was coming downstairs, a pile of linen over her arm. She beamed, "Good morning, Miss Rockington, a beautiful day, isn't it?" Cheerfulness radiated from her, as much a part of her professional image as her mauve and white striped dress and silver-buckled belt. It wasn't assumed, either. Not with that pleasant face and round, wide-open eyes.

Liz smiled back. "Yes, beautiful. I've been out in the gardens. How is my grandfather today?" Extraordinary how easy it was becoming. She could almost believe she really had a grandfather.

"He's sleeping on this morning, it'll do him the world of good. He went off very happily and peacefully last night."

She nodded and smiled again and padded away in the direction of the back quarters, and the house went suddenly quiet again. Liz wandered around the hall. It was spacious and impressive. She didn't know a thing about architecture, but she guessed it would be over a hundred years old, built at a time when boxes were for putting things in, not people. There was a fireplace with inglenooks, a monk's bench and a tall slender clock, as well as the refectory table she'd noticed last night. The polished oak floor gleamed like pale silk.

Mrs. Jackson's voice came from behind her. "It's a lovely old place, miss, isn't it? Too much work, though, these days when you can't get the help."

She had a carpet sweeper in one hand and a house-maid's box in the other, and she was moving stiffly toward the staircase.

"Let me carry something up for you." Liz took the box, and as they went up the wide staircase she said, "Couldn't I help a bit? With the dusting or something? There must be so much to do and I hate being at a loose end."

Mrs. Jackson turned at the top of the stairs, looking quite scandalized. "Oh, no, miss, thank you for offering, but Mr. Brett wouldn't allow that."

"Why wouldn't he?"

"It wouldn't be fitting, with you taking Miss Elizabeth's place." She lowered her head, rummaging in the box for dusters and polish. "And then you're only just out of bed after the accident. Oh, no, it wouldn't be right."

"But I'm perfectly well again now. And anyway, why should Mr. Denton give the orders? It isn't his house, is it?"

The housekeeper straightened up and looked Liz full in the face. "It seems like that sometimes, since... I was going to say since the master's illness, only it was before that. Since Miss Elizabeth left, I think. It's as if the old master started to go downhill then and he's come to rely on Mr. Brett more and more."

Yes, that fitted, she could understand that. "But I still don't see why Mr. Denton should say how the house should be run."

"Somebody has to," Mrs. Jackson said simply. "I'm getting past it now. And I never mind taking orders from Mr. Brett." She was polishing the banister rail absently.

The housekeeper's lips were folded firmly together, but Liz took a chance. "You've known him a long time?"

The mouth relaxed, became almost tender. "Aye, that I have, ever since he was a toddler. It was in the war when his father used to bring him here. Mr. Brett's father and Miss Elizabeth's father were lifelong friends and they served in the R.A.F. together." She shook her head, looking back into the past. "I can see them now in their pilot's uniforms, laughing and making a joke of everything, the way they used to. And Mr. Brett perched up on his father's shoulder, looking as if he owned the world. He was a fine-looking man, Mr. Brett's father." She closed her eyes. "That's how I like to remember him, laughing as if he hadn't a care in his whole life."

"He didn't come back from the war?"

Mrs. Jackson opened her eyes again and stared at Liz as if she'd forgotten who she was speaking to. "Come back? Oh, yes, he came back all right. It was Miss Elizabeth's father, the master's son, who didn't come back."

She picked up the housemaid's box and stumped off along the gallery and around the corner.

Liz wandered downstairs again, through the hall and the drawing room and out onto the terrace. Here were garden chairs with flowered print cushions and a huge umbrella rising from a white-painted table. She sat down and leaned back. She had a faintly guilty feeling that she should be thinking deeply and seriously about all that had happened since the plane crash, but for some reason that seemed impossible. Too much had happened too quickly. There were times in life when you thought out every step carefully—or imagined that you did. There were other times when you simply freewheeled and went along with life, just as if you were being pushed from behind.

She closed her eyes and the sun made a bright pattern behind her eyelids. From somewhere near a dove cooed in its sleepy, monotonous rhythm, and the buzz of bees came from a bank of fuchsias below the terrace. Everything was dreamlike and unreal, and her thoughts moved slowly, as in a dream, too.

Only the day before yesterday her life had been broken into fragments, yet now it had meaning again and a kind of excitement that comes with challenge.

Footsteps sounded on the terrace and she blinked her eyes open to see Brett's tall form, dark against the sunlight. It was frightening the way her heart began to thud. The accident must have left her weaker than she'd imagined if just the sight of a man with a rather overwhelming personality could make her feel like this. It was almost like being in love, only she wasn't in love. She didn't intend to be in love ever again, not the way she had been with Terry. That left you helpless at the mercy of another person.

He stood beside her chair. "Did I wake you up again? I know I said I wouldn't be back until afternoon, but things went better than I expected. I thought it might be a good idea if we went out to lunch, somewhere away from here and from possible interruptions. There's a pleasant hotel out in the country, only a short drive from here. Do you feel up to it?"

"Yes, of course."

"Good. Just give me a few minutes to change into something cooler." He glanced down at his dark office suit. "I'll see you in the hall in five minutes. All right?"

"I'll be waiting," she said.

She watched him stride across the terrace and into the house; moving swiftly, confidently, very much in command of himself.

How many girls had said that to him, in effect? "I'll be waiting." Quite a number, she guessed. Most girls would be willing and anxious to wait for a man like Brett Denton.

But not Elizabeth. The one he loved hadn't wanted him. Liz smiled wryly as she went toward the house. It looked as if she and Brett had one thing in common, even if it was only a negative thing—the pain of being rejected.

CHAPTER FOUR

"READY?" ASKED BRETT exactly five minutes later. He had changed into light-colored jacket and slacks and a dark green silk shirt, and his hair still glistened from the dousing he had evidently just given it.

As they left the house Liz took an interested look around. Heronswood was certainly in the country, but not deep country. The lane soon joined the main road and there were other houses to be glimpsed behind walls and high hedges, a farm, a gas station, a prep school. They passed a red bus with Coventry marked on it.

Brett drove well and rapidly and soon the car turned into the entrance to a country-house hotel. It was an old building, half-smothered in ivy, with a sign Shire Park Hotel made up of separate, gilded letters above the imposing entrance door. The only modern thing to be noticed was the red asphalt parking lot.

"The food's quite good," Brett said as they went in. "Some of the big firms in Coventry arrange to put up their VIP visitors here, so it's got to be."

The way the head waiter greeted Brett left Liz in no doubt that he rated VIP treatment himself. They were shown to a table in a window alcove overlooking the garden. There were few people lunching yet; one middle-aged, expensively dressed couple across the room, and at a large table a party of men that looked like a business conference.

The waiter brought a menu. "What's good today?" Brett asked.

"Rainbow trout, sir. Very special, I can recommend it."

Brett glanced at Liz. "Lovely," she said.

"Melon to start? And would you like wine, shandy or lager?"

"Shandy, please."

"And two shandies," Brett told the waiter.

When they were alone again he looked approvingly at her. "A girl who can make up her mind," he said, and then with a twist to his mouth, "even when it comes to climbing out of windows. By the way, how did you know the old balcony wouldn't come crashing down when you stepped out on it?"

"I never thought of it. It looked solid, the whole house does."

He nodded, "It is; very solid. No cut-price building when Heronswood went up."

"Is it very old?" Liz asked.

"Heronswood? Oh, I suppose it dates from around the beginning of the last century. J.B.'s father bought it when he made his pile starting to build. I expect the idea was that it should pass from father to son. But the war put paid to that."

She said, "Mrs. Jackson told me that J.B.'s son didn't come back from the war." In case he thought she had been cross-examining the housekeeper she added, "I had to try to find out a little about the family."

"Of course," he said rather formally. "That's what we're here for, isn't it?"

But he didn't seem to be in any hurry to brief her. While they ate he told her a little about what Rockington's were engaged on now, which was a big new housing scheme for some of Birmingham's overspill.

"Ghastly word," he said, "but you can't avoid the jargon when you're working in the middle of it all."

"What do you do in the company?" she asked. "I mean, you personally?"

"My nominal title is general manager," he said with a faint smile. "But actually the job has grown around me, like a skin. The day I finished my training I turned up in J.B.'s office and said, Where do I start? and that was that."

"And where *did* you start?"

"Tracking down a load of cement that British Rail was using for a game of 'button, button.' "

"Did you find it?" She leaned forward acrooss the table, interested.

"M'm, eventually, in a siding at Carlisle. I managed to get it back before the men on the site in Birmingham began passing their time playing shove ha'penny along the girders. We were putting up a new three-story block of shops and apartments on Olton at the time, I remember. I had the switchboard girl nearly handing in her cards, she told me afterward." He smiled reminiscently and suddenly he looked much younger. "But don't think my job is all sitting at a desk surrounded by telephones. I get out and about quite a bit."

"Building houses for people to live in must be fun," she said. "I love new houses, all clean and empty, waiting for people to come and live in them. I can never resist prowling around half-built houses if I get the chance."

The wine waiter brought their shandies then and Brett lifted his glass and said, "We'll have to put you on our sales promotion."

She smiled back at him. "I'll take you up on that. I'll be looking for a new job soon."

It was a marvelous lunch and Liz enjoyed every single bite of it. The melon was cool and sprinkled with ginger; the trout, with its sharp, creamy sauce, nestling in a bed of *petis pois* and *fondu* potatoes, was the kind of food that she had read about but never tasted. A long, long way from Dorothy's pickled herrings or the fish fingers of her bed-sitting-room days in London.

She glanced around the dining room: the crystal chandeliers, the thick carpet, the gleaming linen and sparkling cutlery, the tiny bowls of flowers on each table. Terry hadn't ever had the funds to bring her to a place like this to eat. But now it would be different for him. She had a brief devastating picture of him walking into the top hotel in Cape Town, and beside him Frank Carter's daughter (she was glad he hadn't told her the girl's name; that would have made it all worse) in a designer dress, with real jewelry at her neck and wrists, a smooth hairstyle and a breath of French perfume. *Terry and I have both moved up in the world*, thought Liz, with unaccustomed bitterness.

After the trout came a pineapple meringue for her, while Brett chose cheese and biscuits. He said, "We'll have coffee in the lounge. It'll be more comfortable to talk there."

When they had settled down in deep cushioned chairs, with a tray of coffee on the low table in front of them, he said suddenly, "Did you mean what you said just now? About looking for a job?"

"M'm, I'm afraid so." She glanced around the luxurious room and smiled. "This is super, but it isn't really my scene, you know. I'm a working girl."

He was looking at her with the same narrowed, assessing look that she had noticed before. She wished he wouldn't; it made her confused.

He drank some black coffee before he spoke, then he said, "We've come here to straighten out the position, but first I think I ought to tell you about something you should know. J.B. has always had a romantic sort of dream about Elizabeth and me."

"Yes," she said. "I guessed that."

"You did?"

"Something he said the second time I was with him . . . that I knew what he'd always hoped about 'you and Brett.' "

"Yes, that's true," he said, "he had it all planned out years ago. You see, there had always been a close link between our two families ever since Elizabeth's father and mine were at school together, and I think J.B. set his heart on Elizabeth and me cementing the link, so to speak. They used to think that way in the old days. And there were . . . other reasons, which don't concern us now. Yes, it would have made him very happy, only, of course, it didn't work out like that."

She said, "I wondered, did she marry the man? Whoever it was that she left home for? J.B. asked me, you know. It was almost the first thing he asked me."

"And what did you say?" His voice was suddenly harsh.

"I told the truth," she said simply. "My truth, not perhaps hers. I said no. I hadn't married him. That I'd found out I didn't love him after all."

He glared at her and said, "You certainly choose your times to speak out, don't you?"

The easier atmosphere that had been building up between them over lunch had gone. His face was hard again; he looked as if he might be approaching a flash point.

But she didn't care. She splashed cream from a tiny jug into her coffee and her eyes sparkled angrily. "How was I to know what to say? All the help you gave me was to tell me to play it by ear. Which I did."

He went on staring at her and the anger faded from his face. "I'm sorry," he said, and once again she caught a glimpse of the strain he was coping with.

"Was it so fatal to say that to J.B.?" she asked mildly.

"Fatal? No, not fatal. Though it might have repercussions."

"Why?"

He replied with another question. "Will you tell me why you came out so pat with that answer? The bit about finding out that you didn't love him after all?"

"That's easy," She tried to keep the hurt out of he voice. "The story of my life. That's why I was on the plan coming back from South Africa."

He said quietly, "Do you mind telling me about it? Yo don't have to, of course, if you don't want to. But it migh help."

She looked away from him, across the comfortabl quiet lounge, and she thought with surprise that she didn' mind telling him.

She said, with a funny little smile, "The whole of my lif story would go on one page. My parents have both bee dead for a long time. My mother married twice, and I live with my stepbrother and his wife until I'd finished my sec retarial training, then I got a job in London. Six month ago I met a man and we fell in love. When he got a promo tion to the South African branch of his firm it was a ranged that I would join him out there and take a job, an we would be married later when we'd found somewhere t live and so on. But it d-didn't . . . it didn't work out." He mouth began to tremble and she stopped to get herself un der control. "So I came back," she said at last.

He stirred his coffee, not looking at her, for which sh was grateful.

"Was it true—the part about finding you didn't love hir after all?"

She nearly said defensively, "Yes, it was," but instea she said, "No, that was a face-saver. He was the one wh broke it off. He found a better reason for marriage than be ing in love."

"He told you that?"

"He told me that love was a luxury that most men can' afford. Men have to be practical, he said, and leave r mance to women. He was going to marry the managing di rector's daughter. Very practical, don't you agree?"

His mouth twisted, without humor. "He sounds a highl practical type. I'd say you've had a lucky escape."

"That's what I'm trying to persuade myself," she said.

"But you can't believe it?"

She looked past him, out of the long, wide windows, and the flowers and grass outside blurred together. "When you love someone, when he has been all your hopes and dreams, you don't just stop, do you, whatever he does?"

He was leaning back in his cushioned chair and he had that gleam in his eyes that she was beginning to know. "Is it over?" he said. "Finally and irrevocably?"

She nodded.

"Then what you need is something that will take your mind completely off your troubles."

"I've had that, haven't I?" she said wryly. "If all this hadn't happened I would have been back with John and Dorothy, immersed in self-pity."

"I don't see you like that at all, but let that go. The facts are that you're not back with John and Dorothy, you're here with me, and if you're really looking for a job, I can offer you one."

Amazingly her heart lifted. Perhaps it wouldn't be actually as his secretary, she could hardly expect that. But to work in his department, or even to be a cog in the huge wheel of Rockington's, seemed suddenly an exciting prospect.

"Oh, yes," she said, her eyes shining. "That would be marvelous. But it isn't just because you're feeling sorry for me, is it? I'm really quite a good secretary, you know."

He smiled oddly. "I'm sure you are. But the work I had in mind wouldn't require much secretarial ability."

"Oh!" She was surprised at her sudden sharp prick of disappointment. "I don't think I could do anything else."

"You could do this," he said. "The job I'm offering is one that most girls probably don't consider a job at all, and yet I suppose in a way it is. I'm offering you the job of being married—to me."

It wasn't happening, of course. She was either dreaming or she hadn't heard him properly.

"Did you say . . . what I thought you s-said?" Her own voice was tiny, coming from a long way away.

"I asked you if you would marry me."

It was true, then. "Why?" she asked in that same peculiar voice.

He took his time over answering. She watched his face and could tell nothing from it, absolutely nothing.

Finally he said slowly, "You could call it the repayment, in part, of a debt that can never be wholly repaid."

"A debt to J.B.?"

"Yes."

She still couldn't take it in. "Is that the only reason?" she asked, her forehead pleated in puzzlement.

"It's the only reason," he said, "although there would be dividends, as well. It would put your position outside all possible attack or criticism if you were my wife, instead of living at Heronswood in a false position. It would give you security for the rest of your life, because whatever happened I would see that your interests were protected properly."

It was incredible, unbelievable. He was talking about "my wife," and that meant her, or might.

"If you're thinking it sounds like a business arrangement, then I suppose you're right," Brett said. "But then I don't think either of us could claim to have fallen romantically in love at first sight, could we?"

"That isn't very funny."

"No, it isn't," he admitted. "I'm sorry. Here I am, apologizing to you again. It's getting to be quite a habit."

She knew that he was trying to keep the situation from sinking into some unknown depths and she was grateful to him for that.

She realized that she'd been holding her coffee cup between her hands and now she put it down with a little clatter. "If you're really serious," she said, "the answer's no. It's out of the qu-question."

"But are you sure it is?" He leaned forward, hands clasped on the table. "Unusual, certainly, but not impossible. People have married for worse reasons than—shall we call it compassion." He added softly, "I'd love to see J.B.'s face when we told him."

Suddenly she thought, *Oh, so would I*, then she pulled herself together again.

She shook her head. "But you don't know me. You don't know anything about me."

He was smiling at her now, the faintly ironic smile that she didn't know how to interpret. "I'm a businessman," he said. "Quick judgments, quick decisions. We're doing it all the time."

"And are you always right?"

The smile widened a fraction. "About seventy percent of the time. Otherwise we'd be out of business."

She said, "I really don't know why we're going on talking about this. The whole thing is impossible."

"Yes, I imagined you'd say just that." What an incredible man he was—he looked in no way put out. In fact, if she hadn't known better, she might have thought his smile had more than a trace of smugness about it. "However, I'm not going to consider the subject closed finally. See if you can get used to the idea and we'll talk about it again."

He signaled to the waiter and paid the bill. Then he glanced at his wristwatch. "I'm afraid I must call it a day now. I have to go out to a site this afternoon."

Walking out of the hotel Liz felt an inch taller. It was the craziest proposal; all the same it was a proposal, and any proposal would have done wonders, just then, for her self-esteem.

As Brett opened the car door for her she turned and

smiled up at him before climbing in, and her eyes danced. "Thank you for considering me for the job," she said.

"The offer," he said, "remains open."

He slid into the driving seat and slammed the door. Then he frowned. "You know, I haven't given you much information about the family situation after all, have I? Is there anything particular you're bothered about?"

She tried to pull herself together and think coherently. "I'll make a list of questions and you can write in the answers. Will that do?"

"Very businesslike," he said. "So you really are an efficient secretary. Miss...." He stopped, staring at her in a kind of horrified surprise from the driver's seat.

"Do you know," he said, "I've just proposed to a girl and I don't even know her surname."

"It's Hartley," she said. And suddenly they both started to laugh together.

He swung the powerful car out into the road. "I've thought of something better than your list," he said. "I'm going to take you along to meet my sister. I phoned her this morning and said we might drop in. She'll give you all the information and probably in more detail than I could. Her name's Maggie and she's married to Jake Easton, who has a nursery garden. She's five years older than I am, and I think you'll like her."

"THIS IS IT," said Brett, ten minutes later, turning the car in at a wide entrance with a small painted board announcing, J. H. Easton, Nurseryman. Behind a low hedge you could see row upon row of young shrubs and tiny sapling trees. Flower beds were alight with color and just inside the entrance was a trim wooden building marked, Inquiries and Sales. A little further away was a complex of greenhouses. It all looked very flourishing.

Brett stopped the car just inside the entrance and got

out. "Maggie won't be indoors on a day like this. We'll look around first before we go up to the house. Ah, there she is, and she's seen us."

A tall, dark girl in brown denim jeans and a brown-and-white polka dot top was coming toward them, climbing carefully over the rows of plants. As she got near she waved and smiled.

"Hi, Brett. So you managed to get here after all?"

She included Liz in her smile. "Lovely to see you," and to Brett, "it's been such ages—and I've been so wondering—I could hardly believe you'd come even when you phoned."

"We made it," Brett said. "Liz, this is my big sister, Maggie, who used to boss me around when we were very young. Maggie, Liz Hartley."

Maggie pulled off her gardening glove and held out a brown hand, smiling. "Hullo, Liz," she said, "and don't believe him for one moment. Nobody has ever bossed my brother around."

She was tall, nearly as tall as Brett. The same dark coloring, too, with hair brushed back and held with an orange ribbon, and a suntanned skin. She had firmly marked eyebrows, and near-black eyes, just like her brother's, only where his eyes glittered like jet, Maggie's were soft and luminous. The only feature that was completely different was her mouth. There was no hint of harshness or cynicism here, only a wide smile, happy and generous.

She held Liz's hand in hers for a moment and said, "I'm so glad you could come. So many things have been happening, and I've only heard part of it. Can you stay for tea, both of you?"

"Sorry, not for me," Brett said. "I've got to get out to the Queen's Rise site. They've run up against a spot of trouble with the foundations for the new block. I shouldn't be more than about an hour and I'll call back for Liz. Meanwhile, feed her as you think fit."

"Goodness, we've only just finished the most enormous lunch," Liz protested.

"Ah, well," Maggie said, "you can always manage a 'cuppa,' and it'll be an excuse for me to stop working."

They watched Brett drive off and then Maggie said, "Let's go into the house. I'm on my own this afternoon, Jake's out with the van. Our driver's wife is having a baby and he's taken the day off to fuss around at home, no doubt making a great nuisance of himself." She laughed. "Understandable, as it's their first."

She looked in at the open door of the wooden building marked Inquiries and Sales and said, "All right, Pam? I'll be in the house for a while. If I'm wanted you can ring through."

A very young, rather plain girl looked up from the desk. Several large ledgers were open in front of her and she was chewing the end of her pen worriedly. "Okay, Mrs. Easton." Her eyes went to Maggie with schoolgirlish adoration. "I think I'm getting the hang now."

"Good. Don't worry, it'll come right in time."

"That's Pam Baynes, our new trainee," Maggie said as she led the way along a path and around the end of a hedge to where a modern bungalow was hidden from the road. "She's a nice kid, crazy about the open-air life and works like a beaver in the garden, but she's not so bright with the books. You have to be able to tackle anything in this job, so we're being cruel to be kind and giving her a couple of hours a day on the ledgers."

Maggie turned and smiled at Liz as she pushed open the front door. "Come along in and we can talk."

They went into a large back room with a wonderful view over open country. The room seemed to be half kitchen and half living room, the two parts divided by a trellised screen decorated by a feathery climbing plant.

"We fell for the open-plan idea on the ground floor,"

Maggie said as she pulled out a comfortable chair for Liz and retired to the other end of the room to fill the kettle and put cups and saucers on a tray. "We find it suits us very well, being in and out all the time. Also it makes a good shop window for Jake's specialty—houseplants."

There were plants everywhere: on the windowsills, on specially constructed shelves against the wall, on the television set. Every available horizontal surface was occupied by pots and troughs full of color and flowers and every shade of green.

"I've never seen so many," Liz said. "It's like—"

"Like living in the Botanical Gardens, I say," laughed Maggie, "but it's all good for business." She talked on while she made the tea. She had a lovely voice, low and mellow. Through the trailing green on the trellis, Liz watched her moving around and thought that even in jeans and shirt there was something rather elegant about Maggie. She was easy and had a very human warmth about her. Very different from her brother, with his fine-drawn tension, and the grim lines around his mouth. He wasn't always grim, though. Once or twice over lunch he'd looked as if he might have a sense of humor, though she wasn't quite sure. That ridiculous suggestion of his had been no joke, though. She felt the color coming into her cheeks.

Maggie appeared around the screen and set the tray down on a round table. "Now we can talk," she said. "I only know what Brett had time to tell me on the phone and that's not much. Mostly about Elizabeth." She paused, her face grave. "It's been an awful shock. Poor Elizabeth, nothing has gone right for her for the last three years. Funny how one makes just one wrong decision and one's whole life goes haywire. And now—it's all over."

They were both silent for a time and then Liz said, "I sat next to her on the plane. She looked so ... so sad, I thought. And she was so beautiful."

Maggie nodded. "She always had that look, even as a little girl, sort of lost. I never knew her well—she was so much younger than me—but I remember her as a quiet, withdrawn little thing when I used to go to Heronswood with my father and Brett. Brett was nearer Elizabeth's age, of course."

She poured out tea and handed a cup to Liz. "And now this extraordinary mix-up has happened and you're acting as stand-in for J.B.'s sake. That's how it is, isn't it?"

"Yes, that's exactly how it is." Liz hesitated for a moment, then she said, "Do you think it's wrong—to deceive him, I mean? I seem to ask everyone this question, I suppose I still feel a bit guilty about it."

Maggie's dark eyes met hers candidly. "No, personally, I can't feel that it's wrong. I think it's a very human thing to do, in the circumstances, and I think it's very game of you to take it on. You didn't have to. As a matter of interest, why did you?"

Liz felt her cheeks begin to go warm again. She sipped her tea and said, "Well, it was really my fault in the first place. I—I went into his room, not knowing there was anyone there, and when I spoke he mistook me for Elizabeth. He was expecting her, you see. I tried to tell him it was all a mistake, but—" she shook her head "—somehow I couldn't get through to him. And then the nurse came in and—"

Maggie was watching her closely, "And then I suppose Brett bullied you into it?"

Liz met her glance and smiled. "You might put it like that."

"Yes," Maggie said, "I can imagine it very well. Brett's a demon for getting his own way when he sets his mind on something. And he's felt for a long time that he owes J.B. a kind of debt of honor. Personally I would think he's repaid any debt several times over, but Brett doesn't look at it like that." She sighed and picked up her cup. "Ah, well, it's all old history now and it's a long story that doesn't really have much bearing on the present situation, so let's concentrate on putting you in the picture about the Rockington family. How much have they told you already?"

Liz told her all she knew; Maggie sat back and sipped her tea and concentrated. But even with an effort of memory there didn't seem much to tell. Elizabeth's father had been shot down with his plane over Berlin at the end of the war when Elizabeth was a very small baby. When her mother died, not long after, J.B. had brought up his granddaughter with the help of nannies and governesses. She had been a delicate child, suffering from asthmatic attacks and she hadn't gone to school at all until she was about twelve. Then, as might have been supposed, she'd been unhappy and hadn't fitted in. Later on she had gone to a finishing school in France, and then come back to live at Heronswood.

"She never seemed to have many friends around here," Maggie said. "I don't think you need bother about people you ought to know or talk about. There was a French girl called Cécile who came to stay with her once, and Elizabeth went on holiday to Italy with Cécile and her family. That was where she met Gordon. He was working with an Italian film company there."

"The man she wanted to marry?" Liz asked. "Did she marry him?"

Maggie smiled wryly. "Oh, yes, she married him, the silly girl. They were together for—oh, less than a year. Then he got a chance to make a film in America. You knew he was an actor?"

Liz nodded and Maggie went on, "It seems he had gone to Italy in the first place to make some wonderful film or other, but the project didn't get off the ground. Then it turned out there was something wrong with his contract, so no pay! He was absolutely broke. They both lived on Elizabeth's income for a time, but it wasn't enough to keep Gordon in the manner to which he was accustomed—" Maggie pulled a face "—and as J.B. had tied up the capital and he couldn't get at it he got very awkward. Then, when the offer of this part in America came along, he just packed his bag and disappeared into the night."

"And left Elizabeth behind? Just like that?"

"Yes, so it seems. I don't know the details, of course. She may have been glad to see the last of him." Maggie smiled grimly. "I wouldn't think he was exactly the perfect husband. I expect you're wondering how I know all this? Well, Brett made it his business to keep in touch with Elizabeth. He didn't tell J.B. because J.B. simply didn't want to know—or so he pretended. Nominally there was a complete break. But I think Brett always believed there would be a reconciliation at some time or another, so for J.B.'s sake he wouldn't let Elizabeth go into limbo."

For J.B.'s sake? Or his own? "I see," said Liz.

"Once he went to see her in Italy. That was about a year ago. I think he tried to persuade her to come home and patch things up, but she wouldn't. From what Brett said I got the impression that she clung to a hope that Gordon would come back, or send for her. It's always a mystery to me how some women go on and on loving men who treat them badly." Maggie grinned. "I shouldn't talk. I picked a good one."

Maggie poured out second cups of tea and said thoughtfully, "It's just as well, though, that she was Mrs. Gordon Ferrars and not Miss Elizabeth Rockington. The press would have made a big story out of J.B. Rockington's granddaughter being lost in an air crash."

Liz sat straight up. "Oh, goodness—the papers! I'd forgotten about that angle. Has there been much in them about the accident?"

Maggie got out of her chair and took a wad of newspapers from a bureau drawer. "I kept these," she said, handing them to Liz.

The first was a local evening paper with splash headlines: Elmdon Plane Crash. There was a fuzzy picture of the plane and a short piece below with no names given.

"I think it only got in the last editions on Wednesday evening," Maggie said, "and the following morning there was a big story about a soccer player's baby being kidnapped, so it got pushed to the inside of the paper. The national press was getting worked up about a new threat in the Middle East, and the populars were featuring some drug scandal or other. I don't think any of them followed up the plane crash particularly, so...."

The phone rang on the desk and Maggie said, "Yes, Pam? Oh, all right, I'll come over. Ask them to wait a minute or two, please."

She glanced apologetically at Liz and got up, touching the orange ribbon in her dark hair. "Customers. I won't be long. Help yourself to more tea."

Left alone, Liz read through the newspaper accounts. There seemed nothing to connect any of the passengers with Elizabeth Rockington, although in one of the dailies she found the name of Mrs. E. Ferrars on the list of those detained in hospital. She wondered how interested the reporters were, and if they would get onto anything about Elizabeth at the inquest. She thought that probably Brett, with Dr. Winter's help, would see that they didn't.

She drank another cup of tea, and when Maggie hadn't come back she got up and wandered around the big room. Against the side wall was a modern desk, stacked in orderly fashion with papers, catalogs, advertisements. On top of the desk was a plant with tiny flowers of a glorious deep purple, and Liz went across to look closer at it. Beside the desk on a side wall hung an assortment of photographs,

not studio portraits, but snapshots or enlargements. There
was a family group: Maggie in a scarlet dress, her arm
linked with that of a lanky man with tow-colored hair and
creased, smiling eyes, and in front of them two boys in
school blazers so like their father that it was quite ridiculous.

Next to the family group was a rather faded snapshot of
a big, handsome man in R.A.F. uniform sitting on a garden seat beside a frail-looking woman in a knitted suit.
Brett's and Maggie's parents?

Her eyes went to the third snapshot and Brett himself
looked back at her over a gap of ten or twelve years. He
was in white shirt and shorts, sitting on a low garden wall,
a tennis racket under his arm, smiling into the camera. A
young man of eighteen or nineteen, perhaps just starting at
university; a lighthearted boy, secure and happy, trusting
life and finding it good. What had happened to change him
into the serious, almost harsh man he had become?

Liz leaned her palms on the desk and stared at the snapshot as if it could give her the answer. And suddenly the
oddest thing happened. It was like dreaming, only she was
wide awake. She heard Brett say, again, "Do you believe in
fate?" and her own answer, "I suppose, in a way, I do."

When he'd asked her that she hadn't thought much
about it but now she knew—she just knew—that something inevitable had happened. She knew that whether she
wished it or not, her life was linked with these people, that
they weren't strangers at all. It was a strong, very clear impression, impossible to ignore or laugh away.

Liz had always thought of herself as a fairly practical,
two-feet-on-the-ground person. Living with her stepfather,
and later with John and Dorothy, hadn't exactly encouraged an airy-fairy view of life. Perhaps that was why this
feeling she had now was so disturbing, because it seemed
irrational.

She stared again at the picture of Brett and thought, *If only I could see you look like that again, easy, carefree!* At that moment it seemed the most natural, the most inevitable thing in the world that she should try to help him, do anything he needed of her.

It wasn't because she was in love. She'd been in love with Terry and she knew what it was like. This strange feeling she had for Brett Denton was quite different.

So what was it? Perhaps, after her rejection by Terry, she simply had to feel needed by someone—anyone. Yes, she thought, that was the most probable explanation. It was wonderful to feel you were doing someone a bit of good.

Reassured by this pat summing-up of the situation, Liz turned to smile happily to Maggie as she came back into the room.

CHAPTER FIVE

"SORRY ABOUT THAT." Maggie came across the room with her graceful, long-legged walk, and joined Liz at the desk. "Some optimists who imagined they could plant rose bushes in June. Never mind, I managed to put them right on that and I've sold them a nice batch for delivery in November. Admiring my family-portrait gallery, Liz?"

Liz nodded. "These are your boys? And your husband? How alike they all are!"

"Absurdly. All three completely Anglo-Saxon." She pulled a face. "People seeing me with the twins—Simon and Dominic—always look mildly surprised, as if they were trying to make out how anyone as dark as me could have children as fair as all that. Until they see Jake, that is, and then they see why. Jake's forebears must have come from the far north, while Brett's and mine were the Mediterranean type. Actually, my father was half Spanish. Those are my parents, taken just after the war. It's the only one I've got of them together."

Maggie's great dark eyes were soft, thoughtful, as they rested on the faded snapshot of the tall, swarthy man with the tired-looking woman beside him. She said, "The past is so odd, isn't it, everything gets blurred and strange. It's only ten years since my father died, and my mother died the following year, but it all seems like another life."

Suddenly she smiled. Maggie's smile was the only quick thing about her. All her bodily movements were quiet and relaxed, but when she smiled it happened in a flash of white teeth against brown skin. "And this, of course, is brother Brett. Another oldie, but I like it because—" she put her head on one side and the orange bow flopped down "—well, because that's how I like to think of Brett. He looks so cheerful there, doesn't he? Cheerful and young. Sometimes I think it's a pity we have to grow up."

Her eyes rested for a moment on the photograph and then she turned back to the room. "Now I must try to remember what else I should tell you about the Rockingtons. I think you know about as much as I do myself of Elizabeth. There's her husband, of course, but I don't imagine J.B. will refer to him. I don't suppose he'll want to talk about Roger, either."

"Roger? I haven't heard of him."

Maggie pulled out a comfortable chair for Liz and sat down opposite. "No, I don't suppose you have. He faded out of the family history books some years ago. Before Elizabeth did, in fact. Poor J.B. hasn't been awfully lucky with his grandchildren."

"Roger is Elizabeth's brother?"

Maggie nodded. "A year or two older. About Brett's age, actually. We were all kids together, but I used to imagine myself grown up and vastly superior to the others. Elizabeth used to tag along after the two boys. I can see her now, a thin little thing with a worried look, pleading, 'Please t-take me, too. Oh, please!' She would weep if they went off without her. She had a funny little stammer. I don't think she ever quite grew out of it."

"I didn't grow out of mine, either," said Liz. "That was one reason for the mix-up. I spoke to J.B. and I was in such a state that I stammered, and he mistook me for Elizabeth straight away."

"Oh, I *see*...." Maggie drew out the word. "I hadn't noticed it—that you stammer, I mean, but that explains things. I wondered how it all happened."

"Do you think I should know about Roger?"

Maggie's dark brows drew together. "There isn't reall
much I can tell you. Brett knows more about him than
do. They went to the same school, but after—" Sh
stopped abruptly and then went on, "But later on Bre
studied architecture and Roger went to Cambridge. He le
before he completed his course, I don't remember wh
Then he went into Rockington's for a while, but he didn
last long there, either. There was some sort of bust-up wit
J.B. and afterward I heard that Roger had gon
abroad—to South America, I think it was. He and Eliza
beth always had plenty of money—their mother's side c
the family was in the automobile industry and they wer
very wealthy—so I suppose Roger could please himself."

She glanced across at Liz ruefully. "I'm not an awful lc
of help, I'm afraid. Roger and Brett were never friend
after they grew up, in fact they seemed really antagonisti
sometimes. Roger was the wild boy and Brett was steadie
though somehow 'steady' doesn't seem quite the right wor
for Brett, he's too unexpected."

Unexpected, Liz thought, with a twist of her mouth.
That's putting it mildly.

Maggie was saying, "There's quite a bit about the Rock
ington family that I'm very hazy about, in spite of th
friendship that always existed between them and us. Yo
see, about the time everything . . . changed, I was bus
getting engaged and married to Jake, and I was a horri
self-centered little beast. We had our own troubles in th
family, too. It was all a rather fraught sort of time."

Her face changed. The smooth brown skin of her fore
head creased, making her look years older. Whatever ha
turned Brett from a cheerful laughing boy had had it
effect on his sister, too. But she wasn't going to talk abou
it.

"Now then, is there anyone else?" she mused.

"I met a young widow with a little boy in the garden a

Heronswood this morning," Liz said. "Clare Jessing, she told me she was. She seemed to know all about me—about Elizabeth, that is."

Maggie made a wry grimace. "Clare makes it her business to find out as much as she can about everyone. From which catty remark you'll gather that she's not my favorite person. I haven't really anything against her myself, but she's clever and extremely decorative ... and she's fixed her sights on Brett for her husband number two. There have been times lately when I've been afraid she was winning, and I don't want her for Brett—not in the very least."

Liz would have very much liked to go on with this line of conversation, to know exactly why Maggie thought Clare was winning, to try to discover what the relationship between Brett and Clare was, or what his sister imagined it was. If Brett was committed to another woman it made her own situation all the more bewildering.

But at that moment there was the sound of a car's engine right outside the window and a cheery toot on a horn.

Maggie's head shot up. "That'll be Jake back. He's early. I'll go and tell him we're in here."

A minute or two later she was back, holding a big fair man by the arm. "Liz, this is Jake. He knows about what's been happening over at Heronswood."

Jake Easton held out a firm brown hand. His eyes were very blue and deep-set and he had a delightful smile. "Only thirdhand information," he said, "but enough to know you're doing a good job. Maggie and I are firmly lined up behind you, aren't we, love?"

"Firmly," agreed his wife, looking up at him with an expression in her brown eyes that made Liz, for a brief moment, feel an outsider.

Jake Easton lowered himself into a chair. He wore sand-colored slacks and shirt and his fair hair was casually long and bleached almost white by the sun. Liz saw what Maggie meant by saying he was a Northern type. You could imagine his distant ancestors in the prow of a Viking boat.

"Tea all finished?" he inquired.

Maggie was already halfway to the kitchen end of the big room. "Another brew coming up. You talk to Liz while I cope."

Liz said, "I simply love all your plants and I think it's a super idea to have a garden-room like this. That purple one on the desk's my special favorite. What's it called?"

Jake told her, adding for good measure the details of its life history and cultivation.

Maggie returned with fresh tea and a laughing remonstrance. "Darling, you'll bore Liz to death with the technical jargon."

"Not a bit of it," Jake told her lazily. "Liz is that rare and precious creature: a female who really enjoys listening to men talking about themselves and their hobbies. Aren't you, Liz?"

It was all warm and friendly and relaxed, and after the tension of being with Brett, Liz sat back and enjoyed herself. Jake was explaining to her up-to-the-minute ways of cultivating strawberries when Brett came back. It seemed to Liz that as soon as he entered the room the atmosphere changed, became charged; as if an electric current had passed through them all.

Quite obviously he was anxious to leave, but agreed to Maggie's showing Liz around the bungalow before they left.

The bungalow was very modern. Light and airy and labor-saving, with built-in cupboards and wide windows and clear colors against white walls.

"Brett designed it and Rockingtons built it for us," Maggie told Liz, "after we'd tried for ages to get an older house somewhere near. I've always hankered after old houses myself and Jake agrees. But we couldn't find one at our price, so eventually we decided to build on a part of the land here and now we're wondering if we haven't done the wrong thing because Jake is thinking of expanding and there's nowhere to expand to." She shrugged and smiled. "But I expect it'll all work out in the end."

She sounded so confident, so content. She was one of the lucky ones who had married for love. She and her Jake, they were the kind of people who made rubbish of all the dire prophecies you heard about marriage being an outworn institution.

Brett's voice came to them from the living room. "Maggie, are you there? We ought to be getting back."

Maggie called back, "Coming," and said to Liz, "you must come again very soon. And if you need any help, or get stuck over anything, just give me a ring and I'll be right over. It's only a few minutes in the car. Promise you will."

"Just try to stop me." Meeting Brett's sister had put a new complexion on this whole undertaking somehow. It had brought a kind of normality back to what had seemed like a dream up to now.

Back in the living room Brett pulled himself out of his chair when he saw them. He looked different in this house, too, easier and more relaxed. It must be that Maggie's personality had that effect on people.

"Thanks for the tea, Maggie," he said. "And will you do something else for me? Take Liz shopping for some clothes? She's managed to lose hers somewhere between here and Cape Town."

"That," said Maggie, "would be a pleasure, quite literally. Let's go into Leamington, shall we? The shops are pretty good there and it's nearer than Birmingham. When would you like to go? Tomorrow?"

But I can't, Liz thought in a panic, *I haven't any money.* She should have tried to contact John and Dorothy again and she felt a small shock of surprise as she realized that she'd forgotten all about them.

"I'll call for you tomorrow morning, about half-past ten. Will that do?" Maggie said.

When Liz hesitated Brett said, "Good," in his most forceful voice and guided her firmly out to the car.

"Maggie would have had us staying for supper before we knew what was happening," he said, as they drove away and Liz turned to wave. "But I told Mrs. Jackson we'd be back by five. And the late afternoon is usually J.B.'s best time of the day, so I make it a rule, so far as possible, to go up to see him then. Today I thought we might go together."

There was nothing in the words, or the way he spoke them, to account for the way Liz's heart began to thump wildly as she murmured, "Yes, of c-course."

As the stammer caught her she saw his glance flick toward her, returning immediately to the road ahead. But he had noticed she was nervous. There wasn't much that anyone could hide from Brett Denton, she thought, and that didn't make her feel any better.

The car slowed to negotiate a long, narrow bridge over a river and then purred up the hill on the opposite side. After that a small complex of lanes led them quickly to the gates of Heronswood.

"Oh, it is nice and near," Liz said impulsively. It would be quite easy to walk over to see Maggie and that made her feel reassured.

Brett switched off the engine on the gravel sweep in front of the house. "I told you you'd like Maggie," he said. "Most people do. She'll know where to take you to shop. She's very knowledgeable about clothes. She was in the trade herself before she married Jake."

"Was she?" said Liz, interested. "Selling clothes?"

"No, designing. She was getting on pretty well, but she seems to like growing plants better."

He was ahead of her going up the steps and when he

turned to see why she wasn't following, she said, "There's something—I think I should try to get in touch with my stepbrother again to find out if they're back home yet."

He said, "You can call them again now, or I can get Farthingale to run you over later, whichever you prefer."

"I'll try calling first," she said.

He took her to the phone in the small study where she had seen him sitting the night before last, closed the door and left her there. But there was no reply from John's number and when it was useless to wait any longer she put back the receiver and went out into the hall. Brett turned from where he had been standing by the open front door.

"Any luck?"

She shook her head. "No. I can't understand it. It's only about a week since I saw them and there was nothing said then about going away. And I've never known John and Dorothy to do anything on the spur of the moment."

He said, "Is it important? They won't be worrying about you if they haven't received the cable."

"No, it's not that exactly. It's, well, I wanted to ask John to lend me the money to refund my plane fare home. He—the man I was engaged to—offered to pay it, but I'd rather not be under an obligation. And then, if I'm going to buy clothes tomorrow...."

He was looking steadily at her. "You're doing a job for me. We didn't arrange the financial side of it, but if you'll give me the name of your bank I'll put everything straight."

"But not the plane fare, that doesn't come into the job."

"Have you forgotten," he said, "if you hadn't been on the plane you wouldn't have been here to take the job, and J.B. would have had to know—" He stopped, his eyes bleak. "No, let's do as I say."

"If we do it will be on the understanding that I repay it later."

"Don't argue," he said coolly, and he put both his hands on her shoulders and turned her toward the staircase. Although his touch was gentle she had the feeling that if she resisted it wouldn't have made the slightest difference. Up the stairs she would have gone, like it or not.

The day nurse opened the door in answer to Brett's knock and she nodded brightly. "Yes, he's awake and he's had a good day. I think the doctor will be pleased with him when he calls."

J.B. was propped up in the big bed, his eyes closed, his face peaceful under the silky white hair. A small radio on the beside table was playing a Chopin piece very softly. The nurse went over and touched his hand and said something and from the doorway Liz saw his face light up.

His hand groped toward the radio and switched it off. "Come along, my dears, this is lovely. Come and sit down near me and tell me all the news."

Brett put a hand on his arm and said, "I've been taking Elizabeth to say hello to Maggie. We should have been up to see you before, but you know what Maggie's like. We had quite a job to get away."

His voice was strong and ordinary, not in any way a muted bedside voice.

J.B. said, "Ah, I do know indeed. Your sister's the kindest, most hospitable girl alive. You always got on with her, didn't you, Elizabeth?"

He stretched out a hand and she took it in hers and squeezed the frail fingers. "Nobody could help getting on with Maggie, she's a grand person," she said sincerely. "She showed me over the bungalow and I think it's lovely."

J.B. nodded. "Of course, you haven't seen the new bungalow. Yes, we made a good job of it for her, although she really wanted an old house, something with its own personality was the way she put it."

Brett said dryly, "Yes, that's the only romantic notion I've known Maggie entertain. She's very practical as a rule."

Liz reached in her mind for something that would keep the conversation on this light level. She would, if she really were Elizabeth, normally join in, and yet it would be so easy to make a mistake.

She laughed and said, "Oh, I don't know that I'd agree about Maggie. What about those old snapshots she keeps over her desk? She admitted to being sentimental about them."

That sounded easy and harmless and she glanced at Brett for confirmation that she was doing all right. But his face was suddenly hard, his mouth a straight, bitter line. *Oh, goodness, what have I said now*, Liz wondered. Dealing with Brett Denton was rather like picking your way over a minefield, you never knew when a chance word was going to start off a sort of underground explosion. She wished someone would tell her what the shattering thing was that had happened at some time in the past. All she'd had was a word here, a hint there, nothing to make even a guess possible. She wondered if she dared ask him outright, but the very idea made her shake inside. No, she'd just have to go on playing it by ear.

So she chatted on to J.B., telling him how she had encountered Ames in the kitchen garden, and wondered if he would be hurt if she suggested helping him with the weeding, and how Jake had explained to her the modern way of growing strawberries. J.B. held her hand in his and listened with a little smile playing around his mouth, as if all he wanted was to hear her voice and have her near.

Brett stared out of the window in silence and before he spoke again there was a knock on the door and Ethel appeared to say that please, Mr. Brett was wanted on the phone by the office in Birmingham.

"Forgive me, J.B.," he said, getting up. "I'll be back."

When he had gone Liz said, "Would you like me to come and read to you sometimes, J.B.? If you can put up with my silly stammer I'd love to."

"Oh, very much indeed, my dear, it would be something to look forward to." The old man looked delighted. "I listen to the radio, but nurse always wants to fuss around and do things to me just when there's an interesting story on."

"That's settled, then. What book would you like?"

They discussed books and agreed on Dickens. By the time Brett came back they were busily discussing the relative merits of *Bleak House* and *Great Expectations*.

"Nurse is getting slightly restive," Brett announced. "I think she imagines we're tiring you, J.B. And I've brought another visitor. Guess who."

His voice was easy again; he'd evidently got over whatever it was that had touched him on a sensitive spot. In his arms he held the white Persian cat. "Sphinx," he added. "He was sitting hopefully outside the door."

He put the cat on J.B.'s bed, where it purred and rubbed itself against his hand. Brett said to Liz, "Nurse Green's orthodox soul disapproves of cats on beds, but Colin Winter's in favor, and his word goes."

J.B. tickled the cat behind his ear. "If an ancient invalid is not allowed his favorite puss it's a poor show," he said. "That's my beautiful Sphinxy, my mysterious friend! Am I getting dotty in my old age, Elizabeth?"

"Dotty? You? Rubbish!"

Indeed, he looked anything but in his dotage at that moment. There was a new vitality about him that had been missing from the old man she had first seen lying in that bed two days ago, helpless and drained of life, hardly strong enough to raise his hand or to speak.

"He really does seem better," she said to Brett as they closed the door behind them, having promised to come in again later to say good-night. "Do you think he might be...."

"Going to get better?" He shook his head as they walked side by side down the wide staircase. "I'd like to think so, but I'm afraid it's a frail hope. Colin has had two of the top cardiac men in Birmingham out to look at him and they agree that it can only be a matter of time. His age is very much against him."

"It's a heart condition, then? I thought it might be something to do with his having lost his sight?"

"No, that was something quite different. A ghastly coincidence that it should come on shortly before his heart attack. They thought it might have contributed—he was terribly depressed about it at first. Who wouldn't be?"

They'd reached the hall now and by common consent went out of the front doorway, down the steps and around the side of the house into the garden. The sun was getting lower in the sky and the garden was still and warm in the late afternoon.

Brett said, "Let's walk. I want to talk to you."

Oh, no, Liz thought, *not yet. I haven't had time to think.*

But she wasn't going to be allowed time. As they strolled down the path between the flowering shrubs and the smooth expanse of lawn, Brett said, "Well, what's the answer?"

She put up her hand to shade her eyes from the sun. "I thought you said you'd give me time."

"I have. About three hours."

Yes, it was all in character. To him a decision was a swift thing, not something to mull over and fumble around with. Even a decision about the most important thing of all—whom to marry. Or perhaps it wasn't all that important to him, except as it affected J.B. and his own mysterious "debt of honor." Perhaps, now that Elizabeth was gone, any reasonably attractive girl would have done.

She said, "Three hours isn't very long," and as she said it she remembered that three hours ago she had said that the whole thing was out of the question.

"Long enough," he said. "The circumstances won't be any different in another three hours...or six...or twenty-four." He smiled crookedly. "I'm sorry I can't produce any credentials. You have to take my integrity on trust, on the evidence you have already."

He was joking, he must be. No man would ask a girl to marry him in these free and easy times, and use words like "credentials" and "integrity."

She looked up at him and saw that he was perfectly serious. As he had said, this was a business arrangement; it would be conducted on business terms.

Once again he seemed to know what she was thinking. "Are you all that keen on waiting until you 'fall in love' again?"

Suddenly she was back in that bare hotel room in Cape Town. Back with the pain and despair and humiliation. In the cruel early-morning light she had dragged herself over to the washbasin to bathe her face, and her own reflection had stared back at her—white face blotched with red, puffy eyes, straggling hair. *Never again,* she'd thought, horrified. *If this is what loving a man brings you to I don't want any of it.*

Now she said slowly, "I've had all I can take of falling in love. But—to get married—it's such an important thing, and it always seemed to me that it should be final. For always."

"That's how it's always seemed to me, too," he said quietly.

She shook her head. "I don't get it. Marriage a kind of business arrangement! How could it possibly work out?"

"It might. It always used to, you know. It's only quite late on in history that the idea of sentiment and romance entered into marriage. All marriages were arranged ones, and it seemed to work quite well."

They had reached a wild part of the garden now and

were walking along a narrow path overhung by saplings and high-growing bushes, which effectively kept out the evening sunshine.

Liz shivered suddenly. "It seems so calculated. So cold—inhuman almost."

He stopped and put both hands on her shoulders, turning her face to him. "Calculated, yes, I can't deny that very well, can I? But I promise you I'm not inhuman. And not cold, either . . . not unless you wanted it that way."

Before she guessed what was going to happen he had drawn her close against him and was kissing her hard and deep. When he let her go her knees were shaking and if he hadn't kept his arm around her she would have fallen.

She stammered, "What was that supposed to m-mean?"

He touched her cheek with one finger, smiling, and his eyes were very dark. "Not to demonstrate my fatal charm, if that's what you're thinking. Hasn't anyone ever told you that you're a very disturbing young woman, Miss Liz Hartley?"

Terry had told her that, hadn't he, but he'd married Frank Carter's daughter for money and position, all the same. Well at least nobody would ever marry her for her money, that was one comfort.

"Also," Brett continued, "we haven't time for the usual preliminary ploys, and it might have been awkward if you found out, after we were married, that you couldn't bear to have me near you. It does happen sometimes, you know." He was still smiling down at her as he added, "I must say I'm glad it didn't happen this time."

She gasped and shook her head helplessly, half laughing as if she'd just come to the surface from a dive into deep, deep water.

"I think you're the m-most . . . the most impossible man I've ever met. It's all just too fantastic."

"Because I ask you to marry me without all the usual

blah-blah about falling in love," he said. "That's where the danger lies—in the fantasy and the dream. People in love are never honest with each other. But we shouldn't have any ghastly awakening afterward to find we'd been projecting our ideals on each other. We'd know the worst from the start."

"You're serious, aren't you?" she said.

He nodded gravely. "Completely."

"Then what is the worst about me?"

He leaned back against the trunk of a slender silver birch sapling, folded his arms and looked down at her speculatively. "Well, since you ask, you're independent and touchy and you work yourself into huffs. You're somewhat foolhardy and inclined to be oversensitive."

"Fine," she said. "Anything else?"

"Probably." He smiled. "I'll let you know when I notice."

"Thanks, that's big of you. Am I allowed to list your faults?"

"Of course. Any time you like. But the list would be very lengthy, and just now there are more important things to decide. Such as saying you'll marry me."

It wasn't fair that any man should have eyes like his; dark eyes, magnetic eyes, eyes that you could drown in. Maggie's words came back to her: "Brett's a demon for getting his own way." Certainly he was a charmer, and it suited him to use all his charm on her at the moment.

She summoned her will power. "No," she said.

"Really, no?" he said.

It was like thumping your fist against a rock. She wondered how she was going to manage to hold out against him.

"Let's go back to the house," she said.

He didn't argue with her any longer and they turned and walked back along the narrow, overhung path. Once a branch barred her way and he leaned over and pushed it aside. His hand brushed her bare arm and she felt a tingling right up to her shoulder, like an electric shock.

Back in the house Brett said, "Like a drink before supper?"

She needed a clear head and a drink was the last thing she wanted.

"No thanks, not now. What time is supper? I'll need to tidy up first."

"Usually about seven, when I'm in. Mrs. Jackson likes to get it all cleared up early when it's possible."

She went up to her room and sat down on the bed, her knees still trembling.

Don't be a fool, she warned herself. *It doesn't mean a thing, this rather overwhelming physical reaction.* She mustn't let herself be carried away because his touch turned her knees to cotton wool and made her heart behave like Big Ben striking the hour. Before Terry had come along she would probably have mistaken it for love, but now she knew differently.

She got up and walked over to the dressing table and sat looking at her reflection in the mirror, twiddling a crystal bottle of perfume in her hand. She must think harder now than she had ever thought in her life. She must know exactly what course she would take next time Brett asked her to marry him, as he undoubtedly would.

She looked around the beautiful room. If she were Brett Denton's wife she would have a place like this. Comfort. Luxury, almost. Most girls would jump at the chance of marriage to a man who could give them what Brett was offering her. Maybe they were right. Maybe she was too romantic, as Terry had told her.

A little cool objective thought was what was needed, and here, right away from Brett Denton, out of range of the unnerving effect he had on her, was the place to think about what she knew of him.

And how much did she know about him? He'd given her a list of her faults, but what about his?

She knew that he was strong, effective, confident, tough-minded, with a brain that appeared to work with the speed of a computer. That he had a stern sense of duty and obligation, expected people to do what he wanted and had a habit of getting his own way.

Not exactly faults perhaps, but they all pointed the same way, to a man who was hard, almost ruthless. Only once, in all these days, had he spoken to her with any gentleness at all, and that might just have been part of a calculated plan to make her do what he wanted.

She got up and walked restlessly to the long window and stood looking down at the gardens below. Above the shrubs on the right, she could see the tips of the silver birch saplings that fringed the shaded path where only a few minutes ago he had held her closely in his arms and kissed her and said, "Not cold at all—not unless you wanted it that way."

There was a tap on the door and she spun around, her heart in her mouth. "Come in."

But it was only Ethel who appeared in the doorway, smiling shyly. "Mrs. Jackson says supper'll be ready in about five minutes, Miss Elizabeth, and would you like to have it downstairs with Mr. Brett, or I could bring yours up here on a tray if you're not feeling up to coming down again."

"Thank Mrs. Jackson and say I'll come down, will you, Ethel?" She had had quite enough of eating alone in this room.

The little maid's head bobbed up and down and she withdrew as if from the presence of royalty. *What if she knew I was an imposter,* Liz thought. She seemed an honest child; she would probably be horrified.

She went over to the dressing table and retouched her

makeup. Tomorrow she'd buy some of her own, just the basic things; cream, powder, lipstick and so on. She looked down at the array of exotic, expensive jars and bottles that had been Elizabeth's. The colors were all a little too dark for her and the creams and lotions were thickening with age and inclined to cake on her skin. But the worst part was the way she seemed to wince inside every time she had to use Elizabeth's makeup at all.

She brushed a little color onto her cheeks. It would have been nice if she'd been the type who looked fabulous and exciting without makeup at all, but she wasn't. She was inclined to be pale, especially in moments of stress.

She ran a comb through her fine, satiny hair and pushed it away from her face. The real Elizabeth would have looked marvelous, with makeup or without.

Liz sighed deeply. The real Elizabeth had been really beautiful.

CHAPTER SIX

BRETT AND COLIN WINTER were standing beside the refec
tory table in the hall, talking. They stopped and looked u
as Liz came down the stairs and Colin said, "I was just thi
moment inquiring about you. How are you feeling today?"

His voice was quiet and kind and the eyes behind th
gold-rimmed glasses were kind, too. Quizzical, humorou
eyes. Liz said warmly, "I'm fine, thanks."

"That's good news." He watched her as she came dow
the last few stairs in her green dress with the silver buckle
The evening light poured through the long window at the
turn of the staircase, adding sheen to the curve of he
honey-brown hair and her long slender legs. Colin said ap
preciatively, "I must say you're looking wonderful, quite a
different girl from when I saw you yesterday."

"Oh, yes, I'm feeling different, too."

Which was true. It was extraordinary, when she came to
think of it, how well she felt. The anguish of that night in
the hotel bedroom in Cape Town seemed to be light-year
away, instead of less than a week. For some unexplained
reason she felt brimming over with energy.

Colin didn't take his eyes off her as she walked toward
them. Brett turned a little away and said in a rather per
functory tone, "Sure you won't change your mind and stay
for a bite of supper?"

There was a pause while Colin's eyes went from Liz to
Brett and back again. Then he grinned and put his case
down on the table. "You've persuaded me. I've just had a
vision of an empty apartment and the cold ham and limp
salad my daily will have left for me."

"Good." Brett sounded very brisk. "I'll go and warn Mrs. J."

"No, I'll go." Liz stopped him, a hand on his arm. She was supposed to be Elizabeth Rockington, wasn't she? This was her house and this was her job.

She caught Brett's startled expression as she made for the passage, which presumably led to the kitchen quarters.

If Heronswood had, by and large, retained its period flavor, the kitchen was the exception; it had certainly moved with the times. Liz's eyes took in at a glance the modern equipment and the comfortable appearance of natural pine against orange tiles and curtains. Then she pulled up short at the sight of Mrs. Jackson sitting in a straight-backed chair beside the table, one leg thrust out awkwardly in front of her, her face grim with pain.

"Why, Mrs. Jackson, what's the matter? Have you hurt yourself?"

The housekeeper glared. "Oh, don't fuss me, child." Then she remembered her position and added wanly, "Nothing to worry about, miss. My legs gets bad now and then, that's all."

Ethel turned her head from the electric stove, frowning fiercely. "She should be in her bed, Miss Elizabeth, that's where she should be. I know what my mum would say if she was in our house."

"Now then, Ethel, that's enough, you get on with what you're doing."

The reprimand was a pure reflex, but Ethel's mouth went mulish and her neck flushed as red as the tomato-colored pan she was stirring. "You should so," she repeated, and added to Liz, "It's her arthritis, miss. The doctor keeps telling her she ought to rest more."

Mrs. Jackson ignored that and looked up at Liz. "Were you requiring something, miss?"

Hardly the moment to announce the news of an unexpected guest, but it had to be done. Liz pulled an apologetic face and said, "I'm sorry, Mrs. Jackson, but I'm afraid I've come to tell you that Dr. Winter is staying for supper."

A spasm of pain, or irritation, or both, passed across the housekeeper's face and she began to struggle up out of the chair, but Liz put a cool restraining hand over the knobbly old one.

"No, stay where you are, Mrs. Jackson. Ethel and I can manage quite well for once. You just tell me what's for supper while Ethel goes and lays another place at table for Dr. Winter. All right?"

"But . . ." began Mrs. Jackson, her sense of the fitness of things obviously outraged.

"Please!" Liz smiled. "I'd like to."

The housekeeper seemed to be having some inward struggle but it was soon over. Her effort to get out of the chair must have hurt pretty badly. She sank back with a grunt of relief. "Well, miss, it isn't right for you to be working out here, just after your accident and all, but as Ethel's mum would say, 'Needs must when the devil drives,' and I think the Old Gentleman himself has got it in for me today."

She made a valiant attempt at a smile and Liz patted her hand again. "Now you just sit there and direct operations and we'll have things ready in no time."

The orders were soon flowing. Ethel was despatched to the dining room to set another place and Liz was preparing a tray for J.B.

"It's very simple tonight, miss, fortunately. Summer vegetable soup, chicken in aspic with tossed salad and an apricot mousse in the fridge. The soup bowls are in the hot cupboard below the cooker there. I'll be chopping the parsley for garnish while you fill the bowl. . . ."

In five minutes the soup was ready to carry in, the salad tossed, and Mrs. Jackson looking reasonably reassured.

"Thank you, miss, it's really very good of you to do all this...."

Liz picked up the tray and shook her head, smiling. "I haven't done much, have I? But you must let me help, Mrs. Jackson, when you need help. I won't interfere, I promise you. Now, I'll take the soup in and Ethel can carry Mr. Rockington's tray up. What about the nurse?"

"Nurse Sweet has supper later on down here when the night nurse comes."

"Good. Everything's under control then." As she pushed open the kitchen door with her hip, steadying the tray with the soup bowls on it, Liz thought she saw the same startled look on the housekeeper's face that she had seen on Brett's, and she chuckled to herself. How did they expect her to fill her days, for goodness' sake, if she weren't to be allowed to help?

Or was it, she thought sobering, that neither of them could bear to see her in Elizabeth's place doing all the things that Elizabeth herself had once done?

As she came back into the hall Liz saw that Brett and Colin were still there beside the table with the copper bowl of delphiniums. Brett looked at the tray in her hands, eyebrows lifted inquiringly, and she said, "Mrs. Jackson's leg is very painful, so I'm lending a hand."

Colin said, "As bad as that, is it? I'd better take a look at her before I go and make sure she's not missing on her tablets. She can be extremely awkward sometimes...seems to think she ought to slog along without them."

He held out his hand for the tray. "Let me carry that."

But Liz smiled and said, "The soup bowls are rather full. And aren't men supposed to spill things?"

He grinned back at her. "I won't, I promise. I have the lightest possible touch with crockery. I usually have to do my own washing up, you see, so I have to foot the bill for breakages, and that teaches caution."

He took the tray carefully from her and led the way into the room next to the drawing room. Liz followed, and Brett, who had listened unsmiling to this playful exchange, brought up the rear in silence.

Like the drawing room this room overlooked the garden where long shadows lay across the terrace and the lawn. They took their places at an oval table half the length of the room, spread with Madeira lace mats and a centerpiece of roses. The silver and glass sparkled against the burnished wood, the sideboard and the high-backed chairs were lovingly tended to, and not a fleck of dust showed itself anywhere. No wonder, though Liz, that Mrs. Jackson looked tired out if she kept this place up to such a pitch of perfection with only a woman to do "the rough" and one young girl to help.

It was Colin Winter who did most of the talking during the meal, with Liz putting in a word here and there and Brett sitting rather glumly silent. Colin talked amusingly about his struggles with housekeeping when he first took over his apartment in Kenilworth. He talked a little about the partnership practice he belonged to and about the tennis club where he played when he had an hour to spare, and about what appeared to be his greatest interest—the theater.

It was one of Liz's interests, too. When she had lived with John and Dorothy she had regularly queued up at Stratford during the Shakespeare season. She and Colin compared notes on productions they had enjoyed as far back as five years.

Now and then she saw Colin's eyes go thoughtfully to Brett's brooding face and guessed that he was thinking, *Poor old boy, he's been having a tough time of it. No wonder he's not feeling like joining in the chat.*

Yes, Colin was nice. He'd be a good friend, she thought, liking him more all the time.

When supper was over he stood up, reluctantly declining coffee. "I mustn't stay longer, much as I'd like to. I've got a couple more calls to put in this evening. I'll just go along to the kitchen and take a look at Mrs. Jackson and then I'll let myself out. Thanks for the supper and the company; it was great."

He said good-night to them both and went.

Liz began to pile up the plates onto the cart. Brett watched her for a time and then said irritably, "Do you have to do that?"

"Not really. I thought it might help."

"Don't get too carried away with helping. Come and sit down again."

At that moment Ethel appeared with coffee so she could only obey. The little maid put down the silver tray in front of her and Liz said, "Is Mrs. Jackson feeling any better?"

"No, miss, the doctor says she's to go to bed."

"I'm sure that's the best thing. Can you manage, Ethel? What else is there to do?"

"Only Nurse Sweet's supper, miss, and that's all prepared. I can do the washing up afterward. May I take the cart, miss?"

She departed, pushing the dinner cart, which was almost as large as she was herself, with the greatest of care.

Liz smiled. "What a nice child that is!" She picked up the coffeepot. "How do you like your coffee?"

He stared moodily at her. "Um? Oh, black, please."

She passed the cup to him and he said, "Don't get too involved in domestic trivia, will you?"

For a moment her anger flared. "An old woman in considerable pain isn't domestic trivia, surely?"

He was frowning darkly and she thought he was going to pursue the subject, but instead he said wearily, "There's something you ought to know."

At his tone her head shot up. "J.B.?"

"Yes. He's not too good tonight. Colin was rather worried about him. I saw him for a few minutes alone, after Colin had left him, and he looked . . . wretched." He sat holding his coffee cup between both hands, staring down at it. "I felt so helpless, wanting to do something for him, and knowing there was nothing I could do. Have you ever felt like that, Liz?" He looked up at her, his eyes dark with a kind of angry frustration. "Ever watched someone you care about slipping out of life and not being able to do a thing?"

She shook her head dumbly. Her mother had died in hospital. With her stepfather the end had come almost unexpectedly after a long illness, and in any case, although she had looked after him to the very best of her ability, she had never pretended to love him.

Brett smiled grimly. "Then it occurred to me that there *was* something I could do, so I did it. I told him that I'd just asked you—asked Elizabeth—to marry me."

Her breath caught in her throat. "You did—*what?*"

"I told him . . . I'd asked you . . . to marry me." He repeated the words carefully, as if explaining to a child.

"And I suppose you told him that I'd accepted?" To her horror she sounded almost flippant.

His eyes, looking into hers, were steady. "Yes," he said, "I did."

Liz usually liked her coffee white, but now she poured out half a cup, black, and tossed it off at one gulp.

It was too hot and too strong, but it helped. "You shouldn't have done that."

"Do you think I don't know?" he said.

Then, unexpectedly, he smiled. "If you could have seen his face! I might have given him the sun and all the stars on a plate. I knew he wanted it, but I never knew how much."

Because she was oddly moved her voice sounded shakily

accusing as she said, "You make things pretty difficult for me, don't you? It's all very well for you. You seem able to toss out decisions like . . . like a monkey cracking nuts, but I'm not like that. I have to have time to think things out."

If only he wouldn't look at her like that! It was unnerving to feel that someone else was seeing straight into your mind. He probably wasn't, but it felt like that.

He said quietly, "I don't think you do yourself justice. I think you've got a very good intelligence and that you can make decisions if you want to, even big ones."

He leaned toward her, forearms on the table. "I'm not going to plead my case anymore, Liz. I'm afraid you must decide, now, whether it's yes or no."

She said, "Let's get this straight: you mean us to be married—quite soon?"

"Yes."

"But surely . . . wouldn't it be just as good if we were engaged?"

He waved that away impatiently. "No good at all. An engagement wouldn't fill the bill. J.B. needs the reassurance, after all that has happened, that Elizabeth would be safe and secure after he has gone—as far as anyone can be safe and secure in the world today."

"And he thinks you would give her safety and security?"

"He knows I would," Brett said simply.

She nodded. That made sense. The very first feeling she'd had about him, out there in the muddy field near the airport, was of a rock you could lean your weight against.

"So it's marriage or nothing," she said, almost to herself. And then, lifting her head and looking straight at him, "What will you do if it's no?"

His mouth was suddenly hard. "That won't concern you, will it?"

No, it wouldn't. Because if she refused there would be no choice left to him but to tell J.B. the whole truth about her, and that would mean that she would have to leave immediately. Leave Heronswood and never see it again. Never see Brett Denton again, in all her life.

She began to smile. "I think I've got another fault to add to your list. I think I'm stark crazy."

He was suddenly alert, his eyes dark and brilliant. "You mean...?"

"I mean I'm going to take a chance. I'm going to say yes."

He sank back into his chair, drawing in a long deep breath. "My goodness, that's a relief!"

Relief? Or triumph at getting his own way? He'd worked pretty hard on it, she thought with a cynicism new to her.

She studied his face. Now that she had finally committed herself she felt calm. Calm and, in an odd way, elated. Was that what making a hugely important decision did to you? Made you sufficiently cool and confident to view even the formidable Brett Denton objectively?

If she were in love with him she would be dithering now, her mind and emotions all churned up. As it was she felt serene and clear and mistress of herself. It just showed, she decided, that falling in love was a fool's game.

His eyes held hers tensely, his expression unreadable. "Thank you, Liz," he said. "I'll do my best to see you don't regret it." Then, his face relaxing, "Let's drink to our partnership. We'll have a liqueur with coffee." He walked over to the chiffonier in the corner of the dining room. "What's your fancy?"

She shook her head. "I wouldn't know; you choose for me. Liqueurs haven't figured much in my life up to now."

He peered into the cupboard and then back at her thoughtfully. "Let's see, what would suit you? Cointreau? Benedictine? Nothing sweet and sticky, I think. Ah, here we are—Chartreuse. Yes—" he smiled, pulling out a bottle "—I think you're a Chartreuse girl. Cool to look at but with a certain piquancy on closer acquaintance."

He set the tiny crystal glass with its greenish clear liquid on the table before her and, raising his own brandy glass, said, "To our partnership!"

"Our partnership," she echoed, and sipped her drink. "Yes, I like it."

His eyes gleamed teasingly. "Excellent taste you have."

The gleam disappeared. He took out his pocket notebook and flicked over the pages. "Now we can get on with the arrangements. How about—let's see—two weeks from Wednesday?"

She gasped. "You mean for...?"

"For our wedding, of course. Do you feel particularly strongly about a church ceremony? Because if not it would be better to make it as anonymous as possible in the circumstances. Register office, preferably in Birmingham. That should be anonymous enough for anybody. All right with you?"

She wondered fleetingly what would happen if she said no, she wanted to be married in church; that she'd never liked the idea of a register-office wedding. But of course she couldn't make an issue of it. This, she reminded herself, was no ordinary wedding. It was a business arrangement.

She adjusted herself quickly to his change of mood. "Whatever you think best."

He nodded. "Good, I'll arrange it, then. You'll have to give me some personal details, I expect, but we can go into that later." He was still consulting his notebook. "Then there's the matter of reclaiming your possessions. I gather that everything that was found and that hasn't already been claimed is at the police station in Birmingham. I'm afraid you'll have to come in with me to identify anything that is yours. I could take you in on Monday afternoon."

He glanced at her for confirmation and again she said, "Whatever suits you."

"I take it your checkbook was among your luggage?"

"Yes, it was in my handbag."

"H'm, well then, the best way to pay for the things you're going to buy tomorrow will be to have everything put on Maggie's account at the shops and I'll settle with her. I'll phone and tell her."

"Thank you," she said. "I promise not to be too extravagant."

He frowned faintly and she felt as if she had been guilty of undignified flippancy. "You must get everything you need, naturally." He glanced again at his notebook. "Oh, yes, and one other thing. My secretary checked with the travel people and found the cost of your return ticket from Cape Town, as near as necessary, so you can refund the fare money to your boyfriend."

She thought she heard contempt in his voice and for some obscure reason felt suddenly that she would like to call off the whole thing. It was all horrid and humiliating and—

He handed her an envelope. "That's my check for the amount; you can post it, if you like, and let him make what he wants of it. Or you can wait until you get your own bank account working again and send him your own check. Just as you please. There's some spare cash in there, too, for your current expenses."

She took the envelope as if it would bite her. "It's very generous of you," she said stiffly.

Suddenly, unexpectedly, he smiled. "Not at all. As a matter of fact I consider I've got a bargain at the price."

She met his eyes doubtfully, not returning his smile.

"Still bothered about my lack of romance?" His smile seemed mocking now. "I assure you there's always the practical side to marriage, however rose tinted the rest of it."

"Yes, of course."

He leaned across the table and put his hand over hers.

His fingers were warm and vital and again, as out in the garden, his touch was like an electric shock.

"Cheer up, Liz," he said. "It's not as bad as all that." He was laughing openly now, willing her to laugh back.

Some of his own confidence must have touched her, for she felt a bubbly sensation of excitement, of adventure, which she was sure wasn't due to the one small glass of Chartreuse. Her mouth broke into her wide, generous smile.

"That's better," he said. He was looking rather strangely at her now. "Believe me, I really am glad and grateful, Liz, for what you've done and for what you've promised to do. This must have been difficult for you. I'm inclined to forget that everyone hasn't got my own urge for speed and action. Although," he added, his eyes creasing up whimsically, "you didn't do so badly yourself when you climbed out onto that balcony."

"You're not going to let me forget that, are you?"

"Of course not," he said. "I believe in using the weapons that people put into my hands."

Suddenly he became completely serious again. He stood up, draining his brandy glass. "Is there anything else you want to ask me at present?"

She was getting used to his abrupt changes of mood. It was as if he had compartments in his mind and moved from one to another like lightning, but with no carry-over. She guessed that this was something that men could do naturally, but women hardly at all. Certainly she couldn't.

She looked into her empty liqueur glass. "There's one thing—what happens if—if after we're married you fall in love with s-somebody else?"

"We needn't consider that," he said brusquely.

"And if I do?"

His mouth went grim. "We'll cross that particular bridge if we come to it," he said. "Now let's go up and see J.B."

THE OLD MAN LOOKED DESPERATELY WHITE and he lay back against his high pillows as if every spark of energy had left him. But he smiled weakly and held out both his hands. "My dear children, this is wonderful news. The best medicine you could have given me."

Liz took one of his hands and squeezed it gently. "I'm glad."

She felt the feeble answering pressure. "You're . . . happy?"

"Wonderfully happy," she said steadily. Was it a lie? She didn't know. Certainly it didn't seem like one at this moment.

The old man took Brett's hand and joined it to hers. "I don't need to ask you, Brett."

"No, indeed you don't, sir."

J.B. nodded to himself. "It's not everyone . . . can have . . . a dream come true. . . ."

His voice died away and he seemed to be breathing with difficulty. Liz glanced across to Nurse Sweet who was doing something at a side table, one eye still on her patient. She made a little gesture and Liz stood up.

"We're going to leave you to sleep now, J.B., and tomorrow afternoon I'm coming up to read to you, aren't I?" She leaned down and kissed him.

She turned at the door, waiting for Brett. As he followed her across the room the white Persian cat, Sphinx, uncoiled himself from the rug and stretched. Brett paused to tickle the cat absently behind his beautiful silky ears, but his face remained turned back toward the bed.

As they came downstairs Ethel was crossing the hall. "Oh, Mr. Brett, I was looking for you. Mrs. Jessing's just come. She's in the drawing room."

Brett muttered something under his breath as Clare Jessing appeared at the drawing room door. She was wearing a little scarlet dress this evening with a scarlet bow in her pale, shoulder-length hair. She looked more like a model than ever.

She glided across the hall toward them. "Brett—hello! It's been simply *ages*! I just had to come and see how things were."

Her voice was intimate, slightly husky, and she moved her shoulders as she smiled up at him. Liz could almost hear the cameras click. Hold it there, dear. Click. And again. Click. And another one—that's fine, darling.

Clare's eyes slid sideways, just touched Liz with a cool glance, and she said, "Hullo again, Elizabeth." None of the all-girls-together approach today.

Brett seemed to hesitate and Liz saw that even his computer brain couldn't sort out in a split second whether Clare and Elizabeth would have been likely to know each other. She put in quickly, "Clare and I introduced ourselves yesterday, out in the garden. Didn't I mention it to you? I meant to."

"Ah!" She saw him relax as he grasped the point. It was like playing a complicated game, only you made up the rules as you went along.

Brett said, "Come and have a drink, Clare," and they all went into the drawing room. The long windows stood open to let in the scent of lilac. Above the dark shape of the shrubs at the far end of the lawn the last of the sunset was fading in long streaks of gray and pale green and yellow.

Clare took the drink he poured out for her. He evidently knew her preference. She sipped it and said, very gay, "Believe it or not I've achieved the impossible. I've fixed with a sitter for tomorrow evening. I thought we could show Elizabeth some of our swinging Warwickshire night life while she's here. How are you fixed, Brett?" She touched his arm lightly. "Could you get another man?"

He had his enigmatic look. "Sorry, Clare, but no go, I'm afraid. Elizabeth and I have other plans." Deliberately he stretched out his arm and drew Liz against him. "You may as well be one of the first to hear our news. Elizabeth has promised to marry me."

The effect on Clare was startling. Her mouth dropped open, her eyes dilated and all the color went from her cheeks. For a long moment she stared blankly at Brett. Only for a moment though, then she had herself under control again.

"Well, well!" she drawled. "What do you know?"

You had to hand it to her; she'd had a shock and a pretty bad one, but she'd snapped back like a rubber band, and only the two spots of crimson that had replaced the whiteness in her cheeks showed the evidence.

"*Really*, Brett, you shouldn't give people shocks like that, you know. Is it true... you wouldn't be fooling, would you?"

He raised his eyebrows. "I wouldn't be fooling."

She shook her head helplessly, gazing from one to the other of them with exaggerated surprise. "I simply can't take it in."

Seeing that she wasn't going to get any help from Brett, she turned to Liz with pretty appeal. "Forgive the first re-action, and of course congratulations and all that, but you see I thought—I understood from Brett—that you were already married. I noticed you weren't wearing a ring, but of course these days not everyone does. I must have misunderstood."

"Yes, I suppose so," Liz agreed as Brett still said nothing.

She felt rather sorry for the other girl. It was only possible to guess at the relationship between her and Brett, but there had been something there, undoubtedly, even if it only existed as wishful thinking on Clare's part.

An awkward little silence followed. Liz glanced up at Brett's face, but he was wearing an impassive look.

Clare tossed down the remainder of her drink and produced a high nervous laugh. "Well, I must really be getting back to my chores. I've left Timmy on his own. Don't bother to see me out, I'll go across the lawn. Congratulations again and all that."

She smiled brilliantly at them both and went out through the open window and across the terrace.

Liz said, "Shouldn't we have told her the truth about who I really am?"

"Who—Clare? No, I don't think so. The fewer people who know the better, and at present the only ones who know are people I can trust implicitly."

But not Clare, she thought, but didn't say. *And what is Clare to you?*

He watched her face with a flicker of amusement and she knew he had read her thoughts accurately. "I didn't ask you," she said.

He laughed at that. "So you didn't, so I won't answer."

Then his face changed and he glanced at his watch. "I'll have time for two or three hours' work. I brought a whole pile of stuff home with me this morning and it must be got through before I go to bed. Things have piled up in the last few days."

She said tentatively, "Could I help? I'm a good typist."

He looked grim. "You'd need to be a crystal gazer to unravel the snags, but thanks all the same. Miss Johnson, J.B.'s secretary, should be back tomorrow. She's in the run of things and highly competent, and no doubt she'll sort out the mess when she arrives." He looked at his watch again and then at her. "Can you find something to amuse yourself with?"

"I don't have to be amused," she said. "I'm here to do a job, aren't I?"

"A job?" He looked faintly startled. "Oh, that! Yes, of course. You'll have to excuse me, I'm not used to being an engaged man."

She saw the tiredness in his face and said gently, "You don't have to bother about me, you know. I can look after myself. And I want to help, I really do."

She did want to help. She wanted to see the anxious lines disappear from his face, to see him look as he had looked in that old photograph on Maggie's wall; like a man who has life on his side. Was it a forlorn hope?

The tense face relaxed a little. "I believe you do," he said with a sort of surprise. "I really believe you do, though goodness knows why you should." He put a hand lightly on her shoulder and kissed her at the temple, where her hair fell back smoothly as she tilted her head to look up at him. "Good night, Liz, sleep well."

He was almost at the door when she said, "Brett?"

"Yes?" He replied absently and she guessed that his mind had gone forward already to the work that was waiting for him in the study.

"Nothing, really. It was only that I'm...I'm s-sorry."

"Sorry? Whatever for?"

"I don't quite know. Perhaps because I'm not really Elizabeth."

She shouldn't have said it, she knew she shouldn't, but that was what she was thinking, and the words came out before she knew what was happening.

In the silence that followed she didn't dare to look at his face. But she knew only too well as she heard the door close behind him that he must be thinking the same thing.

CHAPTER SEVEN

NEXT MORNING MAGGIE AND LIZ sat with their coffees in the cool, graciously designed restaurant of the Pump Rooms in Leamington. It was another lovely day and outside the sun poured down on the colorful beds of massed flowers, on the wide Parade with its flow of traffic, and, beyond, on the lake and trees and smooth lawns of the Gardens across the road.

Maggie said, "Nice here, isn't it? Reminds you that life isn't all rush and hurry. Still, we mustn't linger too long, I suppose, if we're going to do all our shopping before lunch. And I must admit that I'm simply thrilled by the prospect of spending a whole morning helping you to buy clothes, Liz. Have you made a list?"

"No, I'm afraid I haven't." Liz had had other things than clothes on her mind yesterday.

"Oh, we must have a list." Maggie opened her handbag and took out a pad and pencil. "I'm a great believer in lists—I make 'em all the time myself—and then forget where I've put the lists."

They both laughed, but Liz was uneasily aware that there were things she must say to Maggie and she didn't know how to start. Brett's sister was as friendly as ever this morning, but here in this elegant restaurant in town, in a dress of tangerine and brown patterned wild silk, her dark hair coiled up and gold hoop earrings gleaming against her smooth sunbronzed skin, she seemed less approachable than yesterday, in her old gardening clothes and with her hair tied back with a ribbon.

But her smile was as warm as ever as she wrote in a bold hand, Basics, and underlined it firmly. "We'll stock up on those first, shall we? Shoes, panty hose, scarves, undies, makeup. Then what do you fancy for on top? Summer dresses? Pants and sweaters? Separates or suits? You tell me."

Liz stared out of the window at the wide-open bells of a mass of blue and white gloxinias, and then resolutely back at the girl sitting opposite. "There's something else I've got to tell you first, Maggie. Have you spoken to Brett since yesterday?"

"No. Jake took a message on the phone this morning. I was in the bath. Why, has something happened?"

"You could put it like that. Quite a lot seems to have happened." She smiled wryly. "How do you fancy me as a sister-in-law?"

Liz watched the other girl as she spoke. It was true, you really could see emotions chasing each other across someone's face. Maggie's face, unlike her brother's, normally had a warm, interested mobility when she was talking to you. Now it registered first utter blankness, then startled surprise, then a dawning glimmer of excitement.

"Nothing would delight me more. But—Brett! Are you being serious?"

"I think I must be, although I can hardly believe it myself. Yesterday Brett asked me to marry him. To be exact he asked me three times in the space of a few hours. The way he put it the final time made it almost impossible to refuse."

Maggie's eyes opened very wide. They were the kind of dark brown eyes that usually looked lazy rather than brilliant, but now they were very much alive.

Liz smiled, "You must be surprised."

"Surprised? That's putting it mildly. I thought Jake and I were quick off the mark—we fell in love on Good Friday and we were engaged at Whit—but this beats everything."

Liz dissected a small piece from her buttered scone and said carefully, "I must explain about that angle. Brett and I aren't in love. It will be a sort of arranged marriage, like marriages always used to be; that was how he put it. We're getting married because Brett wants—we both want—to give J.B. the happiness of knowing that his old dream of joining the two families, his and yours, has come true at last. Also, that he may be content in knowing that Elizabeth will always be secure and safe. He is so happy already in believing that his granddaughter has come back. This will sort of round off the whole enterprise."

Watching the other girl's expression grow doubtful and then definitely worried, Liz felt she hadn't made a very good job of the explanation. "Does it sound awful to you?"

"Not awful...no. I know Brett's feeling of obligation to J.B. and I can partly see his point of view, although I think he takes it all too seriously. But—forgive me, Liz, if I'm being stupid—but I can't see why you're doing it. If you were the kind of girl to grab a man just for money or position I wouldn't be asking, but you're not."

"Thanks, Maggie, that's quite the nicest compliment I've had for ages. I wish I could explain in a couple of words, but it's all too complicated for that."

She stopped, her forehead wrinkled, trying to pick out the important points in the situation. "I suppose, first of all, I'm pretty disillusioned about falling in love just at present. And secondly, all this cropped up when I seemed to need an aim in life, something worthwhile that I can do that will help somebody else. That sounds rather pompous, I'm afraid, but can you see what I'm getting at?"

Maggie nodded slowly. "I...think so."

"But you're not in favor?"

There was a small silence while Maggie stirred her coffee thoughtfully. At last she looked up and said, "I'm just a bit scared, that's all. The idea of any two people marrying for any other reason than being in love scares me." She smiled. "You know the old song: 'Love and marriage go together like a horse and carriage'? That's my feeling about it, too. But I'm prepared to admit that something different might work for other people." Suddenly she relaxed with a little gesture that dismissed her doubts. "But I won't be a prophet of doom. You and Brett are two very nice people and I hope very sincerely that it all works out the way you want it. You can count on my support—and Jake's, too, I'm sure. I only hope that Brett...." She stopped.

Liz waited for her to go on.

"Oh, never mind, that's old history. But, Liz, just remember, won't you, that if you need help, about anything, at any time, you can call on me."

Liz felt an odd kind of chill run right through her body, but she said, "I'll remember. And thank you, Maggie."

"Good, that's settled, then," Maggie said briskly, and opened her notebook again. "Now let's make our list. It's going to be even more exciting than I expected. We're going to buy a trousseau." She hesitated, pencil poised. "It is to be a trousseau, is it, Liz? You're not proposing one of those stupid so-called platonic arrangements that never work? It's going to be an honest-to-goodness marriage?"

Suddenly Liz was back in the garden, with Brett's arms holding her strongly against him and his kiss on her mouth, and his voice, deep and not quite steady, saying, "Hasn't anyone told you you're a very disturbing young woman?"

She felt the heat rising to her cheeks. "I imagine we're both human beings," she said dryly. "It's just that Brett doesn't seem to go for what he calls the blah-blah about falling in love."

Her lips twitched as she remembered the way he'd looked when he said that, but Maggie's face was still serious and perturbed. She didn't make any further comment, however, and ten minutes later they went out onto the Parade, list in hand, to begin the thrilling, exhausting business of buying a trousseau.

NEARLY THREE HOURS LATER Maggie delivered Liz back at Heronswood and unloaded the pile of smart carrier bags in assorted sizes, shapes and colors from the back of the Mini.

"There, that's the lot. They look pretty good, don't they? There's only the linen coat to come, the one they've got to take in around the hips." Maggie grinned at Liz. "Nice to be a size ten, I wish I was. I was quite a respectable twelve before the twins came along, but now, alas, no longer!" She glanced at her watch. "Good gracious, it's going on for one. I must dash and get Jake's lunch. You can cope with this lot?" She waved toward the piled-up hall table.

"Yes, of course, and thank you for coming with me. It seemed to make it all a bit more...normal, somehow."

Maggie said, sincerely, "I've enjoyed it. Our ideas about clothes fit in." Impulsively she leaned forward and kissed Liz. "I'm looking forward to having you in the family, and I hope very much that it all works out."

But you don't think it will, decided Liz, waving as the back of Maggie's car disappeared around a bend in the driveway. She stood there for a few minutes more, then she sighed and went back to the hall to begin carrying her trousseau up to the bedroom that had belonged to the girl Brett had loved.

On the second journey down Liz met Nurse Sweet coming up, and they both stopped on the stairs.

Liz said, "Good morning, nurse, how is my grandfather this morning?"

At exactly the same moment Nurse Sweet said, "Mr. Rockington is much better this morning," and added rather coyly, "the news of your engagement to Mr. Denton has done him a world of good."

She adjusted her expression into formality and added, "May I wish you every happiness, Miss Rockington?"

Liz thanked her, wishing she didn't still feel rather a fraud, and they went their separate ways.

Down in the hall Ethel was on her knees polishing the legs of the table. "Oh, dear," said Liz, "do you really have to do that when Mrs. Jackson isn't well?"

Ethel pulled a face and said meaningly, with a jerk of her head toward the kitchen quarters, "She said I was to keep on with me proper routine."

Liz hadn't seen Mrs. Jackson this morning but had learnt from Ethel that the housekeeper had insisted on getting up to cook breakfast. "Although," the little maid had grumbled, "she can hardly move about on her legs, and it's not as if Mr. Brett minds not having a cooked breakfast. Or I could have done boiled eggs," she added. "But she would come down."

In the circumstances Liz had decided that it would be tactful to keep away from the kitchen. Now she said to Ethel, "How are things going out there?"

The little maid pulled down the corners of her mouth. "She's as cross as two sticks. She never even cheered up at the news."

"News?"

Ethel went very pink. "Ooh, shouldn't I have said, miss? But I got so excited about it. Nurse Sweet told me last night that you and Mr. Brett had got engaged, but Mrs. Jackson had gone to bed by then, so I told her this morning. I thought she'd be ever so pleased, but she looked proper grumpy. Have I spoken out of turn, miss?"

Liz laughed at her doleful expression. "No, of course not, Ethel. Everybody will know soon."

The child's mouth stretched into a wide grin. "Ooh, miss, it's that thrilling, isn't it? You and Mr. Brett! You'll make a lovely couple." She remembered how her mum had taught her to behave and composed her face into primness. "I hope you will be very happy, Miss Elizabeth."

"Thank you very much, Ethel." Liz smiled and picked up another batch of parcels to carry upstairs. As she deposited them on the bed she heard a car come up the driveway and stop around the front of the house. Brett come home for lunch? Her heart began to thump nervously.

They had hardly exchanged two words this morning. When she came into the dining room he had almost finished his breakfast, a sheaf of typewritten papers on the table beside him. She thought he looked tired and grim and wondered what time he'd got to bed last night.

He had glanced up when she came into the room, said, "Good morning," in an impersonal way, and stood up immediately, gathering the papers together into his briefcase. "Excuse me, won't you?" he had said with absent politeness. "I'm just off. I've got a full day ahead." And a short time later she had heard the front door shut behind him.

Liz had helped herself to bacon and kidney from the hot plate on the massive sideboard and sat down alone at the table.

It was stupid, of course, to feel a chill of disappointment. But she knew that she'd been hoping for a continuance of his friendly attitude of the previous evening. Now it seemed that they were back to square one; she might have been part of the furniture.

The downcast mood had only lasted for a few moments, then she had pulled herself together. What did she expect, for heaven's sake? This was no ordinary engagement, and they weren't an ordinary engaged couple to exchange loving glances and words loaded with subtle, intimate meanings. It was, as he'd said, a business arrangement, and he was a man with business on his mind in no small way.

She had tried to visualize what it must mean to be in charge of a vast enterprise like Rockington's, and failed, but the effort helped her understanding and strengthened her resolve to help him in any way she could. She would stick to the terms of their agreement and not be touchy and defensive when he seemed to ignore her.

She'd try to think of him as she'd thought of her old boss in London, and he had been difficult and demanding enough, she remembered with a wry grin.

That was her resolution this morning, but now, with the prospect of seeing Brett again in a few minutes, it didn't seem so easy. She glanced at herself in the mirror, drew in a couple of deep steadying breaths, and ran downstairs.

After all this it was with a sense of relief, oddly mixed with something like disappointment, that she saw that it wasn't Brett coming through the front doorway at all, it was Colin Winter.

As he saw her his face broke into a wide smile and he lifted a hand in greeting. "Hi, there!"

He looked very well turned out today in a neat gray suit, his fair hair brushed into a compromise between fashion and professional decorum.

Liz joined him in the hall. "Hi," she said, and smiled back at him, pleased to see him. "You'll find your patient better this morning. Nurse Sweet is very pleased with him."

He said, "Good. That's good news." But he didn't move toward the stairs, or take his eyes off her.

"Brett's on the job in Birmingham, I suppose?" he asked, and when she nodded, went on, "what do you find to do with yourself here all day? Isn't it very quiet?"

"I've got plenty lined up. The gardener's in need of help with weeding, and Mrs. Jackson's a doubtful starter at the moment as you know. I've been in Leamington this morning with Brett's sister, Maggie, shopping for some clothes to call my own. I arrived here with nothing but a very muddy suit and I've been wearing...borrowed things. I've had to try hard not to . . . to remember who they belonged to." Her eyes shadowed, then determinedly she made them smile again. "But I've had an extravagant morning and now I'm all fixed up again."

She didn't intend to tell Colin who had paid for everything; nor to give him the news of her engagement. Let Brett tell him. Let Brett do the explaining this time. He was Brett's friend, not hers, and she hadn't a clue how he would react.

His eyes were still on her, twinkling through the large round gold-rimmed lenses. "You need an excuse to wear a new dress. How about having dinner with me tonight? It's my off-duty evening."

It took her completely be surprise. "Oh, I'm s-sorry. . . ."

She was, too. It would have been pleasant and uncomplicated to go out with Colin Winter.

"Why not?" he urged. "What's to stop you? You're over twenty-one."

"Twenty-two," she corrected with rather a wan smile. Now she would have to tell him.

She went into the drawing room and crossed to the window.

Colin followed her. "Why not?" he repeated.

"Because in my book engaged girls don't go out with other men."

He blinked. "Oh! Forgive me, I didn't imagine . . . you weren't wearing a ring. . . ."

"There hasn't been time for that. It only happened last night."

She watched it dawn on him as she had watched it dawn on Maggie. But if her reaction had been puzzlement leading to delight, Colin's was very different.

"You don't mean—you can't. . . ." He was frowning.

"Brett and I got engaged yesterday evening."

"But he can't," he burst out sharply. "He can't do that."

Keep it light, she thought, and smiled, "Too late, he's already done it. And you're not being very flattering, are you?"

He brushed that aside. He looked deeply disturbed. "Forgive me, but are you sure you're not allowing yourself to be rushed into something you may regret, on the strength of a romantic situation?"

"You think it's romantic?"

"Seems like it to me. It has all the right elements, hasn't it? Almost Ruritanian, I'd have thought. But Brett Denton's no romantic prince, you know. He's my friend, but I wouldn't hesitate to say that in most ways he's a hard man. He has what I'd call the millionaire mentality. A man of action with a brilliant, cold brain."

"Yes," she said. "I've discovered that for myself."

A certain coolness in her voice made him glance at her quickly. "You're thinking it's none of my business? Let's say I feel a certain responsibility for you as my patient. You're very young and you've been pushed into a false position here. Have you no family of your own near?"

"Only my stepbrother and his wife in Birmingham, but they seem to be away from home. I came back from South Africa rather unexpectedly; they wouldn't be expecting me to be in England."

That was as far as she was going to explain herself at the moment to Colin Winter.

"I see." He gazed at her with almost comical concern. She felt like saying she had merely become engaged to be married, not contracted some rare and fatal disease.

She felt his hand on her arm and his voice became very warm and pleading. "Don't do it, Liz. Don't allow yourself to be pushed around by Brett. Decisions taken suddenly are never wise and often turn out the opposite of what one expects. Don't commit yourself yet."

"Too late, I've already committed myself," she said. "It

wasn't something that could wait. You told me yourself that old Mr. Rockington hasn't very long to live."

She thought, *I wish he'd stop going on and on about it.* She found herself wishing that Brett were here to back her up.

Colin was staring oddly at her. "Is that why he wants to marry you? Because Mr. Rockington is dying?"

"Well, of course. What other reason could there be? Your idea of the grand romance was way off target."

There was a long silence. His face changed, his mouth hardened.

Finally he moved his shoulders and gave a little cough. "I see. I'm afraid I've been very stupid. Please forgive me for interfering. I'll go up and see my patient now."

She watched his back as he walked stiffly down the long drawing room and out into the hall. *Oh dear,* she thought with a sigh, *what was all that about? Why the awful disapproval?*

She had liked Colin Winter. She had imagined she had a friend in him. Now it seemed not. That was a very funny look he had given her just then. Contemptuous almost, although probably she had imagined that. She didn't fool herself she was being all noble and self-sacrificing, but she thought she hardly deserved contempt for what she was doing.

Or did he think she was marrying Brett for his money? Yes, that was probably it. Well, she couldn't really blame him; most people would see it in that light. Terry had opened her eyes to that angle.

The white Persian cat strolled across the terrace outside the window, sat down and began to wash his ears in the sunshine. She stared at him absently. How extraordinary, Terry seemed to belong to a different life now. She had loved him, longed to marry him, had wept her heart out in that hotel room when he left her. And now, nothing!

Why? What was the truth about what she was doing?

She had tried to explain to Maggie about needing a purpose, about wanting to know she was doing a bit of good to somebody. All those grand and noble sentiments; they seemed unconvincing now. They didn't even convince her.

Then, why?

Ethel put her head around the door. "Mr. Brett's on the phone for you, Miss Elizabeth. In the study."

Liz turned slowly, her eyes widening. "Thank you."

Then suddenly her heart was thumping in great thuds against her ribs. Her mouth was dry and she passed her tongue over her lips. *No*, she thought, *oh, no, it can't be* that. *It's too ridiculous*. But as she ran across the hall and picked up the receiver her knees were shaking and if there hadn't been a chair for her to sink into she would have sunk onto the floor instead.

"Hullo," she croaked.

"Liz?" He'd evidently recognized her voice, although she hadn't recognized it herself. "Liz, I'm in rather a jam at the office here, and I wonder if you can help me."

"Of course, anything," she said.

Anything, she thought wildly. *Jump off the Eiffel Tower. Swim the Atlantic. Fly to Mars. Any little thing at all.*

His voice, crisp and cool, drew her back to reality. "I found a message waiting here for me from J.B.'s secretary, Miss Johnson. She won't be returning. We can get over that, of course, but what is important is this: before she left I asked her to type some letters and send them off for me. One of them hasn't arrived, apparently. I want to find out if it was written and, if possible, if it was posted. You get the idea?"

"Yes," said Liz.

"Good. Well now, all the work she did at Heronswood is in the office there. Copies of letters, files, so on. Could you have a good look around and see if you can trace anything that would give us a clue about this particular letter? Got a pencil handy?"

"Yes." She grabbed one from the desk and pulled a pad toward her.

He dictated the particulars and she scribbled them down. "Got all that?"

"Yes."

"Right. Call me back then, will you, as soon as you can?" He gave her the phone number and hung up.

In the corner of the study, beside the fireplace, there was a green office filing cabinet. Liz searched through it with great care and concentration, examining every incoming letter, every carbon copy of outgoing ones. But there was no trace of any letter sent to the Otley Timber Corporation.

She moved to the big desk that held the telephone. Three of the four deep drawers were locked. The other held the usual typist's equipment: shorthand notebook, pens, pencils, erasers, ruler.

How about your shorthand, Miss Johnson? Any hope of it being decipherable by another party? Her own squiggles certainly wouldn't be, she thought wryly.

Without much hope she opened the notebook, but here was a surprise. Miss Johnson's beautiful shorthand wouldn't have looked out of place in a textbook. Every stroke was neat, clear, of the correct degree of heaviness, in the correct position above, on, or below the line. Every hook and circle was meticulously formed. She had even found time to put in a few of the dots and dashes, which most stenos leave out, hoping for the best. Every separate day's crop of letters was headed with the date, and the excellent Miss Johnson had even made things easier by writing out in longhand all proper names of companies and individuals.

Bless you, Miss J., thought Liz, beginning at the final batch and working rapidly backward. Eureka! Here it was! Letter to the Otley Timber Corporation, dated 1st June, the day before Miss Johnson left on her holiday. It wasn't scored through to show it had been transcribed. Either Miss Johnson had missed it, being in a great hurry to get away, or two pages had stuck together. But whatever the cause, the letter certainly hadn't been typed.

It wasn't a long or difficult letter. Liz uncovered the portable typewriter on the desk and in a few minutes had the notes transcribed. She read it back, decided it made sense, and telephoned the number in Birmingham that Brett had given her.

It took a few minutes to get through to him and by the time she did she could feel her cheeks burning, but she managed to explain what she had done and to read him the letter.

"Is that what you wanted?"

"Thanks, it's exactly what I wanted. You've done a good job, Liz." There was a pause and she thought he had hung up, but he added, "See you this evening, I may be a bit late."

"Yes, all right, Brett. Goodbye."

"Bye," he said, and rang off.

She replaced the receiver and found she was trembling, just at the sound of his voice. *Stop it,* she told herself, *you're being ridiculous.* But at least she knew now what the score was, and she needn't fool herself any longer about her motives. Against all sense, all prudence, she had fallen crazily, desperately in love with Brett Denton.

On the rebound? She didn't think so. What she felt for Brett bore no relation to what she'd felt for Terry. Who was it had written, "When half-gods go the gods arrive?" That was how she felt about Brett. If she were never to see him again her sun would stop shining and her world would grow cold and die.

"See you this evening," he'd said. And "I may be a bit late." Friendly, casual, almost—domestic. The way a husband would speak on the phone to his wife.

She pressed the backs of both hands against her hot cheeks. *We're engaged,* she reminded herself, *we're going to be married. Somehow I'll make him love me. Somehow I'll make him take back all he said about falling in love. Somehow—however long it takes—everything will come right.*

Meanwhile, life went on and the very last thing she must do was to complicate the situation by letting him guess how she felt about him. Her job at the moment was to do what she had undertaken and to keep J.B. content.

Later on she would find out what Brett expected of her as a wife. Where would they live, she wondered. What sort of establishment would he keep up? A quiet home somewhere, or a shop window for Rockington's? Would she be the little woman in the background, immersed in domesticity, or would he want her to be social, to dress well, to entertain his business friends?

She didn't know and she didn't propose to ask him. Just now Brett had enough on his plate without her bothering him with questions about their future. She would have to go on playing it by ear.

She sat at the desk, idly flicking over the neat pages of Miss Johnson's shorthand notebook. The one word, written in longhand, stopped her short.

She turned back the pages and read, "My dear Brett—"

Just seeing his name there on the page sent her mind into a spin and before she had time to think she had mentally transcribed the first few lines of the script:

My dear Brett, I wish I could write this to you with my own hand, but I have left it too late to do so, and now I cannot. I believe, in spite of what the doctors say, that I may not have very long to live, and before I go I want you to have certain facts in your possession in case difficulties crop up later. You and I—

Liz pushed the notebook back into the drawer and shut it with a click. She had no intention of prying into J.B.'s personal letters to Brett.

Some day they'd have a real marriage, with confidence and trust between them. Some day Brett would tell her his hopes and fears, his likes and dislikes, his ambitions.

She seemed to see his face before her now, that hard, enigmatic face with the keen eyes and straight mouth, and it was almost impossible to believe that he was capable of that sort of love in marriage. *But he must be,* she told herself rather desperately, *he must be.* Because if he weren't then she was utterly lost.

CHAPTER EIGHT

IT WAS JUST AS WELL that Brett was late coming back that evening. It gave Liz a breathing space to pull herself together, and by the time he did come, at a few minutes before eight, she was feeling reasonably calm.

She heard his car drive up and ran out into the hall to meet him. He looked tired and grim as he tossed his briefcase down on the table, and she said immediately. "I'll go and tell them you're in. Dinner's all ready and I waited for you."

He frowned. "You needn't—"

She didn't wait for him to say she needn't have waited, but sped along to the kitchen, hoping that Mrs. Jackson wouldn't be there.

Each time Liz had encountered the housekeeper today she had found her tight-lipped and silent. She might have been suffering pain from her arthritis, or she might have been registering disapproval of Liz's engagement to Brett. Whichever it was, Liz hadn't tried to find out, and now she was relieved to find only Ethel in the kitchen, deep in a *True Confessions* magazine.

Ethel reddened and stuffed the magazine under the cushion of her chair. "She's gone up to have a lay down, miss. Her leg's playing her up again. Dinner's in the oven, keeping hot. Shall I bring it in?"

"In ten minutes, please, Ethel." That would give Brett time to wash and have a drink. "Can you cope?"

"Trust me, miss." Ethel looked very important as she started to bustle around with the cart, and Liz hid a smile and went back to the dining room.

Disapproving or not, Mrs. Jackson had performed the cooking with her usual magic touch. The lamb cutlets were still succulent in spite of their time in the oven; the garden peas had miraculously not dried up; the new potatoes were white and not yellowed, and the gooseberry and cream sweet was fluffy and delicious.

In fact, thought Liz, everything was wonderful. Or was it just because she was sitting across the table from Brett and she could look at him as much as she pleased?

He certainly didn't put himself out to be companionable. In fact, he hardly spoke more than two consecutive sentences all through dinner. That was good, too, she assured herself, it meant that he felt relaxed with her, she hoped.

When the meal was over he stood up and said, "Let's have coffee in the study, shall we? I've got something to give you."

But he seemed in no hurry to tell her what it was. Instead, he leaned his head back wearily against the leather of the armchair and said, "Thanks for your help about the letter this morning. It amazed me that Miss Johnson should have slipped up. I've never known it happen before."

"It could happen to anyone," she said.

"And you could read her shorthand? Very bright of you."

"Not really," she said, flushing a little, "it was very clear."

He sipped his coffee. "Nevertheless, I would have been in a worse hole than I was if you hadn't coped so well."

"It's been a bad day?" she ventured, and thought, *Goodness, this* is *turning into the pattern of a domestic evening.*

"Hell," he said feelingly, and smiled a little. Was he thinking the same thought? Probably. It was disconcerting how often he seemed to know what she was thinking.

"Perhaps," he said, "I'll take you up on your offer of last night. Miss Johnson's not coming back—domestic stress, it seems—and I don't particularly want to bring any of the other secretaries from the office to the house here. The more we keep things to ourselves until after we're married the better."

The casual way he said "after we're married," nearly made Liz choke over her coffee but she controlled herself and said, "You mean you'd like me to do some typing for you?"

"That's the idea. Will you?"

"Of course," she said. "I'd enjoy it. I'm kicking up my heels for something to do at present."

"I thought you and Maggie were going shopping?"

"We did. But that only occupied the morning." She glanced at him with vague apology. "I'm afraid I spent an awful lot of money."

He shrugged as if that was completely unimportant. "Have you seen J.B.? I wonder if it's too late for me to go up and see him now?"

She said, "I only stayed a few minutes, this afternoon. I started to read some Dickens to him and he seemed to enjoy it, but then he dropped off to sleep." She smiled softly remembering how he had looked—calm and peaceful—and how she had felt reassured all over again about what they were doing.

"Nurse said he'd had a tiring morning," she said. "Apparently one of the directors turned up to see him."

Brett's eyebrows went up, but he made no comment. "Perhaps I'd better not disturb him, then. I'll get on with a spot of work instead. There are a few letters I'd like to get done tonight, if you feel like it."

While he was opening his briefcase Liz took the coffee tray back to the kitchen, then she came back and found Miss Johnson's notebook and pen. Brett's dark head was bent over a letter and she sat there, poised for him to begin dictating.

But instead he looked up and met her eyes. "Before we begin on the job, let me give you this." He took a ring box from his inside pocket and opened it. There was a flash of diamond and sapphire in the electric light. "I'm sorry I couldn't fit in the time to take you along to choose it," he said. "But if you'd rather have something else I've arranged for you to go into the jeweler's and have it changed."

She held the tiny box and stared at the beautiful ring against its dark velvet background. Its brilliance seemed suddenly cold.

"It's lovely, thank you very much," she said politely.

"Hadn't you better see if it fits?"

It would have been nice if he'd offered to put it on her finger. Nice and friendly—but, of course, a gesture not called for in the circumstances.

She slipped it on the third finger of her left hand. "Perfect." She held it up for him to see. "A good guess on your part."

He began to sort through his papers. "Not entirely a guess," he said, and left her to make what she could of that. "Now, if you're sure you don't mind a working evening...?"

Liz had always been good at shorthand and found no difficulty in keeping up with Brett's dictation. He watched her at first and then, seeing she was coping, increased his speed until her pen was flying smoothly across the page. There was a certain exhilaration in being able to match his pace.

When he had finished he grinned at her and said, "That's the lot. Think you'll be able to type it all back?"

"Of course," she said indignantly, crossing her fingers by her side.

His grin broadened. "All right," he said mildly, "I wasn't doubting your efficiency. It's rare to find anyone who can keep abreast. We evidently work well as a team. A good augury for our future together, don't you think?"

"I expect so," she said, without smiling. It was stupid to feel hurt because he seemed to be making a joke of it, but she couldn't help it.

"When would you like the letters typed?" she said. "I could do them now if you like."

He glanced at the clock on the mantelpiece. "Good lord, no, it's going on for eleven. Much too late. If you could get them done tomorrow morning I'll come back for lunch and collect them then. I have to come near here on my way out to Daventry. We're putting up some houses here."

She nodded. "I'll do that." She stood up and he got to his feet, as well. "I think I'll go to bed, then; if there isn't anything else I can help with."

He stood looking down at her, an odd gleam in his eyes. "No, nothing else, thanks," he said.

She waited a moment longer. Suddenly the moment seemed vastly important. They were engaged to be married; he had just given her a ring. He hadn't pretended to be in love with her, but surely, if he felt anything at all for her—any tenderness, any gentleness—he would show it now. But he just went on looking at her, without speaking, that strange mocking look in his dark eyes.

"Good night, then," she said.

"Good night."

He went over and opened the door for her and she made her way slowly up to bed. As she went she thought that for all her brave resolutions about making Brett fall in love with her she really couldn't believe that he would.

She was engaged. She was going to be married to a man she loved. And she had never felt so lonely in her whole life.

THE LONELINESS WAS STILL THERE next morning. She didn't even see Brett at breakfast; he must have been up earlier than ever.

"Mr. Brett's been gone this half hour or more. A proper rush he seemed to be in," Ethel told her.

"He didn't leave any message for me?"

"No, Miss Elizabeth, but he said he'd be home for lunch."

Ethel smirked. Well primed by her romance magazines, she no doubt had visions of smoldering passion between the young master and the daughter of the house. *Ha,* though Liz, tipping the coffeepot until it spilled into her saucer, *how little she knows!*

After breakfast Liz typed out the letters. There were a good many of them, but they presented no difficulties, except for one technical word that she wasn't quite sure about. She put them in a neat pile, awaiting Brett's signature, and then sat wondering what to do with herself until lunchtime.

It might be an idea to try again to get in touch with John. She pulled the telephone toward her, dialed the familiar number, and sat waiting.

To her surprise there was a click and a woman's high, precise voice said, "Yes?"

Liz felt a little rush of gladness. They were back, then, her own people. She wasn't as alone as she had felt in this big, quiet house.

"Dorothy!" she cried. "It's you at last. This is Liz. Have you had my cable? Did you know I was back?"

There was a short pause, then Dorothy said, "Just a minute, one thing at a time. I'm afraid I can't take all this in at once. I take it you're back in England for good?"

"Yes. I . . . it didn't work out with Terry, so I came home straight away. There was an accident to my plane as we were coming in to land at Elmdon and—oh, it's a long story. Can I come over and see you and John and tell you all about it?"

There was another silence.

"Dorothy, are you still there?"

"Yes, I'm here. It's just that it's a little difficult at present. You won't have heard, of course, but we're moving down to Kent. John has been promoted and is taking over the Maidstone branch." Dorothy sounded very important.

"Kent...oh, that's a long way away. When do you go?"

"Well, actually John's already there. I've just come back here to make arrangements about moving the furniture. It's all been rather sudden. It's a very busy time."

"Yes," said Liz, "It must be."

Dorothy laughed rather uncomfortably. "I'm afraid I can't very well ask you to come over, Liz. I'm simply up to my eyes in it, you've no idea. We were sorry to hear that your wedding was off, but of course we didn't make any secret about our views, did we?"

"No," said Liz.

"John and I never trusted that man, and we weren't surprised that he let you down." The voice at the other end of the line was becoming shriller. "But I take it you've got yourself fixed up with another job?"

"Oh, yes, thank you, I'm perfectly all right."

"That's good, then." Dorothy's relief was quite audible. "You must write and tell us all your news. If you address your letter to Maidstone branch it will find us. And then you can come down and see our new house some time, when we're finally straight. I'll tell John you rang. He'll be glad to know that you've been in touch."

"Yes," said Liz. "Give him my love."

John had been kind to her in his own way. It wasn't his fault that he had a wife like Dorothy.

She didn't wait to say goodbye. She replaced the receiver and just sat there, looking at nothing.

After a while she took a sheet of notepaper from the desk drawer and wrote to Terry. Just a few lines, hoping that the enclosed check would meet the cost of her plane fare to England. Brett had given her his own check for the right amount and she took it from the pocket of the green frock she was still wearing, put it inside the letter and tucked them both into an envelope. Deliberately she wrote Terry's address and stuck down the flap.

That, then, was that. The end of the chapter, and the beginning of a new one.

She glanced at the electric clock on the mantelpiece. It would be more than two hours before she could expect Brett back. In the meantime it would be pleasant out in the garden.

But first there was something she had to do upstairs, something she had been putting off. Now it must be faced, and her inside tightened at the prospect.

In her bedroom—Elizabeth's bedroom—she pulled back the heavy sliding doors of the wardrobe and, setting her mouth firmly, began to do what must be done. It was a wretched job, taking out all the beautiful clothes that Elizabeth had left behind, folding them and stacking them away in another, smaller cupboard, which held only a shoe rack and some hatboxes. Liz emptied the drawers of lingerie, piled toilet articles and makeup into a white leather overnight case and put that in the cupboard, too, with shoes and oddments. The very last thing to go in was the green dress with the silver buckle on the belt.

She smoothed it down on top of the pile. This was the dress she had worn yesterday when Brett proposed to her. She thought rather bleakly, *It even had to be* her *dress I was wearing when he asked me to marry him.*

She closed the cupboard with a smart click. She would find out from Maggie if there were an Oxfam shop in the district that would take all this stuff. That way, at least somebody would benefit.

The next thing was to hang up her own clothes. Yesterday she had taken them from their bags and draped them over the backs of chairs, without very much interest. But today, looking at them anew, she began to experience that little lift of excitement that new clothes brings to every woman.

Thank goodness for Maggie, she thought. By herself she could never have got into the mood for choosing a trousseau. She had been much too shattered by all that had happened. But now she saw that Maggie's expertise had worked its magic.

Maggie had looked at her with a professional eye and said "With your lovely silky fawn-colored hair and your clear skin you can wear any color there is and get away with it. Not white, possibly, unless you get really tanned, but everything else." Now as Liz took each dress and held it up to herself before the mirror, she began to unwind inside. Appearances weren't everything, certainly, but they mattered a lot to any man, and she really was going to look quite something in these clothes; almost any girl would.

Maggie had chosen something for every and any occasion. There were crisp linen dresses for the garden; pants and sweaters; a casual belted dress in an oatmeal-colored material with a batik scarf in brilliant shades of tomato and citron; a summer suit in heavy ivory Ottoman silk with a short snappy jacket which would do for any occasion—Maggie had said—formal or informal.

For evening there were two dresses; one, ballerina length, a romantic peasant print in cotton voile in shades of lilac and turquoise and white, with pleated, bell sleeves; the other, full-length and dramatic, in cerise and silver.

She slipped out of the coffee-beige pants and top she had put on this morning and, lifting her arms high, let the voile dress slide over her head and body. The deep square neckline flattered her young figure and the skirt frothed out around her long slim legs. She brushed her hair into fawn satin smoothness and revolved before the mirror, the lilac and turquoise shimmering and blending together in the sunshine that poured through the long window.

Your dress, she told herself. *Your very own dress and it suits you. You're Liz Hartley and nobody else, and in a fortnight you're going to marry Brett and some day he's going to tell you he loves you. And that, my girl, is your future all planned out—or as much of it as matters!*

She smiled at herself in the mirror, willing it to happen. Then she got back into the cotton pants and top, hung the dress up in the wardrobe with the rest of her new clothes, and went down into the garden. She would fill in the rest of the morning helping Ames, if he would let her.

The old gardener seemed quite pleased to see her and set her to weeding the raspberry bed. She worked her way conscientiously along the row and Ames retired to the other side of the garden and began very, very slowly to thread a frame with scarlet-runner strings. It was an easy job for Liz; the weeds were nearly all groundsel and chickweed and they came up with satisfying ease. She sang softly as she worked, not thinking of anything, enjoying the warmth of the sun on her bare arms and the smell of earth and growing things, and the quietness of the old garden.

There was a faint mewing sound behind her and she turned, expecting to see Sphinx, the white cat. But instead she saw Timmy, Clare's small son, standing there, his stubby legs planted wide apart, mouth drooping, eyes brimming.

"Timmy, what's the matter?" Liz went down on her knees beside him.

Still whimpering, he held out a podgy hand. It was caked with earth and something else that looked like blood.

"Oh, dear," Liz put an arm around him comfortingly. "Now, what have you done to yourself?"

Even if he'd possessed the necessary words Timmy was in no state for explanations. "Come on, then," said Liz, heaving him up into her arms. "We'd better go and find mummy." Clare Jessing was the last person she would have chosen to meet just now, but this looked as if it might be a minor emergency.

But at the cottage there was no mummy to be found. Clare had evidently gone out and left the ancient Ames in charge of Timmy. Not, thought Liz, the most dependable of nursemaids, for he was very deaf and his sight didn't seem too good, either.

Timmy, safe on his home ground, had started to cry in earnest now. Not bawling, as a child will who is more frightened than hurt, but sobbing in a much more disturbing way. He looked a lost little creature, with his tousled hair and tear-streaked face and grubby little paws. Liz felt suddenly angry with Clare; why did people have children if they weren't prepared to look after them?

"Let's see if we can clean you up a bit, love." She pushed aside a pile of unwashed dishes and deposited him on the draining board.

The shock of the cold water made Timmy howl louder than ever, but soon he stopped and seemed fascinated by the sight of the earth turning to mud in the sink. Liz discovered that the cause of the bleeding was a deep little cut in the fleshy part of the thumb. When it was thoroughly rinsed she lifted him down and poked around in cupboards and drawers for anything that looked like a first-aid box. But there was nothing, not even a packet of bandages. You just had to accept it; Clare would have taken no prize as mother or housewife.

The cut had bled freely, so it only needed covering with a clean dressing to protect if from infection. Finally, failing to find anything remotely clean or newly washed in the kitchen Liz tore off a strip of soft paper towel from the roll and wrapped that gently around Timmy's thumb. Then she sat down with the child on her knee, picked up a picture book from the floor, and settled down to wait until Clare came home.

The time passed slowly and Timmy's small body, warm against her own, got heavier and heavier. By the time Liz heard the front door open he was fast asleep, and so was her arm.

Clare appeared in the kitchen doorway. She was wearing a navy blue outfit, with conventional white accessories. But it didn't look conventional on her; it looked stunning. Her hair was pure silver-gilt today, several shades lighter than it had been yesterday. That fact and the heavy perfume that came in with her proclaimed unmistakably that she had spent the last couple of hours at the hairdresser's.

She stood in the doorway, one hand resting gracefully and casually on the frame. "My, my, what's going on here?"

Timmy stirred but didn't wake. Liz eased his heavy body away from her arm and shook it to disperse the pins and needles that were pricking from shoulder to fingertips. She didn't care for the expression on Clare's face, but there was no point in being unpleasant.

"Timmy gashed his thumb rather badly out in the garden," she said. "I thought I ought to bring him in and clean it up." She looked down at the small hand where the makeshift paper bandage was already stained and sodden. "I think it's stopped bleeding now, but I couldn't find any bandages."

Clare sauntered into the kitchen and stood looking down at Liz, a half smile on her lovely mouth. "Well, many thanks, but you needn't have bothered. He's always bashing himself on something, but he plays up if you make a fuss."

Liz stared in amazement. "But he might have got an infected thumb."

Clare shrugged off her jacket, disclosing satin-brown shoulders. She slid gracefully into a chair and lit a cigarette. "And then again he might not," she said smoothly. "It's the luck of the draw. You just have to take what comes along, that's my view of things."

The darkly fringed eyes met Liz's meaningfully over Timmy's head. "Which is why I'm not weeping bitter tears over Brett letting me down. Bad luck for little me, but you can't really blame him. Brett is just about the most calculating man I've ever known, and that's saying something."

Liz stood up and put Timmy down on the chair, still sleeping. "If you mean what I think you mean, you're being offensive," she said.

Clare blew out a plume of smoke and said, "Oh, darling, be your age! Of course Brett has his eye on inheriting the business. He must know that J.B. wouldn't fancy leaving it all to your dear brother, Roger—not when Roger blotted his copybook so badly in grandpa's eyes." She smiled narrowly. "Surprised I know so much about the skeletons in the family cupboard? Your brother and my late lamented hubby were bosom pals at one time, that's how I picked up my information."

"I don't believe it," Liz murmured, almost to herself. "He wouldn't behave like that—not Brett."

Clare laughed harshly. "Show me the man who wouldn't—they're all the same. You don't really expect me to believe he's marrying you for love, or some other quaint old-fashioned notion, do you? And it would hardly be because he's consumed with burning passion for you, either." Her look slid over Liz from head to foot. "I mean—without putting too fine a point on it—he and I are very compatible in that way. He wouldn't need to look elsewhere, if you follow me."

Liz was beginning to feel rather sick, but she said quite steadily, "Let's get this straight. You're saying that you and Brett have been having an affair and that he's dropped you because he thinks he'll get J.B.'s money if he marries me?"

"Clever girl! Right first time. Oh, don't think I don't feel bad about it, because I do. Brett Denton's a very good prize, with or without J.B.'s money, although I must say I prefer a man with a bit more—well, you know—he's a bit dour, isn't he? Not quite what I'd choose for a good time. Still, he's one of Rockington's top men now, and married to J.B.'s granddaughter he'll doubtless *be* Rockington's pretty soon. He can't lose, can he?"

Liz stood there in the untidy, almost squalid little kitchen, looking down at the other girl, so beautiful, so completely self-assured. Then, without saying a word, she walked out of the cottage and down the path that led back to the garden.

Ames was still fumbling with the bean strings. Liz stood by the row of raspberries looking down at the little pile of weeds she had pulled up. Already they were limp and dying in the hot sunshine.

Reaction was setting in and she found she was trembling all over. Work might help, but she couldn't face any more weeding just at present.

On her way back to the house she met Colin Winter coming across the lawn. She didn't want to talk to him just now, or to anyone else. But she couldn't avoid him.

"Liz, I wanted to see you. They told me you were out here. I wanted to say I was sorry for the stupid way I behaved yesterday. I . . . ." He stopped. "Liz, what's the matter? You're trembling. Are you all right?" In a little movement that was probably partly a doctor's reflex his hand went to her wrist.

She smiled weakly. "I'm not ill. It's nothing. . . ."

He kept his fingers on her wrist for a moment longer, looking hard into her face. Then, with his nice, sincere smile, he said, "If you're not ill, then I suppose it's none of my business. I mustn't make the same mistake that I made last night, must I?"

He shifted his black leather medical case from one hand to the other and said, "I really do apologize for that. You see I—ever since that first night when Brett brought you here after the accident, I felt you were rather special. I hoped you might like me, too."

The warmth in his voice touched her. She said, "Oh, but I did. I do like you very much."

"I'm glad. I thought you might have written me off altogether yesterday. Something you said gave me the impression...."

She grinned, "That I was marrying Brett for his money?"

He flushed. "You must forgive me. A medical training makes one rather objective about human nature. I realized almost at once how wrong I was. You're not in the least that sort of girl. For a man, of course, it's different, and a man like Brett would see things quite differently. He's first and foremost a businessman and I feel sure his interest in Rockington's is more than just a selfish one."

He spoke slowly and carefully. He was doing his best, she saw, to be charitable about Brett, whatever he thought of his conduct. And he evidently thought the worst.

First Clare. Then Colin. And even Maggie had been reserved about Brett's motives. Had she, she wondered, been incredibly naive when she had taken Brett's word that he wished to marry her for the sole and simple reason that it would make J.B.'s last days happy?

Perhaps Brett had said to Clare much the same sort of thing that Terry had said to her: "I want you like hell, Liz, but I'm going to marry Frank Carter's daughter and that's how it is."

No, she thought, Brett's not like Terry. It couldn't happen.

Suddenly she realized that she and Colin were walking toward the house. She pulled herself together. "Are you on your way to see J.B.?"

"No, I've just come from seeing him, and I'm very pleased. He seems to be rallying surprisingly. Well, I must get along, I've two more calls to make before afternoon office hours."

He turned toward the path leading to the front of the house, and hesitated, looking down at her. "I'm glad I had this opportunity to explain. You've forgiven me?"

"There's nothing to forgive."

She smiled up at him, but she scarcely saw him because she was thinking of Brett.

He nodded and his eyes, behind their gold-rimmed glasses, were keen and rueful. "I see," he said. He hitched up his bag. "Well, if ever you need help just call on me."

She watched him walk away around the side of the house. That was what Maggie had said, too, wasn't it? "If ever you need help . . . ." As if agreeing to marry Brett had put her in some awful danger! They didn't know him, she thought. Not Colin, his friend. Not Maggie, his sister. And as for Clare . . . .

She stood for a long time in the sunshine, trying to forget what Clare had said. Then she saw Brett coming toward her from the house and her heart lurched in a way that was becoming familiar. As she waited for him to reach her she thought, steadily, *I love him. I don't care why he wants to marry me, just as long as he does. If he robbed the Bank of England and got caught I'd wait for him to come out of prison.*

As he got nearer she saw the look in his face and ran to meet him. "J.B.?" she said quickly. "It's not . . . ?"

Suddenly the sunny garden was dark and cold and Brett's face was carved from stone.

She said, "Shall I go to him? He might...."

She stumbled toward the house, but his hand was on her arm and before he shook his head she knew that it was too late.

"Oh!" she gasped. "Oh, Brett, I'm so sorry. So terribly sorry...."

He reached out an arm and drew her close to him, without saying a word. He had loved J.B. and he was suffering, and perhaps any other human being would have helped at that moment, just by being there.

But as she felt some of the tenseness go out of his body, with a long sigh, she thought, *I could help him at this moment. I was here and I could help him.*

And that was a kind of heaven.

CHAPTER NINE

FOR A LONG TIME they stood together on the terrace and Brett held her strained against him with a desperate tension. She felt his body hard against hers and all the breath seemed to be squeezing itself out of her. When he slackened his grip she almost fell.

He took her arm and half pushed her down onto the garden seat, and sat down beside her. She could sense that he was getting himself under control again.

"Colin had only just left," she said falteringly. "He was so pleased with J.B., said he seemed to be rallying. I hoped...."

Brett said slowly, with an effort, "No, there was never any real chance. But at least he was happy at the end. Nurse Sweet told me he'd just been talking to her about the wedding. They were arranging to have a little party in his room after the ceremony."

"Oh, don't ... please ...." The words were choked with tears, and it wasn't because now there would be no wedding.

"You mustn't mind so much, Liz," he said, his voice steady now. "You did a good job. Thank you."

She didn't want thanks. What she really wanted—only she couldn't have put it into words at that moment—was to belong here, to be part of the family, to have the right to grieve. But of course she was only an outsider.

She stared straight ahead across the wide lawn, bathed in sunlight, and said slowly, "I can't help wondering, now, if...."

He read her thought, as he so often seemed to do. "If J.B. knows now? I was wondering that, too. But if he does, then he'll know why we acted as we did, and he'll forgive us, have you thought of it like that?"

"No, I hadn't," she said. "It helps."

He covered her hand with his, and his touch was as firm and vital as ever. Liz could have wept when she wondered how, only a few minutes ago, she could have entertained for a moment the suspicion that Clare had put into her mind. Brett might be hard and even ruthless as a business-man, but that he had really cared for J.B. she knew without doubt.

He drew in a deep breath and said, "But life must go on, and there's so much to do." He looked at her as if she were one of the problems he must deal with. "You'd better go to Maggie's for the present. I'll tell Farthingale to run you over right away. Then I'll call her and explain."

This was the old Brett she knew—organizing, shooting out orders. She almost smiled, but instead she said, "But isn't there anything I could do to help if I stayed?"

But of course there wasn't. She had no place here now and her presence would only be an embarrassment. There would be people here for the funeral. Many people, no doubt, for Rockington's was a huge concern. Local folk, too, who might have known the real Elizabeth.

Brett underlined her thought. "No," he said. "There'd be too much explaining to do."

"All right," she said in a small voice. "I'll go to Maggie's if you say so."

He looked at her quickly, surprised perhaps by her un-usual meekness. "You'll stay there, won't you?" A smile that was only a token touched his mouth. "No more climb-ing out of windows, promise?"

As if she were a child! Perhaps that was how he really thought of her. "I promise," she said.

He would feel responsible for her; he was that sort of man. After all that had happened he would want to make some sort of arrangement for her future now that the future he had offered her was no longer viable. Perhaps he would offer her a job in the company?

She put a hand to her head, which had suddenly begun to swim around rather alarmingly.

"Come along," he said. "Let's get you into the car. You're as pale as a little ghost."

She was grateful for his arm around her as they walked to the garage. Brett opened the rear door of the car for her, and gave orders to Farthingale, who was making a rather labored show of polishing the big glossy monster.

The man took the chauffeur's cap from his grizzled head and Liz saw that his eyes were moist. "Yes, sir, I'll take the young lady with pleasure." He hesitated. "Mr. Brett, sir, I've just heard about the master, and may I say how sorry I am." His voice shook and he took out a crumpled handkerchief and blew his nose. "He was always very good to me."

Brett nodded. "He was good to everybody." For a moment his dark eyes were closed.

Farthingale climbed into the driving seat and reversed the car out of the garage.

"Hold on a minute." Brett had his hand on the window ledge. He leaned down and spoke to Liz through the back window. "I'll tell Ethel to pack a few things for you and send them over later."

She nodded. "Thank you." Fleetingly she wondered if it was a special sensitivity that made him know how she shrank from going up to her room just then, or whether he merely wanted to get her out of the way as soon as possible. It didn't seem to matter much which it was.

"All right, Farthingale," Brett said, straightening, and the big car slid away down the driveway.

Liz didn't look back.

AFTER THE HUSHED QUIET OF HERONSWOOD, Maggie's bungalow and the nursery garden were a buzzing hive of activity. Liz welcomed it and enjoyed helping where she could. She found that it took her mind away from things she didn't want to remember, and when she turned into bed at night, her muscles healthily stretched with hoeing and weeding, she slept soundly.

Maggie and Jake were wonderful. They accepted her as one of themselves and made no bones about letting her do as much hard work as she wanted to take on. They asked no questions and kept the conversation away from personalities as much as possible.

That first night Maggie had said to Liz, in her warm easy way, "Brett told me to look after you until he could take over again, and not to let you worry, and that's what I mean to do. Okay?"

"Okay," Liz said, "and thank you, Maggie."

Jake attended the funeral. It was, he told the two girls afterward while they were having supper, a large and important affair as befitted the top man of a company like Rockington's.

"Who'll be top man now?" Maggie inquired. "Brett?"

Jake said he would imagine so. He'd met the other two directors for the first time. Older men they were, and he wouldn't think they took a very active part in the administration.

"They spoke very highly of Brett when they discovered I was his brother-in-law. They obviously think they're pretty lucky to have him in charge."

Maggie looked up from her plate, her dark eyes alight with pride. "So my young brother will be managing director of Rockington's! That's quite an achievement."

"Steady on," Jake told her cautiously. "He's only general manager at present, you know—a paid employee. Being taken on the board is a very different matter. I suppose it depends partly on how J.B. has left his money."

Maggie nodded, and served second helpings of gooseberry tart before she inquired if Jake had heard anybody remarking on the absence of Elizabeth, and if Roger Rockington had turned up at the funeral.

The answer to both questions, her husband said, was no. After that the topic seemed closed.

But Liz remembered it when she went to bed that night. She tried to sleep but couldn't, and over and over again she heard Clare Jessing's mocking voice in her ear. "Married to you, he'll *be* Rockington's pretty soon. He can't lose, can he?"

"I just don't believe it," Liz said aloud, sitting up and thumping her pillow. "Brett isn't like that, mercenary and deceitful."

Why, he had told her explicitly that the one and only reason he had persuaded her to consent to their marriage was to bring comfort and happiness to J.B. for the short time he had left.

Then, treacherously, Terry's words came back to her: "Men aren't little tin gods you know, Liz. They have to be practical and consider their position in the world. It's not dishonest to marry where the money is, it's just plain common sense."

But Brett wasn't like Terry. Brett was honest and straightforward, she was sure of it. And as for Clare's insinuation that she and Brett had been having an affair, that was just a lie told to salve her own pride.

She switched on the light and looked at the bedside clock. A quarter-past two, and she hadn't slept a wink yet. She took a sip of water and in that bleak hour of the morning, faced the facts that for the past few days she had refused to face. All that had happened between herself and Brett Denton had been on a "business" basis; he had made that clear not once but many times. He hadn't fallen in love with her, and he would no doubt be deeply embarrassed if he should find out that she had fallen in love with him.

The extraordinary engagement was now at an end. Brett's motives and his private life were no concern of hers.

The last highly colored days were merely an episode in her life and the sooner she got away and started to forget it all the better it would be.

It was strange that after getting the whole situation into such clear and rational good sense, Liz still couldn't sleep.

A WHOLE WEEK PASSED before she saw Brett again. Then, one evening when she was alone in the bungalow, doing some cooking to help Maggie, a voice from behind her said, "So this is how you spend your time!"

She whirled around, her heart leaping to her throat, every cell in her body responding to his voice.

"It's you," she said weakly. He had surprised her in the middle of beating eggs for a cake and now she fumbled desperately with the egg beater, trying to prop it up against the basin. First it dripped yellow goo onto the table, then the whole beater began to slide. If Brett hadn't stretched out a hand, quick as a flash, five of Maggie's new-laid eggs would have been in a puddle on the floor.

Brett righted the basin and said mildly. "Is this a procedure that can't be left for a second, or may we sit down?"

"Yes, of course." She wiped her hands nervously on a towel, aware that her cheeks must be crimson. "You startled me."

"Didn't Maggie tell you I was coming? I called her about twenty minutes ago."

"I haven't seen Maggie since tea. She's working down at the office and the phone's connected through to there. She's probably busy."

"Yes, probably. There seemed quite a mob of customers milling around as I came in."

They walked to the sitting-room end of the long, open-plan room and sat down opposite each other.

Liz's glance traveled nervously over the trailing green of the plants that almost covered the room divider, over behind Maggie's desk, returning with a quick movement to Brett. Everything between them was changed now and the first approach to the new situation must come from him. She waited for him to speak first, but he sat quite still, looking straight at her. She held his eyes for as long as she could manage, but finally, flushing, turned her head away.

"Well," said Brett, "how have you been making out?"

"Oh, I'm fine, thanks." She wished she could think the same of him. His face showed all the strain and exhaustion that the past week must have brought.

Vividly she remembered those moments on the terrace when he had held her close and seemed to draw strength from her, but that was all over now, of course. He needed nothing from her any longer.

She said, "Would you like a drink? I'm sure Maggie would want me to give you one."

He leaned back in his chair. "No, thanks, I won't. We need to talk and I don't want to waste time. Someone may barge in on us at any moment."

She thought she knew what he was going to say. She had had lots of time in the past week, to rehearse her answer.

He was fair-minded and punctilious, she was sure of that. But she cringed away from the idea that now he must merely think of her as an encumbrance.

She said, "We haven't really anything to talk about now, surely. We made a business contract and now the need for it has gone, so—" she shrugged, with a small smile "—contract canceled."

He ran his fingers through his dark hair, rumpling it. She had never seen him do it before; always he had been without any sort of nervous habit. But it made him more human, she thought.

He smiled back at her, eyebrows raised. "For an experienced secretary your knowledge of contracts is somewhat hazy. You don't just cancel them like that."

"You don't mean ... you can't mean you want us to go on with the original idea?"

"Don't look so horrified, I'm not going to drag you to the altar, or the register office. As they say, the need for that has gone. All the same, those were the plans we'd been working on. Had you made any alternative ones? Your family ...?"

She said wryly, "My family, such as it is, has recently left for Kent and they don't exactly seem to be yearning for my company. And I'm not exactly yearning for theirs," she added with a quick grin. "We shall probably get on very well if we meet once in every five years or so."

He nodded, looking satisfied. "No family ties, then."

"No, I'm on my own. I thought I might go back to London and look around for a job. I have friends there, and you've been very generous." She had enough money in her purse to pay her fare ten times over.

He brushed that away. "I've got a much better idea. I'd like you to come back to Heronswood. I need you there."

She could hardly believe her ears. The colors in the room brightened. The green trailing foliage burst into starry flowers. To go back to Heronswood, to be near Brett. It was too good to be true.

But it seemed that it was true. "I daresay you know what's involved in managing a business," Brett was saying, "and I don't fancy spending quite all my days and evenings at the office. I'm going to be snowed under with work, and if you were available at Heronswood it would take a load off my mind. You could call yourself my personal secretary. What do you say?"

"Oh, yes," she said quickly, "I'd like that very much. If you think I'd be suitable." What silly pompous words one used sometimes!

He burst out laughing. "Suitable? Oh, yes, you'd be suitable, Liz. Very suitable." He stood up. "Let's go, then."

She hesitated. "I was in the middle of making a cake for Maggie."

"Maggie," he said, "won't mind making her own cake. We'll tell her on the way out."

His eyes were still creased with amusement. She had never imagined he could look so relaxed, but now she could see why. He had been under a terrific strain since the beginning of J.B.'s illness and now the strain was ended. He had grieved, but grief must end and life must go on.

She got to her feet. "There's just one other thing. Will you take this back, please?" She had transferred the beautiful diamond and sapphire ring to her right hand when she came here a week ago, and hadn't taken it off since. Now—probably because the fingers on that hand were more developed—she was having difficulty in getting the ring off. She tugged at it, wriggling her hand and fingers, all to no effect.

She said, still struggling, "I wanted you to have it back. I've been terrified of something happening to it when it's not mine. It must be very valuable."

He watched her efforts in silence. Then he said mildly, "Hadn't you better leave it where it is for the moment? It doesn't seem inclined to move."

"All right," she said, "I'll have to try it with soap."

"You do that, but wait until we get home. Go and pack your bag... and hurry."

He gave her a little push toward the door. *Home,* he'd said. *Wait until we get home.*

Obediently, Liz hurried.

BACK AT HERONSWOOD they were greeted by a pale-faced Ethel, who informed them falteringly that Mrs. Jackson had gone.

"Gone?" Brett frowned. "What do you mean, gone?"

His brusque tone had evidently deprived the child of speech and Liz said encouragingly, "What is it, Ethel? What's happened?"

The little maid turned to her gratefully. "Well, miss, she had a fall in the kitchen just after lunch it was, and she couldn't get up again on account of her arthritis, and I couldn't lift her up by myself, and Farthingale had driven Mr. Brett into Birmingham, so we was in a proper pickle, as my mum would say. Then Mrs. Jackson thought on for me to telephone her son in Kings' Heath and he drove over and took Mrs. Jackson back home with him." She looked at Brett timidly. "She was proper upset, sir, but she said she didn't want to be a burden here, and she knew she couldn't carry on any longer. She hoped you'd understand, sir, and be able to manage. She left her address written down and the telephone number. It's in the kitchen, sir, shall I get it?"

Brett nodded. "Yes, Ethel, you do that." His tone was kind now.

When the child had scuttled off he looked wryly at Liz. "You see? You're needed here even more urgently than I thought at first." The new smile was there again, creasing his eyes. "Incidentally, can you cook?"

She smiled back. "I'm not in Mrs. Jackson's league, I'm afraid, but I'm jolly good with bacon and eggs and I turn out a very passable curry. Oh, and my macaroni and cheese is super." Macaroni and cheese had been Dorothy's favorite standby for Liz to cook when she and John wanted to go out, either because it was economical or because Dorothy wouldn't trust her with anything more complicated.

"We'll have macaroni and cheese tomorrow," Brett said seriously, "but right now how about bacon and eggs? I haven't had time for any food since lunch."

It was fun cooking bacon and eggs in Mrs. Jackson's

Ideal Home kitchen once Liz lost her awe of the huge, gleaming electric stove. Ethel spread a red linen cloth on the small round table in the study, and Liz, although she had eaten a hearty high tea only about an hour before at Maggie's, sat down with Brett and tucked into another meal with relish.

They had almond macaroons with their coffee and Liz filed away mentally the fact that Brett considered almond macaroons, the way Mrs. Jackson made them, a treat for the gods.

He transferred himself to a deep leather chair and spread out his long legs. "Superb," he said contentedly. "Perhaps I won't need to advertise for a new cook after all."

"We-ll—" Liz began doubtfully "—I'll give it a try with pleasure if you think I could give satisfaction."

"With a half day off on Wednesday and every other Sunday?" He was laughing openly at her. "No, Liz, you're much too talented to spend your time at the kitchen stove. There, you didn't know I was a feminist, did you?"

In this mood he was like a stranger, but it was too good to question. Outside the light was fading and they sat in the glow of the red-shaded table lamp and drank their coffee, and, and Brett encouraged her to tell him about her week at Maggie's.

And suddenly Liz found herself talking away to him as if they had known each other all their lives. She told him about the new dahlia Jake was hoping would be something special; about how Maggie had taken her to visit the ruins of Kenilworth Castle one afternoon; about the van driver's insistence on taking them all out to the Warwick Arms to celebrate the birth of his first son. She told him one or two amusing anecdotes about customers, which made Brett laugh. It didn't matter that they were Jake's stories and not her own original ones, just as long as Brett was sitting here, happy and relaxed in her company.

She asked him about Rockington's and he told her something of the various building projects they were working on at present. There was a new housing development at Queen's Rise, a factory modernization at Sutton Coldfield, a supermarket in Banbury—

There was a note of zest, of sheer joy of accomplishment in his voice as he talked.

"You love it, don't you?" Liz said.

"The job? Oh, yes, it's satisfying to me, the idea of building things. Always has been." In the lamplight she could see the brightness of his eyes, a dark glitter.

"Maggie was saying that now you'll be head of the firm."

He smiled. "Maggie was jumping the gun somewhat but... well, yes, I suppose I will, if the other two directors will take me in with them. They aren't active members of the firm themselves. J.B. always carried the work load and now someone else will have to do it."

Liz nodded. Her eyes went to his hands, relaxed on the broad arms of the chair. He was so different, so easy and friendly, and there was this new feeling of harmony between them. Dared she risk telling him what was in her mind?

It would be so wonderful to have it all in the open. To ask him straight out whether J.B. had made him his heir; to tell him about Clare's insinuations; to hear him deny them. Most of all to hear him deny them.

She held her breath, her chest suddenly tight, as she hesitated.

But in that moment of indecision Brett stood up. It was almost dark outside now, and he went over and switched on the main light. In the sudden white glare he looked like his old self again, a little less formidable, but still not a man to take lightly. She felt a wave of relief that she had resisted the temptation to blurt everything out.

Brett stretched pleasurably. "It's been very pleasant, taking time off for once," he said, "but conscience pricks. I've got to go back to the office for some specifications before I can finally call it a day. They weren't ready when I left."

"All the way to Birmingham?"

"Afraid so. I've got a site conference in Banbury at ten and I have to have these figures with me. If I don't get them now I'll have to rise at the crack of dawn tomorrow." He stood up. "I'll be away, then. You get yourself off to bed early, you look tired. I may be late getting back. Once I get into the office there's no knowing what I may find to do."

She said, "I'll go and work out a routine with Ethel first, and find my way around the kitchen. How about breakfast? Is eight o'clock early enough for you?"

"Fine," he said. He hesitated a moment. "Good night, Liz, and many thanks for stepping into the breach yet again," he said, and went out of the study.

She heard the front door close and after that the house was suddenly quite empty. But he was coming back, and tomorrow they would have breakfast together. And the next day, and the next—

She walked with light steps toward the kitchen.

Mrs. Jackson's departure had made a different girl of Ethel. She obviously considered that she had moved up several degrees in rank, and Liz found her sitting in a tidy kitchen, all the washing up accounted for, poring over a much thumbed and food-spattered cookbook.

She looked up at Liz, beaming, and scrambled to her feet. "Me mum gave me this when I came here, only *she* never gave me a chance to try. Back at home I used to help me mum with the cooking, and no one never grumbled."

"Well, you can certainly try your hand now," Liz told her. "Come on, let's sit down and sort things out together, shall we? At the moment I don't quite know what's going to happen, but in any case we shan't be able to replace Mrs. Jackson right away, and in the meantime you and I can cope. How do you like that idea?"

Ethel's shining eyes and pink cheeks proclaimed that she liked it very much. Liz sat down at the table with her and together they planned the meals and the running of the house for the week to come. Some of the big rooms could be closed up for the present. Liz would do the ordering and shopping. The cooking they would tackle between them. She would have to consult Brett about what meals he wanted at home, and the times, and so on.

She found herself enjoying the challenge as much as Ethel, as she told Maggie on the phone later.

After Brett had whisked her away so unceremoniously she thought that the least she could do was to call and explain and thank Maggie for her hospitality.

"We enjoyed having you." Maggie's voice came warmly from the other end of the line. "I'm sorry about Mrs. Jackson. I expect doing all that catering on the day of the funeral must have been too much for her, poor old dear. She's been working herself to a standstill for some time past, I've noticed that, but it wasn't any good saying anything to her. She liked her own way."

"Yes," agreed Liz. "I noticed that."

"In any case," Maggie went on, "I don't think she would have wanted to stay now that J.B. has gone. She was one of the old school of domestics—you know, absolutely devoted to the family. She certainly wouldn't want to see Heronswood pass into other hands—even Brett's."

"Brett?" Liz felt a queer little pang inside. "Does Heronswood belong to Brett now?"

"Yes, didn't he tell you? I only heard this afternoon that J.B. made him, virtually, his heir. Roger, the grandson, gets something, I'm not sure how much. But certainly J.B.'s share in Rockington's, and the house, all go to Brett. Of course there'll be fairly hefty estate duty and Heronswood may have to go to pay that, but it's all very much in the air at present."

"I see," Liz's lips felt stiff. "He's very fortunate, isn't he?"

"He is indeed," said Maggie. There was a little silence. Then, "Liz...."

"Yes?"

But Maggie only said, in a rather embarrassed way, "Never mind now, it wasn't anything important. I'll ask you when I see you. I'll pop over tomorrow and see how you're getting along, shall I?"

"Oh, yes, please," Liz said.

When they had said goodbye she put the receiver slowly back in its cradle and sat looking down at it for a long time.

LIZ WOKE to the grumble of thunder in the distance. She switched on the bedside lamp and blinked sleepily at the clock. Ten past two. What a time to wake up, she thought in disgust. She had been deep in a complicated dream in which Brett appeared and she wanted to go on with it. Frantically she tried to remember, but the details escaped like quicksilver, back into the deep recesses of memory, hopelessly beyond recall.

Spots of rain splashed against the window. So the heat wave had broken at last. She switched off the light and padded across the room. There was no moon, and the garden looked very dark and mysterious. Lightning flashed now and again, and there was a small steady glow percolating through the bushes at the end of the shrubbery. That must be a light from Clare's cottage. Probably Timmy had wakened up and demanded attention. He was the timid sort of child who might well be terrified of thunder. Clare, Liz thought, wouldn't at all relish being got out of bed.

She pulled a chair up to the window and sat watching the storm advance and retreat. *Son et Lumière*, she thought, as the gaunt black shell of Kenilworth Castle appeared and disappeared against the sky in a highly spectacular fashion, to the accompaniment of thunder growls.

The rain had passed and the air was hot and heavy. Liz wondered what time Brett had got home from Birmingham. He must have been dead tired, not in the mood to be wakened by any thunderstorm.

She had never been afraid of thunder, but neither could she sleep while a storm was going on. She sat at the window waiting, and it was rather like that other night when she sat here waiting, and Brett had come back to tell her that Elizabeth was dead.

How long ago? A couple of weeks at the most, and it seemed like years.

He had had a bad time; all the worry, the responsibility. And now it was over and it all belonged to him—the company, the house—

But she didn't want to think about that just now.

The thunder was dying away in the distance now, the lightning switching off to an occasional flicker. There was only the light through the bushes from Clare's cottage. Finally that went out, too. Timmy must have gone to sleep again.

Liz rose and stretched. Sleep was possible again, and if she were lucky she would pick up that dream where it had broken off.

Then a flicker of lightning showed her something moving on the lawn below, a tall figure coming through the gap in the hedge from Clare's cottage.

Liz stood in the dark room, one hand gripping the curtain, her knees weak. But even before the next flash of lightning came she knew.

It was half-past three in the morning, and Brett had been with Clare.

CHAPTER TEN

IT WOULD BE FUTILE to try to persuade herself that it made no difference, because it did. She had jumped at Brett's offer to stay on at Heronswood because she thought it might give her a chance with him.

How idiotic can you get, she asked herself at intervals all the following day. What did she think she had to interest a man like Brett? What had he ever done or said to make her think that?

The engagement had been merely a business arrangement, as he had pointed out. The marriage, if it had taken place, would have been an arranged one, in the literal sense of the word. She began to wonder now if he would have gone as far as to marry her had J.B. lived. Perhaps he would, she just didn't know. She didn't really know anything about him, she decided, except that certainly he had never pretended to feel anything at all for her.

And now he would probably marry Clare. She tried to think that they would suit each other very well, both of them worldly, ambitious, cool, hard.

Oh, but Brett wasn't hard. She recalled how he had spoken of J.B. with deep affection, how his face had softened when he looked at the old man. No, Brett wasn't all hard. It was simply that only certain things got through his shell of reserve. And a romantic attachment certainly wouldn't be one of them.

Liz slept badly that night and was up very early. Brett came down geared for business, ate his breakfast with sheets of specifications spread out on the table beside him, and left for Banbury as soon as he had finished.

Up to then he had hardly spoken a word to Liz, except "Good morning," accompanied by a brief, preoccupied smile. But now she said, "Will you be in for lunch?"

He pulled a wry face and said, "I don't think so. I've got to go over to the Queen's Rise site immediately after the Banbury conference."

"And dinner?"

"I'll try." He glanced through the open front door where Farthingale was waiting with the car. "Sorry I can't be more definite. The penalties of looking after a worried executive! Try to bear up, Liz." He gave her an enigmatic little smile, picked up his briefcase and went out to the car.

When he'd gone Liz helped Ethel with the housework and did her share of preparing meals for the day. Later in the morning, Maggie arrived and, hearing that Brett wasn't expected home for lunch, whisked Liz back to the bungalow with her.

Jake was out interviewing a customer. At half-past twelve he telephoned to say that he wouldn't be in until later, so the two girls decided to have lunch on a tray in the garden room. The thunder seemed to have passed over without bringing rain and the big glass doors were thrown open to the bright blaze of flower beds outside.

Maggie offered Liz a ham sandwich, took one herself, and said in her quiet way, "Look, Liz, the last thing I want to do is to pry, but I can't help wondering how this new situation is going to affect your plans. It's no use asking Brett, he's an oyster, but I just wanted to be sure that you are ... well, that you come out of all this business on the right side, so to say. You've been such a brick in the way you've tackled everything that I suppose I feel a spot of family responsibility."

She heaved a sigh of relief. "There now, that's out and I feel better. Now, tell me to mind my own business."

Liz laughed. "Of course I won't, I'm very grateful. It's a

luxury to have someone taking an interest, a luxury I haven't really had since my mother died, years ago." Because you couldn't really count Terry, could you? His only interest was in himself. "But don't worry about me, Maggie, I'll be fine."

Fine, except that the small glimmer of hope at the end of a dark tunnel seems to have blotted itself out, and now I'm groping in the dark.

She cut her sandwich carefully into two. "Brett has asked me to stay on at Heronswood for a while, just to help him over this next very busy patch. I'm used to office work, I can do some typing for him in the evening, and now that Mrs. Jackson's gone I can lend Ethel a hand to keep the house running smoothly. I don't think Brett has had time to make any plans yet, and it suits me to have a job and somewhere to live."

Maggie looked down at Liz's ringless hand. She had managed to get the sapphire and diamond ring off her finger before she went to bed last night.

"And I suppose," Maggie said tentatively, "that the engagement is off?"

"Definitely off. It was never more than a kind of business arrangement."

"Um, pity." Maggie's dark eyes were thoughtful, but she didn't pursue the subject, and soon after she had to go down to the office to relieve Pam who was waiting to go home for lunch.

Liz said that she wouldn't wait for a lift but would enjoy the walk back to Heronswood which, Maggie told her, shouldn't take more than about twenty minutes or so. Liz checked with her on the best route and then set off in the afternoon sunshine.

Maggie had given her a way that avoided the main roads almost entirely and she walked briskly. Walking was a relief from thinking, and the Warwickshire countryside was at its best in June, with the great trees not yet grown heavy with leaf and the hedgerows still freshly green. There was a scent of hay in the air, larks trilled somewhere up out of sight, and the hum of traffic on the Coventry road, half a mile away, could be ignored.

Not so the blue car that suddenly appeared around the corner of the lane and came speeding toward her. She stepped quickly into the side of the road, but the car slowed and pulled up beside her.

"Well met, it couldn't have been arranged better." She saw Colin Winter's pleasant smile and the gold rims of his glasses glinting in the sunshine. "Hop in and I'll run you back to Heronswood."

She would have liked to say she was out for a walk, but there was no way to say it that wouldn't have sounded rude, so she murmured her thanks and slipped into the passenger seat as he leaned across and opened the door.

"But you were going the other way," she protested.

He smiled and reversed the car skillfully in the narrow lane. "I'm going your way," he said firmly. "My next patient can wait another ten minutes for me. As a matter of fact I've just come from Heronswood. I looked in to, er, to see how Mrs. Jackson was getting along."

He switched off the engine and flicked her a look that said quite plainly, "I went to see you."

Ignoring it, she said innocently, "Poor Mrs. Jackson, she was really in a bad way. She's gone off to her son's home to be nursed. She was quite worn out; she must have worked herself to a standstill."

Colin Winter was a direct young man. "Look, Liz," he said, "let's not beat about any bushes. I'm sorry to hear about Mrs. Jackson, but it's your welfare that concerns me. How are you, after all that's been happening? I thought of looking you up at Mrs. Easton's, but decided to wait awhile."

"Oh, I'm fine," she said. "Absolutely recovered."

"Forget about the medical angle," he said. "It's the personal one I'm interested in. I want you to tell me how things are with you. I've been in on this charade of Brett's since the start, and I think I have the right to know."

He had a squarish jaw and it was very firmly set at the moment. "What exactly do you want to know?" she hedged.

"I want to be sure you're all right." Almost the words Maggie had used, only this time they were spoken in a very determined and not at all apologetic tone. "I didn't like the way Brett made use of you at the beginning, only I had my patient to consider then and I had to admit that from his angle it might have been the best thing. But when I heard about that phony engagement . . . well, I admit it made my blood boil."

She said very quietly, "Why?"

He flushed a little. "Well, I should have thought it was obvious."

"No to me it isn't."

He shrugged. "Well, if I must spell it out, there's very little doubt in my mind that by allowing J.B. to believe that he was going to marry into the family Brett was insuring his own future."

She looked straight ahead at the winding sunny lane. "I seem to remember you once told me that you believed in Brett's integrity. And yet you can believe that of him?"

"Anyone can be wrong." He smiled faintly and added, "I'm not so pompous as to blame him for what he did. He had a good deal at stake. What I blame him for is doing it to you."

Oh, goodness, she thought, *how can I stop him saying it*? She should have realized what all this was leading up to, and now it was too late.

He turned toward her and said earnestly, "Liz, I think you know how I feel about you. Normally I wouldn't have rushed things, but this hasn't been a normal situation. I take it that you'll be going home now to your own people. Will you give me your address? Let me come and see you very soon?"

It was time to get this straight. She said, choosing her words with care, "You've got things wrong, you know. Don't think I'm not grateful for your ... your interest, but please do accept that I'm perfectly capable of looking after myself, and nobody makes use of me without my consent. Brett has asked me to stay on at Heronswood for a while, to do some secretarial work and help Ethel to run the house. It's only a temporary arrangement, but it suits me for the moment."

How stilted can you get, she thought ruefully, but at least she had kept her voice cool and steady. *I'm learning*, she congratulated herself; *perhaps one of these days I really shall be master of my fate and captain of my soul*. It was a pity it sounded so bleak.

Colin was digesting what she had said in silence. Then he looked down at the bare fingers on her left hand. "But the so-called engagement is over?"

"Of course. The only reason for it was to avoid giving J.B. a dreadful shock and unhappiness when he had such a short time left. The only reason," she added.

"Yes," he said, very skeptically.

Liz wasn't going to rise to that and there was another silence. She moved restively in her seat. After the open freshness of the lane the inside of the car, even with the windows wound down, began to feel stuffy and there was a smell of gas mingled with upholstery.

She said, "I think perhaps I should be getting along, if you're going to run me back."

His head jerked up. "Yes. Oh, yes, of course."

He switched on the engine. Then, with a hand on the gear shift, he turned to her and said ruefully, "Sorry, I rushed my fences. Something I thought I'd learned not to do. I'll remember in future."

It was only a few minutes back to Heronswood in the car. Colin drove right up to the front door and Liz got out of the car and turned to thank him.

"My pleasure," he said. And then, "I shan't be visiting here now, of course. May I call you some time?"

It sounded sufficiently vague, and this didn't seem the time to force the issue further.

"Yes, of course," she said.

"Good." Her hand was resting on the car's window frame and he leaned across and covered her fingers with his own with a long, firm squeeze. "I warn you," he said, smiling, "I don't give up easily."

She watched him drive away. Even when the car had disappeared she still stood there. *Oh, dear*, she thought. *Oh, dear, oh, dear*. Then, slowly, she turned to climb up the steps.

She hadn't seen Brett standing there, beside the heavy oak front door. When she did her heart leaped wildly and then plummeted down as she saw the expression on his face. His mouth was set in a hard line, and he was frowning. She recognized the look; she had seen it often before, during her office career. It was the exasperated expression of a busy man, engaged on important business, who considers he has been let down or kept waiting by some irresponsible chit of a typist.

With a sinking heart she ran up the last few steps. "Are you waiting for me? I'm so sorry, I didn't expect you home so early. Maggie called for me and took me to lunch at the bungalow and—"

He cut short her gabbled explanations with a somewhat curt, "Never mind. Will you come and take down some letters for me now?"

She hurried after him into the study, grabbed Miss Johnson's notebook and pen from the top drawer and tried to compose herself to take dictation.

"Got all that?" he asked, ten minutes later. "You can type them afterward. There's no hurry, but I needed to get it all down while it was fresh in my mind. Just now I'd like you to come along with me to Queen's Rise. It would be useful to have you to take some notes. Can you be ready in—" he glanced at his watch "—in five minutes?"

She scrambled to her feet, her wrist aching with gripping the pen tensely in the effort to keep up with his dictation.

"I'll be ready," she said.

The Queen's Rise building site was much like any other building site—a desert, it seemed to Liz, of red earth dotted with bulldozers and other more unfamiliar machines. Foundations had been marked out, and stacks of bricks, timber and pipes were scattered around the site in what seemed a haphazard fashion, but probably was all according to plan.

"Here we are. Come along." Brett was out of the car almost before it stopped. He paused a moment to give instructions to Farthingale, and then set out briskly across the hills and valleys of the wasteland, toward a wooden hut marked Site Supervisor. Liz scurried after him, dodging between a concrete mixer and a pile of pink-primed door frames under a flapping cover of plastic sheeting.

Inside the hut an oldish man with a rubbery face and a cheery grin looked up from a table covered with papers and forms. Brett greeted him as George, and the two men immediately went into a huddle over a large plan, which Liz, by peeping between their shoulders, saw was marked Bar Chart Program.

At last Brett straightened up and said, "Good. I'll have a gang over from Banbury tomorrow and you can go ahead with excavation. I'm on my way to Birmingham now and

I'll get them to put the work-loading chart in the mail for
you. Okay?"

"Okay, Mr. Denton." George nodded, but his little
screwed-up eyes were beaming at Liz, stationed just behind Brett's elbow.

Brett glanced around. "Oh, yes, George, this is my new
secretary, Miss Hartley."

George got to his feet and extended a large rough hand.
"How d'ye do? Hope you'll be happy in the job, Miss
Hartley."

Liz smiled back, "Thank you, I'm sure I shall."

Brett was already outside the hut and she trotted breathlessly after him, clutching her notebook and pen. But
Brett, as he strode about the site, examining the pegged-
out markings, pausing to measure by eye and occasionally
getting out a tiny instrument in a case and squinting
through it, made no attempt to give her any notes. She began to wonder why he had brought her with him at all.

Finally, when they were back in the car, he said with satisfaction, "Looks pretty good, doesn't it?"

She saw with surprise that he was referring to the desert
of red earth and bricks and pipes. To·her it looked like
chaos, and she was at a loss to know how to reply.

He seemed to notice her for the first time for about half
an hour. He smiled. "Poor Liz, you can't appreciate the
layout of our elegant mews-type modern housing, can
you?" His tone was faintly touched with irony, but she
thought she detected a kind of proud satisfaction, as well.
"Never mind, we're going to the Birmingham office now
and I'll show you the finished drawings."

He put his head back against the luxury cushioning of
the seat of the car and said, "If you open the top of that little leather locker thing you'll find a duster. For your
shoes," he added in explanation.

She glanced down at her black pumps, which were

smothered in red earth. When she had managed to get most of it off she noticed that Brett's shoes were in the same condition, and hesitated, duster in hand.

Then she saw that he was laughing at her, his head still back, his dark eyes surveying her frown of indecision.

"No, Liz, it's not part of secretary's job to clean my shoes, if that was what you were wondering." He took the duster from her and rubbed the earth from his own shoes.

Passing her back the duster to stow away in the locker his hand touched her own for a moment and what felt like an electric current ran up her arm.

No, she thought, *no, no, no! I'm just his secretary and it's a good job and I'm lucky to be here, and there's Clare Jessing. So be sensible and very soon you'll get over it. You might even fall in love with Colin, in time, which would be a very sensible thing to do.*

The Birmingham office of Rockington's turned out to be a big old house in a part of the city that had once been the moneyed quarter, where all the successful new captains of industry had built their solid Victorian residences. Now, the directors' belt was a long, long way farther out, but this district still kept a kind of dusty, faded charm.

"This," said Brett, leading the way into the house, "was originally the Rockington family residence in the days when they had such things. J.B. lived here himself when he was a little boy. I think he was about ten when his father bought Heronswood and decided to turn this place into an office. I think J.B. rather liked the idea of not losing sight of the old home altogether."

Inside, the house had evidently been ripped apart and put together again as a modern office. Brett led the way upstairs and along a corridor with doors opening off on both sides. The end door was marked General Manager. Mr. B. Denton. He opened it and stood aside for Liz to enter.

"My domain," he said. "Come along in."

The office was small but comfortable, with the best of modern furnishing: a thick gray carpet, a large tidy desk, a couple of comfortable scarlet-upholstered chairs, a polished cabinet against the wall. There was even a wide window overlooking a long stretch of garden at the back.

Liz went over to the window immediately and looked out, turning back to him with shining eyes. "Oh, how lovely to have a view! So much nicer than the expanse of glass and concrete you see out of most office windows."

"I think so," Brett said. "I've got a tiny apartment on the premises, too, up on the top floor, but I haven't used it for some time now, except on odd occasions when I've been working very late. I've made my base at Heronswood; J.B. liked it that way. I think he was lonely after Elizabeth left."

His tone was so matter-of-fact that she glanced briefly at him, but his expression didn't invite any comment.

He opened a drawer in the desk and pulled out a sheaf of drawings in a folder. "Look, this is how Queen's Rise will be when it's finished if all goes according to plan."

She studied the immaculate colored drawings. "It's beautiful. You'd never imagine from the way it is now that it could ever look like this."

The terraces of neat little mews houses with their blue front doors had a vaguely Regency look, and the linking roads fitted into the surrounding width of grassy expanse, with trees and shrubs, as if some fairy godmother had whisked a wand and planted them there.

"We're keeping the old trees here, and here, and over here," Brett told her, pointing them out on the drawing. "In fact the whole idea of the development is to fit it in to the original landscape, which was parkland to begin with—part of a very old estate."

"I like it tremendously," Liz said, and thought he looked pleased. "I think houses are much nicer than apartments although I suppose apartments have their advantages."

"Sometimes the're the only solution to a housing problem," he said.

Then, to her surprise and delight, he began to talk about his ideas on building, his aims and ambitions for Rockington's. As he talked, standing beside her at the window, now and then going over to the desk to get out drawings to illustrate a point, Liz saw more how single-minded he was about his work. His dark eyes glowed brilliantly, his whole face lost its gravity and became expressively alive.

When he paused she said, "How lucky you are!"

"Lucky?"

"Yes, surely it's the luckiest thing in the world to love your work so that it gives you everything you need in life."

He looked oddly at her, then he laughed. "You're always surprising me, Liz, by the habit you have of hitting nails bang on the head. I wouldn't quite agree with everything in life, but ... well, yes, I suppose in some ways I have been lucky."

The door of the office opened and a tall, spare, grizzled man came in. "Ah, Brett, I've been looking for you. They told me downstairs that you'd just come in."

His tone was formal. That, and his austere looks, gave him a chilly and faintly forbidding air.

Brett seemed to Liz to stiffen a little, not antagonistically, but rather as a junior master might do when the headmaster walked into his classroom.

"Good morning, sir." He walked over and pulled out a chair, but the elder man shook his head.

"I only have a few minutes. I wanted a word with you about the Raikes business. Wheeler and I were talking it over last night, and we consider...."

He broke off, his eyes going to Liz, by the window.

Brett said, "This is my new secretary, Miss Hartley, replacing Miss Johnson. Had you heard Miss Johnson left us rather suddenly? Domestic trouble."

The gray-haired man nodded in Liz's direction as Brett said, "Mr. Cox is our senior director."

Liz murmured, "How do you do, Mr. Cox?" and, like a well-trained secretary, melted from the office, closing the door silently behind her.

She wandered along the corridor. At the far end there were three doors marked, respectively, Mr. J. B. Cox, Director; Mr. R. A. Wheeler, Director; and, at the very end, next to the fire escape, Mr. J. B. Rockington, Managing Director.

Her eyes lingered on the last name, as she thought that soon, probably, Brett's name would be there, and some vague feeling of the inexorable flow of time came to her. Then she heard Brett's voice calling her, and she went back along the corridor.

"That's fixed that," he said. "If you'd like to come back and wait for me I'll be about half an hour, and then we can go home." She sat down in one of the scarlet leather chairs and proceeded to wait, trying in vain to stifle the little thrill that his use of the word "home" always gave her.

IN THE WEEK THAT FOLLOWED life fell into a kind of pattern. Brett left early in the morning and when he had gone Liz attended to the domestic side of the house and helped Ethel—who was gaining confidence by leaps and bounds—with the preparation and planning of meals. Maggie usually rang up some time during the morning to ask if she could help in any way, by shopping or ordering. She couldn't come over, she said, because Pam was off sick with a summer cold and Maggie had to spend all her spare time looking after the office and sales.

After the housework was arranged and under way, Liz did any typing remaining from the previous day and kept the files straight. Some time in the early afternoon Brett would return to pick her up, and Farthingale would drive them in the big, black director's car, to one or other of the sites where Rockington's had work in progress. Liz enjoyed these trips, but Brett used her services so seldom that sometimes she felt almost superfluous. She wondered why he bothered to take her with him, but she certainly had no intention of asking him. She loved tagging along with him, impressed by the way he handled the myriad details of the work, noticing how the men all appeared to like him, from the foremen right down to the youngest apprentices. He was the kind of man, she thought, who commanded respect effortlessly from those who worked under him.

They had supper together and afterward Brett worked in the study, only occasionally asking her to take dictation. Liz usually filled in the time between then and going to bed watching television with Ethel in the kitchen, or beginning to find her way around the library, listing the books she wanted to read, and trying not to wonder how long she would be there to read them.

She usually went to bed early so that she would be ready to get up in good time the next morning, and she kept her curtains drawn tightly so that there was no possibility of seeing Brett make his way to or from Clare's cottage across the lawn. What he did was his own business, she told herself firmly, but she would rather not know.

Of Clare herself she saw nothing at all; certainly she didn't come to Heronswood, but then, Liz thought, she wouldn't need to, would she?

Colin phoned her twice. "Just to make sure you don't forget my existence," he said, after explaining that the local doctors were being rushed to death by a mild virus infection, which was going the rounds of the schools.

"You're going to have dinner with me as soon as we're clear of this," Colin warned her masterfully.

Liz laughed and said lightly, "Am I?"

She would enjoy going out with Colin as long as he

didn't get too serious. She had had enough emotion recently to last her for a very long time, and until the wounds were all completely healed she was determined to remain cool and levelheaded and make up her own mind about things instead of being swayed by her feelings. She and Brett seemed to be establishing a friendly, calm relationship, which she enjoyed. He talked to her about his work, now and then even asking her opinion about the details of built-in wardrobes or fitted kitchens and appearing to take her reactions seriously.

In this calm atmosphere Liz began to wonder if she could not be content, perhaps, to be a career girl. She saw herself as growing into a position of responsibility where she would be invaluable to Brett and he would rely upon her in many different ways. And if doubts arose when he stood close behind her, pointing something out, or when his shoulder brushed hers, or their fingers touched momentarily, she firmly pushed aside her wild rush of excitement as something merely physical, which would disappear eventually.

She might, in fact, have gone on fooling herself for quite a long time if something hadn't happened on Friday afternoon to jerk everybody out of routine.

Liz had just finished lunch and was starting work on some schedules that Brett would need this afternoon, when Ethel tapped at the study door and came in, looking very pink and round-eyed. "Miss Elizabeth, your brother is here to see you."

Behind her, Liz saw a tall, fair man of about thirty. As he walked nonchalantly into the study she had time to notice that his eyes were very light blue and his clothes were exquisite; altogether he looked remarkably like something from the Sunday color supplements.

She had no time to decide what she should do or say. After a momentary flicker of startled surprise in those light blue eyes, the newcomer came across to where Liz sat at the desk, leaned over and kissed her cheek.

"Greetings, sister mine. Nice to see you again."

There was amusement in his voice, but something else, too. He looked and sounded like a man who measured up an opponent.

As he straightened Liz saw Ethel still hovering in the doorway, eyes goggling.

"Thank you, Ethel, that will be all," she said, and the little maid withdrew with obvious reluctance.

Liz drew in a steadying breath and swiveled around in her chair. "You're Roger Rockington, of course. I've heard about you."

"That's a comfort, anyway." He slipped into an easy chair and took out a cigarette from a gold case. "I was beginning to wonder if I really was who I thought I was. I must admit it's a jolt to acquire an unknown sister at my age."

The blue eyes passed appreciatively over Liz's body in its sleeveless emerald green dress, and her beautiful silky long legs.

He smiled quizzically. "My life, it seems, is full of surprises just now. First I get notice from my grandfather's lawyer that the old boy has passed on. Then, when I fly back to claim my birthright I hear I've been bypassed in favor of another fellow—one Brett Denton, my boyhood rival. Returning to the ancestral home to offer fight with swords or pistols, I find a beautiful stranger claiming to be my long-lost sister, Elizabeth. If that doesn't sound like the beginning of a Victorian melodrama, you tell me what does."

She stared at him speechlessly, wishing Brett were here to deal with this situation, trying to recall what Maggie had told her about Roger Rockington.

He leaned back in his chair and eyed her speculatively

through the smoke of his cigarette. "I hope you appreciated the subtlety of my act in the presence of the maid, but now I think I should be let into the mystery."

Suddenly his blue eyes became as cold and hard as steel and all the banter left his voice as he said, "As you're certainly not my sister Elizabeth, who the hell are you, and what exactly is the game?"

A quiet voice from behind them broke in, "I think perhaps you'd better let me answer that question. Hullo, Roger, I thought we might possibly be seeing you soon."

Liz spun around to see Brett standing in the doorway, and in spite of the mildness of his tone, there was something in his face as he looked at Roger Rockington that made her tremble inside with fear.

CHAPTER ELEVEN

BRETT CAME FARTHER into the room. "Well," he said to Roger, still lounging back in his chair, "what do you want to know?"

Roger grinned. "Shame! Is that the only greeting you have for an old buddy! After all these years!"

Brett flicked him an unfriendly glance and said, "We never were buddies, as you well know, and I'm quite sure you wouldn't be here if you didn't want something."

The other man raised his eyebrows at Liz. "Charming fellow, our Brett, don't you find? Always did have a winning way with him. All right, old boy, I'll tell you what I want to know. But first let me explain that I met an old friend of mine, Clare Jessing, on my way up to the house, and she brought me up-to-date about several interesting events that have been going on around here lately. I must admit I was staggered to hear that my sister, Elizabeth, had come back, even more surprised that she had got herself engaged to you, Brett, when I happen to know she has a perfectly good husband already. But the topper came when I was ushered in here by the maid and presented with this delectable young lady as Elizabeth, the said maid having evidently been conned into believing it, as the decorative Clare has, too. I rather think some explanation is called for from you, Brett."

Liz looked from one man to the other and shivered, feeling the tension between them like a living thing, with poisoned roots reaching back into a past unknown to her. She stood up, pushing back her chair. "I'll go if you don't want me," she said.

Brett turned to open the door for her, but Roger was there first, moving out of his chair with an agility that she wouldn't have thought he possessed.

"Oh, no, you don't, my dear," he drawled, his eyes resting on her in a way that made her squirm inside. "You're in on this little game of Brett's up to your pretty neck, so we'd better have you here, too, while we get it sorted out."

The study was a somber room in the daylight, facing toward the thick-growing shrubs at the side of the house. In the evening, with the lights on, it was warm and cozy. Now, although the sun was shining it did not reach this window and the room was dark. Brett's eyes, fixed on Roger Rockington, were dark, too. Liz recognized that look of his by now and knew that he was keeping himself under firm control. She felt a wriggle of fear as she wondered what would happen if that control should ever snap.

She looked questioningly at him and he nodded, so she sat down again beside the desk as he turned to Roger, saying curtly, "All right then, let's have an answer to my question. What do you want?"

Roger left the door and went back to his chair. "First of all, I want to know where my sister is and what this little masquerade—" he waved toward Liz "—is in aid of."

Brett told him, standing very still, one hand resting on the desk. He spoke rapidly and fluently, completely master of his expression. Liz watched his face as she listened, seeing him marshall his facts with the speed of lightning. She had never heard him talk at length before. This was how he would conduct a business meeting. She could well imagine him putting forward his ideas with force and precision, carrying the others along with him. Oh, yes, he would make a brilliant chairman of the company, she thought, with admiration and a funny kind of pride—as if he belonged to her. As if he ever could!

When he had finished there was a short silence. Then

Roger sucked in a breath. "So that's what happened to Elizabeth! Poor old Betty, she never did have much luck, did she? He slanted a provocative glance at Brett and added, "She might even have done better to marry you, as granddaddy always wanted."

Liz saw Brett's hand clench by his side, saw a muscle in his jaw tighten. Roger must have seen, too, for he held up a placating hand. "All right, all right, I know. It was all my fault. But I thought I was doing it for the best—protecting my sister's interests and all that. I didn't know that J.B. was going to step in and sort out the mess for you. But I might have guessed, I suppose. You were always J.B's angel boy who could do no wrong, weren't you?"

Brett turned abruptly and walked to the window, looking out on the dark shrubbery. "Don't treat us to all that again, Roger. Just tell me what you want and then get out."

Roger leaned back in his chair, thrusting his hands into his pockets, forehead wrinkled below the stylishly cut fair hair. "There's just one thing I'm still puzzled about. You've told me how you persuaded this charming young lady—" he waved a hand toward Liz "—to fool J.B. into believing his long-lost granddaughter had come back to him, but—"

"She *was* coming back to him," Brett put in very quietly.

"All right then, I'll give you that, she was coming back to him. So you decided to gladden his last days by your little plan. Very commendable! But Clare Jessing tells me you also spread it around that you and the, er, mock Elizabeth were going to be married. That wasn't quite so commendable, was it, my dear Brett?"

Brett said dangerously, "What exactly are you getting at?"

"I'd have thought it was obvious. As Elizabeth's husband, the plums were all there for your picking, weren't they? I take it that was what you hoped for, and you were betting on a winner, as things turned out."

Brett turned from the window and gave the other man a hard straight look. "So that's the line, is it? I wondered when we should get around to it. Out with it, Roger, what are you trying to say?"

Roger smiled. "I want half of everything J.B. left to you, Brett."

Brett said, "Don't be a fool, you know that's out of the question."

"Is it? Why? Because then you wouldn't be in the running to be Rockington's top man, would you, Brett?"

Liz stared at the fair man lounging back in the chair, and was appalled. She couldn't follow all they were talking about, but this Roger was incredible. He was so like the smooth "baddy" from an old Hollywood film that it was almost laughable.

Brett was staring at him, too, but he didn't look in the least like laughing.

"I really don't think," Roger went on, savoring his own words, "that you're going to be top man at Rockington's anyway. I very much doubt if Brer Cox and his fellow directors would want you as chairman of the board if they knew the kind of trick you'd played on a dying old man in order to get there. Of course, if you see things my way and hand over the money I wouldn't dream of mentioning it to them. No doubt you could still stay on in your present position, but...."

"Get out," said Brett very softly.

For the first time Roger's assurance seemed to falter.

"Out!" repeated Brett, coming a step or two nearer.

Roger laughed then, unpleasantly. "Always the little gentleman! I thought at least you'd invite me to tea. Ah, well, you're bigger than I am, Brett, so I won't stay to argue." He pulled himself up lazily and grinned at Liz. "Bye, sweetheart, sorry our acquaintance has been so short."

With a hand on the doorknob he turned back to Brett.

"Don't forget what I said, will you? I promise I mean every word of it."

Brett waited to hear the slam of the heavy front door, then he shrugged and glanced at his watch. "I have to be out at Kimson Green by three. We'll have to get a move on. Are you ready, Liz?"

"Yes, I'm ready." She hesitated. "Brett, is he, I mean, he isn't really hard up, is he? He doesn't appear to be, but...."

He burst out laughing. "Hard up? Roger? Why, he inherited a fortune from his mother's side, and J.B. settled a large sum on him some years ago. No, don't waste your sympathy on Roger."

"Then why?" She wrinkled her brow.

He looked down coolly at her as they walked into the hall. "Why all the histrionics, you mean? Roger's like that. He's one of the people who simply love making trouble. He's a thoroughly nasty piece of work, Roger Rockington, and he hates my guts, always has done since we were at school together."

Yes, Liz thought, *you'd make enemies at school as well as friends. Leaders always do, it's one of the penalties of being a born leader.*

"Brett—"

"Um?" He had taken his briefcase from the hall table and was rifling the papers inside.

"Can he do anything, do you think? Make trouble with the directors? Because...."

He looked up from what he was searching for, and his face had gone hard. "Look, Liz," he said, "just forget it, will you? I'm not interested in Roger Rockington, nor in what trouble he imagines he can stir up for me, and I don't respond to blackmail. So come along, there's a good girl, or I'm going to be late."

You didn't argue with Brett Denton when he spoke in

that tone. Liz picked up her handbag and followed him out to the car.

MAGGIE WALKED IN THAT EVENING as Brett and Liz were finishing supper. She came across to where they were sitting at the table and said, "Hullo, you two. The drawing-room window was open, so I walked in."

Brett pulled back a chair for her and she sat down next to him with a smile of thanks. Liz, surveying the two of them across the table thought how alike they were, and yet how different: Brett's darkness had a dominant masculine quality, whereas Maggie's was warmth and softness, lit by humor.

Her dark eyes sparkled now as she said, "Do you let your secretary off the hook on weekends, Brett? Because I hope to steal her for the next two days. How about it, Liz? We're having a small party on Sunday evening, just a buffet sort of thing. I thought you might enjoy it after the way Brett keeps your nose to the grindstone here." She laughed up at Brett, but there was a faint edge to her tone and his eyebrows lifted a fraction.

Liz said, "Oh, I'd like that very much, Maggie, only I'm not sure if Ethel can manage by herself yet."

Brett said shortly, "Of course she can. There's no reason on earth why you shouldn't go off for the weekend if you want to."

He didn't sound exactly gracious, but Maggie said gaily, "There you are then, Liz, it's all fixed. I'll call for you around ten tomorrow morning."

"I'll bring Liz over," Brett said. "I have to go into Birmingham, to the office. I can drop her off on the way." He pushed back his chair and stood up. "Now, if you'll excuse me I've got some work to get on with. Ask Ethel to bring my coffee to the study, would you?"

When the door had closed behind him Liz said ruefully,

"He didn't seem awfully pleased. I wonder if I ought to leave him to Ethel's cooking."

Maggie grinned. "Do him good. Brett's such a demon for work himself it never occurs to him that other people might like to take time off for some fun. He seems to have got out of the habit of having fun himself. Couldn't you persuade him to come along to our party, Liz?"

"Me persuade him?" Liz was amazed. "I haven't any influence, I just do as I'm told. Well, mostly," she added, remembering the sparks that had flown between them when they first met.

"Well, do your best."

Ethel came in with coffee and Liz poured a cup and said, "Take this to Mr. Brett in the study, will you, please?" When the little maid had gone she burst out suddenly, "Maggie, I'm worried."

"About Brett?"

Liz nodded. "In a way. Roger Rockington turned up earlier today."

"Roger? Oh, dear, what did he want?"

"It was all rather horrid. He made me stay and listen because he said I was—I was involved."

Maggie said, "Go on," and her dark eyes weren't lazy any longer.

"Brett asked him why he'd come and he said he wanted money. He wanted half of everything that Brett had inherited from J.B. and if he didn't get it he'd make trouble."

Maggie looked staggered. "Half? Why, the colossal nerve of the man! After the way he walked out on J.B. and left the business and everything. Then to come and . . . and . . . goodness, it's incredible what some people expect." She paused, frowning. "How do you mean exactly, make trouble?"

Liz said slowly, choosing her words, "It seems he's found out about my pretending to be Elizabeth. And that

Brett was going to marry me and let J.B. believe it was Elizabeth he was marrying." She looked at Maggie very straight. "He accused Brett of planning the scheme so that he'd be sure of inheriting J.B.'s position in Rockington's."

To her surprise Maggie burst out laughing. "Why, it's too ridiculous. Why, Brett's the very last man to—nobody who knew him would even entertain the notion that he would behave like that." She was suddenly quiet, looking at Liz. "You don't believe it, do you?"

"No," said Liz.

"Well then, my advice is, forget about it, and about Roger Rockington. I'm sure the directors won't listen to any tales he tells them. They know Brett, he's worked for them and with them for years and years. Don't worry, Liz, it'll all be all right."

She sounded so confident that Liz was almost persuaded that she was right. But after Maggie had gone and Liz sat alone in the big, shadowy drawing room, the worry came back.

Liz had worked in business long enough to recognize the type of Mr. Cox, the head director. He was, she was sure, a man who would never let personal opinions—even loyalties—cloud his business judgment. If they were going to vote Brett onto the board the directors couldn't afford to ignore an accusation that would throw doubt on his integrity. Brett would have to explain and justify his actions. Remembering Brett's face earlier today, proud and arrogant, as he ordered Roger out of the house, she wondered if he would be prepared to respond to a slur on his honor with excuses and justifications.

She only wished she could be as sure as Maggie that it would all be all right. Brett's work meant everything to him, and she couldn't bear it if all his ambitions were put at risk because of her. Because she had climbed through a window.

LIZ ENJOYED HER WEEKEND. Being with Maggie was always fun, and there was laughter and high spirits and plenty of work to do at the bungalow. She helped Maggie with the party preparations, chatted with Pam in the office, did some layering of strawberries under Jake's supervision.

The party on Sunday evening went with a swing. It was a still, warm evening, and the French windows of the garden room were thrown open onto the lawn. Jake had strung Chinese lanterns between the trees and a couple of floodlights lit up the bright flower beds. "All good for business," he chuckled.

Maggie and Jake seemed to have lots of friends. Cars rolled up and soon the bungalow and garden teemed with people. Only, for Liz, nobody had any deep and vital importance because she hadn't managed to persuade Brett to come, and it was no good searching the crowd for a sight of his brooding dark eyes, the carved bones of his face.

The party was half over and Liz was going around the lawn with a tray of drinks when she encountered Colin Winter.

His face lit up. "Good, I thought you might be here, that's why I took up Mrs. Easton's invitation. I rang you at Heronswood earlier this evening but there was no reply."

No reply? She knew that Ethel's father was calling for her, but Brett should have been there. That was the excuse he had made for refusing Maggie's invitation, that he would be catching up on work for the whole of Sunday.

Evidently there was something more important than work. He would, of course, be with Clare, Liz thought, with a sick, empty feeling inside.

Colin took the tray out of her hands and parked it on a table. He linked his hand firmly through her arm and said, "I want to talk to you."

Liz looked at the milling guests. "But I'm supposed to be helping Maggie...." Getting involved in a serious talk with

Colin was the last thing she wanted, and at this moment he looked very serious indeed.

He wouldn't be put off. "They've probably all had far too much to eat and drink already. Come on."

Short of making an issue of it, she had to go with him. He took her across the lawn and along the driveway to the open space between the main road and the office hut, where the overflow of visitors' cars was parked.

"Let's sit in my car, we shan't be interrupted there."

He unlocked it and opened the rear door for Liz to get in. When she hesitated he said rather grimly, "Don't be alarmed, this isn't an invitation to dalliance. I really do have something I want to say to you."

When they had settled themselves (and in spite of his reassurance, Liz had squeezed herself well into the corner) Colin said, straight away, "What I want to tell you is that I've got the offer of a hospital appointment in London. I put in for it some time ago, but I didn't think I had a serious chance. Now, it seems, the man they appointed has dropped out and I'm next on the list. It's a wonderful opportunity for me; specialization in the field I'm particularly interested in. There's a house that goes with the job, everything laid on."

Liz said warmly, "That's simply marvelous, Colin. I'm so glad and I really do congratulate you."

"Thank you, Liz." He turned toward her, but made no move to touch her.

In the dim light Liz could only see the other cars pressed in all around them, the shape of the wooden office hut, the dark mass of trees between them and the road.

"I think you can probably guess why I'm telling you this. I'm asking you to come with me, Liz, to marry me. You're the girl I want for my wife, I knew that almost as soon as I first saw you. I suppose that doesn't sound very romantic. Perhaps a doctor's training doesn't leave much room for romance. But I think you're a wonderful girl, Liz, and I'm sure we could make a—a jolly fine life together. Please say you will."

What a funny, conventional proposal! She could have laughed, but she wouldn't have his feelings hurt for anything in the world. Dear earnest, practical, nice Colin! It would be the most sensible thing she had ever done to accept.

She swallowed and said rather helplessly, "Oh, Colin, I'm sorry. I'm...I'm t-terribly flattered, but, I'm sorry."

There was a long silence and when Liz couldn't bear it any longer she burst out, "I like you so much, Colin, and I wish it could be different, but you see I'm—I'm in love with somebody else."

"Yes," he said heavily, "I was afraid of that. It's Brett, isn't it?"

She leaned back with a sigh. "Yes," she said, and admitting it was pain that was also luxury. "It's crazy and weak and there's no future in it, but there it is. It would be wrong to marry anyone else, feeling as I do. But I—I don't want to talk about it."

He urged, "I'd wait. You'll get over this in time. It's all been so dramatic and highly-charged. You'll feel different after a little while. Let me keep in touch, and perhaps, later on...."

"No," she said sharply. "It wouldn't be any use. I'm sorry, truly, but I don't love you, Colin."

He didn't say another word. He opened the car door for her and she got out. Here, the lights from the road percolated through the trees. She could see Colin's face, very pale and taut, and the large gold-rimmed spectacles that were so much a part of him.

He said, "Would it be rude of me to leave? Can you find your way back alone?"

"Of course." She was miserable because she had hurt him.

He stood there, looking at her silently, then he got back into the car and began to maneuver it toward the gateway.

Liz didn't wait. Slowly she made her way back to the bungalow, wishing that she didn't like Colin so much, wishing that he'd been angry, wishing that she'd never met Brett Denton. If she hadn't, she might have gone on believing that what she'd felt for Terry was love. Now she knew that that had been a pale affair compared with this shattering firework display that exploded inside her whenever she saw Brett, or even thought of him, which was most of the time, for he was always there, in her mind and her heart. She ought to get right away from this madness, but leaving him was unthinkable—not unless he sent her away.

"Liz, are you there?" It was Maggie's voice, calling into the darkness outside the radius of light from the swinging Chinese lanterns.

"Yes, here I am."

"Brett just arrived." Maggie spoke slowly, worriedly. "He says he's called to give you a lift back. I tried to persuade him to stay on, but he won't."

Liz reached her side and they turned and walked toward the bungalow. Maggie continued, "I saw that you were with Colin Winter. I didn't know what you'd want to do, so...."

"Colin had to leave. I walked to his car with him. Maggie, Brett's all right? He's not ill, or anything?"

Maggie shook her head. "No, it's not that, but ... Liz, I may be imagining things, but I've got a feeling something's wrong, something's happened. Brett seems so, oh, I don't know, exactly. But look after him, will you?"

Liz's steps slowed. "Maggie, do you think—could it be something to do with Roger Rockington?"

Brett had been so casually dismissive about Roger's visit. Maggie had been so sure that the directors wouldn't listen to anything he said against Brett. Had they both, Liz wondered uneasily, been whistling in the dark? She was cold suddenly. Rockington's was Brett's life work, she knew that, and if anything happened to threaten his position there....

She quickened her pace. "I'll go and pack straight away."

At the edge of the lighted lawn she stopped and turned to the other girl. "Thank you for my weekend, Maggie, I've had a lovely time. And...shall I phone you?"

They both knew what she meant. "Yes, please," Maggie said, "you do that."

She leaned forward and kissed Liz's cheek and then, with her usual long, graceful step, she went back to her guests.

IT WAS A SILENT DRIVE BACK to Heronswood. When they got there the big house was in darkness. Ethel's father wouldn't be bringing her back until late; there was a birthday in the family and the celebrations were likely to be kept up.

The hall had a forsaken appearance, empty and chilly. Liz shivered and pulled her coat around her.

Brett glanced around him and then back at her and said grimly, "Something of an anticlimax, is it? Cinderella after the ball?"

She wasn't sure whether that was meant to be a joke, but she laughed anyway. "Of course not. But it is a bit cold, don't you think? I'll put the fire on in the study. What would you like to drink, something hot?"

"Nothing for me, thanks."

She was kneeling on the rug, trying to cope with the big, old-fashioned gas fire. Her hand shook as the match spurted and went out. She struck another and this time she was successful. The fire burned with a pale limp flame.

"Supper, then? I could rustle up some in no time."

Or had he had supper at Clare's?

"No, nothing."

Silence fell again. He leaned a hand on the carved mantelpiece and stood silently looking down at the fire. Liz got to her feet uncertainly, wondering why he'd bothered to call and bring her back. She saw what Maggie had meant, though: something had happened, something was wrong. She wondered if he intended to tell her.

She waited until she could bear the silence no longer. Then she moved toward the door. "I'll go and tidy up in the kitchen."

"Wait, Liz." His most peremptory tone. She turned and came slowly back to where he stood.

"Sit down," he said, and she sat by the desk.

"I think you should know what's going on," he said, "because it may concern you and your position here. This evening I had a phone call from James Cox. You met him, didn't you?"

She nodded. "That day you took me to the office."

"He asked me to go and see him and I went over to his house. He told me what I already knew, of course, that I was being considered for an appointment to the board of directors of Rockington's. He also said that Roger Rockington had been talking to him."

"Oh!" Her eyes widened, her hand flew to her mouth. This was what she had half expected, but now it had happened she couldn't think of anything to say.

"Apparently Roger carried out his threat. I imagine he made quite a colorful story out of it." The contempt in Brett's voice made her wince. She knew he wasn't blaming her, but she'd been so very much involved, and she still blamed herself for much that had happened.

"But the directors wouldn't take his word against yours," she said indignantly. "They must have understood when you explained what happened, and how it happened."

"What makes you think I explained?"

"Well, surely, didn't you?"

"No," he said.

She stared at him, horrified, but his face told her nothing. Not explain? Not put things right?

She knew she shouldn't have argued with him in this mood, but she couldn't stop herself. "Then let me tell them, if you won't. I'll go and see them."

"No, thanks," he said curtly. "I've no intention of offering a justification of my actions to anyone. I've worked for the company for ten years. They've had plenty of time to make up their minds about me. They either take me on trust, exactly as I am, or they don't take me at all."

"But people don't take you on trust," she pleaded desperately, "they just don't, and you can't expect them to if you refuse to give them the facts." She got up and put a hand on his sleeve. "Please let me go and see them. I was as much involved as you were. It was my responsibility that it all started in the first place. You told me that yourself."

"Did I?" He sounded as if he didn't care very much.

Summing up all her courage, she blurted out, "Don't you want to be a director of Rockington's, to carry on J.B.'s work? That's what he wanted, wasn't it?"

She had broken through his reserve at last. He had always been so grimly self-controlled, so very much master of himself, but now he rounded on her with a fury that made her draw back, fear prickling down her spine.

"Oh, for God's sake don't go on about it. I've had about as much as I can take and I don't want any more from you. Just keep out of the whole affair in future, will you?"

Without another glance at her he strode out of the room, and a moment later she heard the heavy front door slam behind him.

CHAPTER TWELVE

IN THE SILENCE THAT FOLLOWED the angry slam of the front door the house felt desolate. Shivering with cold and nerves, Liz sank to the rug in front of the gas fire and held out her hands to the warmth.

Where had Brett gone? She hadn't heard him start up his car. So he would be at Clare's. He'd gone for peace, for solace. Clare would know better than to interfere. Clare had all the calculated feminine tricks at her fingertips to build up a man's wounded masculine pride. Liz felt sick inside as if someone had punched her.

Her eye caught the telephone on the desk and she scrambled to her feet. She'd ring Maggie, tell her what had happened, ask what was best to do. But then, her finger on the dial, she stopped. She had a sudden picture of the garden room full of people; of Maggie taking off the receiver, pressing her palm over her ear to try to hear what Liz was saying above all the noise and chatter of the party. No, better leave it until tomorrow.

She kept the big desk very neat, ready for any work Brett might want to do. Her shorthand notebook was there, waiting. Well, she wouldn't be wanting that again. If Brett was determined to ruin his career he wouldn't be needing a secretary. And even if he wasn't, he'd made it quite plain tonight that he wouldn't be needing her. She felt hollow inside, hearing again his parting words, thrown at her with a kind of bitter, exasperated rage: "Just keep out of the whole affair in future, will you?" She might as well go up and start packing here and now. She'd been nothing but a trouble and embarrassment to him right from the start.

With a nervous, repetitive gesture her thumb flicked through the shorthand notebook that had been Miss Johnson's. Then, out of nowhere, came the memory of the letter she had noticed days ago, the letter to Brett, dictated by J.B. Quite deliberately she leafed back through the pages until she found it.

Yes, here it was, as she'd remembered, dated 25th April, beginning, "My dear Brett...."

She sat there staring at Miss Johnson's beautiful shorthand, not yet allowing herself to transcribe a word. She might be wrong, but she had a feeling that this letter could be the answer to many things. It could hold the key to the future—Brett's future, anyway.

But it was a private letter, and you didn't read other people's private letters, did you?

"No," said Liz out loud. She thrust the notebook into a drawer and slammed it shut.

She couldn't read the letter, of course she couldn't. And yet if it contained something that might help Brett? He was already being absurdly rigid about the whole thing; shouldn't she try to help him, even if he threw her out for her pains? Wasn't there a time to forget your principles if you could help someone you loved?

Liz wasn't making excuses for herself. She just knew, within minutes, that she had to read that letter.

As before, Miss Johnson's beautiful neat shorthand presented no difficulties to her.

My dear Brett, I wish I could write this to you with my own hand, but I have left it too late to do so, and now I cannot. I believe, in spite of what the doctors say, that I may not have very long to live, and before I go I want you to have certain facts in your possession in case difficulties crop up later. You and I, and of course Pilkington Senior, are the only ones who know that you are my legally adopted son, and knowing Roger, I believe it not impossible that he might try to make trouble for you later on.

I think you know that my dearest wish is that you should carry on in the company where I leave off. Roger turned his back on it and on me, and thus forfeited any further interest in it. I don't want to rake up old history now, but you should know that he had a very liberal settlement from me when he came of age. He also inherited a considerable fortune from his mother. You need not have any qualms that when I name you my heir you will be taking anything that should have gone to him. As for Elizabeth, she, too, is well provided for by way of settlement, although I was careful to ensure that her capital could not be realized, either by her or *anyone else*—you will know to whom I refer. Certain securities and family property are entailed and these will go, by right of succession, to Roger, but the bulk of my private estate, including my interest in the company, and Heronswood, I am leaving in your hands, my dear boy, and I am sure that they could not be in better hands. I know, because you have promised me, that you will do all you can for my dear Elizabeth, if ever she needs help. It is the greatest regret of my life that there is this rift between us, especially as I could have avoided it. Now, Brett, I am very tired and I must stop. God bless you, my dear son, for that is how I think of you.

Liz closed the notebook and sat staring down at the desk, her eyes thick with tears.

So Brett must have known right back in April that J.B. intedned to make him his heir. Nothing that had happened since—not the masquerade, not the short-lived engagement—nothing had made the slightest difference to the inheritance. Brett had only to show this letter to the directors to clear himself of any suspicion. Why wouldn't he? Why? Why? She thumped her fist on the desk in useless frustration.

She knew now what she would do. She would wait up for Brett, tell him that she knew about the letter, plead with him again not to risk his future for stupid pride. What did it matter how angry he was with her? He could throw her out of the house if he wanted to. She had nothing to lose, but he had everything.

Ethel came in just before midnight, flushed with excitement, and obviously anxious to chat.

"Wouldn't you like a nice cup of cocoa, miss? It's so late, and you working on like this! Shall I make you one?"

Liz turned from the desk and said, "That would be lovely, Ethel. Make one for yourself, too, and we'll have it together in the kitchen. It'll be warmer there."

The sweet, hot cocoa and Ethel's graphic and detailed account of the birthday party relieved some of Liz's cold misery, but after a while the child's eyes were drooping and Liz sent her off to bed.

Ethel yawned and admitted she did feel a bit sleepy. "But you look washed out yourself, miss, if you don't mind me saying so. Aren't you going up, too?"

Liz smiled. "Not yet. I have to wait for Mr. Brett to come in."

When Ethel had gone the house seemed even more silent than before. Liz settled herself in the chair by the desk, swiveling around to face the open door into the hall, so that she wouldn't miss seeing Brett when he came in and he couldn't help seeing her.

What never occurred to her was that he wouldn't come in at all.

LIZ WOULD HAVE SWORN that she had been awake through the night, counting each tinkling chime of the clock in the hall. She had been absolutely sure that she couldn't possibly sleep a wink. But now, incredibly, the sun was filtering through the crimson velvet curtains and she was sprawled across the desk with her head on her arms.

The clock in the hall struck seven. Painfully, for her arms had pins and needles in them, she got out of the chair, turned off the gas fire, and dragged herself upstairs. The door of Brett's room stood open and a single glance told her that the bed hadn't been slept in. She went on to her own room, pulled off her shoes and, almost falling onto the bed, dragged the eiderdown over her and was dead to the world.

Next time she wakened it was almost nine. By ten o'clock she had bathed, dressed, made a show of eating the bacon and eggs that Ethel had cooked, and still Brett hadn't come home.

Liz began to pile the breakfast dishes onto the cart, it was no good waiting any longer for Brett. The front-door bell sounded and she jumped nervously. It might just be Brett. If he'd lost his key....

She heard the quick patter of Ethel's footsteps crossing the hall. Then the sound of voices, and her heart sank because the man's voice wasn't Brett's.

Ethel appeared in the dining-room doorway, holding out a large square envelope. "A man just brought this for Mr. Brett, miss. He says he's Mr. Cox's chauffeur, and his instructions are that Mr. Brett is to have the letter urgent. Shall I tell him it's all right? He's waiting."

Liz took the envelope. It was of expensive, hand-pulled paper and was addressed to Brett Denton Esq., in thin, precise handwriting. The words "Private. Urgent" appeared in the top corner, underlined.

Liz said, "Will you tell him that Mr. Brett isn't in at present, but I'll see he gets this the moment he returns."

"Yes, miss." Ethel went out and there was quite a lengthy conversation at the front door. But eventually it seemed that the chauffeur was satisfied, for the door closed and then everything was silence again.

Liz looked down at the envelope in her hand. No good trying to guess what it contained. Good news, bad news, it might be anything. But one thing she felt sure of: it was connected with what Brett had told her last night. And if that were so it was vitally important, and somehow she must find Brett and give it to him.

But Brett was at Clare's. She felt absolutely convinced of that now. Her heart started to thud heavily. She couldn't go there looking for him. She couldn't.

Pushing away the thought, she pulled the telephone toward her and dialed Maggie's number. There was a longish wait and then a sleepy voice replied. "Liz? Oh, hullo, love, I'm dead to the world. My goodness, who'd give parties? It must have been half-past three when the last of 'em went home. There's a real Monday morning atmosphere around here this morning, I can tell you. Even Jake's feeling it, poor sweet. How are things with you, Liz?"

No, Brett evidently wasn't there. Liz said automatically, "Oh, I'm fine, thanks. I just wanted to say how much I enjoyed the party. It was lovely."

Next she tried the office in Birmingham. No, the receptionist told her, Mr. Denton hadn't been in this morning. She knew for sure because Mr. Cox had been inquiring for him earlier. Was there anything she could do?

"No, thank you," Liz said. She replaced the receiver and sat looking at it, a sick hollow feeling settling in her stomach.

She slipped the envelope into the pocket of the white blazer she was wearing over her slacks and went out onto the terrace. There, across the lawn and behind the spinney of silver birch trees, was Clare's cottage, and there she was sure she would find Brett.

Only she couldn't go there, she simply couldn't.

Sphinx, J.B's white Persian, came stalking softly along the terrace. He had accepted Liz as part of the household and now he brushed luxuriously against her legs, purring like a small dynamo. She stopped to caress the soft white fur and he stared into her face, his green eyes huge, their pupils narrowed to a tiny slit in the bright sunshine.

She stood up abruptly. Seeing Sphinx still reminded her of that first day, when she had climbed through the window, and nearly tripped over Sphinx on the white carpet, and J.B. had wakened, and.... She had started something that day and, pride or no pride, she knew that she would have to see it through to the end.

The lawn was springy under her feet. She passed through the gap in the bushes and the spinney closed over her, the leaves brushing her hair. She went swiftly on, trying not to think, intent on getting there and getting it over and done with as quickly as possible.

After she had given Brett the letter there would be nothing to keep her at Heronswood. She would put a few things into a case and leave straight away.

Her toe caught in a protruding root and she almost fell. She steadied herself, her hand against the trunk of a tree. This was the place where Brett had taken her in his arms and kissed her; where he'd said, "Hasn't anybody told you you're a very disturbing young woman?"; where he'd asked her again to marry him "on a busines basis."

Her steps checked for a moment, then she hurried on again. She could see the back door of the cottage now, in a narrow gap between the trees. She'd knock and Clare would open the door, with something clinging and exotic draped around her lovely body. "I have an urgent letter for Brett," she would say, and Clare would look at her speculatively, triumphantly.

Or Brett might open the door himself, his dark eyes sleepy, his hair tousled....

Liz paused to get her breathing under control. It was then that the back door of the cottage opened and Clare emerged. She was wearing a little scarlet suit with black gloves and shoes and she carried a shiny black leather overnight case. She called to someone inside the cottage, "I'll put this one in the trunk, shall I, darling?"

Liz drew back as if she had been slapped. From inside the cottage a man's voice answered, but she couldn't hear what he said. So this was what Brett had decided: to cut loose, to take J.B.'s money and go off with Clare. This was what he was really like.

She leaned her head against the silky silver bark of a tree. She wanted to turn and run, but her legs wouldn't move. *I've never known him at all, then, never known anything about him. Never for a moment.*

She heard Clare's voice, scolding Timmy now. "You just sit quiet in the car and behave. I said *quiet*, did you hear me?" A smack, a high-pitched wail. Then Clare calling to the cottage again, "Hurry, darling, we don't want anyone from the house snooping around."

Liz tried not to look, but her head seemed to lift itself against her will. A man came out of the cottage, carrying two large suitcases. He put them down and turned to close the door. She saw that it was Roger Rockington.

She stood quite still until the car had gone, the sound of its engine dying away to a snarl in the distance. After that it seemed deathly quiet under the trees. Liz said aloud, "Brett, I'm sorry." Then she turned and walked slowly back to the kitchen garden, where Ames was scraping soil from his boots.

When he saw Liz he muttered something about going off for his dinner, wound a long knitted scarf around his neck in spite of the hot sunshine, and shuffled away.

The old garden was very peaceful. From somewhere out of sight came the soft syncopated call of wood pigeons.

Far, far overhead an unseen plane was tracing a snail-trail of white vapor against a pale blue sky. The smell of sun-warmed growing things hung in the air.

Liz sat down on an upturned wooden box. She was in a dreamworld of miracles because Brett hadn't been with Clare. She'd been so certain he was there and she'd been wrong. She felt that nothing would ever surprise her again.

So that when she saw Brett walking along the path toward her it seemed quite natural and she smiled at him as if last night had never been. Miracles were still happening, because he smiled back and, although his face was drawn with weariness, there was something in his smile that she had never seen there before, something that made her heart shake almost painfully.

He stood looking down at her. "Room for one more?" he said. She shifted along on the wooden crate and he sat down beside her. There was just room for two of them.

"It's been a long night," he said. "I never knew War-wickshire was so big. You don't notice it in a car."

"You've been walking?"

He lifted one foot and showed her a dusty, scuffed shoe with the heel worn down. "At one period I found a hospi-table haystack. It was surprisingly comfortable. When I woke up I hitched a lift back. There's nothing like a night in the open for clearing one's mind."

She waited, saying nothing.

"I've been working on what you said last night," he went on at last. "There's been a good deal of dead wood to hack away, but most of it's gone now, I truly believe. Liz, will you come with me to see George Cox and explain how everything happened? I'd be glad of your moral support."

She turned to him, her eyes like stars. "You'll go? Oh, Brett, I'm so glad. Of course I'll—but I nearly forgot." She took the letter from her pocket. "This came for you about half an hour ago."

He took it and turned it over in his hands deliberately. "Liz, before I open this, there's something I want to ask you, and you can forget all about business propositions, because this is something quite different. I don't know what's in this letter, but whatever it is, even if it means starting a new life, a new career somewhere else, will you marry me and share it with me? Because I'm no good at all without you."

She looked up into his face and saw it was true. She wasn't dreaming. Her eyes were misty and her mouth trembled. "Yes," she said. And then, uncertainly, "You did ... you did ask me to marry you, didn't you? I wasn't imagining it?"

"You certainly weren't imagining it. And you said yes. I'm holding you to that."

His arms were on her shoulders, turning her around to him. She looked into his eyes and it felt like drowning. She said shakily, "I didn't take so long to make up my mind this time. I'm learning."

"Oh, Liz, Liz," he said in an odd, rough voice. Then he pulled her into his arms and kissed her, and for a man who had spent most of the night tramping the lanes he seemed curiously unfatigued. The old wooden crate now seemed to hold the two of them with plenty of room to spare, and the bees kept on buzzing and the wood pigeons calling, just as if nothing earthshaking had happened.

When he stopped kissing her at last he still held her close. He said, his mouth against her hair, "Last night was hell. I thought I'd lost you, and everything was black and horrible."

She said, "It was horrible for me, too. I thought you were with Clare."

"With Clare?" The amazement in his voice was real. He drew away and stared at her. "You thought ... you thought I was having an affair with Clare?"

She nodded. "She spelled it out for me. And . . . and I saw you one night coming back from her cottage about, oh, it must have been after three o'clock. It . . . seemed quite likely. She's very attractive."

He looked grim. "And selfish, and lazy, and on the make. No, not for me, thanks. Yes, I remember that night now. I'd been working very late in Birmingham. I got back about midnight and heard the little boy screaming. I climbed in through a window and found that Clare had gone out and left him on his own. I stayed with him until she got back, hours later, and then I tore a few strips off her." He looked satisfied. "I haven't seen her since, nor given her a thought. You believe me?"

"I believe you," she said, and thought, *I'll never doubt you again. Never for a split second.*

"And you won't hold against me all that rubbish I once talked about marriage being a business arrangement? I doubt if I really believed it myself, even at the time, but you see, I'd been carrying around an outsize chip on my shoulder for ten years."

"Ten years? That's an awful long time."

He nodded. "I'd like to tell you now, then we won't talk about it again." His arm tightened around her and she waited.

"I daresay you knew my father was a flying man in the war. He was an ace fighter pilot—decorations, medals, star-billing, the lot. To me he was just simply a god, I think. But when the war was over he had to come back to a small family printing business. A small business, after the kind of life he'd had for six years! We never knew what was happening, we took the super-goodies for granted. Then, just about the time I was leaving school, the whole thing crashed. It must have been the thrill he missed, the danger, the excitement. I think now I can understand, in a way. The business was on the rocks, the men thrown out of a job. He'd gambled it all away, my mother's capital, too, the lot. Then he took his car out to a high mountain pass in Wales and drove it over the edge."

She couldn't say a word. Things like this happened, you heard about them, but they didn't touch you. Anger and compassion welled up as she pressed closer to him.

"I don't think about that time any more than I can help, even now," he said. "It was like dying. It was J.B. who—well, it sounds dramatic, but it was literally true—who saved me then. You see, he'd lost his own son in the war, and in a way I think he put me in that son's place. He lent me money to pay my father's debts and to finish my education and then he took me into his business. He had the sensitivity to understand that I would wish to pay it all back to him. I finished paying last year."

Liz said, "I wish, oh, I wish I'd known you then. I wish I could have shared it with you, the heartbreak and everything."

He smiled at her very tenderly. "I believe you do," he said. "I really believe you do."

"And Elizabeth? Did you love her?"

He thought about that. "When she died it was like another life, like watching someone else's story on a screen. I suppose, if things hadn't blown up around us, we would have married. We were boy and girl sweethearts, as the saying goes. Our two families were very close, and J.B. always wanted it, especially after his son was killed."

A touch of the old grimness came into his face. "That was Roger's malice," he said. "He never lost a chance of getting one up on me. Even when we were kids it was always like that. It wasn't very difficult for him to convince Elizabeth that I didn't want her, that she'd just be a burden to me, and to convince me that she could do better than a fellow with a load of debt around his neck. Years later we sorted out what had happened, Elizabeth and I, and how

Roger had manipulated the breakup between us, but by then it was too late, and anyway it didn't seem to matter very much." He smiled and added, "I suppose the iron had entered my soul by then."

There was a silence as they sat very close, arms entwined, her head against the roughness of his coat, the sunny fragrance of the old garden all around them.

Liz said, "When did you know you—you wanted me?"

"Very soon," he said. "As you've remarked once or twice, I'm pretty quick off the mark, too quick probably. This past week I've had to exert a good deal of control not to blurt it all out. I wanted this proposal to be calm and dignified, after my last effort. Have you forgiven me for that, love?"

She said demurely, "I've forgiven you."

Five minutes later he said, "It'll be good, living here with you. Is that what you'd like, to live at Heronswood?"

She frowned a little. "Can we afford it?"

"Just about," he said, smiling.

"Then I'd love it. I always hoped I'd be here when the raspberries were ripe . . . and they nearly are," she added leaning forward to part the leaves and show him. "But Brett, the letter! We forgot the letter."

"So we did," he said, but he didn't sound unduly perturbed. He pushed a finger inside the flap and broke the seal. "What do you guess, Liz? Do they want me, or don't they?"

Suddenly she was absolutely, gloriously sure.

"They want you, Brett," she said, and she added, so softly that he had to lean forward to hear, "but not nearly as much as I do."